SHAKER MADISON

The Suitcase Murders

Steve Whitman

<u>Important Notice</u>

ISBN-13: 9781539871071
ISBN-10: 153987107X
Library of Congress Control Number: 2016920354
CreateSpace Independent Publishing Platform
North Charleston, South Carolina

Forward

I would like to dedicate this book to my two German Shepherds that I had the great pleasure of owning for many years and to the dogs of the K-9 units all over this country that serve and protect us everyday. Although this book is strictly fictional, several of the mannerisms, capabilities, and personality traits of Barrett have been directly taken from my good friends, *"Mr. Schultz"* and *"Handsome Hoag"* that I owned for more than twenty-five years. Their loyalty and dedication to making my family safe will be long remembered and although they left us several years ago, their dear memories will be forever with me.

Table of Contents

CHAPTER ONE
The Past Catches Up

"I hear him too, boy" as I grabbed Barrett by the head and massaged his neck. *"There's no doubt he's out there, but the big question is....where?"* Barrett gazed up at me with his deep, yellow eyes panting and licking his chops. Then turning his head, he looked to the right of us and stared off in the direction of a large clump of evergreens, pawing the ground slightly. *"Oh, that's where he's hiding....pretty sneaky....ehh?"* Barrett quickly stood up on all fours and moved forward slightly without hesitation, showing that he desperately wanted to search for the criminal, but I held him back by the scruff of the neck. *"You're in too much of a hurry, boy.......we need to figure this one out......have a little patience, okay?"*

As my eyes scanned the empty woods around us, there was nobody else in sight from the search team. Barrett and I had been hunting the escaped criminal from the State Prison for about two days now along with the other law personnel. Unfortunately, they had spread themselves out too thin throughout the woods and since this country was rugged and unforgiving territory we had lost contact with them several hours ago. Patting him on the head I said softly, *"This is not going to be an easy one, boy....we don't know if the man is armed or not....we're gonna have to take this one slow."* Barrett pawed me, showing me that he was anxious to do his job, and while rubbing his head I acknowledged his ambition and restlessness.

Gazing into his eyes I could not help thinking back a few years ago, to a time when things were not very pleasant for me. A time when my own existence had become a pitiful one and how I hated the world and everybody in it, including myself. A point in my existence when all things meant little to me and wished that death had come knocking on my door, taking my worthless life away. Then as my mind rambled on with more distant thoughts my eyes scanned downwards suddenly bringing a smile to my face for I was looking at the animal that had literally brought me back from the living dead.

It was 1954 and I had just been discharged from the army, having served in the Korean War and World War II conflicts. Decorated a few times in those two living hells, I had received the Bronze Star, Silver Star and Purple Heart, but like most of the men who returned, I had no idea what was in store for me. The popularity of the Korean War had waned and the public had grown indifferent opinions about it, including the men who served in it. All I knew, coming back to my hometown of Middleton, Maine that it was a welcomed sight and since all my limbs were intact, it was just an added bonus. Sadly, there were far too many of my fellow soldiers that I had served with in the Korean War that had lost their limbs due to combat or frost bite injuries. Often the temperature plummeted below zero degrees with a constant wind, creating a cold that a man could not believe was possible. Living with hypothermia during that time was a normal existence and frozen limbs had become a common everyday occurrence. In reality, the cases of frostbite claimed more fingers and toes than any shelling or combat situation during the war. Yes, looking down at my hands and feet, I was indeed fortunate to have arrived home entirely intact.

One of my closest friends from high school, who did not serve in the war, by the name of Benjamin Morse, became a member of our town's police force. He was one of the so-called *"lucky ones"* that had a hearing problem and was declared 4F. Not eligible to serve, he continued with the police department, and eventually became chief. A straight and always *"true shooter,"* we remained close friends during the war years by writing back and forth. Coming back from Korea, we happened to meet by chance in a local coffee shop one day and he convinced me to join the force. Since I had been involved in special operations for missions behind enemy lines, my knowledge had involved intelligence and reconnaissance work. Trained as a Army Ranger, my combative skills were second to none as I specialized in knife fighting and hand-to-hand combat. Along with my size, Ben was convinced that I would be a *"natural"* in law enforcement. Standing at six feet, two inches, and with over two hundred-twenty pounds of lean muscle mass, I definitely looked the part, but I was hesitant at first, due to my horrid experiences overseas on the battlefield. The chaos and the amount of death that I had witnessed was something that I wanted to leave behind as the nightmares still came to visit me every night. Expecting to be exposed to some of that again through police work, I initially refused him, but Ben was the type of person that never gave up easily. He worked on me for several days after that explaining the exposure to homicides and violence would probably be minimal due to our small town being a nice and quiet place. After all, with a population of only about eight hundred this made violent crime almost nonexistent. So after much thought and deliberation, I decided in the summer of 1954 to become a proud member of the Middleton Police Department.

Not long after joining the force, I became reacquainted with a woman by the name of Jane Reilly that had been a few years behind me in high school. We never really knew each other during our school years, but it did not take me long to realize that Jane was a great woman and we immediately hit it off in many ways. She loved the outdoors like I did and when we both had the time off from work; we usually spent every waking moment together exploring our picturesque surroundings. The area we lived in contained so many lakes and thousands of acres of pristine woods that it made a paradise for outdoor types of people.

Camping, hiking, and canoeing were only some of the activities we enjoyed together and it wasn't long before Jane even joined me on a few deer hunts. It was not long after our meeting that I fell deeply in love with Jane and realizing we were meant for each other, six months later, I asked her to be my wife.

After we were married, times were good and because of my previous military training and experience in the Army, I was quickly promoted to the position of detective, even though I was only thirty-one years old. I had greatly assisted our department by solving a few robberies and even saved a couple of people from certain death in a bad automobile accident when they lost control on an icy section of highway. Their vehicle had flipped over, down a steep embankment into a small ravine that was adjacent to a deep gorge. With the fire department's help along with my previous Ranger training, I was able to repel down the cliff to reach them, just before their balancing car went over the supporting edge, falling more than six hundred feet to the river below. Consequently, the town fathers were more than happy to shower me with a few commendations and when a detective slot opened up, they immediately picked me for the job.

Yes, those years were a good time in my life and looking back on them now, I only wished that we had stayed in our small town. Life was simple then and I should have seen the *"forest through the trees"* as we often say up here, but several years later I was offered a detective's position in Harrisburg, Massachusetts where the pay was much higher. A larger city with a bigger police force than our little town, I thought there would be more opportunities for advancement. My wife and I agreed that the move would be a positive one, thinking the additional money would come in handy for purchasing a new home and starting a family. Taking the position and after renting an apartment in Harrisburg for a couple of months, we then purchased a new home on Putnam Street. Sitting at the end of a cul-de-sac and being a ranch style house with three bedrooms and two baths, we thought this home would be an ideal location for us to start a family.

My new detective's job was going extremely well except for my relationship with the chief who I was constantly at odds with, as he never agreed with my investigative methods. Chief Roland Morin on many occasions brought me into his office for a *"little talk"* as he often put it, only to blast the hell out of me. My veteran colleagues on the force, who never understood his attitude as well, often took me to the side and tried to help be through those tough times. On several occasions they even covered for me and this only irked the chief to a greater extent. Soon I found myself with every dirty job that Morin could find, but I tried not to let it bother me and just went with the flow, hoping that the mess would eventually work its way out. It was obvious what the man was up to, but it still puzzled me and I often tried to figure out what his motivation was. Many times, I thought the real reasoning behind it was just plain jealousy because of the positive results I generally got from solving my cases. Sure, I intimidated witnesses and pressured suspects for answers sometimes, but I did get results and the rest of the department appreciated my work. Money laundering, bookie operations, and prostitution rings were only some of the activities that I had put a stop to in our city and members of the city council were grateful for it. The chief, on the other hand, was never impressed and his belittlement of me never stopped in front of the men. For my good police work and due to political pressure, probably initiated through the mayor's office, he was forced, from time to time, to give me some recognition and an increase in salary. Of course, this only added to his frustration and hatred of me along with him saying many times, *"Just because you have a few friends around here, Madison, don't think you're invincible to your eventual demise because guys like you always screw up and when they do.....I'll be there waiting to pick up and throw away the pieces."*

Yes, despite of the chief, my life and career were going well, that is until that fateful day in October when a female body was discovered down by the river. When I got the call, I never realized at the time what a life-changing event that it was going to be for me. An angler had discovered a large black suitcase in a secluded area along the banks of the Nashua River and being curious, he opened it. To his horror, he found a woman entirely nude and it was obvious by the piece of ripcord that adorned her neck she had been strangled. Tied, utilizing a slipknot the cord had left a deep, red impression around her neck and the strangulation had been so brutal that it caused the whites of her eyes to redden due to the internal pressure from the ruptured blood vessels. Additionally, the woman's legs and arms were broken at the kneecaps and elbows, respectively so her body would fit into the restricted space and her long, black, silky hair had been severed near the scalp and stuffed in her mouth by the killer.

Evidently, the murderer had struck her across the face with his fist or a blunt object, breaking some of her teeth, as some of them had pierced her lips. After closer examination, there appeared to be no other injuries to the woman's body, including any defensive wounds, but there was no doubt in anybody's mind that a maniac, with a severe hatred of woman, was now on the loose and the main question that blitzed through everyone's head was, *"When and where was he going to strike next?"*

By the time my partner, Russ Wilson and I arrived at the crime scene, several officers and emergency personnel had already contaminated the area with their footprints and movements. Russ was not happy with the situation and went on a tirade about it, severely chastising the men and telling them they were a bunch of fools for being so careless. As his ranting went on, I quickly grabbed him by the shoulder and tried to calm him down. *"It doesn't really matter, Russ.....look at the embankment leading down to the river....see the flattened brush along it?....it's obvious the killer tossed the suitcase from up above and it rolled down here....we need to go up top."*

Unfortunately, when we searched the area on top of the embankment we found nothing. There were no tire marks, footprints, or any signs of a struggle. The fifty-foot path that led down to this location from the paved road was void of anything as well.

There were some old discarded beer bottles and trash near it, but along the path there was not a single visible footprint. *"I guess the recent rain did a number on this place, Russ....by the looks of the erosion on the trail, if there was anything here, the thunderstorm washed them away."* My partner squatted down, looking up the narrow path and with disgust in his voice, replied, *"Yeah, it sure did...if there was anything here....it's long gone now."*

That was the first victim as the second murder was discovered only a few months later when another large suitcase was found near some active train tracks along the Nashua River. The suitcase, as in the previous situation, had been dumped over an embankment and allowed to tumble towards the river, coming to rest along the water's edge. Again, coinciding with the previous MO, a sledgehammer of some kind had been used due to the heavy contusions and breakage of bone at each joint in the woman's limbs. Sadly, by the amount of bruising present on the body, it was evident that the victim was alive when the killer did this and since the woman's suffering must have been immeasurable, it only confirmed our initial thoughts about the sick killer's profile. As before, no real evidence was ever collected from the scene, as it appeared that the nude body had been cleaned of everything. As a result, it became extremely obvious to everyone working on the case that due to the lack of fibers, fingerprints, and other forensic evidence we were dealing with a very conniving and shrewd killer who knew how to hide evidence from the police.

It was not long before the city bosses erupted in a full scale panic, as the realization of a serial killer running around loose might eventually wind up plastered all over the local newspapers. Every day our chief received more and more pressure from City Hall, asking to speed up the investigation and find the killer that was roaming our city. With the heat turned up on him, the chief generally took out all of his frustrations on us, often causing severe dissension among the ranks. At one of the departmental meetings, he went so far as to chastise the detective division for dragging its feet and threatened disciplinary action if we did not come up with a suspect. We were working around the clock with little sleep, following up dozens of leads given to us by our snitches and informants, but all of them proved to be useless. As our list of suspects dwindled to almost nothing, we soon found ourselves with no where to turn and with the political pressure bearing down hard, the pressure cooker we were all working in was about to explode.

Adding to our misery, several City Councilors constantly visited the station in secret, saying ugly comments to us such as, *"Our police department must get off their lazy butts and protect the citizens of this city.....we know what the real problem is.....all of you men just don't care about what goes on here....the only thing you people care about is getting your paycheck and early retirements.... look around you, this place has become nothing, but a country club...... well, gentlemen, if the council does not see some results soon, you better believe some heads are going to roll."* Of course, hearing all of those snide remarks from them on a daily basis only sent what little moral we had left in the department down the *"shit chute."*

Being the lead investigator, I was taking the brunt of the harassment and the more crap that came down on me, the greater the chief seemed to enjoy himself. Often I would see him chuckling when the city councilors came into the station to take another shot at my staff and me. In addition, as soon as they left, he would add to our grief by ripping us in front of the other men. His words burned in my mind as he hollered disgusting things like, *"Madison, you're a disgrace.... a useless piece of crap that doesn't deserve to wear a badge.....all you do is sit around and suck your thumb like a preschooler who is waiting for someone else to solve the case... meanwhile, the killings go on and why we ever hired you is beyond me......as far as I am concerned, you and the rest of your task force should be made to pack up your bags and get your asses out of here!"*

Needless to say, the stress and the criticism wore on me and soon I looked for ways to avoid the pain. My drinking was on the increase and before I knew it, a couple of belts in the morning were necessary to keep me going, but even with the excessive drinking, I kept doing my job. My dedication to the investigation did not waiver as I pursued every lead on the murders, trying everything to solve them. However, all of that came to a grinding halt on October 1, 1961.

I will never forget that day when I left to go to work as it was a beautiful fall Monday morning. That weekend, my wife and I had just finished remodeling the third bedroom, making it into a nursery for our new bundle of joy that we were expecting the following March. As with all young couples expecting their first child, we were full of happiness when we received the news and turning the bedroom into a nursery was a project that we both had enjoyed working on as it only brought us closer together. Even my drinking had subsided a little during those months and although there was still a mess going on at work, my daily life regained some normalcy to it. I was in control again and even making some progress with the investigation, all of which helped me to stay sober. Dealing with problems at work in a sensible way and starting to behave myself, Jane was extremely grateful as well. Even during all the turmoil and while working fulltime, she remained supportive and was always willing to listen about the problems I was dealing with at work. Above all, she kept my spirits up, and helped me through those tough times, but as I said before, all of that changed on that fateful day.

My wife had an appointment with her doctor, late that afternoon and while she was driving to his office, her car was rear ended by someone at an intersection. Not a serious collision, but still shocked by the accident, Jane immediately got of her vehicle to see if the person was injured in the other car. Without any warning, the other driver apparently backed up, then swerved his car at her, while pressing the accelerator to the floor. In an instant, the love of my life and my unborn child were gone forever as she was instantly killed. There were two eyewitnesses to the accident, but due to their distance from it, they were unable, unfortunately, to identify the man driving the car. In my mind there was little doubt that the driver had murdered my wife and it should have been classified as a homicide, but for some reason it was officially labeled both as an accident and a hit and run by our department. That was bad enough, but with a serial killer on the loose, the chief refused to spare any men in finding my wife's killer. In fact, he was insistent that my wife's case take a back seat to everything and he personally instructed everyone in the department to spend their entire time and resources on the serial killer case. Although I tried on my own time to track down some of the multiple leads that came into the office, without additional help, it turned out to be a senseless cause. Naturally, his apparent lack of support and *"give a shit"* attitude only caused more disdain in me and my hatred grew towards the chief in the coming months.

My life began to spiral downhill after that and more often than not; I tried to find answers in a bottle. Things got so bad, that I was often drunk on duty and my partner, Russ Wilson, covered for me several times by putting his own job on the line. On many occasions, I went to work in a stupor and would even drink during the day. In fact, there were several instances at the end of my shift that I was not capable to drive home from the station. My partner knew I always had a flask beneath my suit coat and that I would at times take a few *"hits"* from it during the day, but like a *"good"* partner, he never said a word to anybody. Even with my *"pickled"* memory, I remembered at least a dozen times leaving my car at headquarters and letting my partner drive me home in his car. Realistically, I knew my days were numbered, but I did not really care anymore. So what if I had become a liability to the chief or to the department. Booze had a firm grip on me now and it was the only thing in my life that mattered. Plain and simple, I was nothing but a drunk.

Chief Morin hated me and relished in my demise as he watched me go downhill, showing little sympathy while he continued his harassment. Many times, he brought me into his office, slammed the door shut, and put on a show for everyone else in the department. Yelling at the top of his lungs, how I was a disgrace to the uniform and should be thrown off the force. However, even with all of the drinking, I was still doing my job and this only stuck in his craw, making him actually feel sick over the situation. Realistically, Morin was a predator boss and he was just waiting for the right opportunity to finally catch me in the act and end my career. Well, he did not have to wait very long, because six months after my wife died, that day finally came too.

My drinking was totally out of control at that point in time, as I needed more of it during the day when I was on duty. A few sips from the flask were no longer enough and I was actually hiding bottles everywhere to keep myself going. My partner had warned me several times about it and even took me home several times during the middle of the day, due to *"sickness"* on the job. Nevertheless, did that stop me? Hell no, since I often carried a pint of Vodka on me and had several other bottles stashed in my locker at work and in the city car in order to satisfy my cravings.

It became truly amazing to me where a person could find places to hide a bottle in a vehicle. Being creative, some of them included the heater vent, in the trunk underneath the spare tire and behind the rear bumper, secured in place by some electrical tape. Then as my need for the stuff increased, so did my imaginative thoughts on where to hide it elsewhere. The beauty of Vodka was it did not smell and I soon discovered it was easy to hide it in bottles of soda and even in my coffee. To supplement my *"stash,"* within a short period of time I was concealing it in my locker at work in mouthwash bottles and placing it in my orange juice in the refrigerator that all of the detectives used to keep their lunches during the day. However, in one particular instance, I almost had a heart attack when the cleaning boy decided to explore our refrigerator for something to drink. I had forgotten my *"orange juice"* at work one afternoon and had to return after hours to retrieve it, fearing that it might be discovered. Like always, my *"little voice"* was right, because as I rounded the corner into the break room, the young kid had my orange juice container up to his lips. Knowing that my secret was about to be blown, I swiped it from the kid quicker than Bob Cousy could take a basketball away and saved my ass.

I became a master of deception and was always one-step ahead of the chief that is until my heavy drinking starting going into the late night hours. Drinking until after midnight and needing to go to work before seven am had become a real problem. That is when I discovered the beauty of *"uppers"* and their powerful effects for getting you up in the morning. They were *"miracle pills"* to me and an answer to my prayers as they made me sufficiently function throughout the workday. When I first started taking those, for about a week or so, I never went to bed. Sleep was no longer a necessity as I worked all night and day, along with my drinking. Soon, it became very apparent to me that this was a short road to an early death, but being as smart as I was, there was only one answer to my dilemma. That is when Quaaludes or *"downers"* came into my life, as they helped me to sleep. Being a cop, both of these highly addictive drugs were very easy to get and before I knew it, I was a full-fledged *"pill junkie."* Along with my drinking, I was like a yo-yo going up and down into the depths of hell one minute and being on top of the world the next.

Then one particular day as we were riding together in our detective's vehicle Russ sitting in the passenger's seat eyed me with a concerned look. While I was trying not to pass out from the previous night's binge and with seriousness in his voice he said, *"You gotta get yourself straightened out, Shake.....have you looked at yourself in the mirror lately?.....you're a walking dead man for Christ's sake....this is getting real serious and I don't know how much longer I can cover for you....take some advice, I know that the chief is on to you and it won't be much longer before he's going to have you by the balls."* I rubbed my face vigorously with my hands, trying to get my wits about me, but my morning *"uppers"* had not kicked in yet and my head felt like a bowl of mush. *"Yeah...I know,"* I mumbled. *"Life doesn't mean that much to me anymore, Russ... the other night, I felt like eating a bullet, but do you know what stopped me?"* As I stared at my partner with glazed over eyes he replied, *"No, I don't....what did make you stop?"* Reaching for the pint bottle in my jacket pocket, I quickly decided to take my hand away from it as I had never drank openly on duty in front of Russ and my conscious was trying desperately to hold me back. *"I didn't eat a bullet because my gun was missing and I couldn't find it.....that's why, as I didn't have a clue where it was.....plus, I couldn't even get up to look for it because I was too loaded......imagine that, too drunk and messed up to even kill yourself.....how bad is that?"*

My throat was parched as if sand had been poured down it and with my sweaty hands shaking, I rubbed them together hoping to get my nerves under control. Russ seeing me do this, glanced at me for a second from his driving and gently touched me on the shoulder. *"Shake, do you know why I haven't turned you in?.... because even though you are a drunk, you are still worth more than anybody else in our department, including myself.....hell, there isn't a door that I wouldn't go through with you."* I smiled back at him and tapped him on the arm. *"Thanks, partner.....partners need to stick together to get through the heaps of shit that are piled on us...... after all, if we didn't have each other, who would we have?"*

As my partner's eyes welled, I knew he was thinking back to when I had saved his life. A few years ago while investigating a robbery we needed to question a couple of suspects at their home. While knocking on their door, I noticed one of them in the house had slightly pulled the curtain aside at a window. Being partly lucky, I guess and acting by instinct I pushed Russ out of the way of a .357 magnum, hollow point bullet. That day he could have left his wife, but as he put it, *"You saved my life, Shake.....because of you, my wife will see me come home tonight.....from this day forward, I will always have your back and don't you ever forget it."*

I never forgot what he told me that day. Maybe, I was still using those non-cashed chips to protect my drinking and putting my partner on the spot was only part of the cashing in process. Sadly, for me, I really could have cared less about what he had said because my drinking was the most important thing in my life. In reality, I was nothing but a drunk, a man who avoided hangovers by staying drunk and a person who would do anything to get more of the stuff. My loving wife and unborn kid were gone; my job was probably lost, so in my mind to drink myself into oblivion was not that bad of an idea at all. To be blunt, my entire life had been tossed in the crapper and far as I was concerned, if I had ended it all by eating a bullet, it probably would have made me the happiest man on earth.

CHAPTER TWO

Free fall

It was about two months later that my partner and I were on our way to conduct our investigation of a robbery that had occurred at a drug store on Park Street. The storeowner had been severely pistol whipped by the thief and it had landed him in the hospital for more than three days. We had spoken to him previously, but due to his condition at the time, we felt another interview was necessary to clear up a few details. Although, he had been seriously injured and was lying on the floor in a semi-conscious state he was still able to get a good look at the man as he cleaned out the cash drawer. He described his assailant as someone with a medium build, with blonde hair and a fair complexion. The thief was wearing a black, leather, biker jacket and he estimated his age to be around eighteen to twenty two years. Having undergone such turmoil and physical harm, the toughest thing for the owner to accept was the crook hurt him badly for about twenty-three dollars.

When we arrived at his place of business and entered through the front door, to our amazement the shopkeeper with desperation on his face was being held at gunpoint with his hands in the air. The blonde haired man holding the gun had a biker jacket on, telling us that he was probably the same person who had previously robbed the place. Upon seeing us step into the store, the thief immediately bolted out the back door to the alley and disappeared. Quickly, we both pulled our guns and told the shopkeeper to stay where he was. *"You take the front, Russ....I'll go out the back,"* I hollered, dashing for the rear door.

My head was pounding from last night's safari and sweat was running down my forehead into my eyes, causing them to burn. Trying to wipe the perspiration away with my sport jacket sleeve my stomach was in knots as it reminded me that I had not eaten in several days. I was living on booze now and food had become a non-essential part of my diet as I rammed the back door open into the rear alley. Looking left, then right, I saw the suspect head deeper into the alley and immediately took off on a dead run after him. Being in such bad condition I swear within a few steps I was winded and nauseous. Bending over and placing my hands on my knees, I threw up some bile on the pavement and looked up while wiping my mouth with the back of my hand. Seeing the suspect trying to open a side door into another building I pointed my gun at him and hollered, *"Freeze!"*

Within seconds after cocking and pointing my Smith and Wesson at him, what little was left in my stomach came up through my throat and I hurled the disgusting yellow liquid all over the ground. My throat burned from the bile as I tried to steady myself and regain my equilibrium. When I moved my eyes back to the suspect, the world started spinning out of control, and before I knew it, blackness came over me.

I do not know how much time had passed, but as my left eye opened, I realized I was flat on the ground on my back, with my partner and two other officers towering over me. *"Are you alright?"* my partner desperately asked. Quickly sitting up I looked around and saw a body lying on the ground about ten yards from me. *"Yeah, I guess so....what's up with him?"* pointing to the lifeless body. *"You don't remember?"* Russ immediately replied. Trying to get my focus, I opened and closed my eyes a few times, working the haze from my vision. Suddenly realizing that the back of my head was sore to the touch, I rubbed it gently, answering, *"I don't know....I remember stopping the suspect, but everything went blank after that."* My partner pointed to my gun lying on the ground next to me. *"I checked your weapon, Shake....it's been fired and that boy over there has a bullet in his head....the worse part is, he has no gun.... it appears he was unarmed."*

Shocked, I immediately tried to stand up, but the dizziness overwhelmed me, causing me to grab my partner for support. *"What do you mean there's no gun on him....you saw it, Russ....he had a gun, I know he did."* Standing erect I stumbled over towards the body, wiping the sweat from my eyes and to my astonishment discovered that the young kid had taken a bullet to the forehead above the left eye. His head was lying in a large pool of blood, telling me that the back of his head must have been blown to pieces due to the impact of the blast. As I gazed down at the lifeless body, the pounding in my head was so immense that I could barely keep my eyes opened and as I scanned the scene my partner was correct as it appeared there was no weapon in the kid's hand or anywhere near the body. My mind was in a total fog, mostly due to the hangover, but my head and neck were throbbing as well, telling me I was undoubtedly struck from behind. *"I don't know what's going on here, Russ...but I know..."* Just then, a familiar voice came up from behind me and I knew it was the chief. *"What do we have here?......oh, look at that now....my, my.....don't tell me we have another Madison screw up on our hands?"*

My partner quickly responded, *"Believe it or not chief, this boy was robbing the drug store owner again....we chased him out the back and it looks like Shake was forced to take him down, sir."* The chief stood over the boy, peering down at him and then his eyes began searching the scene, looking for any additional clues. After a few moments, a big smirk came to his face as his eyes passed over to me. *"I see your weapon, Madison....but, where's the kid's?"* Rubbing the back of my neck, I peered back at him. *"Well, he had a gun....I saw it and Russ did as well....didn't you partner?"* Russ scratched the side of his face, looked down at the boy and then back to the drug store. *"Well, Wilson...did the kid have a weapon or not?"* the chief demanded. *"Ahh...ohh...yeah...I think he did, sir.... yep, I remember....yeah, he did have a weapon, chief....I think it was*

17

a two inch snub....anyway the shop owner can testify to that." Chief Morin rolled his eyes in disgust at Wilson and then he looked me up and down. *"Well, the shop owner can't help you now, Madison, because he's as dead as a door nail behind the counter....looks like he died of a heart attack or something and with no weapon found on the suspect, your tit is probably in the wringer....it appears that you are going to finally pay the piper for all of the bullshit that you have been pulling off around here as it looks like you're going down for this one, mister."*

Speechless, I tried to shake the cobwebs out of my head, knowing that things did not look good for me and seeing the joyful expression on the chief's face only confirmed my worse fears. Chief Morin, staring at the both of us, stepped forward a few steps and got into our faces. *"I don't know what's going on here, Wilson, but I suspect you are covering up for this guy....let me give you a little piece of advice....don't....that is, if you value your career because this piece of drunken shit is going down, way down into a deep dark hole and I'm going to make sure he does....Madison, give me your badge...as of now you have been put on administrative leave and are under official investigation."*

I removed my detective's badge and glanced at it for a moment, then handed it slowly to him. Seeing the perpetual grin on his face I replied, *"Well....you got what you wanted, Morin....but I'll tell you one thing right now....the boy was armed and I was hit hard from behind....can't you see whoever did that, shot the kid with my gun?....it's pretty damn obvious, isn't it?....even you should know, that I would never shoot an unarmed person, especially a kid......or has your judgment been so corrupted by your deep desire to screw me up the ass that you have put the blinders on?"*

The chief walked to the side of me, grabbing my shoulder and turned my body to look at the back of my neck. *"There's not a mark on you, Madison....there's not even a red spot back there....nice try, but you've been caught in your own lie!"* Quickly, I moved over towards Russ and pulled down my collar, showing him the back of my neck. *"What about you?....what do you see?....it must be red, isn't it?"* Wilson after examining my neck looked over at the chief and then back to me with an expression of regret. *"Sorry partner... I don't see a damn thing....maybe he just didn't hit you hard enough, Shake....or he used something that wouldn't have left a mark....that must be it, chief....don't you think?"*

The chief, seeming to be disgusted with the both of us, began watching the other officers secure the scene. After a few moments, he walked over to one of them and started giving additional instructions while pointing back at me. *"What do you think he's doing, Shake?"* my partner asked putting his hand on my shoulder. I glanced at him saying softly, *"What ever it is....I'm sure it's not going to be in my best interest....the man has been after my butt for a long time, Russ and I'm afraid he's finally caught me with my ass hanging out the window on this one."* As the other officer nodded his head, listening to the Chief's instructions, Morin was jabbing his finger at him and it was obvious by the expression on the officer's face my remaining days on the force were numbered. Appearing to have finished their discussion, the chief and he walked back over to us. *"Officer Dolan will take you back to the station for your statement, Madison....your partner will remain here, on the scene with me."*

Knowing the chief was purposely splitting us up, I realized that he had other plans for me and they were all bad. *"Don't worry Shake, I will take the chief through the whole thing,"* my partner said while he followed the chief back over to the body. As officer Dolan motioned for me to follow him over to his patrol car, my head was finally starting to clear a little and I noticed that the lab boys had come on the scene. They were taking photographs from every angle and the chief was right in the mix of directing everyone. He was really enjoying himself as the smile on his face told me that while he gave out instructions to the investigative team and there was no doubt, as I watched him; he was taking no chances of screwing up the investigation.

Entering the patrol car, I glanced over at the chief and his head rose up noticing that I was departing the scene. A sarcastic grin developed on his face as he glared at me along with a twinkle in his eye. He took his finger and made a slicing gesture across his own throat, making my hatred for the man explode inside me. While I sat down in the patrol car and closed the door, he kept staring at me with amusement almost looking like he had just put Dillinger behind bars. Then suddenly, while the car was backing up, he waived his right hand in mid air while smirking at me and mouthed the words, *"bye..bye."* My contempt for the man bloomed while the driver drove forward and glaring back at him, I gritted my teeth, saying, *"Go to hell, you bastard."*

When we got back to the station my so-called *"statement"* or should I say my interrogation began. I had many friends on the force and they were usually behind me, but I had my enemies too. I believe that most of them were due to jealousy, because my success record on apprehending criminals was very high. The chief had always been against me too, even though my conviction rate made his department look good in the public's eye. Because of this, he always obtained more funding for his budget through City Hall when he asked for it. That was a good thing, since the chief was always acquiring new equipment and sending us for additional training, making our department one of the most progressive in New England, if not the country. However, constantly seeing my picture in the newspapers and hearing my voice on the radio describing our crime solving victories was too much for the chief to take, as he wanted all the glory and commendations for himself. Myself, I could have cared less about the publicity, especially after my wife was killed. All I wanted to do was drink and catch a few *"bad guys,"* but now I found myself in a much darker place than where I had been for the past year. There was no doubt that my enemies in the department were coming for me with everything they had to kick me off the force and if they got lucky enough, put my ass in jail.

The chief had assigned Officer Dolan to lead the interrogation and this was a clear sign of things to come. Dolan, one of the chief's henchmen always had it out for me, since I became a detective before him even though he had several more years of experience on the force. The man was a hothead that did not deserve a detective's badge, but eventually because of some political pressure he finally got the gold badge a year later. However, in my opinion, due to his flaring temper and total disregard for a person's rights, he should have never received the position. In fact, due to his incompetence on a case about two years ago, which I exposed his ineptness on he swore that one day he would *"dance in the streets"* when he acquired his revenge for what I had done to him. Never getting over the delayed promotion and the criticism, it was obvious by the recent turn of events that he was about to have his day in court.

Well, that time had come as I looked at him sitting across the table from me in one of the interrogation rooms. He had the biggest smirk on his face, looking like a kid who had just gotten a big bowl of ice cream with all the toppings and was about to embark on devouring it. The other two officers serving as witnesses were part of the chief's hit squad as well, so I knew the session was going to be a real *"picnic"* for me. The questions they were about to ask me would be definitely slanted and not have my best interest in mind. In addition, I was still hung over from the night before and my mind was still not free yet from the drugs and the booze. Everything was all mixed up in my head and with my memory, still a blank I knew the whole questioning session was going to be nothing but a disaster. Trying to plow through my brain for answers during the interrogation a shocking revelation came to me as my blood was never taken for analysis and that was something I could have kissed them all for not doing. What a rookie mistake I thought for not doing it, but in no way was I going to remind them of it now.

After giving my full statement, they allowed me to leave and I immediately went home to bed. I had not slept in days because of the *"uppers"* and when my head hit the pillow, I literally passed out. In reality, I did not go to sleep, but went into a low-level coma, not hearing or seeing anyone for several nights. It was not until a few days later, that I received a phone call to report to the station for *"additional questions,"* but when I arrived, I discovered that the real reason was for blood sampling. I guess from what I was told, the chief went ballistic when he found out that everyone had forgotten to take my blood on the day of the shooting. In fact, he even suspended a couple of them for a few weeks, but the damage was done, as my tests eventually came back negative for alcohol. The explanation why it showed nothing, even made me laugh a little as I had been out cold for a couple of days and was not able to drink. Otherwise, my blood would have jammed the needle right off the scale.

As the weeks followed, there were several meetings with the District Attorney's office, which considered my written and verbal statements of the incident along with my partner's version of events. Russ had backed up my testimony regarding the presence of a gun, even though I think he never actually saw it. He was directly behind me when we had entered the drug store that day and the kid probably bolted out through the back door before he got a good look at it. The doctor's examination of my neck proved inconclusive as to the injury that I had supposedly received from my assailant, but at least internal affairs and the DA were made aware of it. With the shop owner dead from an apparent heart attack, there were no other available witnesses to support my story about the kid having a gun. That meant I was probably going to jail for a very long time, since the charge of involuntary manslaughter was hanging over me and the chief was licking his chops with the thought of it dropping on me.

Then a strange thing happened, a private citizen by the name of Henry Willingsworth came forward. He testified that he saw someone running from the alleyway, shortly before my partner came sprinting down the sidewalk towards the entrance to the back street. Not wanting to get involved at first, he had held back his eyewitness account. However, later reading in the newspapers that a cop might be railroaded into serving a twenty-year sentence, he came forward and gave his version of what he saw.

Unfortunately, the man was partially deaf and could not testify to when the sound of the gunshot echoed from the alley. However, his statement was enough to save me from the *"big house"* as there was enough doubt placed in everyone's mind to have the charges dropped, but my days on the force were definitely over. Due to a plea bargain and at the chief's insistence, I agreed to resign from the force.

No job, no wife and with no life in front of me, I continued to drink and pop the pills. Soon the bills started piling up and any savings I had quickly disappeared. The bank foreclosed on my house and with no place to go, I was forced to live out of my car. Still being sick in mind and body, I continued taking the *"medicine"* labeled Vodka to drown my sorrows and wipe out the memories of the past. Day by day, my health declined and soon my chest became filled with fluid, telling me that my days were numbered. Almost at the end of my rope and with nowhere else to turn, I decided to head back home to Maine.

When I arrived back in Middleton, things did not change for me at all, as my drinking and drug addictions had followed me home. I managed to scrape up a few dollars from turning in a whole life insurance policy that my wife and I had on each other, but this only enabled my addictions. The only good thing that came out of it was a bed at the motel on Main Street where I would pass out for days at a time. Every morning was the same, however, lying there, anticipating the pain that I was going to endure by placing a foot on the floor before I attempted to get out of bed. My craving was so high at times, that it throbbed through-out my body and caused my hands to shake uncontrollably from withdrawal. However, a sigh of relief would come as I knew my medicine was close at hand because over on the end table, a bottle of vodka always sat, waiting for me when I needed it most. With only a few quick gulps, the pain drained from my body as the clear liquid burned the back of my throat like razor blades. As a result, the shakes magically disappeared and my body relaxed from the liquid nourishment, leaving me at peace with my surroundings.

The vicious cycle of pain and relief would come and go everyday as if I was on an endless merry-go-round of self-destruction, but it was life as I knew it and nothing in the future was ever going to change it.

One morning, however, waking from a multi day binge, I laid there in the motel, sick and hung-over, thinking about my *"friend"* on the nightstand, anticipating its relief that it would give to me. Finally managing to gather enough strength, I reached for the bottle of Vodka and brought it to my lips. Immediately fear exploded inside of me as I realized there would be no relief this horrid morning as the bottle was entirely empty. Knowing I had to face the God forsaken world with no assistance from my liquid savior, a sudden terror enveloped my mind. Throwing the empty bottle across the room in a full-scale panic, I leaped from the sweat-ridden bed and stood up. Immediately, my head began to spin and my vision blurred as I tried to search for another bottle. Maybe I had hidden a *"sleeper"* for emergency purposes I thought....it must be here somewhere!

Stumbling around the darkened room, I began frantically pulling the drawers out of the dresser and threw the few clothes I had in them around the room. With no success of finding a bottle, I continued my frenzied search under the bed, on the desk, and in the bathroom. Dumping out the wastepaper baskets onto the floor and scattering the trash all over the place, only a few empty bottles rolled across the floor and clinked together. Picking up one of them and gazing upon it with dismay, I threw the bottle at the TV screen, demolishing the picture tube into a thousand pieces. Out of my mind with anger, I grabbed a wooden chair from the desk and whipped it with all my might at the wall to the right of the sofa chair, puncturing several holes in the plaster. Thinking that the solution to my problem might be beneath my bed, I picked up one side of it and hurled the mattress with frame and all at the bathroom door, hoping that a full bottle would magically appear.

Finally, exhausted, with no place else to look and at my wits end, I suddenly realized that a trip to the liquor store without some liquid courage in me was inevitable. As I stared at my watch, the face of it was blurry, as if it was covered in a mist or dense fog and rubbing my eyes, trying to focus, the hands of the watch slowly appeared. It read 3:10, but was it morning or the afternoon? God forbid, if it was the morning. That meant the package stores would be closed and with many more hours to go before any possible salvation, what was I going to do?

Staring at the large picture window with the drapes drawn across it and desperately wanting to know if it was day or night, I ripped down the dingy curtains. A flash of lightning blinded my eyes, hurling me backwards against the opposite wall and as the sun's rays penetrated the room I staggered towards the door, holding one arm across my eyes. Grabbing the doorknob and attempting to open the door, a bolt of realization shot into my soul, telling me the knob would not turn. Trying with all my strength the doorknob still did not move, so I began yanking at the door in desperation, hoping to be released from my prison, but no matter how hard I pulled, it remained tightly closed. With no hope in sight, I began kicking and swearing at it, thinking that the heavy metal door might magically open, but alas, it did not move.

Seeing no success and with two closed fists, I hammered the door, trying to pound it into submission, but no matter how hard I struck it, it laughed at me and my futile attempts. Suddenly realizing I was trapped like a rat with no way out and crazy with fear, I began throwing myself at the door. As my body rammed up against it repeatedly, the bruising started to take hold on my flesh, but I cared little about that, as I wanted out and nothing was going to stop me. Out of control and crazy with thirst, I began screaming while throwing myself against it. *"You bastard!....you can't hold me!....let me out!"*

After several minutes of trying to break the door down and with my body drenched in perspiration along with several bruises, the room started spinning and my stomach felt like it was turned upside down. Unexpectedly, yellow bile began flowing out of my mouth and down my shirt as I began heaving my guts out.

Wiping the excess from my mouth with a shirtsleeve and bent over in pain, I gazed up at my enemy, wishing I could smash it down. With one last desperate attempt, I dove at the door hitting it hard, but with it stopping me dead in my tracks, I fell to the floor in a heap. Feeling hopeless and sorry for myself, I began to sob, wondering why God was treating me this way. Lying there, half-conscious, I suddenly felt a need for the bathroom, but trying to stand I fell backwards against the door and slid to the floor. Struggling to move I rolled onto my side, wishing that my legs would work again, but my body was too weak, too helpless, and without any more thought, my pants suddenly became saturated with urine.

Still lying there, on a soak-ridden carpet, I mustered up enough energy to make one last ditch effort and raised my arm, reaching for the coffee table, praying a bottle was there. Then with the room still spinning out of control and making everything a blur, the bright rays of sunlight weakened, leaving me in partial darkness. As my body shivered from the cold clamminess on my skin, blackness gradually came over me and soon I realized that death had come to pay a visit. Suddenly a state of calmness overwhelmed me along with a feeling of peacefulness, making everything serene. Closing my eyes and immersing myself in it, I reached out and grabbed its dreadful hand, letting it steal me away.

CHAPTER THREE

Born Again

I do not know how much time had passed when I opened that first eye and looked around the room. Even though my vision was messed up, I could tell something was different as the smells were not familiar and the bed I was in seemed strange to me. As both of my eyes slowly opened, I realized this was a different place as there were strange pictures hanging on the walls and the big picture window from my motel room was missing. *"Where in the hell am I?"* I thought, trying to raise my head off the pillow. Turning to the right, a chair was draped with my clothes and they appeared to have been recently washed as they were neatly folded along with my shoes and socks. I was entirely naked and the crisp sheets felt good against my body as I sat up against the headboard. *"At least I'm not dead,"* I thought, *"but where could this be?"* Rubbing my face, I discovered my ratty beard had been shaved off and my face felt as smooth as a baby's bottom. No longer did I stink from body odor and personal hygiene neglect, which led me to think, *"It's obvious that someone cleaned me up..... but who?"*

Suddenly, I heard footsteps coming and the door to my room opened. A tray of food appeared and to my astonishment, holding it, was my old high school friend, Ben Morse. *"Well, welcome back Shake.....looks like you had a pretty bad go of it."* Shocked on who was before me, I sat up, straightening myself against the headboard. *"Where am I?....is this your house?"* Ben placed the tray on a table beside me and sat down on the edge of the bed. Staring at me with a smile, he answered, *"Yeah...you're at my place....good thing when the call came into the station, we were shorthanded and I was there to take it...if one of my men had found you, your treatment would have been a lot different....from what I saw, you really busted up that hotel room, but good."*

As my eyes scanned the walls I asked, *"How long have I been here?....I don't remember a thing."* Ben chuckled, replying, *"I wouldn't doubt it....you've been here almost four days now....when I picked you up, I didn't think you were going to make it....in fact, I might have mortgaged my house on it as the ole booze had taken its toll on you for sure....most of the time you were screaming out of your head as the bottle tried to keep a hold on you...hell, the shrieks you made while you were drying out were chilling at times, but after a few days they seemed to disappear."* I grabbed him by the shoulder and shook him slightly. *"Thanks...sorry I was such a pain in the ass to you, but things have been pretty bad for me lately.....I hope you didn't miss work because of all of this."* Ben took the coffee cup off the serving tray and handed it to me, motioning to take some. *"You better drink this...it will help you with the remaining DT's that you have.....and by the way, I was able to get a nurse that I know at the hospital to care of you....she is downstairs right now and that's who prepared this breakfast for you...her name is Andrea Carlson."* My hands were still shaking a little as I took the cup from him and placing it up to my mouth I dribbled a little. *"I've been through hell, Ben....with Jane being killed last year and the recent trouble that I had with the bad shooting, I guess living and I just didn't get along anymore."*

Ben stood up from the bed and patted me on the shoulder. *"Yeah...I heard about the shooting....sounds like you might have gotten a rotten deal out of that, but we can talk more about that soon enough....you better get some food in you now and I'll tell Andrea that you are awake.....she'll be up to see you real soon."*

Ben, while walking to the door stopped, turned his head, and smiled back at me. *"Just want to let you know something from the get go...there is no booze in this house, so don't bother looking for it...okay?"* I nodded my head and he slowly opened the bedroom door to leave. Upon him closing it, I took another sip of the herbal tea and looked at the breakfast tray. On it were a few hard-boiled eggs that were pealed along with some buttered toast and sliced melon. My stomach was still in knots, but I knew eating something was essential so I forced the contents of the tray down. The first few bites of the eggs made me gag, to tell the truth, and I thought they were going to come right back up on me, but as I progressed through the rest of the items, the taste of food became more tolerable.

Finishing breakfast, I leaned back on my pillow and rested my head against it, trying to keep my mind from spinning. My equilibrium was still a little shaky and my internal organs were reminding me of the severe punishment I had put them through the past few months. My stomach was not used to food and with the constant rumbling that was coming from it; I did not know how much longer it was going to stay inside of me. Without taking any chances, I located the bathroom door that was attached to the room, thinking if I needed it in a hurry; I would know where to go. Concentrating on stopping the room from turning and twisting, I stared at the ceiling, trying to fix my eyes on the overhead light fixture. Being half in a trance, time passed quickly and it was only a few minutes later that a knock sounded at the door. As it opened, a dark haired woman entered, dressed in tight, black slacks and a white, form-fitting blouse. A few buttons were undone at the top of it, which revealed her more than ample breast size and along with the blouse fitting snugly as well, it was indeed a pleasant sight. Along with a pleasing smile, she was a beautiful woman of about thirty years of age, with long, black hair to her shoulders, which shined in the daylight that was emanating through the large bedroom windows.

As she walked towards me, her slender figure in tight fitting pants definitely caught my attention and while placing her hand on my forehead to determine if I still had a fever she said, *"I'm Andrea...looks like you have decided to come back to live with us for a while longer, haven't you?"* She grabbed my wrist and glanced at her watch, taking my pulse and while doing so I smiled back at her. *"Are you the one that cleaned me up and washed my clothes?"* Letting go of my hand quickly, she felt my forehead again. *"Yep... and I washed everything else you had....you needed it."* Embarrassed slightly, I pulled the sheets up a little. *"Sorry to have put you out like this...your name's Andrea right?.... just want to let you know that I've had it tough lately and things...."* Instantly growing a disgusted look, she abruptly cut me off while picking up the tray. *"Don't want to hear about your troubles, Mr. Madison.....especially your kind as all of you drunks have the same pitch....I have seen and heard it a hundred times before working at the hospital...you know, how sorry you feel for yourselves...your life is always the worse and no one else can comprehend your problems...that no one understands you and that you desperately need sympathy....like you, they all want a shoulder to cry on and someone to listen to their bullshit....so buddy, I'm going to save you a lot of time and effort..... don't go there with me because it won't do you any good."*

She picked up the tray and swiftly left the room while I sat there at first, appalled at the way she had spoken to me. However, as the time passed, I suddenly realized that what she had just told me was the truth and it had cut into me deeply. Self-evaluating myself for a few minutes, I began to grasp that maybe it was about time I faced the facts and got off the *"pity pot."* Yes, my wife was dead, killed by a hit and run asshole that had no right to live anymore, but was I honoring her memory by drinking myself to death? *"This is ridiculous,"* I muttered to myself. *"Here I am close to death and for what?....sometimes I guess you need a kick on the side of the head and boy did I just ever get one from a complete stranger....one who could see right through me and not be taken in by my stinking words of self pity."* Disgusted with myself, I jumped out of bed and dressed quickly, hoping to catch her before she left the house.

Opening the door to my room and going downstairs I heard talking coming from the kitchen and as I rounded the corner, Ben and Andrea were seated at the breakfast table. *"It's good to see you up and around, Shake...why don't you take a seat and join us,"* Ben stated while moving a chair out from the table. *"You've met Andrea already....Andrea, this is Shaker Madison...a good friend of mine."* I cautiously shook her hand with a half heartened smile, replying, *"Yeah, we met...I guess by now she knows just about everything that she needs to know about me....oh, and we just had a pretty good conversation, too."*

Sitting down, my eyes never left her as she flashed a small grin back at me with a partially blushing face, replying, *"Sorry, I got a little feisty up there, but I have been working a lot of hours lately..... little sleep, I guess, has finally caught up to me."* I glanced over at Ben and then my eyes found her again. *"No problem, Andrea...it's alright that I call you that, isn't it?"* Nodding her head in agreement, I continued with, *"Sometimes a fellow just needs to hear the real truth about himself before he even has a chance of getting back into life.....don't you agree, Ben?"* My old friend winked back at me. *"Yeah, Shake...I guess we all need that from time to time.... take you for instance...when I found you a week ago, you might say the coroner should have been called instead of a nurse...you look pretty good now, but back then I would had laid odds that you were going to end up on a cold slab down at the morgue.....you have to give credit where credit is due, Shake.....Andrea was actually the one that pulled you through this."*

As we sat and talked, I realized that my old friend was not going to coddle me, as he was extremely blunt with his opinions. Andrea, had softened a little, but she was still laying it on the line about me sobering up and becoming a useful human being again. I could tell by her attitude that she had seen enough of my kind, and far as she was concerned if I made it....that was great.....if I did not, well let's just say she was not going to lose any sleep over it. To my surprise though, both of them seemed to very supportive, and they were both sincere in their wanting to see me make it as a sober human being again. In fact, Morse even offered me a job of dispatcher back at the station. *"You need to get back into* the swing of things, Shake," Ben said lighting up a cigarette. "Idle hands are the devil's workshop and with you, it's suicide....plain and simple....so how about it?....would you like to take the job and come back working for me?"

Hearing those words made me recognize it had been a long time since I felt useful and as I took a sip of coffee, sitting back in my chair, my mind was bombarded with thoughts of the past. Could I stay sober? Was my friend taking a huge gamble on me for nothing? Or did he see something in me that gave him the confidence that I would straighten myself out? On the other hand, was he just being a good friend and felt some charity was in order? I did not want to hurt anymore of my friends and colleagues as I had done plenty of that already and at first, my only thought was to get out of there as quickly as I could. The sharp thoughts of, "Maybe I did kill that kid in the alley.....after all, I was definitely out of it that day with all the booze and pills in me......being in another black out, I could have probably done anything without remembering it ....even kill someone for God's sake." While all of this was continually running through my mind, at the same time, I knew this was the end of the line for me. If Shaker Madison was ever going to live another day, he needed to take drastic action by getting off the booze and cleaning up his act. After mulling it over for several moments, I glared back at him, answering, "Sure...I would love to take the job....and I can tell you another thing, Ben, I won't let you down....you can count on that."

Therefore, from that day on, I became the new dispatcher for the Middleton Police Department, taking over for a person who had recently retired. It was a far cry from a detective's position and pay, but it gave me the badly needed confidence that I yearned for. Performing a job while remaining sober was necessary for me to feel that I was a part of society again and Ben did not have the blinders on when he decided to take a chance on me, as he knew I was headed for a real uphill battle in keeping my sobriety. So after several months of adjusting to my new job, I guess that is when Ben decided that we would take a little trip together as I was about to meet something that would forever change my life.

As part of the Selectmen's new law enforcement development program, the police department was in the process of acquiring some dogs for their newly formed K-9 unit from a man that lived further north of us near the Canadian border. Ben had asked me along to help with the selection of two pups from the litter that would later go on for special training. Being a dog lover all of my life, he knew I would quickly jump at the chance and he was right. The breeder specialized in German Shepherds that had a long history of being *"working dogs,"* which were utilized in police work and his reputation for providing excellent animals was well known throughout law enforcement. Their sense of smell and hearing were much keener than regular dogs and their physiques were unparalleled in the attack dog industry.

When we arrived at his house that was surrounded by various kennels, to my surprise, the breeder was of Indian descent. A very tall man with a deep complexion, his braided jet-black hair glistened in the sunlight as we approached the house. Greeting us on the porch, I could tell from his firm handshake that he had spent many years working in the woods as a logger. His hands were extremely rough and strong along with several scars, telling of the many mishaps that he had experienced working in the woods. As we entered the small rundown house, the pups were in the living room, playing with each other. The breeder had isolated them to one corner where their food and water dishes were by utilizing a temporary fence made out of chicken wire. Seeing the pups munch each other and roll around, it immediately brought a grin to my face and as we took a seat to further observe them, the Indian stated, *"So, what you men think?....they all nice pups, are they not?....especially one with tan collar."*

Eying the dog that the Indian was talking about, he had placed different colored collars on each pup to differentiate between them. Thinking that was a terrific idea, my eyes examined the little fellow he had identified with the tan collar. He was a standard black and tan German Shepherd with good bone structure and sitting next to him was another dog with a blue collar that was similar in stature. They both looked the biggest and healthiest of the pups, so I was anxious to vent my opinion. *"Those two look like the ones, don't you think?"* I said pointing out the two dogs to Ben. Looking closer at the pups, studying their bone structure and overall appearance, Ben replied, *"I think you're right Shake, but don't look now...there is someone else that is trying to make friends with you."*

Not knowing what Russ was talking about, I looked behind me, and to my surprise, there was a solid jet-black colored pup with huge paws sitting right next to me, licking the heel of my shoe. He was much larger than the rest of the pups in the room, being almost twice their size, and his face was entirely covered in black fur. With his feet being so large, it made him look a little funny and awkward as he walked around to the front of me. Reaching down with my hand, he immediately licked it several times while keeping his eyes shut. *"What you doing here?"* the Indian said loudly. *"Come on...back you go."* Quickly, he scooped up the pup with him squirming wildly in his arms. *"No more that!"* the Indian said while he spanked him on the butt. While the pup still struggled to get loose, I stood up and walked towards the man. *"Where are you taking him?"* I demanded. The Indian stopped walking away from me and turned holding the pup from the withers. Holding it out at arm's length he declared in a disgusted voice, *"This from litter I have out back....they half wolf, half dog......all useless....nothing you want.....those much better,"* pointing to the other puppies on the living room floor.

As I approached the Indian, the pup bit his hand while at the same time squirming to get free. Wincing from the shock of the bite, the Indian let go of the pup and he flew from his arms at me, causing me to catch the little guy in mid-air. Immediately, the puppy licked my face and then started chewing on one of my ears. *"Looks like he's taken a shine to you Shake,"* Ben said as he patted him in my arms. *"Heh there!....you still have puppy teeth you little bastard...that hurts!"* as I pulled him away from my head and looked at his cute black face. Holding the puppy up in front of me and admiring him, I glanced over at the Indian, saying, *"How much?"* Still pleased with the fur ball in my arms and after I gave him a few additional pats, the Indian observing us shook his head in disbelief. *"For that?....hell, I try to get rid of them.... they, no good! ......even make lousy watchdog......big man, you take him.....no charge.....he last one..... if no one take him soon......well, just say..... good thing you want him."*

Knowing exactly what the Indian meant, I held the pup tighter in my arms, replying, *"This big guy is going home with me, then..... are you sure I can't pay you something for him?....maybe for the food he's eaten already?"* The Indian immediately chuckled as he pointed at the half wolf pup. *"White man have no idea how much that can eat!....you take him....good luck!"*

That is how my life changed forever and for the better too. You see, Barrett and I became great friends as the months went on. We were inseparable as he came to work with me everyday after that. I tried leaving him home at first as a pup, but no matter what type of cage I locked him in, he always escaped. Barrett would then tear Ben's house up by gnawing at the furniture and pulling down the curtains, but his favorite was to chew up the bedroom pillows and spread the goose down everywhere. After all, Ben was good enough to let me stay with him for a while and ripping up the furniture was not in the plan, so since he was the chief and the boss, Barrett ended up going to work with me everyday.

As he grew, the dog filled out matching his enormous feet and his coat turned to a silvery jet-black color. His deep yellow eyes and black face made him look fierce and intimidating, but in reality, he was very disciplined. He always listened to my commands and was very obedient especially whether he was needed for protection or not and his keen nose soon became apparent during our play sessions together. One of our so-called *"training exercises"* involved taking a black golf ball and throwing it into the woods at night for him to find. I instructed him to sit while I threw the ball and after it had come to rest, I would then release him. No matter how deep in the woods I tossed it, he never failed in returning the ball to my feet, looking for another throw. For hours, we would play that game and I swear that is how I developed a rotator cuff problem years later in my right shoulder.

Additionally, Barrett was a great swimmer and often pulled me to safety during our *"practice rescue missions"* while swimming together at one of our nearby lakes and it was nothing for him to swim a mile or so, pulling me along while holding his tail.

His understanding of language became very apparent as the months passed as well. Since there was no doubt that learning commands was easy for him, too easy in fact. It soon became obvious that he had the uncanny ability to comprehend and understand, almost in its entirety, the English language. Amazing to say the least, later it became necessary for me to spell out words that we did not want him to recognize, but that was short lived, as he soon understood the spelling of some of the most common words.

Truly, a remarkable animal, Barrett could also sense people's inner feelings as well and would often comfort them when they were down in the dumps by placing his head on their laps, allowing the person to pet him. Having that unusual ability, he helped many people in the department deal with their daily frustrations and always brought a smile to their faces. All of the men loved him dearly, especially Ben, who often played with him at his house. Both of us, tossed tennis balls at Barrett and he would catch them in mid-air as if they were a fly ball. The only problem was we went through a tremendous amount of tennis balls as many times Barrett crushed them with his powerful jaws, ending their usefulness.

At one year old he was more than one hundred pounds of solid muscle and could easily drag a two hundred pound man across the floor. His athletic ability was astounding, often leaping a six-foot high fence with a single bound while chasing down squirrels and catching them for a tasty meal. Speed and quickness was in his repertoire as he could catch houseflies in the air or easily outrun a skittish cat. However, upon catching it, he never hurt the animal, only mouthed it gently a few times, and then always let it go. He heard people's voices where a human could not and we always knew when a distant thunderstorm was approaching, because he sought shelter in a bathtub or other secluded place. Gunfire or other loud noises never affected Barrett, but the rumblings of a thunderstorm sent horrible chills through him and he never stuck around for them either.

We slept, ate and worked together, twenty-fours a day. Where I was, Barrett was...it was just that plain and simple. I was alive again, wanting to work and before long, seeing the changes that were occurring in me, Ben placed me back on active duty again as a detective along with my newfound friend.

Soon we were solving petty crimes together, by seeking out shoplifters and robbery suspects. Many times, Barrett's nose would come into play by tracking the criminals from the crime scene to where they lived, even if they had driven in a vehicle back to their home! How he managed to do that, nobody including myself could ever figure out, but Barrett would do it, and it was not just once, for he did it many, many times. So many, in fact, that the crooks in our small town got really scared and petty crime dropped by over fifty percent. We were an unbeatable team and because of him, my life improved tremendously as well, but it was not just due to Barrett. Andrea had come into my life too, as we saw more and more of each other through the coming months. She came to love Barrett as I did and he became fond of her as well, but the only problem we had, he had become overly protective of Andrea and always placed himself between her and the person she was addressing. Everybody needed to be constantly reminded to show their hands at all times and not make any sudden movements towards her because if Barrett felt Andrea was threatened in any way, he grabbed the individual by the arm with his powerful jaws, reminding the person to behave. Thank God, it never went beyond that, since I could have only imagined what he would have done to them.

▲ ▲ ▲

Staring into those bright yellow eyes brought back all of those memories as I stroked the back of his neck and a broad smile came to my face as I asked, *"So...how do you want to handle this, boy?"* Barrett pawed me and sat up straight, looking to the right of him and back again at me. *"You want to go right...ehh?"* I chuckled, stroking his fur and rubbing one of his ears. Barrett stood and motioned with his body that he was ready to go into action as he moved slightly to the right. *"You hold on there for a second....like I said we have to be careful with this guy....if he has a weapon we could be walking into a hornet's nest."* Impatient, he pawed me once more while licking his chops and lunging towards the right. *"Okay...okay...you can take the right, but you are going to wait for my signal before you make your move.....you got that?"* Again, Barrett motioned as if he was going to bark in agreement, but remained quiet, only licking me on the side of the face.

Taking one last look around and seeing no one else from the search team, I grabbed the side of his head and reaffirmed my concern. *"Okay...you be careful now and wait for my signal...no heroics today...you got that?"* Barrett looked off to the right and I let him go. Within seconds, he had disappeared into the brush, without a trace, and I was on my own. Opening the chamber of my Model 27, .357 magnum, I spun the cylinder and verified the gun was fully loaded. Closing it, I began my approach to the left side of the small group of evergreens that were ahead of me, being careful where I stepped to avoid the snapping of any small twigs. Thinking I was fortunate that the forest floor was covered with a thick moss, thus making the advance easy and quiet,

I systematically made my way over to a large hemlock tree that was directly west of the evergreens. I figured they would give me excellent cover and provide a better vantage point to begin negotiations with the escaped criminal if he was still there. However, knowing Barrett, he was never wrong, especially about these types of things, and as I worked my way over, a partial human face became visible through the thick evergreen branches.

I froze immediately in my tracks and gradually slid my body behind the huge hemlock tree. Then in amazement, I saw Barrett up in a leaning, blown down tree about ten feet off the ground staring at something below him. Evidently, he had climbed up the leaning trunk to better position himself. Glancing downward at me with enthusiasm written all over his face, Barrett was definitely anticipating the assault on his victim below. Immediately, I shook my head telling him no and to stay put, but by his reaction, there was little time left before he took his own initiative on the suspect. Knowing there was no time to lose, I hollered, *"Corey!... This is the Middleton Police Department...you are completely surrounded....come out with your hands in the air and no harm will come to you!"*

The woods fell silent with no response and as I glanced up at Barrett, he was readying himself to pounce. *"Last chance Corey!.... come out with your hands up!"* Suddenly, I saw the prisoner's face through the branches and as his body became more exposed, it revealed that he had a handgun pointing in my direction. Within a split second, he aimed the weapon and fired a quick shot. Bang! A piece of bark blew off beside my head from the tree that I was behind, causing me to flinch from the flying debris. Quickly looking around the trunk to return fire, I saw Barrett leap through the air from the blown down tree and disappear into the brush below.

All of a sudden, screams filled the air and while deep loud growls and snarling partially drowned them out I heard, *"My God, he's got me!....ahhhhh!.....ahhhh!.......get the bastard off me!"* Within an instant, I ran to the clump of evergreens with my pistol at the ready and bursting through the branches into the small clearing, the sight in front of me brought a smile. With a look of terror on the prisoner's face, Barrett had him backed up against a large pine tree, snarling, and exposing his large canine teeth. Noticing immediately, that my partner had badly bitten the prisoner's right arm and that his weapon was lying on the ground, I knew the man was ready to surrender. Several sets of teeth marks decorated the rest of his body and a large gash extended from the convict's elbow to his wrist. The prisoner's clothes were torn in many places and there were signs of blood oozing through his exposed white tee shirt. Barrett's yellow eyes were no longer showing the unconditional love that they often exhibited to me, but looked evil and menacing as they glared up at the criminal. *"Get him off me!"* the man cried out trying to put more distance between them by pushing his back up against the tree. Holding his right arm with his left and with his clothes ripped to shreds, the convict's eyes were wide open and glaring. There was little doubt by the prisoner's face that he was scared half to death, wondering if the mad beast was going to finish him and hearing the man yell at me to get the dog off him, saliva was spraying from his mouth while the sweat poured off his face.

"I told you to get him off me!" the man hollered again. My chuckling turned into a grin as I replied, *"Alright boy......that's enough......ease off the man before you give him a heart attack."* Barrett promptly turned his head and looked at me, removing the snarl from his face, and sat back on his haunches while still staring at the man. *"Don't move buddy...or else the dog will have you again and this time I won't call him off."* The convict, sweating bullets with scratches all over his face kept looking at the dog with fear. *"That's not a dog....it's a God damn beast....I've never seen anything like that in my life!"* Hearing that, Barrett immediately snarled at him and got up on all fours, ready to attack again. *"That's alright boy....I know you don't like him and want to play with him some more, but we have to bring him back in one piece...so back off."* Seeing the dog glare at him with hatred in his eyes, the prisoner pushed himself against the tree again. *"You talk to that*

thing like he understands you or something....he's a damn menace I tell ya....look at it!"

Barrett inched closer to him, sending even more fear into the escaped convict and while watching the spectacle unfold in front of my eyes, I calmly pulled out a cigarette. *"You better not talk about him like that as he understands everything you are saying about him......I hate to say it, but anymore talk like that and he's going to get you again!"* The convict looked at me with bewilderment, replying, *"What kind of shit are you trying to pull on me?....that dog can't speak!"* I chuckled while picking up the dropped handgun and glared back at him. *"No, he can't speak... at least the way we do....but he understands every word that you are saying about him and he doesn't like it...do you boy?"* Barrett growled deeply and raised his upper lip even more at the man as he glanced back at me for a second, telling me I was right. *"Okay...nice boy...I really like you....you are my friend,"* the convict said extending out his hand in friendship. Immediately, Barrett lunged at him, taking a mighty snap at the outstretched hand, sending the convict into full panic mode up against the tree again. *"What the hell is the matter with him?...I'm trying to make friends with him!"* Hearing those words sent Barrett into full attack mode while I lit up my cigarette. After taking a puff, I answered, *"He doesn't like that word....never has....so don't say it, unless you want to start losing some body parts...in fact, he's look-ing at your crotch right now!"*

Smirking at the prisoner, I chuckled while Barrett stared him down and soon tears exploded from the convict's eyes. Covering his crotch with both hands, he said loudly, *"I can't believe it!.... he doesn't like what word?....f..r..i..e?"* Immediately I stopped him by holding up a hand and saying, *"Hold on there....he can spell too!"* The convict's eyes rolled back in his head, as he could not believe what he was hearing. Reluctantly, he tried to sound con-vincing, but the tone in his voice told me otherwise. *"Okay...nice dog...that's it, nice doggie...I really like you,"* and the man tried to extend his hand again. Barrett immediately returned to my side and sat down, appearing like a normal dog, but he continued to emit low growls at the man. I patted him on the head and stroked his neck while he looked up at me with a huge smile on his face. The escaped prisoner watching us, pointed to Barrett. *"That dog is half human for Christ's sake....where in the hell did you get him?"* Stroking his fur some more, I replied, *"Oh...he's my buddy...we are partners."*

My eyes began scanning the woods and not seeing a sole, I looked down at Barrett. *"Could be some time before the rest of the search team catches up with us...why don't you go and find us something to eat."* He did not move at first, so I motioned with my head and pointed to the left of us. *"Go on now...you're done here...don't worry I have him covered."* Barrett glanced back and forth between the convict and me, trying to decide if it was okay to leave. *"I told you, it's okay...now go and get us something."* In a flash, Barrett disappeared into the woods and I turned to the prisoner. *"You better take a seat over there and behave yourself while I gather up some wood.....remember, if you try and make a break for it, the dog is out there and your ass will be his."*

As I started to gather a few pieces of dried pine that littered the ground, the convict sat down on a log. *"Where in the hell did he go lawman?"* Picking up some more sticks while keeping my eye on him, I replied, *"He went to get us something to eat....we might as well enjoy a little lunch before the others get here."*

It was only about fifteen minutes later, when Barrett reappeared in front of us with a large rabbit in his mouth. My partner casually walked over to me, dropped the fresh kill at my feet, and then took his place beside me while not taking his eyes off the prisoner. By that time, the fire was blazing away and I had rigged a small spit. Skinning and dressing the rabbit out with my knife, I pushed the handmade spit through it, placing it over the open fire, and within minutes, the area was filled with the aroma of cooking meat. *"Why does that damn dog keep staring at me?....tell him I won't run, okay?....and by the way, do*

I get some of that?.....I haven't eaten in days," the prisoner asked *staring at the rabbit, cooking over the open fire.* I could tell by the smacking of the prisoner's lips that he was starved, so I decided to have a little more fun with him. *"He comes first,"* I replied pointing at Barrett. *"Then me....if there is anything left, you can have it."*

Right away, a disgruntled look came over the convict's face as drool started to flow out of the corner of his mouth and while it dribbled down his chin, he exclaimed, *"You'll feed a God damn dog before a human being?....what in the hell is the matter with you anyway?"* Barrett growled a little and his head turned toward the man. *"I told you to keep your mouth shut and not to talk about him.....if you keep it up and finally piss him off enough, he might not quit on you this time."* Gazing at me, the prisoner sitting on the log readjusted himself, which immediately caused Barrett to rise to his feet. *"You better not move too much,"* I warned. *"He gets particularly aggravated when he has to watch someone close, especially when his dinner is about to come off.....you better keep still or be willing to suffer the consequences."*

Seeing that the rabbit was a golden brown, Barrett nudged me with his nose, telling me that it was time. As I lifted it from the fire, he watched me closely, but his eyes were on the prisoner as well, letting the man know that he was *"still on the job."* As I tore the rabbit into pieces and placed them on the log in front of him, the convict was intently watching me. Wiping the drool from his mouth, the convict blurted, *"Looks like there's plenty of rabbit...I should be able to get a piece."* Chuckling, I looked up at him. *"You don't know how hungry my partner is,"* as I tossed Barrett a piece. Catching the meat in mid-air and after three mighty chews, Barrett swallowed it whole, looking for more. The second piece disappeared as quickly as the first and then his eyes focused in on the remaining rabbit. Picking up the last two chunks, I motioned with one of them to Barrett and he quickly gave a little bark signaling he was ready for another.

Throwing it to him, he gulped it down and sat there licking his chops. *"All right if I have this piece, boy?"* extending the piece out to him. Seeing it was the last piece, the prisoner sat up straighter on the log, saying, *"He's a God damn pig...how about me?"* Barrett sniffed the fourth piece in my hand, sat back on his haunches, and while turning his head at the convict, his upper lip snarled slightly. Looking back at me, he woofed, telling me it was okay and I bit off a piece and started enjoying the sweet taste of the meat. The prisoner stared at me with hatred in his eyes, watching me pick away at the carcass while I enjoyed each and every morsel. With only bones left, I tossed them to Barrett and he quickly crushed them in his powerful jaws and swallowed them. The prisoner stared at both of us with disgust. *"That's really shitty....that pig over there ate most of it and you finished off what was left....you didn't even give me a smell of it.....both of you are just plain assholes."*

Barrett quickly got up and faced the man, getting into his attack stance. A deep growl came out of him, while his white teeth glimmered in the sunlight. Barrett lunged at the man a couple of times, causing him to jump to his feet and force his back up against a tree. With a full face of terror, he looked in every direction for a means of escape. *"I wouldn't try that if I were you.... he would have you within three steps...I warned you about ridiculing him...now, I don't know if I can call him off."* The convict realizing it was hopeless, looked at Barrett and pleaded, *"I'm sorry boy....I take back everything I said....really I do!"* Laughing out loud I commanded, *"Alright Barrett, that's enough......the man says he's sorry....it's okay!"*

Still wedged up against the tree, the prisoner's eyes were still wide, expecting at any moment he was about to be made into dessert. *"I told you, that's enough!"* I hollered, motioning with my hand for Barrett to come. Suddenly, the deep growling stopped; Barrett's head turned, and looked behind us. Focusing his full attention to that portion of the forest, I knew he was onto something. Peering off in that direction, I exclaimed, *"They're coming...aren't they, boy?"* My partner turned away from the convict and his tail began to wag, looking like a long lost friend was about to appear. Within a few moments, Ben and a few other officers emerged about one hundred yards from us and I waived my arm overhead. *"We're over here, chief....everything is okay!"*

CHAPTER FOUR
My Old Life Returns

As I drove back to my place, Barrett and I planned to celebrate the apprehension of the escaped prisoner who had been serving fifteen to twenty years for armed robbery. Being a convicted felon, he had little to lose, and since we were able to return him to the *"Big House"* without taking a scratch it was a real plus. *"I think we both deserve a little treat tonight, boy....what do you think?"* My partner, sitting in the front seat with his head out the window and enjoying the fresh breeze on his face, glanced over at me. Smiling from ear to ear with a rhythmic panting, Barrett licked his chops and moved over next to my leg, putting his head on my lap. Rubbing his ears, a familiar grunt came from him enjoying my affection, as I added, *"I think a huge steak is in order.... don't you?"*

Barrett's head immediately perked up and his bright yellow eyes gazed up at me, anxiously agreeing with my assessment. After pawing my leg a few times, he began staring out the windshield, searching for the grocery store that he knew was coming up in a few blocks and after letting loose with a few short barks; he wildly licked the side of my face and shoved his nose into mine. Interfering with my driving as I tried to keep the car on the road, I pushed him aside and patted him on the head. *"Hold on there.... we'll be there in a second and don't worry......you'll be able to pick out your own."* Barrett seemed satisfied with that as he sat back down on the seat, but as I turned into the parking lot, the thought of what was about to come was just too much for him. Instantly, he stood up with his head out the window, wagging his tail, smelling the air that surrounded him, as he knew his reward was very near.

The owner of the grocery mart, Paul Seeley, being a dog lover himself, allowed me to bring Barrett into the country store on a regular basis. Always greeting us at the front entrance today was no exception, as he opened the door for us. *"Good afternoon, men.... doing a little shopping today?"* I shook Paul's hand, replying, *"Yep... we just apprehended that Corey fellow who escaped from the prison the other day and thought a little reward was in order....do you have any nice steaks?...I think we both deserve one."* Before I could even finish my sentence, Barrett had disappeared around the corner, and I knew immediately where he had gone. As Paul and I walked over a few aisles, the display cases showing the meat selections came into view and sure enough, there was Barrett with his paws on the glass, staring straight ahead at the full case of steaks. While walking up to him, he intermittently threw several glances back and forth at us, but his main attention was definitely on the beautiful cuts of meat behind the glass. Going behind the counter, Paul chuckled as he grabbed a sheet of waxed paper from the top of it, saying, *"I suppose you already have yours picked out...don't you, Barrett?"* Immediately, my four-legged companion began pawing the glass case at a huge chuck steak that was over two pounds in weight. *"You don't want something better than that?"* I asked. *"You know there are some nice sirloins over here."* Barrett shook his head at my suggestion and again pawed the glass case. Laughing aloud, Paul added, *"Heh...he knows what he wants,"* as he removed the huge steak from underneath the glass. Shaking my head a little and patting Barrett a few times, I replied, *"Yeah, that's one thing about my buddy here, Paul....you might say his stomach goes more for quantity than quality....besides with those 'choppers' of his a tough steak means very little to him."* My partner's eyes became wide as he glared at the steak on the weighing scale, thinking about the feast that he was about to enjoy. *"Give me two of those sirloins, Paul...the ones that have a little more fat on them....I'm sure my buddy here will enjoy that as well when I trim it off."* As Paul wrapped the huge chuck steak, he roared with laughter, gazing at Barrett's antics. *"The way he's looking at yours, Shake, you better keep a careful eye on them....otherwise; he might gobble up those too!"*

Getting back into the car with our newly found treasures, Barrett began steadily pawing at me while eying the paper bag in the back seat. *"Be patient, boy...we're almost home...plus, we have to wait for Andrea to get home from work."* Immediately, he shoved his head underneath my arm with excitement and began licking the side of my face. *"Yeah, I know...she's a good girl and you love her, too....it will be good to see her tonight."*

Pulling out, onto the main highway, my thoughts quickly turned to Andrea and a smile came to my face. We had been seeing each other seriously for more than a year now and our relationship could not have been better. Getting along well together and having the same interests created a strong bond between us. Additionally, her feelings towards Barrett were immense as she loved the dog dearly and often played with him in the backyard. Seeing them together always brought a lot of joy into my heart and when we all wrestled on the lawn, the memories it gave me were precious as Barrett would *"attack"* us and gently mouth our arms and legs, making us both laugh hysterically while we played with him. I do not know who had the most fun, to tell the truth, but looking back on those picturesque times as I drove back to my house only caused me to grin from ear to ear.

Within a few minutes, we turned into the driveway, and right away, I noticed a strange car parked in front of the house. Andrea's vehicle was already in the driveway, but I had no idea who the other car belonged to and while opening my door, Barrett jumped out of the passenger's side window and bolted for the front door. As he approached it, his nose went to work sniffing the threshold and his upper lip snarled, telling me something was not quite right. *"What's the matter, boy?"* I said while quickly walking up to the front stoop. Reaching it, the front door opened and Andrea appeared, flashing a huge smile. Seeing her, Barrett immediately dropped his head, let out a slight cry with some soft whimpering, and rubbed his head against her. However, it was only seconds later when he returned to full alert.

"I heard both of you had some success today," Andrea said while patting Barrett on the head. Displaying to her the paper bag in my arms, I replied, *"Yeah, the 'bad man' is back in his cage... thought we should do a little celebrating tonight so I picked up some nice steaks from Paul's on the way home."* Barrett looked beyond Andrea and his lip began to curl again. *"What in the hell is up with you?"* I asked grabbing him from behind the neck while Andrea looked behind her. *"There's someone here to see you, Shake....he just got here a few seconds ago and says he's an old friend of yours."* Entering the house, I instructed Barrett to behave himself and while doing so, my mind kept thinking who the person could be and rounding the corner to go into the living room, I was totally taken back. There standing next to the couch to my amazement was my old partner, Russ Wilson.

Seeing me, he immediately took a few steps towards me and extended his hand. *"Nice to see you, Shake...it's been a long time."* Barrett let out a low, extended growl and I quickly reprimanded him for it. *"What's got into you?....he's an old buddy....say hi to the man."* Russ surprised at seeing the huge animal, backed up a few steps. *"He's a big one...isn't he?"* Chuckling, I replied, *"Yeah... he's my new partner...this is Barrett....Barrett, this is Russ...say hi."* Barrett did not move and his eyes glared at Russ, almost trying to stare him down, while watching his every move. Russ seeing the dog's reaction to him, softly said, *"He's not too friendly, is he?"* Surprised, I reached down and rubbed the back of Barrett's head, trying to get him to relax. Usually, he did not act this way, unless I told him to do so or he felt that Andrea and I were threatened. This was something new and being a little shocked at his reaction, I pulled him closer to me. *"That's enough now...I told you it's okay...say hi."* Barrett reluctantly put his paw out and Russ bent down to shake it. *"Glad to meet you, Barrett....Shake and I have been friends for a long time."* Immediately, Barrett backed up and growled, exposing his white teeth showing that he was more than ready to take a piece out of him.

"What in the hell is the matter with him, now?" Russ asked, backing away towards the wall. Chuckling, I replied, *"I don't know....he usually doesn't act this way....it must be left over from our past few days out in the woods searching for the escaped prisoner or its the word you just said....it's okay, boy...settle down."* Caressing him by the head, Barrett finally became at ease and sat back down next to me. *"You can't say that word around him, Russ....you know the "f" word.....for some reason it really bothers him."* Russ, looking perplexed, chuckled slightly. *"You mean f..r..i.."* Quickly, I interrupted him, *"You can't say the letters either...he can spell."* Russ waived his hand at me. *"Don't give me that shit......you know, this is your old partner that you're speaking to ......you can pull some of that crap on other people, but me?"* Andrea watching all of this smiled and reached out to join me in petting Barrett. While admiring the animal, she added, *"He can you know...actually, he's more human than most people...and smarter too!"* With everybody laughing, Barrett scanned all of us with his eyes and seeing that we were enjoying ourselves, finally felt at ease enough to lie down on his bed over in the corner of the room. Promptly closing his eyes and folding his paws in front of him, he appeared to fall fast asleep.

"Russ, I guess you have met my girlfriend Andrea already.... Andrea, this is Russ Wilson from the Harrisburg Police Department....we were detectives together there for several years," I said reaching for a glass of water on the table. Being very polite Andrea responded, *"Mr. Wilson, glad to meet you."* Russ chuckled, *"Oh please, Andrea....Russ is the name...I think we can forgo with the formalities."* Pleased that Russ seemed to like her, I gave him a little smirk, asking, *"So, what brings you around to this neck of the woods, Russ...you on vacation or something?"*

My old partner sat back down on the couch and motioned by showing the pack to me if it was all right to light up a cigarette.

With a nod of my head, he promptly lit one up, and blew out the match while Andrea and I took a seat. Taking a drag off it, he let out the smoke and sighed a little, thinking for a moment. Suddenly his demeanor turned serious and looking me in the eye he said softly, *"I need to talk to you...alone."* My eyes threw a quick glance over at Andrea and she immediately got up from her sofa chair. *"I have to get supper ready anyway...I'll take the steaks into the kitchen and get started, Shake...okay?"* Nodding my head in agreement, we watched Andrea disappear into the kitchen and Barrett seeing her go, quickly got up and followed her. *"That dog of yours, keeps a close eye on her....doesn't he?"* Russ commented as he took another drag from his butt. Smirking a little, I replied, *"He sure does...never really lets her out of his sight.....especially if she is cooking a big steak for him."*

With us both chuckling, Russ seemed relieved that she had left the room and leaning back against the couch, he looked down for a moment. After working with him for a long time, I knew when a problem was running around in his head and this time was no exception as he was trying to find the right words to drop on me. *"You know, I haven't seen you looking this good in a long time, Shake.....life here appears to agree with you."* Pulling a cigarette out myself, I lit it and shaking out the match, I took a heavy drag from it. Exhaling the smoke and nodding my head, I smiled back at him. *"Yeah, this place has been good for me, Russ....you might say, the furry guy in there and that woman saved my life....I was in pretty tough shape when I got here, but life is better now and I thank God for that everyday."* My old partner was avoiding eye contact with me now and seemed deep thought about something. I knew whatever he was thinking was not very good, but being curious I asked, *"So, you never answered me...are you on vacation or is this house call for another reason?"*

Thinking some more, Russ took a deep drag on his cigarette and exhaled slowly, filling the room in front of him with wispy smoke. *"You remember the last case that we were working on?"* Like a flash, my thoughts returned to Harrisburg and all of the horror blitzed through my mind. While gritting my teeth, I sighed heavily, and slowly counted to myself, hoping to keep my composure. Then looking up at the ceiling, still trying to calm myself down, my eyes lowered and I stared back at him. *"Yeah, you mean the serial killer case with the suitcases?....why?...did you ever get him?"*

Russ crushed his butt out in the ashtray on the coffee table in front of him and leaned forward with his arms on his knees. Gazing at me, his mood turned grim, appearing like he was attending a funeral for a close friend. Then with an expressionless face he replied, *"No...we didn't....in fact, he's killed three more in the past few years.....same MO.....you know putting the young girls into suitcases to dispose of the bodies."* Being in those shoes before, I recognized the look of desperation on a man's face when a case was not going well. Before any time could pass, he added, *"To be honest with you, we're in a bad fix, Shake....the political pressure has been really building lately and the mayor has been relentless.... he's on the chief everyday and you know what that means...the boss has had us working day and night on this case with no vacations or leave time at all.....the morale sucks and I feel a reprisal from the men is coming very soon....you know how hard a case like this can be on everyone."*

Yeah, I knew what a situation like that could be. The stress was unbelievable at times and soon some liquid encouragement was needed to numb the pain and relieve the anxiety. That was one life I did not want any part of anymore and the area I had escaped to, by being back in our little town, was my cure for Russ's current condition. My old partner showed all the signs of being a broken man with his hands shaking as he put the cigarette to his lips while his eyes danced all over the place. Russ's mind was going at full speed now and any pleasant thoughts he might have had at one time were long forgotten. He was in a world of shit and the bags underneath his eyes and the dark circles around them only confirmed my suspicions.

"Russ, have you asked for help from the State boys or even the Feds?" My old partner's face turned red with a look of revulsion.

"No, not at all....the mayor and the city council have tried to keep this under raps......going so far as to release things to the public which would imply that this was not the work of a serial killer but were separate and unrelated instances.....they even have tried to pass them off as simple deaths due to drug overdoses and natural causes....you know how important tourism is to our city along with the University...if the word ever got out about there being an active killer on the loose, our economy would go in the dumper."

Things had not changed I guess, as I continued to think back to when I was hired by the Harrisburg Police Department. Appearances were always foremost and the city being a friendly and safe place in the public's eye was a top priority with the political establishment. In many instances, cases were squashed from the public to dampen their severity in order to keep the city like the Land of Oz. An image of limited crime where people could live with their doors unlocked, having absolutely no fear for their safety and well-being was always foremost. Evidently, the powers to be still had their heavy hand on the police department and the chief was still bowing to their wishes in order to keep his high paying job. It was a sick way of conducting business, but it was the government way of life for the City of Harrisburg.

"Okay...things are still bad, but what does that have to do with me?....after all, I'm out of there.....they ran me out of town on a rail....I'm the guy who supposedly killed a kid without a gun, murdering him in cold blood.....don't you remember that?" Russ rubbed his face with his right hand and I could see the stress, emanating from his eyes. Suddenly, Andrea hollered from the kitchen, *"Are you guys almost done out there?....I'm starting supper."* Quickly, Russ responded loudly, *"Just a little more time...we have a few more items that need discussing."* Andrea let out a laugh, *"Well, don't take too much longer....I have an impatient officer of the law here in the kitchen who wants his steak....don't know how much longer I can hold him off!"* Grinning, I hollered back, *"Well, tell him he's just going to have to wait a little longer."* As soon as I said that,

a deafening bark came from the kitchen and Andrea added, *"You see?....someone doesn't agree with you."*

Smiling, knowing Barrett must be chomping at the bit, I looked back at Russ who leaned forward again and stared at me. After a few moments of gathering his thoughts, he said, *"We want you back....we need your help on this."* Those words cut deep into my soul and all the pain from those past years came rushing back into my body. The horrid thought about those mornings, afraid to get out of bed because of the pain kept running through my head. The binge drinking, the pills, and how every day was a struggle to survive, pierced through my mind like a spear. Losing my wife, my house, even my health, all of it went down the shitter in that city, and with every passing moment, the thoughts of going back to that hellhole ripped through my mind, causing me to shiver. After all, the past couple of years had finally given me peace and tranquility, as if I had gone to heaven. Being able to breathe fresh air and live again was something I deeply treasured and now I was going to throw all of that away to live in hell again? In a flash, I exploded with, *"No God damn way, Russ....there is no chance that you are going to convince me to go back there....I hated that place and that bastard they call a chief.....I suppose he put you up to this..... well, he can go to hell too!"*

My old partner looked off to the side, hoping to think of another set of words he could throw at me. *"Actually, the chief was dead set against it, Shake...in fact, he went totally ballistic when he heard what was going on.....the Mayor and City Council approached me about getting you back as they heard you were doing so well up here....to tell you the truth, I had no interest in bringing you back to our city, not because you wouldn't be of use, but because you were finally living a good life here......believe me, there was no way I wanted to drag you back into our snake pit of problems."*

Maybe I was not listening or really did not care to see his point, but I decided to put the kibosh to his further attempts. *"Well, the Mayor can go screw himself as far as I am concerned.... and those city councilors can go with him.....because there's no way*

I am going back with you....that's a disgusting cauldron of corruption and I want no part of it......so why don't you just sit your ass right back down in your car and head out, okay?"

He knew I was extremely angry and realizing that I was not coming around to his way of thinking, he reached on the side of the couch, and picked up a small brief case. Placing it on the coffee table and opening it, he pulled a piece of paper from it that was encased in a plastic wrapper. Continuing to stare at it for several moments, I finally asked, *"What's that?......a formal request by your asshole superiors, asking me to help you?"* Russ shook his head slightly and rubbed his chin, still staring at the single sheet of paper. *"Before I hand you this...I just want to tell you that this was not my idea....it was the Mayor's....I thought the chief was going to kill me when he found out that I was headed here with this."*

As he handed me the paper, my arms were paralyzed, and I did not reach for it at first. Actually, the amount of apprehension that was going through me was immeasurable of what the paper might contain, but after he held it out in the air in front of me for several moments, I finally decided to reach for it. Grabbing it, Russ did not let go at first and added, *"Remember...this was not my idea."* With my hand shaking slightly, he let it go and I brought the single sheet of paper into my field of vision. It read:

To all members of the Harrisburg Police Department

I know you are out to stop me....why, I do not know, for I am ridding the earth of its evil and its worthless human beings ......I have eliminated several so far, but there is more to do.....many others will follow as these creatures of the night need to be removed from our society as they suck the very essence from it.....you might have had a chance to stop me, but that was until you sent your best away....oh, Shaker Madison, how I miss you!.....you were my nemesis!...oh, to have you back here, to challenge me!.....not like these others who are so inept......

So, Shaker Madison, here are a few clues to help you along your way....the boy in the alley was not your fault and you didn't kill him either, but I know who did.....catch me and learn his identity.....this I promise you..........

Signed:

The Traveling Man

P.S. if that's not enough.....then, who killed your wife?....catch me and I will tell all!

My heart sunk as I read the type written note. Old, suppressed thoughts of my murdered wife came alive in my mind, stinging my stomach, making it turn and growl from the ugliness. *"Of course this is not the original note, but a type written copy,"* Russ said, as I continued to stare at the letter. *"The original was made up from letters taken from magazines and newspapers......we are looking at it closely back at the lab as it may give us some more clues."* Handing the note back to him, I looked towards the kitchen. Andrea was standing at the stove and Barrett was sitting beside her, waiting patiently for his steak, which was being broiled in the oven. The pleasing sight caused me to grin a little, but the pleasantness of it quickly dissipated when my old partner said, *"Sorry to have laid this on you ole bud....but we are in real trouble....I don't know if the killer is being truthful about everything, but if he is, it could mean full reinstatement for you."*

Glaring back at him with a cold hearted stare, I said, *"I could care less about the reinstatement...my new life is here now with those two,"* as I pointed towards the kitchen. *"They mean everything to me, but if this guy is serious about knowing who killed my wife, it might put a different light on the situation...maybe with a little luck, I can finally put that ugly portion of my life to rest."* Russ stood up and walked over to the large bay window, looking out into the front yard. *"You have a nice place here, Shake...you seem* to be at peace now and I would totally understand if you refused to go back there."

I picked the note back up, reread it, and when I was done, I tossed it into his briefcase. *"I'll have to discuss it with her in there, but if I do decide to do this, my chief will have to give me a leave of absence....and that could be a problem."* Russ chuckled as he allowed the curtain to fall back in place, eyeing me with a wink. *"That won't be a problem at all, Shake.....luckily, your boss has already given the okay to our chief and from what I have been told, you can take all the time you need on this.....plus, authorization by the mayor has been given to our department to pay for all of your expenses...you will be provided a room at the Spirit Arms Hotel and all your meals will be paid for....you remember that place, don't you?"*

How could I ever forget the Spirit Arms Hotel? That was the place where we had made a huge bust on a bookie operation and a prostitution ring. It was one of my last cases before I went on a uncontrollable booze binge. The owner of the place was supposed to go to prison, but like similar situations we had been involved in, he had a slick lawyer who got him off with ten years probation. The worse part of it was, the owner of the place was a good friend of mine and I had always regarded him as a *"straight shooter"*, but all of that changed when the bust went down. With all of the illegal activities that were going on in that place, he should have gotten twenty years in the slammer at least. However, with money comes power and since hiring a high priced lawyer was within his grasp, he got off. All of which only reinforced one of my old favorite adages. *"How much justice can you afford?"* Nevertheless, that is how our legal system worked and being in law enforcement, that was something you had to accept. Let it get to you and a trip to the funny farm was surely in the cards.

"I'll give you a call tomorrow and let you know my decision, Russ.....like I said, those two in there mean everything to me and they have to be willing to go along with it." He closed his briefcase and picked it up off the table while shaking my hand. *"Good...I'll*

head back now and tell the mayor and the chief of our meeting... *don't worry Shake, if you decide to return, I'll have your back on this."* As he left through the front door, I watched him walk out to his vehicle, and before he opened his car door, I hollered, *"Just like when you testified that you saw the kid with the gun, right?"* Russ opened his door and smiled. *"You can take that one to the bank, Shake."*

As he drove away, I knew he had lied for me and that was because he was a faithful partner. Russ was a good man and I trusted him because he was always there for me, even when my life was in the toilet. Closing the door, I could not help to think what must have been going through his mind as he drove back to Massachusetts. There was no doubt he had a hard time coming here, but he also knew how much I wanted to find Jane's killer, and strangely enough, the *"traveling salesman"* who was a cold blooded killer was probably going to help me in doing that.

Walking back into the living room, I realized that Barrett was nowhere to be seen. Then, all of a sudden, I saw the rear door to the kitchen open and amazingly, Barrett nonchalantly came walking through the door. Turning around, he jumped on the door to close it, and walked over to his water dish for a drink.

Awe struck, I walked into the dining room, and Andrea was busily setting the table. *"Do you know what I just saw, Andrea.... that damn dog opened the back door by turning the door knob with his teeth and walked in here like he owned the place....when in the hell did he learn to do that?"* Before I could say another word, while she placed the plates on the table she asked, *"So are you going back, Shake?"* Surprised, I replied, *"I suppose you heard our discussion....I knew Russ was talking too loud."* Andrea started putting the silverware out and glanced over at me with a stern look in her eye. *"You think you can handle something like this?.... after all, you have only been sober for a few years...with all of the pressure that comes in a case like that, you could end up on skid row again....have you really thought about what it might do to you?.... to us?"*

Oh, she was right. Seeing Russ and talking about the case was bringing back a pack full of memories and drinking was one of them. Standing there, with no real defense, I calmly said, *"I might be able to find Jane's killer if I go back......you can understand that, can't you?"* Andrea threw the napkins on the table and leaned on a chair, staring at the backyard through the picture window. I knew she was disgusted and wanted to give me a piece of her mind, but being so upset, she was having a hard time getting the words out. Approaching her, I saw a tear starting out of the corner on one eye and she promptly wiped it away. *"I think you're making a huge mistake by going back there, Shake.....that place will bring you nothing but a lot of heartache and misery....stay here with Barrett and me....we are your family now."* Wrapping my arms around her from behind, I kissed her gently on the neck while hugging her. *"I know you're worried, but I will be okay...after all, Barrett will be with me and you know how he can be."* Quickly she broke the hold I had on her and rapidly turned around, facing me with astonishment. *"So Shaker Madison, you are taking the dog, too?....leaving me to face this alone?....constantly wondering as every minute passes if you are back on the bottle lying in some gutter somewhere in a drunken blackout or even worse, dying with a few bullets in you?....no, I won't put myself through that...not alone anyway....if you go back to that damn place, then don't think I'll be waiting here when you get back...because I won't be."*

She quickly went over to the kitchen counter, grabbed her purse, and swiftly walked towards the front door. Prior to reaching it, she stopped for a second, took off her apron, and threw it at me, hollering, *"And you can cook your own God damn dinner, too!"* As I caught the flying apron, she opened the door and went outside, slamming it behind her, almost taking it off the hinges. Barrett trotted to the front entrance looking back and forth at me, confused on where Andrea had disappeared. Pawing the front door a few times he turned around and sat down, staring at me with his deep yellow eyes. *"You too...ehh?....you're against me going back, aren't you?"* My furry partner stood up and stretched by placing his paws out in front of him and after crouching, turned and went back to the front door. *"No...she's gone, boy....there's no use going after her either...she's too pissed right now, but she'll be back eventually....come on, let's finish dinner."*

As I walked back into the kitchen, I could see dark smoke bellowing from the open oven door. Quickly retrieving the steaks out of it and placing the broiling pan on top of the stove, smoke filled the room to the ceiling. *"I hope you like your steak well done,"* as I picked up one of them up off the pan with a fork. *"Looks like they got a tad over cooked."* Holding up the blackened piece of meat, Barrett slowly approached me, with his eyes staring at the steak. Sitting down next to me, his eyes left the plate and met mine, while his upper lip lifted slightly. *"I know...I screwed it up, but that's the way it goes....don't worry, they'll still taste good."* I grabbed the plate with the steak and put it down on the floor next to his bed. Barrett slowly walked over to it and sniffed it a few times, then stared back at me. Seeing that he was displeased, I firmly stated, *"You don't like it?...well, I am afraid it's going to have to do."*

I snatched up my steak along with some of the mashed potatoes, green beans, and sat at the table. Trying to cut into my steak, I soon found that it was too hard and dried out, as it was like a piece of inner tube. Eventually, after a lot of effort, and cutting a small piece off, I placed it in my mouth and began chewing it. It was burnt to a crisp and the heavy deposit of charcoal around it coated my entire mouth with soot. While gnawing on it, I glanced over at Barrett and he was just lying on his bed, staring at the steak on the plate. I swear the piece that was in my mouth was like shoe leather and after chewing it several times; I spit it back on the plate and took a sip of milk.

Sitting there disgusted with myself, suddenly out of the corner of my eye, I noticed Barrett had gotten up on all fours and had grabbed his steak with his teeth. *"Well, that's better,"* I muttered to myself. *"At least he's going to eat his."* Then abruptly, he spun his head away from me and with the steak in his mouth, walked over to the trash basket, and dropped it in. Sitting back on his haunches, he barked at it, and then eyed me for a second. Glimpsing down at my pathetic, burnt to a crisp steak for a second, I looked back at Barrett while his eyes returned to the trash basket. Picking up my steak with a fork, I said, *"Okay...I get the idea."* And as I threw the steak into the trash I added, "Come on.....*you're right.....let's go back to the store and get another one."* So with Barrett jumping up and down while wagging his tail with enthusiasm, I grabbed my car keys off the kitchen counter and we both headed for the door, back to Paul's.

CHAPTER FIVE
Back Again

My old partner Russ Wilson was right, when Ben got home that night and I was able to reach him at his house he had already been contacted by the Harrisburg Police Department. Although, not keen on the idea of me leaving, he had agreed to grant me a leave of absence in order to assist the city on their serial killer case. He knew how much I wanted to find Jane's killer and to tell the truth, I think he would have come with me, if he could have as Ben knew Jane very well in high school as he had dated her sister for about a year before she went off to college. Like all relationships at that age, she found someone else while attending school and was married a few years later. I do not think Ben ever got over that, but he always liked the family and got along well with Jane. He did not come out and actually say it, but by the tone in his voice, I think he was glad I was going back to solve the mystery of Jane's sudden death.

As I drove down Route 1 to Massachusetts, my thoughts went back to those old school days and most of those memories always brought a smile to my face. Barrett, sitting on the front seat, could always tell when I was in a good mood and would often give me a lick now and then, showing his approval. Crossing the state line and seeing the sign *"Welcome to Massachusetts,"* however, brought on a completely new set of feelings. All of the pain from years past regarding the job and my wife's death began to work on me. Before I knew it, my hands were starting to sweat and holding onto the slimy steering wheel became more difficult. Barrett knew something was up as he promptly moved over and put his head on my lap. Caressing his head a few times I said aloud, *"I can't fool you, can I?....I'm afraid ole boy we are entering a very dark place....a place that I thought I would never see again......a place that is full of nothing, but ugliness and pain.....well, hopefully, you will be able to keep me on the straight and narrow, right?"* My furry partner's eyes gleamed with affection towards me and after closing and opening them a few times, he licked my hand. Smiling down at him, I stroked the back of his neck, saying, *"That's right...you're gonna help me through this, aren't you?.....that's the one thing I can depend on in this shitty world that we all live in and that's you, ole pal....you are always there for me."*

It was about three hours later when we arrived in Harrisburg and as we started to drive down Main Street into the city, all of the familiar buildings came into view, especially the liquor stores. As we passed by them, the sick part of my subconscious mind began to speak to me, reminding me of all the *"good"* times that I had missed for the past few years. *"Just one...that's all you'll need to take the edge off and then you'll be okay,"* the little voice whispered in my ear. *"You know you can handle it now....after all, you have been a good boy.....you deserve a little reward, don't you?"* Gripping the steering wheel tightly and almost tearing it from the column, I hollered, *"No!"* Startling Barrett from a comfortable sleep on my lap, his head shot up and he immediately stood on the seat, looking in all directions expecting to see a bad buy. Rigid as a board, in full attack mode, he was more than willing to chew up anything that was in sight and trying to calm him a little, I reached over and affectionately rubbed his neck. *"Sorry, ole boy..... I didn't mean to wake you......it's just the old demons keep coming back, but don't worry.... everything will be okay."*

Just then, City Hall came into view and I knew the police station was right around the corner. Taking the right down Church Street, sure enough, several patrol cars were visible outside the station and noticing a parking space across the street, I pulled in.

Shutting the engine off and sitting there for a moment, I tried to collect myself while rubbing the back of Barrett's neck. He nestled his head underneath my arm and gave me a quick lick on the side of my face, while wagging his black, bushy tail. *"I'm glad someone is happy about being here,"* I said aloud while opening my door. *"Well, let's go in and face the music, partner."*

Crossing the street to the building, standing in front of the main doors, there were a few officers that I did not recognize. I could tell their eyes were fixated on us, probably not believing what they were seeing, as Barrett followed along side of me. Approaching the building one of them said, *"You can't bring that dog in here, sir...it's not allowed."* Stopping, I turned to them. *"I'm Detective Shaker Madison...I have an appointment with the chief... and far as the dog?....where I go, he goes."* Surprisingly, one of them quickly opened the door for us. *"He's expecting you, sir"* and as we both entered the station, I heard one of the officers say, *"That's the guy that used to work here...he's some kind of hot shot detective from up north now....I guess he's taking over the serial case."*

Walking up to the front desk and speaking through the glass at the desk sergeant while showing my identification, I was amazed on how little the place had changed. It was an old building that badly needed some fresh paint as the walls were peeling in several areas and the tiled floors were heavily worn and dirty. A musty smell filled my nostrils and the air actually felt heavy, almost seeming to be void of oxygen as I tried to fill my lungs. *"The chief is expecting you....go right in, Madison...you know where his office is."* Hearing that voice, I knew immediately who it was, but due to his massive weight gain, I had been completely fooled at first. *"Thank you, Sergeant Hill,"* I responded as he pushed a button, which released the locking mechanism so we could open the massive door to the rear offices. As we rounded the corner, the sergeant stood, looking over the counter and noticing the huge bushy tail, waiving back and forth in the breeze behind me, he quickly hollered, *"Heh....wait a minute!......where the hell do you think you're going with that!"* Stopping for a second, I smiled back at him. *"Don't you know who this is?....it's Detective Barrett from the Middleton Police Department....his reputation is well known!"*

I could not help from snickering a little as we continued down the long, narrow hallway towards the chief's office. Several officers were busily crossing the hallway back and forth in front of us, going to various rooms and each time they got a look at Barrett, their expressions were priceless. Some of them actually threw their backs against the wall in fright and others just stopped dead in their tracks, staring at the intimidating sight as we walked by. Barrett was not fazed in the least as he calmly followed beside me to the chief's office, looking in each room as we passed them. Occasionally, he would glance up at an officer who was standing still like a statue with his back up against the wall, trying to give him more room to pass. As he continued down the hallway, Barrett licked his chops several times, which only drove the officers to rise even higher on their tiptoes, causing me to grin as we passed them by.

Reaching the chief's office the receptionist behind the desk looked up at us and became immediately startled when she saw my sidekick. *"What is that?"* she said loudly. *"And who are you?"* Smiling, I replied, *"I'm Detective Madison and this is Barrett, my partner....the chief is expecting us."* The secretary stared at Barrett as he sat beside me, panting with his tongue out. *"Well, I know he was expecting you, Mr. Madison, but I am sure he is going to have a fit about your so called partner....you better get rid of that before he sees him."* Standing up from behind her desk, she knocked over a stapler and it fell with a thud, hitting the floor. Bending down to pick it up, I held my hand out saying, *"Hold on lady...Barrett, you know your manners better than that, don't you?"* Immediately, he retrieved the stapler from the floor and offered it to the woman. Cautiously, she took it from him while looking at me with awe in her face. Gingerly taking the stapler from his mouth, she exclaimed, *"A person not knowing any better might think he understood you."* As Barrett returned to my side and sat again beside me, I replied, *"Oh, he does...every word....and he can spell too."*

With a face full of amazement, the woman sat slowly back down in her chair and buzzed the intercom. *"Chief....Detective Madison is here."* The intercom answered, *"It's about time he got here......we have been waiting for over an hour......send him right in!"*

With a lukewarm smile, she motioned for us to go around her to the chief's office. Staring at Barrett the whole time as we passed by, she leaned her head forward to get a better look at him. Without warning, my partner turned and licked her face, sending the shocked secretary back into her chair. *"Come on...never mind her....we have work to do,"* I said staring back at him. Seeing the astonishment on her face, I added, *"You should be flattered Miss.... usually, he does not take to strangers like that."*

Motioning with my head for Barrett to follow me, we entered the chief's office, and found several men sitting in chairs throughout the smoke filled room. The chief, who was behind his desk, stood, and went to put out his hand, but suddenly took it back, exclaiming, *"What in the hell is that thing doing in my office!.... get that God damn animal out of here!"* The rest of the men in the office rose quickly out of their chairs, showing fright on their faces on what had just come into the room. *"Hold on everybody... this is Barrett, my partner,"* I declared, hoping to put everyone at ease. The chief, still startled on what was in front of him, promptly replied, *"Your what?....that's a dog, for Christ's sake.....Madison, don't tell me you never sobered up!"* Those words hit me hard and I realized that this was not going to go very well, but a familiar voice came from behind me to the rescue. *"It's all right chief....I know the dog and he's okay....no need to worry about him...just don't say one word."*

The chief looking puzzled, replied, *"What word?...what's this shit about?"* The voice was from my old partner, Russ Wilson, and as he walked over to the chief's desk, he grabbed a note pad and pencil from it. Writing something on the pad, he then handed it to the chief whose eyes grew wide. Confused, the chief demanded, *"Why in the hell did you write it on the pad?"* Russ smirked back at the chief, saying, *"Because the dog can spell, sir."* Immediately the chief flew out of his chair, waiving the pad in his hand at him. *"What the hell is this shit...telling me a dog can spell...this word that you wrote, 'friend' what is ...."* In an instant, Barrett's mood changed for the worse and he growled at the chief, showing his huge canine teeth. Chief Morin backed away from his desk to the wall. *"That dog is a killer!...look at him!"* Quickly grabbing Barrett by the scruff of the neck, I replied, *"Leave him alone, boy...the chief is going to help us out on this case.....back off!"* Barrett immediately calmed down and sat beside me while Morin seeing that the dog was under control, moved forward to take a seat at his desk. The other men, being shocked out of their wits, took their seats as well, but all of them kept their eyes on the jet-black beast. Knowing that everybody was still staring at my dog and me I knew an explanation was in order. *"I'm sorry, sir....for some reason that word just drives him crazy, but he's all right now....look at him, he's as calm as a cucumber....don't worry he won't be a problem."*

Russ, pointing at us added, *"He's right, chief....the animal is very well behaved and always listens to Shake....he's really smart, too....Shake, why don't you demonstrate what Barrett can do?"* Chief Morin was staring directly at me and I knew what was going through his mind. He was trying to rationalize the whole situation and determine whether we were going to be allowed to stay or told to *"hit the road."* Noticing a small paperweight on his desk, I reached over and picked it up. Holding it in my hand for a second, I rolled it around, studying it and then tossed it to the chief. As he caught it, I said, *"Put your hands behind your back and place the paper weight in one of your hands, chief, but don't divulge which one.....then hold out both fists in front of you."*

Standing up at his desk, the chief reluctantly did what I had asked and then extended his arms out towards us. *"Barrett.... tell the chief which hand the paper weight is in."* Getting up on all fours, he stared at the chief for a second, who was about ten feet away from him. Making him uneasy because of his staring, yellow eyes, the chief blurted, *"Madison, he looks like he's going to take a bite out of me for Christ's sake."* Chuckling, I replied, *"No...he's just thinking that's all....pretty soon he will make his choice."* After a few moments, Barrett sat back on his haunches and raised his right paw. Observing this, I remarked, *"The right one?....is that where it is?"* Barrett immediately produced a soft bark and I looked back at the chief. *"It's in your right hand, sir."* Morin slowly opened his right fist and to everyone's amazement, the paperweight appeared. A man sitting next to Russ sighed in awe, declaring, *"I never would have believed it unless I saw it.....how in the hell did that dog do that?"*

The chief placed the paperweight back on his desk and rubbed the side of his face with his hand, trying to grasp what he had just witnessed. *"Yeah...okay Madison, how did he do that?"* Rubbing the back of Barrett's neck, I looked over at the chief. *"Oh, he can do lots of things....actually, that was only a small sample of his capabilities...since, he's been my partner, we have solved a lot of cases together and I know with a great deal of sincerity that we can solve this one too, that is if you let us work together."*

Leaning back in his chair, Morin surveyed the room with his eyes, peering at each man for a second. *"Gentlemen, I guess Madison here, has proven his point...I have no objections.....in fact, if he had a pet yellow canary that could solve this case, I wouldn't have a problem with that either!"* Sporadic laughter broke out with Russ adding, *"Give Madison some time, chief....he'll probably come up next with that."* That caused the entire room to erupt into hilarious laughter and I knew then that Barrett and I were in.

With the chief nodding his head, exclaimed, *"Okay, gentlemen.....let's get down to business....,Madison, you know most of the men in this room except for Lieutenant Harley as he came on board about two years ago....he is heading up the investigation along with your ex partner, Russ Wilson."* I reached over, shook hands with the person, and noticed right away that he was a fairly big man, but surprisingly, his handshake was weak and he seemed to be timid about meeting me. Maybe it was because of Barrett sitting beside me, but something about him was telling me that this man was not a leader, but a follower and should have never been put in charge of an operation such as this one. *"Glad to meet you Harley...this is Barrett, shake hands with the man."* Barrett quickly extended his paw and Harley cautiously took it, hoping all of his fingers would go back with him once he retracted his hand. Shaking his paw, the fearful look in Harley's eyes were tell tale, and it only confirmed my original impression of him.

The other men in the room were William Stone from the forensics lab and a very well dressed man in a three-piece suit by the name of Marty Sloan who was representing the Mayor. While working for the city years ago, I had several confrontations with the man, as he was a little weasel who sneaked around, trying to get dirt on everybody. I had always despised the man since he was nothing more than a snitch that secretly reported everything back to the mayor. Because of his antics, Sloan was never well liked by anyone and was often shunned by most of the city employees. At that time, the city was extremely political, and the mayor had just been elected to his third consecutive two-year term and of course that had been helped along by using all of the information that he had learned through his rat. The mayor had dirt on everybody, including other politicians, and he used that information to the hilt, which only furthered his political power.

All of the department heads were wary of the mayor, including Chief Morin who was originally appointed by him during his first two-year term. Morin had not risen through the ranks, but had been brought in from the outside by the mayor and his henchmen. This only caused a lot of dissension within the department since many other men thought they should have been considered for the position first, but the mayor had his own agenda. In fact, that was his normal course of business for the other city departments, since the fire chief and planning direc-tor were both hired by the mayor from the outside too and this worked to his advantage, because all of the department heads served at his pleasure. As a result, the political machine that he had built was very strong and calculating, which explained why a serial case of this magnitude could be withheld from the public. The thoughts of a killer running around loose had all been erased from the newspapers and the public by his deceitful machine.

"Madison, after this meeting, you'll sit down with Harley and be brought up to speed on this thing....since you were together for several years, Wilson will be reassigned as your partner.... I'm sure you'll be in agreement with that." I wanted to fight him on this, as I had grown very accustomed to my current furry partner, but I knew if I said anything, it would have only opened up old wounds with the chief and me. *"That would be fine, sir....I am looking forward to working with Wilson again."* The chief smiled, *"That's good...I'm glad you have decided to become part of the team again... I guess you've changed."*

Hearing those words emanating from him, hit me along side of the head like a ball peen hammer because I had not changed, at least as far as my feelings toward the man. There was never any love lost between us while I worked for the City of Harrisburg and everybody knew it. In fact, he was the driving force behind my suspension and the one who actually kicked me off the force when the shooting occurred. Thinking back to that horrible point in my life, his words at that time still singed my sole. *"Madison, we have no room in our department for killers of unarmed teenage boys...I knew in my heart that something like this would eventually happen.......you are a disgrace to the uniform and to this city......your drinking has finally caught up with you and I am glad to see you go....the only thing I regret not doing is being able to put your ass in jail!"*

During the past several years, those words revolved in my head like an endless tape recorder, playing over and over again. It almost drove me mad, listening to those vile words, but with God's help, I kept my sanity and experiencing his non-threatening actions today along with his smooth talk was actually making me nauseous. To tell the truth, I started to have reservations about coming back here, but I knew it was the only way that I would have even a chance of finding Jane's killer. Therefore, I decided to keep my mouth shut, play the game, and let the chief go on with his performance.

"Harley, give us an update....where are we on this thing?" the chief ordered as he poured a glass of water out of a pitcher that was on his desk. The nervous Lieutenant rustled some papers together on his lap and cleared his voice. *"We have identified the fifth victim; she is Ellen Sullivan, Caucasian, 25 years old....she lived alone over on Putnam Street and was employed as an escort agent.....no living relatives that we can determine....like the others, she was strangled with parachute cord and found in a large suitcase down by the Nashua River.....there doesn't appear to be any sexual assault.... however, it appears she was severely beaten with a blunt instrument....as in all of the other cases chief, no finger prints or other evidence was recovered at the scene."*

Morin clasped his hands together in front of him on his desk, while he stared back at the detective. *"And the press?....how are we handling that?"* Harley looked around the room at everybody and then lowered his head. *"Ahhh...we are going to use the hit and run scenario, chief."* Instantly, the chief stood up from his desk and looked out the window, giving his back to us. *"You think that's smart?....after all, we already used that one on the second victim.... the press can be pretty stupid at times, but that dumb?....I sincerely doubt it...you better come up with something else that we can use."*

Sitting there and listening to all of this go on, made me cringe a little, as the formation of the cover up was in full swing. With everyone in total silence and not offering anything, I decided to give them a little gift. *"Chief...if I may...why not keep it a Jane Doe for the time being and tell the press she was found on the outskirts of the city and we are waiting for the coroner's report....tell them that she must be from out of town as no one has filed a missing person's report as of yet....since, we knew she resided alone and has no living relatives, that kind of a story should be able to stand up for a while."* Quickly, the chief turned around, saying, *"Now, that's what I call good police work...good job, Madison...you hear that, Harley?.....we'll go with that story for now."*

Harley looked up from his papers, I could tell he was still nervous about the whole situation and was intimidated by the chief's assertion. *"Okay, sir....I'll make up a press release and run it by you before we go public.....hopefully, they will buy into it."* Morin grabbed the water glass from his desk and took a few sips, staring at me, and then glanced at Sloan who was taking notes. *"I suppose you have everything written down Marty....are you going to take care of informing the Mayor?"* While writing a few more words down on his pad, the executive assistant grinned, looked up, and answered, *"Yep...I think he will be pleased....looks like Madison will be a good addition to the team....don't worry, Madison.....I will be giving the Mayor a full report and your help on this will not go unnoticed."*

"That little weasel," I thought. *"He'll tell the Mayor alright..... after being instrumental of getting me kicked off the force, now I was supposed to buy into his bullshit?"* Rubbing the ears of my partner, I could tell by Barrett's eyes he did not really care for the people around him, reaffirming the old adage about dogs being good judges of people. Amazingly, throughout history, it seemed that most dogs had an instinct for character determination and how they managed to do it was anybody's guess.

"What else, Harley," the chief asked while he took a seat at his desk. *"You must have something else by now....it's been several months and I haven't seen anything cross my desk."* Harley glanced for a second at me while he put his pencil down on his pad. *"Well, I would like to go over everything with Madison before I file my next report....I am sure he will have some things to add once he reviews all of the evidence, sir."* Saying that, Harley grinned at me, which told me that he was glad I was getting involved. He was off the hook for now with the *"new boy"* on the block and it could not have made him any happier. *"Okay, Harley...I'll go with that, but like I said, Madison....after this meeting you'll go with the team and take a closer look on what we have, but from now on, leave the damn dog at home."* Knowing that was not going to fly with me, I immediately stood up which got Barrett alerted as he came to

attention on all fours. *"That's one thing I won't go along with, sir... where I go, he goes...it's as simple as that....you don't know it, yet, but this partner of mine is the best damn cop in the room....he'll help solve this case, but as any detective knows, he has to be able to see all of the evidence."*

Morin took another drink of water and pursed his lips, thinking. There was no doubt he was taken back by my insistence and knowing the chief's history, everyone in the room was waiting for him to blow up. By not being able to call the shots, his anger usually got the best of him, but this time it was a rude awakening for him as there was even more fuel for the fire. After all, there was someone directly in front of him who the chief despised, giving orders on what he was going to accept. That was something that Chief Morin could not swallow as it was sticking in his craw, forcing him to swallow hard. Rubbing his face with his hands, he stared back at me, waiting for me to continue with my demands, hoping that I might go *"over the line,"* but I remained silent along with the rest of the men.

Then to everyone's surprise, the chief stood up from his desk and looked over at Sloan, saying, *"Tell the Mayor we had a good meeting today and we are making some progress...inform him that Madison has taken full responsibility for this case and he should have a report filed along with Harley within a few days to both our offices."* With a slight grin, he then turned his attention towards me. *"Okay, hotshot....you say you want your buddy here with you at all times...well, you got him, but I'm telling you one thing....you better have some God damn results on my desk by next Monday morning because if you don't, I'll kick that sorry ass of yours all the way back to Middleton along with that mangy mutt and I'll make sure that all of the press knows about it too before I do it.....that means your new found reputation will go down the crapper as well."*

"What a nice man," I thought as I gazed upon the chief's grinning face. Trying to keep my temper under control, I gritted my teeth, hoping the pretentious man would die from a heart attack in front of me. There was little doubt now that the chief had

finally revealed his true feelings about Barrett and me in front of several witnesses by illuminating the fact that he hated me, plain and simple, but why? For some reason the chief still had an ax to grind and he had now set me up to take the fall if the investigation stalled in its tracks. All the niceties he had expunged on my old partner and my chief back in Middleton to get me back here was simply a con and that stupid grin of the chief's face told me that, as he wanted me to fail so he could drive me out of town on a rail in disgrace. Not taking the bait and fulfilling his need for a confrontation, I simply stared back at him while Barrett did the same. Then, out of the corner of my eye, I saw my partner's lip begin to curl upwards, showing that he had little respect for the man. Nudging him, Barrett's attention turned to me and rubbing his snoot I replied, *"Anything you say, chief....don't worry we'll find your killer."* That only irritated the chief more as he cleared his throat, responding, *"Well, if nobody has anything else to add....."* As we all looked at each other, waiting for someone to speak, the chief with a reddish tinge to his face, shuffled some paper work and blurted, *"Okay, gentleman, the meeting is over...let's get back to work!"*

Almost immediately, everyone in the room rose to their feet and began filing out of the office. Nearing the door, Harley who was to the left side of me, grabbed my shoulder to get my attention, but Barrett was right on him, getting between us. Showing that he was displeased by Harley's actions with a deep growl, the detective jumped back saying loudly, *"For heaven's sake man... doesn't that dog of yours like anybody?"* Chuckling, I hand signaled Barrett to go on ahead of us and as he left the room, I smiled back at him. *"That's one thing about my partner, Harley.... he always has my back....from now on, just be careful how you come up on us...you do that and you'll be just fine."*

CHAPTER SIX

The Sit Down

As we moved into the next room, Harley, Wilson and another officer who I did not recognize, sat down at the large oak table, and opened up their brief cases. Barrett took his place beside me and while we both observed the men around the table, I was hoping that the strange man would be introduced. *"This is Detective Robinson, Shake....I don't think you men have met,"* Russ said as he took out some photographs and spread them out on the table. Shaking his hand I replied, *"No, we haven't...I take it you are relatively new here."* Robinson quickly pulled a pack of smokes from his pocket and offered me one. *"Yeah, I am...started about two years ago, along with Harley here....came up from Southern Georgia where I used to work in a small town outside of Atlanta."* Taking a cigarette from him, he lit mine, then his, and after taking a huge drag off it he asked, *"You're presently working north of here, aren't you?"* Picking up and studying a photograph while slowly exhaling the smoke from my cigarette, I replied, *"Yeah, it's a small town outside of Bangor...this one, I remember this girl....wasn't she the first victim?"*

Russ threw a quick glance at the photograph and went back to sorting out some more of the papers. *"Yeah, Shake...she was identified as Carla Harju, age 24, Caucasian, a local drug addict with no priors, except for being picked up a couple of times for her night time activities."* I gazed at her face in the picture and recalled the day she was found, down by the Nashua River, packed into a large suitcase. She had been strangled by the killer with parachute cord and left naked. The killer had broken all of her limbs in order to fit her into the restrictive container while most of her long, black hair had been cut off and stuffed in her mouth. Except for a few minor scratches, there were no signs of any blunt trauma. Harley picked up another photograph and while scanning his notes commented, *"You must remember this one too, Madison....this one however, was never identified....a Jane Doe, age approximately 25, Caucasian, strangled and left naked in a suit case by the river as well...by the needle marks on her arms, there's little doubt she was a druggie and probably a prostitute like victim number one....except for the broken arms and legs, as in the previous victim, there were no signs of any struggle or defensive wounds."*

As I gazed at the crime scene photographs, thoughts of my pathetic life during that time came barreling into my mind. My drinking was out of control, as I had just come off a three-day binge on Vodka over the long weekend. Investigating the scene that day my hands were shaking uncontrollably and the twisted, nauseous feeling in my stomach was almost too much to bear. Breaking my stare of the victim's photo, I peered over at Robinson who was gathering up some more papers along with additional pictures. *"You say, Robinson that she was never identified, ehh?.... what about victims three and four?"*

Hearing my request, Detective Robinson laid out two more sets of photographs on the table. *"This is victim number three, a Kyle Swanson, age 28, Caucasian.....she was easy to identify, since she worked in City Hall for the Planning Department.....she was found strangled in her apartment where she lived alone...when she didn't report for work one morning, an officer of ours went over to her place and that's when the body was discovered....we hushed it up by saying she had a heart attack."*

As I grabbed one of the crime scene photos, which contained a close-up of her face, it was obvious to me that this crime scene did not have the same MO as the other murders. Tossing the photograph back to him, I asked, *"This one appears to be out of sync with the other victims...for one, this body was not found down by the river......why have you placed this one under the same auspice of the killer?"* Russ picked up another photo and handed it to me. As it came into view, Robinson seeing my eyes focusing in on it, added, *"As you can see, she was strangled with the same type of cord and next to the body is a large suit case, ready to take her on a little trip, Madison.....additionally, she was found naked like the others.... we think the killer must have been interrupted by something and was scared off before he could go through with his normal disposal and dumping ritual."* Scratching the side of my head and taking another drag off my butt, I handed the photo back. *"Okay...what about the fourth?"*

Robinson picked up another pile of papers and handed them to me. *"This one is a little different, but we still think the same guy did it.....Tina Hendricks, age 29, Caucasian....worked as a night receptionist over to the Spirit Arms Hotel....she was found naked in a suit case down by the river and was strangled with the same type of parachute cord..... the difference with this one is..... the victim was bludgeoned numerous times and several areas of the body were heavily bruised, including some brutal head wounds by a blunt instrument....there was no evidence of semen found in her vagina or on her body, but a majority of her blonde hair had been chopped off and stuffed in her mouth as you can see from the photographs...this coincides with the other murders.....the glitch is, by the great number of ruthless trauma wounds to the body, it looks almost like it was done by a homicidal maniac.....It might be a little too messy for our boy as it almost looks like a revenge killing.....this is something we have not seen before on this case."* After studying the photograph, I handed it back to him. *"Or maybe the nut is progressing, Robinson, and he needs more violence to satisfy his appetite....that may be the reason for the overkill."*

Surveying the table, there were numerous photos and each one was very clear, showing all of the evidence that Robinson had mentioned during his synopsis. He was correct, as the fourth victim, Hendricks, had been beaten with something numerous times. In fact, her entire body was almost completely covered in bruises and puncture wounds as she was bloodied from head to toe. Running several theories through my head, one in particular stuck. There was no doubt that the killer had possibly gotten careless or this victim meant more to him somehow and she had caused him to go berserk. Thinking for a moment, I placed the photo back on the table. *"What about the fifth victim?....I think you said her name was Ellen Sullivan....was she strangled too?.... do you have the photographs of that one with you?"*

Quickly, Robinson went to his brief case and pulled out another file. Taking a photo from the pile, he showed it to me. From the briefing, Robinson had left out one important detail during his summation and it was extremely obvious from what I saw. *"Looks like she was severely beaten, Robinson.....and there are multiple contusions around her neck and torso along with several stab wounds.....plus, her face looks like Sonny Liston used it for a punching bag...God, this woman was totally cut up.....why wasn't this mentioned during the meeting?"* The detective looked at the photograph and pursed his lips, thinking for a moment. I could tell he was taken back by my comment as he reached for another cigarette and with his hand shaking, fumbled with the pack while taking one out. *"I guess, I just forgot.....didn't seem that impor-tant....we know it's the same guy because of all the other evidence... as you can see from the photo, the cord, suitcase, etc. are all there..... all of these are critical parts of his MO...so what's the big deal?"*

Harley, who had been sitting quietly through all of this, sud-denly came alive to come to Robinson's rescue. *"Yeah, Madison.... what is the big deal?.....it's obvious we are dealing with the same man here....this nut job kills with the same type of cord and puts his victims in a suit case for Christ's sake...plus he throws most of them down by the river....just because Robinson left out a minor detail during the briefing, it doesn't mean we have to get our panties in a bunch...does it?"*

There was no doubt that Harley was trying to cover for Robinson and being his partner, I should have expected it.

However, Russ had his head down and seemed to be in his own little world, not wanting to make eye contact with me. That made me think a little, as I knew something else must have been going on that I was not privileged to.

Definitely not agreeing with the man, I could not help myself from answering his hollow remark. *"Well, I think it makes a huge difference, Harley...it's obvious by the fourth and fifth victim that we might have more than one murderer to deal with or if it is only one man, he must be growing in his animosity towards women as his killing is becoming more and more violent....it's as plain as day that strangling his victims is no longer fulfilling his needs....he needs more violence, more aggression to feed his obsessive appetite and with that comes a greater desire to kill.....unfortunately, it usually leads to more killing along with an increased desecration of the bodies.....by the department covering up these murders with hit and run scenarios along with other reasons, aren't we misleading and harming the public?....in my opinion, I think we are....it's obvious that there is a violent and smart serial killer on the loose and the public needs to know about it so they can take their own appropriate actions to safeguard themselves.....by shoving these under the rug, aren't we doing a great injustice to our citizens that we are sworn to protect?"*

The room fell silent after I had said my peace. My old partner, Russ Wilson, did not even look up at me as my eyes scanned everyone around the large oak table. When my eyes hit Detective Robinson's, he quickly looked the other way, but Detective Harley was another matter. Being made of different stuff, he stared right back at me, daring that I continue with my onslaught. *"Well... what do you guys think?...am I right or not?....keeping this from the public is not the way to go."* Still no one responded, but after a few moments had passed, Harley leaned back in his chair and chuckled. *"You tell the chief and the Mayor that, Madison....in fact, I want to be there when you do, so I can watch them kick your ass all over this town."* That was it as I had lost my patience with my fellow detectives. *"Alright...when the next victim cries out from her grave with her throat slit or her dismembered body is found in some back alley...how are you all going to live with yourselves?....I know I am not going to be able to do it...that would bother the hell out of...."* Harley quickly stood and interrupted me. *"Yeah, that's right, Madison...it would really bother you.....being the weak son of bitch you are...it would probably cause you to hit the bottle again and sink to the bottom where you belong!.....wallowing in your own self pity!"*

Immediately, I stood up to take on Harley. If he wanted a confrontation, I was more than happy to oblige him, and while getting out of my chair, Barrett became alarmed as well. He stood on all fours staring Harley down with his fiery, yellowish eyes, while his upper lip pulled back slightly, exposing his brilliant white canine teeth, which informed the man that one wrong move was all it was going to take, before he had a set of jaws locked on him. Harley seeing the threat, pointed at me, and with firmness in his voice said, *"You can stick that dog up your ass, too...I'm not afraid of that mutt...I'll put a bullet in him before he even gets to me."* Harley reached inside his suit jacket to pull the snub nose .38 from his shoulder holster. Seeing that, made me burn inside with anger, but before I could react, Russ sitting beside him put his hand on Harley's chest. *"Enough of that Harley...don't be an asshole... Madison was just trying to make a point about this mess and if you would listen for once, maybe you might see his side of this...besides if you try and pull that gun of yours, that dog over there would chew you into mince meat before you even got it out....I've seen that dog work and believe me, I'm saving your life right about now...so keep it holstered."*

Russ winked at me, keeping his hand on Harley's chest while Barrett licked his chops, hoping that Harley would make a move, as he was ready to leap over the table and have him by the throat in a blink of an eye. The air was saturated with tension as we all looked at each other, thinking how the situation was going to play out. *"My God,"* I thought, *"This is the team that is supposed to solve this case?....and we are about to unload guns at each other?"* Harley, lowering his hand slightly away from his holster, seemed to calm down a little and Russ observing this gradually removed his hand from his chest. My old partner glared at him, saying, *"For heaven's sake Harley, let's sit down and discuss this rationally....after all, we are all on the same team, aren't we?"* Harley while staring at Barrett glanced back at Russ. *"Well, you can tell that partner of yours to keep that damn mutt away from me....or else he'll get a .38 piece of lead from my buddy here, "* as he patted his chest.

By this time, I knew our relationship was going nowhere, but I still wanted to make my position perfectly clear to him. *"Alright Harley...my dog will keep his distance, if you behave yourself and leave the petty ass threats at home....however, if you ever harm him, I won't use a .38 on you or even my .357 with hollow points.....I'll beat you to death with your own leg, after I blow it off first with a shotgun loaded with a one ounce slug!"* Russ knowing Harley's temperament quickly interjected. *"Alright guys....that's enough male dog pissing around here...both of you have marked your own territory well enough and know where you both stand....so let's get back to work on this thing....okay?"*

Harley slowly sat back down and I did likewise while Barrett seeing that the threat was over, circled once at my feet, and laid back down. Within seconds, Harley unloaded with, *"Madison, I think your problem is that you have been away far too long to remember how this place operates....maybe you should give the Mayor a visit and get reeducated....then, you might understand what we are up against around here....if you don't know it yet, our hands are tied and the chief isn't calling the shots either."*

I knew what he was talking about, but did not realize that it had gone that far. When working for the department several years ago, things were changing, as some of our directives that we received from the chief's office seemed bizarre. Everyone knew that the chief was getting political pressure put on him in certain cases, but it was obvious by the recent comments and actions by the chief, that it had gone way beyond that. It was becoming clear to me now that the department had become a total political arm of the Mayor's office and that meant good police work was now a distant memory. *"Yeah, maybe I will, Harley....after all I've never met the Mayor one on one and it should prove pretty interesting to do so."* Harley acknowledged what I had said by a quick nod of his head and buzzed the intercom to a secretary in the other room. *"Call the Mayor's office, Ann and see if he is free today...Madison would like to see him."*

I gave him a head nod as well, thanking him and started to spread out the various photographs of the victims in front of me. Placing them in a single row, I was immediately taken back by all of their beauty and youthfulness. *"What a shame,"* I thought to myself, *"to be cut down in the prime of life like this....all of them strangled, stuffed in suitcases and tossed out like they were pieces of garbage....the guy that's doing this is got to be sick and now it looks like to get his kicks he has to cut or beat them up as well.....there's no question we haven't heard the last of this nut."*

Just then, I felt a cold nose against my arm and out of the corner of my eye, I saw Barrett trying to look over the end of the table. *"You want to look at these too, I suppose,"* as I moved to the side a little. Promptly leaping up, he rested his two front paws onto the edge of the table, and began gradually moving his head back and forth, looking at all of the photographs. Wearing a puzzled look, Robinson asked, *"What the hell is that mutt doing?"* As I looked around the table, all of them were staring at Barrett, and by the looks on their faces, I figured they were thinking the same thing. With a slight grin at them, I answered, *"He needs to look at these to get a feel for the case and the type of individual that we are going after....he's pretty intuitive, you know."*

Harley immediately broke out in laughter and Robinson followed with, *"You can't expect us to believe that shit, can you?.....the dog is just curious on what you have been looking at and he's probably just missing the attention that you normally give him...that's all."* I did not want to fight with the guy and decided to allow him to think what he wanted to. While Robinson was spewing his doubtfulness, I noticed Barrett was paying particular attention to the third victim as he kept staring at it. Finally he turned his head, looking for a reaction from me and giving him a few pats I said, *"I know....this one is different, isn't it?"* Harley noticing what the dog was doing, quickly added, *"I have seen some hocus pocus bullshit in my time, but what you are trying to pull off on us, Madison, is really ridiculous....look at this guys...he's a damn con artist."*

With all of them laughing, Barrett removed his paws from the table and landed on the floor. He began walking to the door and stopped, turning his head, expecting me to follow him. Observing his actions I surmised, *"You've seen enough, I take it....time to go?"* He gave a muffled bark while I stood up and I could not help from noticing that the other men were still laughing. *"You guys can think what you want to, but that detective standing by the doorway is probably smarter than all of us put together...in fact, he's probably working a lead already."* That is when the roar of laughter developed into a howl, as they all turned red in the face. Some of them even had tears rolling down their cheeks as they pointed at Barrett, mocking the *"furry detective."* Detective Harley, trying to control himself, broke from his laughter for a moment, saying, *"Yeah...he's a detective alright, Madison...I suppose he demands extra pay for his good work, maybe even a bonus.....like premium dog food or even a nice bone!"* Again, another wave of hysterical laughter came from the men when they heard that come from Harley. Standing there, watching all of them enjoy their laughing session, I returned fire with a contemptuous look, answering, *"No...it usually costs me a juicy steak."*

That was too much for my old partner, Russ Wilson, who choked on his cigarette and gagged on the smoke as he began a coughing fit. For a moment, because of his severe hacking and cherry redness in his face, I thought he was a goner. Then, a woman walked into the room while all the men were still howling and said, *"I never knew police work could be this much fun.... all of us can hear you throughout the station!"* Their laughter started to subside a little and Ann while shaking her head added, *"The Mayor can see you now, Madison...but you need to get right over there because he has several meetings this afternoon."* Harley, still snickering and wiping his eyes looked over at her. *"Tell him Madison will be right there with his highly skilled partner.....and please inform the mayor not to worry about his 'high' pay affecting the city budget because the so-called expert works for Purina dog chow!"*

That began the ruckus all over again as the men reared back with even louder laughter. I guess it was contagious because Ann started to giggle, but she managed to blurt out, *"You can go over now, Madison....he's expecting you."* Motioning to Barrett, we both started to leave and while we walked down the long hallway, the laughter was still flowing from them. Stopping for a moment and looking back at the room in disgust, my eyes then scanned downwards, peering at my faithful friend. *"That's alright....those guys don't know what you're capable of....do they, boy?"* Barrett answered me by pawing my leg and while we went out the front entrance door and began walking to the car, I looked across the street at City Hall. *"That's where that asshole lives, boy....wait till he gets a load of you!"*

CHAPTER SEVEN

Mayor Logan

Walking up the City Hall granite steps, Barrett as always was right behind me. As several people exited the building, the looks we received were priceless. Most of them, once their eyes fell upon my furry sidekick, moved over to the other side of the steps to avoid us. That was one good thing about having Barrett as a partner, no matter how crowded the situation we generally found ourselves in, there always seemed to be a path left opened for us.

The Mayor's business office was directly on the left as you entered the building through its massive doors and turning the corner, entering his office, you came upon the secretary's reception area. It was a very small room, containing a single desk facing the doorway, along with a few chairs against the opposite wall for waiting guests. The office was paneled with dark oak from the floor to the ceiling and all of the finished trim around the doors were thick and heavy, giving the impression of grandeur. As soon as we rounded the corner, the secretary upon seeing Barrett was immediately taken back by the huge animal. Her eyes grew to twice their size and she gasped while trying to move away from her desk. *"Hi...I'm Detective Madison and this is my partner, Barrett....we have an appointment with the Mayor."* She continued to gaze at Barrett in astonishment while he returned a cold stare. Almost frozen in her tracks, she did not respond to me, and knowing that she was still mesmerized by what she saw, I added, *"Stop your staring Barrett and say hello to the lady."*

Barrett had a habit of doing that and with his black face and deep yellow eyes it only made people feel more uneasy. I tried to break him of the habit many times, but having little or no success, I accepted the fact that there was little I could do about it. With us going around her desk, the secretary cringed, and continued to back away from him while still sitting in her chair, which was on rollers. *"Don't worry Miss...he's a good boy,"* and as I said that Barrett placed his head on her lap and nestled his huge head against her, allowing the young woman to pat him. A slow smile developed on her face as she stroked his black fur and Barrett acknowledged the young woman by licking her hand. *"My...is he a big one...I've never seen a dog like that."* Chuckling, I replied, *"That's because he's half wolf."* Just as I said that, a feeling of regret came over me as a look of terror immediately enveloped her face. She yanked her hand away and Barrett sensing something was wrong moved back away from her. Knowing that she was about to have a heart attack, I calmly responded, *"Wolves are great animals, Miss...having organized families, they are true to one another and actually get along great with humans...that is if you treat them right."*

She appeared to relax a little and cautiously reached over her desk to buzz the intercom. *"Mayor...Detective Madison is here to see you...plus, he has something with him....ughh...should I let them both in?"* There was a brief pause for a moment and then a voice commanded, *"Yes, I know who they are...let them in."* Surprised, the secretary got up and opened the door behind her. *"Go on in,"* she said and motioned for both of us to enter the next room. Barrett, being anxious, immediately went ahead of me and before I could even take a few steps, I heard a lot of commotion with someone hollering, *"What the hell is this?....Maryanne!...there's a wild animal in here.....call the police!"*

Quickly rounding the corner and entering the office, I almost broke out into hysterics because of the spectacle that was in front of me. Mayor Logan was actually standing on his desk and holding a large wooden pointer that was used for presentations as a defensive weapon. His eyes were wide and his hair was all messed up, which added to his scared *"out of his wits"* appearance. Barrett was simply sitting in front of his desk, with his right paw extended, while the Mayor was desperately waiving the pointer back and forth, trying to keep him away. Seeing me, he hollered, *"Get that damn thing out of here!"* and I immediately whistled to get Barrett's attention. *"Go lie down, boy....over there in the corner, while we get this brave gentleman off his desk!"* I could not help from snickering while Barrett moved over to the side of the room, and although I tried to hold it, the laughter finally escaped me. Seeing my reaction to his precarious situation, the Mayor while getting down from the top of his desk, loudly said, *"You think it's funny do you?.....what the hell is the matter with you?....bringing something like that into City Hall....that dog is a menace, look at him.....he can't wait to take a chomp out of me!"*

Barrett was lying down now and was panting slightly with a happy expression on his face, which exposed his large canine teeth, but it was hardly a look of aggression. *"Oh, for heaven's sake, Mayor...he's perfectly harmless...look at him, he's happy to meet you....aren't you, boy?"* Barrett immediately gave a little woof in acknowledgment and looked for attention from me. As I sat down in the chair beside him, I stroked his head and looked up at the Mayor who was sitting back at his desk, intently watching our every move. *"You see?....perfectly harmless...his name is Barrett, Mayor, and he's my partner."*

The Mayor continued to stare at us, trying to think on how he was going to respond to me. *"Your partner?.....well, Madison.... from now on you can leave your damn partner outside!"* Chuckling, I replied, *"Can't do that, Mayor...you see, where I go, he goes.... but don't worry, we don't plan to be around here for very long.... we intend to solve this case as soon as possible so we can go back home....don't we, boy?"* Barrett immediately placed his head on my lap and pawed me, agreeing with my assertion while the Mayor looked on with amazement. *"You might think that dog understands you, Madison."* I looked back at the Mayor who was trying to rearrange the papers on his desk and replied, *"Oh, he does.... every word...so don't talk ill of him, Mayor....he doesn't like it when people do that."* The Mayor's face turned red and his anger boiled as he stared back at us, letting me know that he thought I was trying to pull a fast one over him. *"Well, I guess if he makes you perform your job better and this case gets solved....he can stay, but if I hear any complaints about him, it's off to the pound with him until you're done here....you got that?"* Stroking Barrett's back, I replied, *"Don't worry, he won't be a problem....I can assure you of that."*

From a side door at the rear of the room, Marty Sloan suddenly appeared and when he entered the room, his eyes immediately fell upon Barrett. Startled, he stopped dead in his tracks and stared, while Barrett's upper lip began to rise a little. Whispering, I said, *"That's enough, boy...leave him be."* It was obvious that Barrett did not care for the Mayor's assistant and as he moved closer to Mayor Logan to hand him some papers, Barrett's eyes were on him like a hawk. Sloan remarked, *"I see you have met Madison's friend, Mayor...pretty intimidating...isn't he?"* Both of them with their eyes glued on Barrett looked like frightened school children who were about to take their first ride on a roller coaster. To break the ice, I blurted, *"Well, Mayor...you are probably wondering why I wanted to see you."* Nodding his head slowly, both men still had their eyes fixated on the large animal and I could tell by their body posturing that they were getting ready to bolt at any moment at the first sign of trouble. Smiling back at the both of them, I added, *"Well, I've never met you officially Mayor Logan and I wanted to get your thoughts and personal opinion about the case....it might help me with the investigation."*

Breaking from his stupor, the mayor replied, *"Ahh...yeah... the case....well, as you know we have a very serious situation here, one that this city needs to resolve...our economy and way of life is being threatened by this lunatic that has been roaming our streets.... drastic times call for drastic measures and I knew when you worked*

*here before that many cases were solved under your direction.....
you always seemed to get results and that's what this place needs
as our police department so far has proven to be totally impotent....
we have had five people murdered in this city so far and what do
we have to show for it?....nothing, absolutely, nothing!....all I hear
coming from that building across the street is that we are working
on it, sir...pretty soon we should have something, sir....we are doing
our best, sir......crap like that with no results!"*

Logan threw a disgusted look at Sloan who had taken a seat
beside his desk, hoping that he would join in on his tirade about
the police department, but the mayor's assistant kept looking
down at his pad while taking notes. The frustration in the may-
or's face was evident and as I stroked Barrett's back, I replied,
*"From what I have seen so far, this is a complicated case.......in order
to solve it, I am going to need the complete cooperation from the
department and from everyone else......and that means no interference from anyone."*

The Mayor got up from his chair and walked over to one of the
many windows in the office, looking out onto Main Street. With
his back facing us, he declared, *"Don't worry, you'll have it...espe-
cially from this office....the chief was against bringing you back here,
but I insisted on it...for some reason, Madison, he seems to have a
real hair across his ass for you and because of that I was forced to
pull rank on him...he even threatened to quit, if I brought you in
on this, but I wanted you back.....especially when I heard that you
had beaten the bottle and was doing some good police work again...
apprehending that escaped convict a few days ago was a great thing
you did...a real service to our society and we need some of those
same type of results around here, don't we Marty?"*

As the Mayor turned his body to see his reaction, the assistant
only glanced up for a second from taking notes while nodding his
head. Then the Mayor's eyes returned to me as he walked back
over to his desk. Leaning on it and peering down at me, he declared,
*"Are you going to be able to help us out on this, Madison?....I mean
find the killer and get this city back to some kind of normalcy?"* I

glanced down for a second at Barrett who was peacefully sleeping. *"Yeah, we can....but like I said; we will need a free hand in this... no interference from anyone, no matter where the case might take us."* Logan's eyes bugged out a bit, answering, *"When you say 'we', does it mean that dog and you?"*

I stood up from my chair and Barrett immediately woke, while I answered, *"Yes...you see I do not work unless he's with me...he's my full time partner as I have no faith or trust in anyone else..... and by the way Mayor, he's one of the best detectives that you can have working this case....you are indeed very fortunate to have him here."*

The Mayor reached for his pipe on his desk and stuffed it with tobacco from a pouch that he took from his top drawer. Lighting it, he began puffing heavily on it while his wide eyes studied my furry companion. Barrett, not being intimidated, stared right back at him, letting him know that he was ready to go to work. *"Well, like I said, if it makes you feel better, Madison, having him along... so be it...but remember, I don't want to hear any complaints about him attacking or biting someone, you got that?....otherwise the dog officer will have to take care of him."*

That was the worse thing the Mayor could have said, since Barrett hated being associated with the *"criminal"* dog element that had to be taken in by the *"law."* Immediately, a deep growl radiated from within him as his eyes glared back at the Mayor. *"What the hell is the matter with him?"* Logan asked while rearing back in his chair. *"Mayor, you insulted him and he does not take kindly to people who do that....calling him a criminal that needs to be taken to jail...you better say you're sorry."* The Mayor looked at me with bafflement on his face. *"You can't be serious, Madison....that thing actually understood what I just said?"* Chuckling, I replied, *"You bet, every word......you better say you're sorry...otherwise you might not like what he does."*

Mayor Logan glanced at Sloan beside him, but he only shrugged his shoulders not saying a word. Then the Mayor's eyes moved over to Barrett who by this time was standing on all fours, with his teeth exposed, and a slight growl was still emerging from him. Sighing a little, Logan clasped his hands together on his desk, saying, *"Ahhh...I'm sorry...didn't mean anything by it, Mr. Barrett."* Upon hearing that, Barrett's behavior quickly changed and he rubbed up against me, telling me that he was ready to leave. *"Well, if there is nothing else, Mayor....Barrett and I are ready to go to work."* After shaking his and Sloan's hands, we headed for the door to the secretary's office and as we exited, I heard the Mayor say, *"Well, I'll be damned...the dog actually understands English, Marty....what do you think of that?"*

Heading back to the hotel to get settled in, we had to pass several of my old sources of *"medicine"* as there were numerous package stores along the way. Most of them were *"Ma and Pop"* operations, which I had grown to know the owners personally as that came in very handy at times when I was short on cash and needed to ask for a little credit now and then. I do not think there was a package store in Harrisburg that I did not have a credit arrangement with at one time or another, but it was a necessity, since at that time I could have never lived without it. As they say, *"When the monkey scratches, you need to itch."*

Pulling into the Spirit Arms Hotel I noticed that A&E Liquors was across the street. That was one of my *"old watering holes"* and of course, I knew the place very well and being a small store, it had the typical neon sign on the front of the building that was flashing the word *"Spirits"* in red letters. Seeing those words flashing brightly in the dusk air, a dryness came to my throat, which caused me to swallow hard, thinking about those days not so long ago. Taking my eyes from it and stopping the car at the main office to the motel, I saw Zack Thompson through the picture window at the front desk. He appeared to be busily shuffling paper on the counter and organizing it into piles. I had not seen the man since going out on my final *"toot"* a few years ago, but was still surprised on how much he had changed. He had always kept himself in good shape, but now with an enlarged girth and totally bald, he actually looked older than a man in his mid fifties.

Even though I had busted Zack several years ago, during a *"sting"* operation, I still considered him a friend. I never understood why he got involved in a prostitution ring and the numbers racket, but I assumed it was because of money. There were many rumors floating around town at the time that he owed the mob a lot of money, due to his gambling debts, and his uncontrollable thirst for high maintenance women. Surely, a combination that would bring any man down, he succumbed to making easy money, and that spelled the end for him, but as I said, we remained friends throughout the whole convoluted mess.

Opening the office door, the attached overhead bell rang out, which immediately gained his attention. *"Well, I'll be....they told me you were back, but I did not believe it...how are you doing, Shake?"* Extending his hand, he noticed Barrett behind me and added, *"I have heard a few things about the fellow behind you, too.... how are you doing, boy?"* Zack had always been a dog lover too, so I knew there was not going to be a problem with Barrett staying with me. *"Oh, I'm doing fine, Zack, and so isn't Barrett....don't be rude, say hi to the man."* My partner quickly raised a paw, bringing a smile to Zack's face, and when he shook it, he glanced up at me, saying, *"He's a beauty, ain't he?"*

After rubbing Barrett's head a little, Zack went behind the counter and opened up the register book. *"I guess you'll be staying with us for quite a while, Shake, but you won't have to worry about a thing....the city is picking up the tab for everything including the continental breakfast we have in the back meeting room every morning...other meals you will have to fend for yourself, since we do not do them, but I guess you must remember that."* Signing the register, I asked, *"The case that I will be working on...they told me downtown that one of the victims worked here."* Zack's face became increasingly solemn as he slowly turned the registration book around, verifying if I had filled it out correctly. *"Yeah, Tina Hendricks....she was a great gal, Shake....worked with me for about seven years...she started out as a housemaid and worked her way up to helping me manage the place.....in fact, she was on duty here *when it happened."* I could see the anguish bloom in his face and it was obvious that talking about the woman was tearing him apart, but he went on. *"There was blood all over the breakfast room floor when I woke up that morning, Shake...it looked like the place had been turned into a slaughter house and there was no sign of her.......* *when I saw all of the blood, my heart sank as I knew what must have happened.....poor girl, they found her down by the river, beat to shit."*

Seeing that he was really welling up, I decided not to push him anymore and quickly changed the subject. Handing me the keys to my room, I asked, *"How's your mother doing, Zack?"* Immediately, he turned to look away from me and started moving papers on the shelves behind him. *"She passed on about a year ago, Shake....the doctors said it was a massive stroke....I guess she never knew what hit her and by the way you're in room 106...it's on the west wing."* Having not spoken to him since his arrest, I wanted to bury any bad feelings between us. *"Zack....I hope you don't hold any hard feelings against me.....I mean, I was just doing my job and if I hadn't busted you, somebody else would have."* Busily working on his papers, he kept his back towards me the whole time, probably wishing that I had gone away, and while glancing up for a minute at the wall looking straight ahead, he replied, *"I know you were just doing your job....hell, I was pretty messed up back then, but I'm straight now....so don't worry about it....there's no hard feelings at all."* Returning to sorting papers and still not facing me, I knew it was time to leave him alone, and as I opened the door I added, *"Sorry to hear about your mom, Zack... she was a good woman."*

Going back to my car, I kept thinking about his mother and since Zack had lost his dad early in life, how sad he must be for him with her gone too. His mom had brought him up alone and knowing that they were really close, I looked back at Zack in the office as he stood there, still staring at the wall where I had left him. *"Poor bastard,"* I thought to myself. *"He really misses her.... she was everything to him."*

After parking the vehicle in front of my room, I opened my motel room door and flipped the switch to the left of the jam. Turning on the light, I found the place surprisingly comfortable and nice, as there was a small refrigerator in one corner of the room along with a TV on a wooden table opposite the foot of the bed against the wall. Several cheap, but nice pictures adorned the walls and the carpeting had just been cleaned, giving the room a nice fresh smell. Barrett quickly jumped on the bed and laid down while his eyes roamed the room. *"Couldn't wait to go to bed....could you?"* I said while putting my suitcase on the stand in the corner. *"Well, we have work to do....so get your butt up."* With a slight moan and some grunts, Barrett jumped off the bed and came to sit beside me at the large coffee table that was in an adjacent sitting area, to the left of the entrance door as you walked in. Fully furnished, there were two sofa chairs along with a desk and telephone, which created a perfect setup for me to do my work.

Opening up the large manila envelope that Detective Robinson gave me, it contained individual files for each of the five victims. Spreading them out on the coffee table, I removed the crime scene photographs and arranged them in order. The similarities became immediately apparent as all of the women had been strangled with nylon parachute cord and were found naked. Most of them had their hair removed by the killer, and for some sickening reason it was stuffed inside their mouths. However, this was not the case with victims three and four as Kyle Swanson and Tina Hendricks still had their hair intact. Four of the five victims were discovered by the Nashua River, while Kyle Swanson's body was found in her apartment. The first three victims had not been physically mutilated, except for victims one and two who had their limbs broken. Tina Hendricks, the fourth victim, had been severely beaten, almost giving the impression that the killer went berserk on her and the fifth victim, Ellen Sullivan had been stabbed repeatedly and beaten by a heavy, blunt object.

"The crimes are basically the same, but they're different too," I said aloud to Barrett. *"What do you think?"* My partner looked

over the pictures and pawed at the third victim, Kyle Swanson, who was lying on the living room floor next to a large suitcase. *"Yeah, I know what you are seeing....there's something strange about this one, isn't there?"* Barrett woofed slightly and put his paws out in front of him, stretching his back while he kept his eyes on me. Taking a magnifying glass out of my briefcase, I began closely examining the pictures while Barrett licked the side of my face and nudged his head next to my body, anxiously looking for more attention. *"You're a big help,"* I said, *"All you want is to have me rub....."* Suddenly, I was stunned on what appeared through the magnifying glass. Not believing my eyes at first, I had to scan each crime photo again with the magnifier to verify in my own mind what I had discovered. *"Yep...there's no doubt about it, ole boy...the strangle knots on the third and fourth victim are not the same as the others...look, see for yourself."* Barrett again licked the side my face and stuck his face along side mine, looking at the photographs. *"Victims one, two and five, the killer used a slip knot, but victim three has what appears to be a thief's knot and it looks like four has a square knot."* Thinking to myself aloud, I mumbled, *"The thief's knot is an improperly tied square knot...hmmm....that's funny, the square knot is a basic knot used in Boy Scouting....why would the killer use three different types of knots?...plus, there's no question that the slip knot is far more efficient at killing than the other two....doesn't make any sense."*

Gazing at the third victim's crime photo, I noticed the large suitcase beside the body in the living room, opened, and with nothing in it. Mumbling to myself, *"Her hair is intact, too....the suitcase is basically the same size as the others, but she was found in her apartment...I guess the killer could have been interrupted and that might explain why she was found there....possibly being rushed, he used an inferior knot as well."*

Grabbing the fourth victim's picture of Hendricks, there was little doubt that this was an *"overkill."* She had been brutalized throughout the head, chest and abdomen. Several bruises were apparent along her inner thighs and there was even a puncture on her left foot. *"This one was banged up like a hammered piece of beef,"* I thought to myself, *"the previous ones were not...why?"*

Scanning the fifth victim who was another prostitute, it challenged my stomach, even though I had seen dozens of crime photos and had observed my share of death and destruction in the Korean War. The woman had been stabbed repeatedly throughout the torso and was beaten to a pulp since her face and body were covered in multiple contusions and abrasions. Almost unrecognizable, her face resembled hamburger and most of her teeth had been knocked out. Her lips were split in many areas and her nose was off to the side, indicating it was severely fractured. The victim's eyes were totally swollen shut and the discoloration of her face had every color of the rainbow. Her left arm had been broken at the elbow and her stomach area was totally black and blue from the heavy blows that she had received. Most of her long blonde hair had been removed and stuffed in her mouth, making her cheeks bulge as if she was a chipmunk. The tell tale nylon cord was tightly tied around her neck utilizing a slipknot with the loose end dangling down around her feet. *"Hmmm....,"* I thought, *"there is much more nylon cord left on this one...looks like he had thoughts of hog tying this one by attaching the arms behind the back to her feet."*

Returning the photographs in my hand to the table, I leaned back in the sofa chair and rubbed my eyes. Glancing back down at them, the ugliness of the case started to work on my mind. *"So many young girls...,"* I thought. *"Look at them...all of them brutally murdered by some sick piece of shit out there who's lying in wait for his next victim and by the condition of the fifth girl, he's getting worse...more violent...more daring...God knows what he is going to do next."*

The strain of working the case in front of me was bearing down hard now and I could feel myself slipping back into the depression that I had fortunately escaped two years ago. Maybe Andrea was right and I was not ready to take on a case such as this. Rubbing my face with my hands, I placed them out in front of me and stared at them. Watching them shake, my palms were dripping with sweat, telling me that my anxiety was about ready to explode. The thoughts of *"just one drink"* started to enter my head and I quickly stood up, causing Barrett to rise as well. As I walked back and forth in front of the pictures lying on the coffee table, I kept rubbing the back of my neck, trying to remove the tightness in it. However, the more I rubbed, the more I thought about drinking and how all of the pain and anguish that had invaded my body would be eliminated with just one swallow. Looking out the large picture window, I caught myself gazing at the package store with its bright flashing neon sign. In a desperate attempt, I pulled the curtains shut, hoping to remove the vision from my mind, but the quart bottles of Vodka would not disappear. Shutting my eyes and shaking my head, the revolving of bottles spun in my thoughts and as they began to spin faster and faster, dizziness took hold of me.

Leaning my back against the wall, opening my eyes wide towards the ceiling, and trying to get my senses back, Barrett sat there looking at me with concern in his eyes. *"What are you looking at?"* I said aloud. My furry partner did not move, but kept his distance while his eyes glared at me, hoping that I was not going into a full-scale rant. *"Never seen a man have a bad day, ehh?... well, this man knows how to turn a bad day into a good one.....I'll show you how to fix this situation.....come on, let's go."* With that, I whipped my hotel room door open and motioned for him to come, but Barrett just sat there, looking at me. *"Don't give me any shit, now......get your ass up.....come on, let's go."* Barrett realizing I meant business stood up with his head lowered, looking very sad, and walked slowly towards the opening. Upon reaching the threshold, Barrett gave me a quick subdued glance and after sticking his head outside for a moment, he reluctantly followed me out the door.

CHAPTER EIGHT
The Bottle

As I crossed the street with Barrett, there was only one thing on my mind now and that was something, which would give me relief. The case and its helpless victims would have to wait as I was on a far more important mission. Getting my hands on a bottle meant everything to me now and as I opened the glass door to the package store, a young man dressed in a bright, red shirt with an A&E logo was sitting on a stool behind the counter. Leaning up against the wall with his head down and appearing to be fast asleep, upon hearing the bell ring from the door opening, he immediately looked up. Seeing what was coming into the store, he blurted, *"Mister, there are no dogs allowed in here."* Not giving him a second look I immediately went over to the shelves containing the hard liquors and as my eyes searched, there to my right I found several brands of Vodka. *"Smirnoff, there it is,"* I mumbled to myself as I grabbed the quart bottle off the shelf and hugged it like a helpless baby walking over to the cash register. *"I told you mister, that there are no dogs allowed....get him out of here or I'll have to call the police!"* Smiling back at him and taking my wallet out to pull some money from it, I flashed my detective's badge at him. *"Relax...I am the police....besides he isn't a dog...he's a wolf... aren't you, boy?"*

While giving him a few pats Barrett grinned, staring at the boy with his jet-black face, exposing his huge, sharp teeth. Immediately, an expression of fear came over the young man and as he nervously tried to put the bottle in a paper bag, it ripped, forcing him to get another one. Chuckling, I handed him the money and the clerk opened the cash register to retrieve my change, while his eyes remained fixated on Barrett. With wide-open eyes, it was obvious that the poor boy was scared out of his wits and wanted no part of my furry sidekick. *"You want to hurry it up there?"* I said as the monkey on my back sunk his claws in, reminding me what was on the counter. Still glaring at the dog, the young man gave me my change while stumbling all over his words. *"Ahh...Ahh...is that dog; I mean that wolf.....is it safe for him to be on the loose like that?"* Swiftly grabbing the bottle off the counter I headed for the door, opened it, and turned my head at him. *"Oh, it's safe alright, but he can't stand young guys in red shirts."*

Barrett quickly turned around, facing the boy, and growled with saliva dripping from his mouth. The sight sent the young man into a full-scale panic attack as he backed up against the cigarettes and cigars in the display case on the wall. Adding to the horror, Barrett stood tall and then crouched slightly, looking like he was going to strike at any moment. Bumping into the case, the boy knocked several packages to the floor along with many individual cigars as he tried to put distance between him and Barrett. Laughing and going out the door, I could not help to take a second look at the young man, up against the wall, as his eyes were wide like saucers and his face was entirely white with fear. Waiting for Barrett to catch up with me I laughed aloud, saying, *"That was a pretty good show you put on in there.....I think the poor kid shit his pants!"*

Walking across the parking lot, Barrett scampered to get along side of me and upon reaching the street; we had to wait to cross. There was a continuous line of cars as the traffic was heavy and with no break in sight, I became agitated from the wait. Standing there, clutching my little *"friend"* in the paper bag, my throat was so dry that I could barely swallow. With the orange sized lump in my throat along with the anxious feelings that were almost out of control, I squeezed the bottle in my arms, as it was the only thing preventing me from going insane. *"Why does there have to be so much God damn traffic in this town?"* I thought, watching the cars go by us. *"Why don't they hurry up and let us cross, for Christ's sake."*

However, the parade of cars continued and the monkey on my back was growing more impatient as every second passed. His claws were set in me deeply now, causing me to envision the taste of Vodka, making my cravings soar. I was yearning for that initial feeling of razor blades down my throat, since what followed was pure ecstasy, a true feeling of contentment and happiness. Licking my lips, feeling the paper bag against my body, and seeing my room across the street where I could get some desired relief only made my hunger grow. With my patience running out and with no end in sight of the long line of cars, I finally held up my badge. Walking out into the traffic I shouted, *"Police business!... hold up there!...stop!"*

With one hand outstretched in front of me, the cars starting stacking up as they came to an abrupt stop. Pleased that access to my room was finally in reach, I scurried across the highway with Barrett, almost looking like a young boy who had just stolen a watermelon out of the next-door farmer's patch. Then suddenly, I heard a loud crash echo through the damp night air. Halting my escape for a second, I glanced back, and saw that a car had crashed into the back of another one, crushing its trunk, folding it up like an accordion. Then another loud crash occurred when two cars collided next to them. With all hell breaking loose, people started furiously blowing their horns and hollering at us to move faster across the four-lane highway. Walking in front of the cars that were stopped and being disgruntled with their actions towards us, I gave them all my middle finger, which only infuriated them more. Finally reaching the other side, there were people already exiting their cars, attending to the persons in the accident. I looked down at Barrett and motioned with my hand. *"Come on, boy...let's get the hell out of here before the heat shows up!"*

As we hurried back to our room, I still heard people hollering and horns blowing from several cars at the accident. Looking back over my shoulder, there were several people scurrying about and it was only a matter of time before the cops showed up along with an ambulance. Knowing to be detained for questioning was not in our best interest, I yelled at Barrett to move faster. Pulling the key from my pocket and quickly opening my motel room door, we both bolted into the room. Before closing the door, I detected that lights from emergency vehicles were already approaching the chaotic scene. *"Well, we got out of there in the nick of time, boy....seems the troops have arrived,"* I exclaimed, slamming the door, and throwing the security chain into place.

My nerves were killing me now as I clumsily took the quart of Vodka out of the paper bag and placed it on the coffee table. Grabbing a glass off the desk, I sat down on the couch and with a gleam in my eye, stared at the bottle in front of me. Wringing my hands from the sweat in my palms, I could barely swallow as the back of my throat felt like a desert. My heart was racing with excitement and as I gazed at the bottle, I knew relief was only an arms length away. However, as my conscious battled with my inner self, I realized that my guilt was staring me in the face, telling me that this was the end if I took that first drink. Then a little voice spoke to me. *"Go ahead...it's all right....just one...that's all you need and the pain will disappear....you know what it feels like to have all the anxiety and anxiousness just fade away.....after all, you've been there a thousand times before when that precious, clear liquid slides down your throat, giving you that beautiful relief you seek....go ahead, you'll be just fine."*

Continuing to gaze at it, the bottle began to go in and out of focus, almost disappearing from my sight. Placing my elbows on my knees and my hands under my chin, I desperately concentrated on it, but it remained blurry, almost surreal. Opening and closing my eyes several times attempting to clear my vision, I tried to make sure the bottle was actually there and not a dream. *"I know it's there.....I just bought it for Christ's sake,"* my mind kept telling me. *"It has to be real...but why can't I see it?"* Desperately, I leaned forward and with my eyes big as silver dollars and glaring, I finally saw the words *"Smirnoff Vodka"* magically appear, giving me untold relief that this was reality and my *"medicine"* was truly there on the table for the taking.

With joy exploding throughout my body, I suddenly felt a stare upon me. Turning my head to the left, I discovered Barrett sitting at the end of the coffee table. His yellow eyes were glaring at me and I could almost feel him telling me that this was wrong and not to succumb to my addiction. The guilt started to build in me again, causing my breathing to be hard, if not impossible. I looked down at my trembling hands and attempted to wring them out again, while the anxiousness started choking me, causing me to loosen my collar so I could get a breath. Finally, throwing my body against the back of the couch in desperation, I glanced over at Barrett who was still sitting there and looking at me with sadness in his eyes. His constant stare penetrated my suit of guilty armor and drove my inner feelings to a point where I thought I was losing my mind. Finally, out of despair I yelled, *"What's the matter with you?....can't a man have a drink once in a while?....why don't you mind your own God damn business and go lay down."*

Not bothered in the least by my outburst, Barrett kept staring at me, working my conscious to the next guilt level, which caused me to plead, *"You don't understand, do you?....I need this......besides it will only be one....I'll leave the rest for another day."* In a frantic attempt to release my pain, I lunged forward and reached for the bottle.

Suddenly, a loud ringing noise echoed throughout the room, interrupting me from my quest. It was the phone on the desk and my first thought was not to answer it. After all, I was on a personal mission now and obnoxious phone calls were not going to interrupt my quest for peace and tranquility. As the phone rang many more times, it was obvious whoever was calling was not going to go away that easily, and reluctantly I jumped off the couch to answer it. Picking up the receiver in almost a panic I said, *"Hello....Madison here....it's your dime."* The voice on the other end answered, *"Shake?....Russ Wilson calling.....just wanted to touch base with you about tomorrow...thought I would pick you up, so we could visit some of the crime scenes together and go over the files...what's a good time for you?"* Thinking for a moment, I realized that sleeping in tomorrow was not going to be an option and that meant my drinking spree was surely going to be hampered. Desperation set in, as my mind searched for an answer to my dilemma. *"Well, Russ...ahh...ahhh.....we don't have to get a real early start do we?....why don't you come by around ten o'clock?"*

There was silence on the other end for several seconds and I began to wonder if my ex partner might know that I was up to my old tricks again. Not waiting for an answer, I added, *"Well, how about nine o'clock then?"* Quickly, Russ answered, *"Are you okay, Shake?....sounds like you are a little anxious about this whole thing."* I knew it was going to be hard to pull the wool over my old partner's eyes and my mind went on an immediate search mission to find the right words to cover my tracks. *"Oh...everything is just fine, Russ...Barrett and I are just about ready to go to bed....come to think of it, why don't we get an early start tomorrow morning so we can hit this thing hard.....how about eight o'clock?"*

Waiting for Russ to answer me seemed like an eternity, as that beautiful bottle on the coffee table beckoned to me, telling me that a land of peace and tranquility was only seconds away. The case, Russ, and the whole investigation had taken a back seat now, and the thought of pouring down my throat what was contained in that bottle was overwhelming my mind. The vision of multiple quarts of Vodka circled within my head as I sat there desperately hoping that my suggestion of eight o'clock would be sufficient to get rid of him. *"Yeah, that sounds great, Shake...I'll pick you up then.....see you in the morning."*

Hearing the click of the receiver and the monotonous dial tone brought incredible relief. I was finally free at last to gather up my little friend on the table and begin our exciting journey together. Putting the receiver down, I suddenly heard the rustling of papers and turned my head to see what was happening. To my surprise, Barrett had grabbed the neck of the Vodka bottle and was trotting away with it. *"What the hell are you doing?....come back here with that, you little bastard!"*

In a full-scale panic, I reached over the table to grab the bottle from the furry thief, but he was too quick for me, and before I knew it, he was well on his way to the bathroom. Stumbling over the coffee table, I made a mad dash towards the bathroom door and just as I reached it, Barrett was holding the bottle over the bathtub. Before I could say another word, he let it fall and with a loud crash, the bottle broke into a hundred pieces. My little *"friend"* was lost forever and as I watched the booze flow down towards the drain, my whole life seemed to go with it. With red-faced anger, I glared at my fury companion, wanting to wring his neck, but Barrett just innocently sat there, looking straight at me with his right paw raised.

At first, I felt betrayed, lost and not knowing which way to turn, my thoughts rapidly turned to hatred towards the hairy beast. After seeing the entire bottle of booze disappear down the bathtub drain, I wanted to kick the shit out of him, but realizing my situation was hopeless I just hung my head and plopped on the floor in regret. Burying my head in my hands, I started to cry for my loss, and mourn its passing, but then a cold wet nose nudged my cheek. As Barrett pawed me and licked my face, the depression and thoughts of the bottle suddenly left me, just as quickly as they had invaded my mind in the first place. Rubbing one of his ears, he showed even more affection towards me by nestling his head on my lap. With calmness coming over me, I looked at my furry partner with contentment in my eyes. *"Well, partner...looks like I owe you another one....a steak that is....you certainly pulled my butt out of the fire again."* He answered me by licking my hand and the flood of serene feelings flowed through me like a rush of adrenaline. Looking at the white enameled tub with shattered glass in it, I said aloud, *"Yep...you sure did, my friend...you saved my ass....come on, let's get to bed...we have a busy day tomorrow."*

As I got up and stared at the broken bottle in the tub, I thought, *"Yeah...broken glass...that would have been my life....broken to shit again, if it wasn't for him."* Heading for bed, Barrett was settled in before I even started to undress. Laying my shirt on the back of the chair, I started to take off my pants and suddenly the sound of snoring filled the room. *"Look at you,"* I thought, glancing at him sprawled out and taking most of the bed. *"You are quite a partner."* Lying down on the bed as well and trying to squeeze in, I adjusted my pillow and looked over at the snoring beast. With a smile, I gently patted him on the side, saying, *"I wouldn't have it any other way."* And with that, I turned out the light and went to sleep.

▲ ▲ ▲

Surprisingly, the next morning came quickly, but I had a good night's sleep, as the thoughts of booze had not appeared in my dreams at all. Being thankful for that and opening one eye, I noticed that Barrett was out of bed and at the front door. Whimpering slightly, I knew he was telling me that it was time for him to find some woods. Climbing out of bed, I put my pants on to let him out, and upon opening the door, he quickly disappeared behind the hotel. Stepping outside and closing the door behind me, my eyes began scanning the parking lot. The sun was already up, and I could not help from noticing that it was going to be a beautiful day. The sky was a vibrant blue, absent of any clouds and glancing up at the sun, its rays felt so good on my face. I had made it through another night without a drink and I was still sober, something that I could be forever thankful for. Knowing Russ would be here any minute, I suddenly grasped that there would be no need for hiding today. Facing him would be easy as the need for a pick me up was not going to be necessary this morning, which only made me feel good inside.

As Barrett came back from around the corner, a vehicle pulled up in front of my room and parked. *"Good morning...beautiful day isn't it?"* Russ said exiting the car. *"Yes, it is,"* I replied opening the door to my room. Approaching me, he asked, *"You have break-fast yet?"* I stepped inside and began gathering up my files from the wooden coffee table while he watched me along with Barrett. Noticing that Russ was looking around the room, I knew right away, what he was searching for. *"Don't worry, Russ......despite the temptation across the street, I made it through the night without a drink."* Taken back a little by my words, Russ cleared his throat, seeming almost embarrassed about his thoughts. He moved over a few steps toward the TV, not saying a word, and while I grinned at him, picking up my stuff, I added, *"No...I haven't had breakfast yet, have you?"*

Going out to the vehicle and opening the back door for Barrett, Russ watched him hop into the back seat. Closing the rear door, he moved up to the driver's side and looking over the roof of the car, he exclaimed, *"No...thought we would grab something down at the local diner....I know the owner and he loves dogs...Barrett shouldn't be a problem."* Entering the passenger's side, I chuckled. *"That's good, Russ....I owe Barrett big time and I think steak and eggs is what he's got in mind."*

When we arrived at the diner, my old partner was right about Bill Parsons the owner, for he was more than happy to serve all of us, including Barrett, as he truly loved dogs. Of course, his plate had to be on the floor and not on the table, but at least I was able to repay my furry friend for last night's rescue. *"So tell me Shake, how is Miss Carlson doing?"* Russ asked buttering his toast. Smiling, I answered, *"Oh, she's doing just fine....quite a girl, don't you think?"* Putting the butter knife down on the table, Russ took a bite of toast and grinned. *"She's a good looking woman, Shake.... you should consider yourself pretty lucky in landing a girl like that.....and a nurse too, that should come in pretty handy later in life."* Nodding my head, I patted Barrett, answering, *"Yeah, you're right Russ....we are both lucky to have found her, aren't we boy?"* My faithful friend raised his head and with a gleam in his eye, confirmed my answer while he hoped for an additional morsel from me.

"So, what do you think about the case so far?" Russ asked while sipping on his heavy, ceramic coffee cup. I wiped my mouth with a napkin and rubbed my chin, thinking for a moment. *"I went over the files last night before going to bed....did you know the killer used three different knots on his victims?"* Russ looked surprised as he dug back into his eggs, answering, *"No...never noticed it."* Taking a drink of coffee, I glanced down at Barrett who had finished his feast and was quietly sleeping at my feet. Knowing that he was content I replied, *"He used a slip knot on victims, one, two and five .....number three had a thief's knot and four had a square knot."* Russ put down his fork and placed his elbows onto the table. Resting his chin on his hands, he said, *"That's strange...a slip knot is more efficient for killing.....why would he have used a substandard one on two of his victims?"* Resting my coffee cup back on the table, I gazed out the window for a second at the people passing by, and grabbing my coffee cup I responded, *"That's what has been bothering me....the killer might have been pressed for time for some reason with the third victim and could have made a mistake in tying the knot, but the fourth was found by the river, wasn't she?"* My old partner nodded his head. *"Yeah, she was, but not in the same vicinity...her body was found about two miles upstream from the others."*

Leaning back in my chair, I looked out the window and noticed the newly constructed gas station across the street. *"Russ, the city is growing right along, isn't it?"* Finishing up his home fries, Russ chuckled. *"Sure is...there's a new developer in town...he's been buying up land like crazy around here...in fact, I think he must have five or six large subdivisions under construction....all toll, there's got to be at least eight hundred homes involved."* Sipping on my coffee, I handed Barrett a leftover piece of bacon under the table and he promptly snatched it up. *"The guy must be rich,"* I said placing my cup back on the table. *"Where did he come from?"* Russ patted his mouth with his napkin. *"Don't know exactly, Shake....I heard he's from down south somewhere....Georgia, I think....he came into town about six months before you left.....you must remember that, don't you?......his company is the Veratex Corporation and you can*

110

see their signs all over the city....I guess he's also into apartment buildings....some of them he tears down and rebuilds, while others he rehabilitates for the homeless and the poor....he's a big man here in town and a staunch supporter of the Mayor....some day, I'll have to introduce you to him."

Finishing up my eggs, I downed what was left in my coffee cup. I tried to recall the man Russ was talking about, but at that point, in my life because of my heavy drinking I was lucky to have known my own name. That year after my wife's death was nothing but a living hell and to tell the truth it was really an extended blackout, so remembering a detail like a strange builder coming into town was just wishful thinking.

Barrett noticing that I had finished breakfast, sat up next to the table and patiently waited for me. *"Looks like somebody is ready to go to work,"* Russ chuckled. Rubbing Barrett's forehead, I replied, *"Yeah, he's anxious...a new case always gets his blood going....before you know it, he'll be heading for the door."* Just then, the waitress strolled over to our table and said, *"Anything else gentlemen?"* It was obvious she was a little nervous since she kept staring at Barrett while I pulled my wallet out. *"No, that's okay... we've had enough...what's the damage?"* She tried to hand me the bill, but Russ swiftly scooped it up from her. *"No, partner...this one is on me to welcome you back, but from here on out, if that dog of yours is going to eat like that, you can pay for the rest of the meals!"* Smiling, I tucked my wallet away in my suit coat and flashed a sheepish grin. *"Russ, to level with you.....the only reason he ate that much was that he knew you were paying!"* With both of us laughing, Russ's eyes looked left then right, realizing that Barrett had already left he asked, *"The dog's gone....where the hell did he go?"* Pointing to Barrett pacing back and forth at the door, I shrugged my shoulders. *"Do you see what I mean, Russ?....when it's time to go to work, he's always the first one to punch in!"*

With both of us still chuckling, we exited the diner, and because the traffic was heavy and noisy on Main Street, Russ needed to raise his voice a bit. *"Well, Shake.....where do you want* to start?" Opening the rear passenger's door for Barrett, I replied, *"Let's begin at the last crime scene....victim number five...I believe her name was Ellen Sullivan."* Russ nodded his head as we piled in and while he started the car, we noticed an old man walking down the sidewalk. *"Well I'll be....Shake....here comes old man Thompson....you remember him, don't you?"*

My mind immediately went back to the old days, working as a detective for the city. Old man Thompson had been a deeply respected businessman in town, but had lost everything due to gambling debts and bad investments. Unfortunately, his wife left him as well with their four kids and had gone to Florida to begin a new life. Totally devastated and depressed over the whole stinking mess, he took to the bottle. Cheap wine, whiskey or anything that contained alcohol was the only nourishment that he ever consumed after that. Barely weighing one hundred pounds now, he was very fragile, dirty, and unshaven. Shuffling along, it was obvious that death was following close behind the poor man and seeing the sickening sight caused my thoughts to recall staring at the bottle last night with glee and brightness in my eyes. The picture was very clear in my head last night as I sat there, anticipating the good time I was going to have, drinking myself into oblivion. Seeing old man Thompson now in his deplorable condition suddenly sent a shiver up my spine as I imagined myself walking down Main Street like that, penniless, and in a drunken stupor. Staring at the old coot and reliving those horrible times, out of the blue, I felt something cold on the side of my face and realized it was Barrett, nestling his nose against me. *"That dog really cares for you, doesn't he Shake?"* Waking from my daydream, I patted Barrett on the head, saying, *"You wouldn't believe how much even if I tried to tell you, Russ....he's my best friend."*

CHAPTER NINE
The Hunt Begins

When we reached the crime scene of the fifth victim, I immediately recognized the area on the banks of the Nashua River, as it was within about two to three hundred yards of victims one and two. This section of the river was very well secluded, but easy to access, since there were several dead end streets that stopped short of the river. The ends of these streets were thickly wooded and undeveloped, giving the killer a perfect spot to dispose of the bodies. This told me that our perpetrator or *"perp"* that we commonly referred to them as, knew the city well and was familiar with the area. Given a disposal site such as this gave us little chance of a probable witness, as the killer would have been in and out of this place within seconds.

Stopping at the end of May Street, Russ pulled a thick manila envelope out of his satchel that was next to him on the front seat and removed several pieces of paper from it. Taking a few minutes to get his bearings, he then began reading the summary. *"Ellen Sullivan....age 25...she was discovered near the river about three weeks ago....the victim had been strangled, badly beaten and cut up, but like the others she was found naked in a suitcase with her hair cut off and stuffed in her mouth."*

Getting out of the vehicle, Barrett immediately went to work sniffing the ground, and while he circled the immediate area back and forth, he paused at several locations for a few seconds. *"Gee...he doesn't waste anytime, does he?"* Russ jokingly said. As

I watched Barrett make a bigger and bigger circle with his nose to the ground, it became obvious to me that he was conducting his normal search pattern. *"Yeah, he doesn't, Russ....the dog just loves to work.....by the way, where did they actually find the body?"*

Russ pointed to a stand of brush about twenty yards from us that were at the top of the banking. *"There...underneath that large maple tree....like some of the others, her legs and arms had been broken."* As we walked over to the brushy section, my eyes scanned the ground for any clues, but due to the number of footprints, I saw, it became apparent to me that this area had been well covered. *"This location is almost identical to where victims one and two were found, Russ....If I remember right, they were found at the end of Fourth Street."* Nodding his head, my old partner pointed up the river. *"Yeah...your memory is good, but those suitcases were tossed over the banking and had fallen towards the river...I think he might have been aiming for the river with this one, too, but it fell short.....or maybe for some reason he just left it at the top of the knoll."*

Standing in the center of the crime scene, we watched Barrett make his rounds as he was still working the area and with his nose to the ground, he busily investigated every square inch that he trotted across. *"I don't think he will find anything, Shake...we covered this area pretty well...hell, I think we must have had thirty officers searching this place.....the suspect probably brushed out his foot prints and kept the car on the pavement as there were no signs or evidence of anyone stopping here."* While I continued to watch my furry partner work the scene, I pointed him out to my old partner. *"If there is anything here, Russ, he'll find it....that nose of his is incredible...you wouldn't believe what he has discovered at other crime scenes....just when you think that you have been beaten and there is nothing to be found, he ..."* Suddenly, Barrett came to an abrupt stop, pawed the ground, and looked back at us. *"Like I said, Russ...it's only a matter of time."*

Quickly we moved over to where Barrett was sitting and examined the piece of ground that he had pawed. Kneeling down, I looked closer and beneath the dirt, it appeared he had partially uncovered what looked like a small metal plate. *"What the hell is that?"* Russ asked with a confused look. I reached in my coat pocket, retrieved a handkerchief, and began brushing more of the dirt away from it. Within a few moments, a six-inch square piece of metal was revealed, and as I picked it up with the handkerchief, a folded piece of paper that was beneath it came into view.

Seeming pleased and proud on what he had discovered, Barrett put his nose down next to it, and quickly backed away, sitting on his haunches. Observing the gloating pup while extending his paw out, I remarked, *"Yeah....okay....I know..... good job....you've done it again,"* and I shook his paw. Russ rubbing the side of his head looked at Barrett and then at the piece of paper. *"That dog is something else again, Shake.....he has some real smarts."* Smirking a little, I looked up at him. *"Oh, for Christ's sake, Russ....the dog has a big enough head as it is... don't blow it up anymore."* As both of our eyes turned to my furry friend, he sat there with a huge smile on his face, panting and soaking up our admiration of him, appreciating that we were pleased with him. That was one thing about Barrett; he enjoyed being the center of attention and always knew how to get it.

Taking a pen out of my pocket, I poked at the folded piece of paper on the ground and opened it, revealing some pasted letters taken from several newspapers and magazines. I began reading it aloud:

"Welcome back, Madison....I knew you would return as staying away was not in your veins and finding this, means that your furry friend is with you too....that's good....really good because it will only make this little game a bit more challenging .....tell the others that number four is surely on

the way and remember, you won't have a chance of being cleared unless you bring me in, for I am the only one that knows all!....think back to that sweet and pretty little wife of yours.....it hurts doesn't it?......picking her poor, broken body up off the pavement.....how you held her limp and lifeless body in your arms, wishing that you could put her back together........beat me at my game and you will have your answers.....be warned though, I doubt that you are up to the challenge....having a little trouble staying sober are we?....well, after I get done with you, you'll be lying in the gutter somewhere out of your mind on booze and knowing that will make my victory complete!......so my good friend, enjoy your little quest for the truth as you step back into the darkest pits of hell!

Good luck !
the traveling salesman

Oh, by the way.....let's keep this between us, okay?....because if you release this note to anyone else, I will immediately stop my cleansing of your city and move on....then, you will never know who did that pretty wife of yours!.... plus, I know what happened in that alley and it was not your doing....gives you a little incentive, right?......and now to leave you with a little clue, my inept detective to think about.....'there are none so blind as those who will not see'.......now, you think on that for a while........"

As I stared off into the distance, almost in a trance, Russ squatted down next to me and seeing that the note had genuinely gotten to me said softly, *"This guy really has it in for you, doesn't he?....and what does he mean by the fourth victim is about to die?....he's killed five already."* Trying to remove the painful thoughts from my mind by rubbing my forehead I replied, *"I knew there was something funny about this case....I told you about the different knots that I* discovered....it really made me think and now with this note from the killer, we are probably dealing with at least two different nuts or maybe even three!"

Barrett gave a sharp bark as he looked at the both of us. "I swear that dog gives me the 'heebee geebees' sometimes, Shake," Russ said standing up. "You can't say a word without him listening in and giving his opinion....if I didn't know better, I would say he's a detective that was reincarnated into that thing." Chuckling, I stood up as well, holding the piece of paper by my handkerchief. "I doubt there are any prints on this, Russ...our killer is too smart for that, besides he's made a mistake already....his scent must be all over this and Barrett has gotten a good whiff of it....don't worry, if we ever come upon him, he'll let us know."

Retrieving an evidence bag from the car, Russ carefully placed the note in it, and sealed it. Walking back to the vehicle, my old partner noticed Barrett was still searching the area, making his circles as he was doing before. "He never quits, does he?" Russ commented, placing the evidence bag in the vehicle. "Tell me, Shake....what are we going to do about this note from the killer?.... looks like he means business about not bringing anybody else in on this, but realistically, we can't suppress this evidence.....can we?"

Leaning against the car, I lit up a smoke and offered one to Russ. Taking one, I lit his as well and we both began taking some heavy drags from our butts, thinking about the situation we now found ourselves in. "Well, if this guy is telling the truth, Russ..... and he does know who killed my wife....you know what my vote is going to be." Russ took another drag and held the smoke in for a second before exhaling it, followed by a heavy sigh. "You know, Shake... .I'm caught between a rock and a hard place on this...if the chief ever finds out that we are withholding evidence, my job will go down the shitter, but quick!" He took another drag and expelled the smoke quickly, adding, "But I know how much your wife meant to you... and the son of a bitch that ran her down needs to pay for it....never mind the possibility of clearing your name with that shooting in the alley, but how do we know if this guy is for real?.....when you think about it, how can this psycho know so much about everything.....he might be just yanking our chain on this and to tell you the truth, I really don't know what to do."

Pursing my lips and thinking for a moment, I noticed that Barrett was trotting over to us. He was panting and licking his chops as he sat down next to us, hoping for a drink of water. Looking down at him, I declared, "Look at you...there's a river over the banking you damn fool....you can get a drink from there!" Upon hearing that, Barrett immediately got up and disappeared over the banking, rustling down through the brush. Russ took another drag from his butt and finishing it, he crushed it against the side of the car. Watching Barrett disappear into the woods, he grinned back at me saying, "Like I said, that dog gives me the creeps."

Waiting for Barrett to come back, Russ and I continued to talk about what we were going to do. It was evident by his mannerisms that he was uneasy with the whole mess and was thinking about the definite possibility of losing his pension. He was ten years older than I was and had been on the force much longer, making him that much closer to retirement. A twenty-year pension was right around the corner and expecting him to jeopardize everything for me was a tall order. However, Russ had always been a straight shooter with me, even through the years of my heavy drinking, where he often covered for me. He always backed his partner, which he had proven repeatedly, as when he lied for me about seeing the gun in the kid's hand. I knew he did not see it, but with his testimony, it saved me from the slammer and now I was not going to force him into anything. If he was going to be in on this, it had to be his decision alone and no one else's, especially mine.

Suddenly, we heard growling and a ruckus coming from where Barrett had disappeared to. Both us went running towards the noise and as we got to the top of the slope, Barrett came trotting up with a rabbit in his mouth. Chuckling, I said, "It must be time for a coffee break, Russ......Barrett's hungry.....let's go." Russ watching my fury partner devour the rabbit in a few gulps, looked over at me in amazement. *"Like I told you, Shake...that dog is not a dog....he's as human as either of us!"*

Piling back into his vehicle, we started our trek over to the coffee shop, and Barrett with a full belly was lying on the back seat, snoring away, oblivious to anything around him. *"That dog of yours, does everything hard doesn't he?....I mean he works hard, sleeps hard...I bet he even plays hard."* Russ had done it now, because in a flash Barrett was up and jumping all over him as he was driving, licking his face and pawing him from one side of the head to the other. *"Shake!...what the hell is he doing?....tell him to leave me alone, I can't see to drive!"* Laughing, I blurted, *"You said the magic word, Russ.....and he does love to play, you know."*

Realizing we were headed for an accident, I instructed Barrett to lie down and to behave himself, which he promptly did. Russ continued to wipe his face from the slimy saliva with his handkerchief and while glancing back at Barrett in the rear seat who was staring at him with wide eyes, said, *"Look at that damn mutt.... he can't wait to go at it again, can he?"* Chuckling, I lit up a cigarette, exhaled the smoke out the window, and reached behind to give Barrett a few pats. *"Some day I will tell him something that really gets him riled up and then you'll have some real fun on your hands with him, but that's for another time....besides you are trying to drive and I really wanted to get to the coffee shop in one piece!"*

About ten minutes later, we arrived at Cliff's Doughnut shop and were enjoying some of his well-known pastries. I had ordered Barrett a fresh cruller and a carton of chocolate milk, which he considered some of his favorites. Usually, the establishment was packed full of people and was a hangout for the local politicians, but since we arrived close to lunchtime, that crowd had already been and gone. That did not bother me in the least; in fact, it was a Godsend, since they would have pounded us for answers about the case and of course, they would have made some political speeches along the way about our department in order to stir things up a bit. That was one thing about this town and others that I had worked in. You could always count on the city council-ors visiting the local coffee shops, hoping to gather up some addi-tional votes. They appeared to be constantly campaigning all the time and the act of conducting city business to accomplish any-thing always seemed to be the furthest thing from their minds. So seeing the coffee shop with only a few people in it and politician free, actually brought a smile to my face when we entered it.

As Russ took a bite of his jelly doughnut, he sneaked a portion of it to Barrett who was underneath the table. Actually sucking it out of his hand, my fury friend gently took the piece, leaving Russ very surprised. *"He can be real gentle, can't he?"* Russ commented taking a sip of his coffee. I did not answer him as my mind was stuck on the note we had just found and a blank stare had over-taken my face. Staring out the window, in another world, I sud-denly heard Russ say, *"Earth to Shake...come in please."* Realizing my thoughts had gotten the best of me; I broke my stare and gazed back at him. *"What do you think he meant Russ, by, 'there are none so blind as those who will not see?'.....that's actually a quote out of the bible......don't tell me we have another religious nut like we had in the Anderson case."* Russ shook his head, placing his cup back down on the table. *"No...I don't think so, Shake....In that case, which was about five years ago, Anderson dropped scripture passages on the two people he murdered....plus, he was not a serial killer.....he just wanted to kill his wife and her lover who were screwing around behind his back while he went to work....if you remember, he tried to throw us off the track, by making us think a nut was doing all of the killings, but we eventually figured it out and got him....I'm sure if you think back hard enough, you'll remember the particulars on that one."*

I recalled the case all right as the department was sure it had a serial killer on its hands. It was not until Russ discovered that the young male victim was a lover of the wife who was found a day before him. They had kept their secret relationship *"under wraps"* from the public for several months, but the husband knew about it. Evidently, due to sickness and by chance, the husband found both of them in bed because he went home early from work one day. However, the husband was clever, since he posed the bodies in various ways to make it appear it was an act of random violence as the wife was found seated on a park bench with her throat slit from ear to ear, looking like she was waiting for the bus. While her lover was found a day later, sitting alone in his car, stopped at a traffic light. He had been strangled and with no other apparent wounds along with his wallet missing, it looked like he had been robbed and at first, the department considered these two murders as not being related to each other.

Later it was determined that the husband had actually been waiting for his male victim at his house, by hiding in the back seat. Putting two and two together, it appeared that the boyfriend was evidently trying to make a break for it by leaving town, once he saw what had happened to the guy's wife, but the husband never gave him a chance to do so. Initially we were all fooled on that one, but Russ discovered the link days later by finding a witness at one of the hotels putting the cheating wife and boyfriend together. From there on it was just old-fashioned police work that put the husband behind bars, but it was Russ's hard work and dedication in finding the clues that eventually broke the case.

"Are you seeing anyone, Russ?" My old partner did not hear my words as his expression was blank and he seemed to be caught up in the past. *"Well, are you?"* I asked again. Breaking from his stupor and taking a sip of coffee, he replied, *"Nah....no time for women I guess....you know how police work can be......and to tell the truth, a good woman is hard to find, but when you do.....it kinda makes a man feel whole, if you know what I mean....gives him a reason to get up in the morning and face this rotten world we live in."*

All of a sudden, I saw Russ's demeanor change as he became caught up in the past again, probably thinking about his wife who had left him for a local bum. Why she left him for such a low-life, I never quite figured out, but she did and it devastated Russ. Thinking that must be the reason for his blank stare and since it happened many years ago, I thought it would be safe now if I poked around a little bit more. *"So...no girl friend, ehh?....maybe it would be good for you if you took some time to find a woman."* Russ rolled the cup between his hands, staring at it, and thought for a moment. Then he glanced up at me, shaking his head. *"No.... after Martha left me, I never found anyone else as she was the love of my life.....I gave her everything.....house, cars, jewelry, but she turned out to be a no good whore.....going with that piece of shit and screwing me, but good......well, you know the whole story on that one, Shake....no sense stirring the bucket of shit, is there?"*

I could see that period in his life still bothered him and me reopening old wounds served little purpose, as he wanted nothing to do with them. Quickly deciding to get back to the case, I asked, *"Well, where do we go from here on this thing?"* Immediately he snapped out of it and looked out the window at the people passing us by on the sidewalk. *"Look at them, Shake....going on with their daily lives....not realizing what we are dealing with.... anyone one of them could be next, you know.....take that blonde for instance....she is about the right age and she's pretty, too....who knows, we could find her down by the river in a few days."* As we watched the woman pass us by, even Barrett sat up and stared at her. *"Shake...I don't know where you got that damn dog from, but he seems to be aware of everything around him....nothing ever gets passed him."* Stroking his fur, I glanced at Russ, smiling. *"Nope.... he sees everything and his mind is always working.....plus he's as loyal as they come....he's the best damn partner a man could ever want."*

Just then, the waitress came over and I took out my wallet to pay the check. Handing her a five-dollar bill, I told her to keep the change and she promptly disappeared behind the counter towards the cash register. *"Russ, I would like to know a little more about the woman that worked for the city....I believe her name was Swanson, you know the one that was found in her apartment."* My old partner took the last sip of coffee from his cup and pursed his lips. *"Not much to tell, really....she went to work for the city about two years ago, taking the job of Assistant Planner in the Planning Board office.....I believe she came from a small town in upper New York State where her previous position was a planner for about three years..... a very intelligent girl, she graduated from Boston University in 1955 magna cum laude.....single with no boyfriend, work seemed to be her only interest......a very pretty and talkative girl, she was well liked by everyone in City Hall...Don Birmingham, the head of planning, hired her out of six applicants and was generally pleased with her job performance....we interviewed him extensively, asking the routine questions, but there was nothing out of the ordinary with her life....no enemies...no broken hardhearted boyfriends or anything like that..... if you want to talk to him, I can arrange it.....who knows?...you might come across something we missed."*

I lit up a smoke and took a couple of drags on it, pondering what Russ had just said about the girl. This murder was still bothering the hell out of me, as it did not fit the profile of the killer. The girl was well educated and had a good job, while the others were transients and prostitutes for the most part. In addition, her body was found in her apartment and not down by the river like the others. *"Yeah, maybe Russ,"* I replied after exhaling a huge amount of smoke. *"But I'm still really interested in Swanson's personal life.....is her apartment still vacant?"* Russ replied, *"Sure is.... with no immediate relatives, we decided to secure the place.....the owner had no problem with us doing that since the building is currently under renovations by the Veratex Corporation....you know, Charlie Shields, the developer that I told you about."* That was a coincidence I thought and immediately I asked, *"What about the other people in the building?....did you question them?....did they see or hear anything?"*

Russ pursed his lips again, trying to come up with an appropriate response to my curiosity. *"Unfortunately Shake, the building at the time was in the process of rehabilitation and had very few tenants....the only other one in the building was an elderly lady on the first floor who was partially deaf and she really doesn't go anywhere and keeps to herself....her son visits from time to time, gets her groceries once in a while, and does the banking for her....other than that, Kyle Swanson was the only other tenant, living on the second floor.*" Standing up in the booth, Barrett immediately stood with me. "*Let's take a trip over there, Russ....I would really like to see the apartment for myself and I am sure my four legged buddy here wouldn't mind doing a little sniffing around as well.*"

CHAPTER TEN

The Apartment

Arriving at Swanson's apartment building, I was surprised at its location as the three-story brick structure was located on Spring Street in the southwestern part of the city. This area was well known to be a particularly bad section of town, especially for a young woman, who was single and lived alone. Some of the local businesses had even closed due to the constant vandalism and their storefronts were boarded over with plywood. Of course, typical graffiti had been sprayed all over them in various colors of paint, which only added to the eeriness of this part of town. As we all got out of the car, Barrett immediately went to the front entrance, and started working his nose around the stoop. He seemed to be fixated on it and almost immediately, began scratching at the partially glassed door, showing little patience for us to reach it. Russ observing him, pointed towards the building. *"He never stops, does he?....look at him.....the mutt just keeps on going."* I chuckled back, motioning for us to step up the pace. *"No, he never quits, Russ....like I said, he loves to work."*

Opening the glass front door, which was partially covered over with plywood, Barrett immediately followed the scent to an apartment further down the hallway, which was adjacent to the staircase that led upstairs. Walking back and stopping halfway between the apartment door and us he sat, looking for me to react to his find. *"That's where the old lady lives that I told you about,*

Shake....apartment 1C....come on, Swanson's apartment is on the second floor."

Motioning for Barrett to follow us, the smell of fresh paint filled the air as we climbed the recently refurbished wooden stairs. The oak steps glistened in the sunbeams that penetrated a very large skylight at the top of the stairwell and while taking each step, I was amazed how ornate and grandiose the staircase was with its beautiful oak hand railings and raised panel wainscoting. Being extremely wide, it was easy for all of us to climb them together, side by side, and while we did, I could not help to think about the building's history. The embellished architectural style was definitely from the late 1800's during the *"Gilded Age"* and upon studying the detail work; it became obvious to me that great care must have been taken during its construction. *"This Charlie Shields fellow that owns the Veratex Corporation, Russ..... does he always rehab buildings like this?....I mean completely redo them?"* Russ, who was already out of breath before we reached the second level, stopped and grabbed the hand railing for support. *"Yeah, that's why the Mayor likes him so much....he takes old stuff that is junk and renovates it into a show place, making it useful again....the rehab program has really given the Mayor a good image and with it happening all throughout the city, he's almost guaranteed to be reelected this fall."*

Reaching the top step, Barrett immediately bolted for the third door on the left down the long, narrow hallway and stood waiting for us. The sheet rock that had been installed was newly taped and plastered, waiting for its final sanding and painting. Surprised, by all of the construction, I commented, *"With all of the construction going on in this place and the noise, it must have been really tough to live here."* Russ, opening the door to the apartment with a passkey that he took from his pants pocket, grinned back at me. *"Yeah, that's why the rent was so cheap I guess......from what we've learned, he let her live here for practically nothing, but it was good for the young woman and it was actually beneficial to Shield's company as well....you know, having some people living here during the rebuilding process rather than leaving it vacant."*

When the door opened, the scant contents of the living room came into view. A single chair and sofa, which had a coffee table between them, were the only pieces of furniture that decorated the room. Several magazines about fashion wear littered the table and there were dozens of books on a wooden shelf behind the stained, worn out couch. Barrett's nose was in high gear as he made his search pattern around the furniture and coming upon the sofa chair, he suddenly stopped. Sitting there, he looked up at me, almost wanting me to come down to his level to take a look and Russ lighting up a cigarette, acknowledged the find. *"Looks like that dog of yours doesn't miss a trick....that's where we found her.....lying next to that sofa chair....she had been strangled like the others and a large suitcase was found next to her.....as mentioned in the briefing, the killer must have been interrupted by something and left in a hurry."*

As my eyes scanned the adjacent rooms, off to the left was the bedroom door, and next to the living room was the kitchen, which was separated by a Formica counter top. The open-air concept made the one bedroom apartment appear to be much larger than it was. *"I take it that the department dusted everything in here for prints?"* Russ nodded his head, answering, *"Yeah, the killer must have worn gloves because the only prints we found were hers..... we discovered some of her personal effects on the counter such as a handbag and wallet, but all of it came up empty.....we even went to work and tore her closet apart along with the dresser in the bedroom, but in a nut shell we ended up finding no clues whatsoever."*

There were a few pictures on the walls, but they were just some cheap seascapes along with other typical scenery paintings. The wallpaper was soiled in many places and there was evidence of heavy wear on the decorative moldings around the doors and baseboards. Most of them were severely scratched and dented, indicating the many years of heavy use and neglect. To top it off, mice excrement was obvious along the baseboards at several locations and numerous spider webs decorated a few corners of the room. Amazed to say the least at the apartment's condition, I turned to Russ, asking, *"Why would she have moved into a place like this?....you'd think that the developer would have remodeled the place before she moved in."* My old partner took a drag off his cigarette, while his eyes scanned the old place. *"Like I said, Shake, that's why the rent was cheap....she was only paying twenty-five dollars a month to live here."* Chuckling he added, *"A real bargain don't you think?"*

Opening several of the kitchen cupboards, there were only a few dishes and glasses along with a couple of sets of severely scratched silverware in the drawers. Most of the cabinets were entirely bare and had very little dried foodstuffs in them. While examining the rest of the kitchen, nothing really jumped out at me, as it appeared that she had very few possessions, which was not unusual for a young person.

With my eyes drifting back towards Barrett, he was still sitting beside the area where the body was found. Patiently waiting, I walked over to him and patted his head while still looking around the apartment. *"Seen and had enough?"* Russ asked. Nodding my head, I replied, *"Yeah...but this fellow hasn't......watch this, Russ.... you are about to see my partner go to work.....Barrett!.....search!"*

Immediately, Barrett's full attention left Russ and me as he began circling the apartment. With his nose to the floor and while passing each piece of furniture, a full evaluation of them was performed by Barrett. At various locations throughout his search, he would stop for a moment, and his eyes would roam the floor and surrounding walls. You could tell by the expression on Barrett's face that he was all business and concentrating heavily on the situation at hand. After about five minutes of roaming back and forth in the living room, he trotted around the counter top, and entered the kitchen area.

Continuing his intense search, he finally stopped at the refrigerator and pawed at it. Seeing that we were not reacting to him quickly enough, he became even more excited, and began scratching at it. *"Looks like your dog wants something to eat....* *some investigator he is,"* Russ chuckled as he walked towards him. *"Well, there's nothing in there....we removed all of the food months ago."* Laughing, Russ opened the refrigerator door, and sure enough, it was completely empty. My old partner looked down at the furry detective and said, *"See, nothing in there...you are out of luck."* Hearing those words did not faze Barrett in the least as he jumped up with his front paws on the shelves inside the refrigerator and began barking with even more enthusiasm. *"What the hell does he want now?....can't he see that it's empty, Shake?"*

From Barrett's reaction, I knew something else was going, but to my surprise, upon opening the top freezer door, there was nothing in that as well. However, Barrett was still insistent as he kept pawing the shelves and barked at it. Russ began to laugh extremely hard and being barely able to get the words out, he stumbled over them. *"Ahh....ahhh.....that dog must be really hungry, Shake......or maybe he's just a typical traffic cop who needs another coffee break along with a doughnut!"*

My old partner seemed to be really enjoying himself as he watched Barrett paw the empty shelves, knowing that my little experiment had failed to show him anything. *"Before you split a gut, Russ....something is going on here....Barrett doesn't act like this unless there's a reason for it."*

Carefully examining the inside of the appliance and then the outside, it became apparent that the refrigerator had been installed in a space between the end of the counter and an existing wall to the left. It was a tight fit, however, as there were gaps on each side of it of only about an inch in width. With a pen light that I carried with me, I attempted to peer down both sides of the appliance to the floor. Seeing nothing, my attention turned to the back of it. *"I think we need to pull this away from the wall, Russ."* I grabbed the front of it, to move it forward, and Wilson seeing what I was up to, pulled on the refrigerator as well. With both of us working at it, the appliance was easily moved about two feet forward away from the wall. Quickly, I shined the pen light behind it and searched the area, but there was nothing on the wall or the floor. *"You see anything?"* Russ asked. Shaking my head, I replied, *"No...not a damn thing....I can't understand it..... why in the hell is Barrett so...."* Suddenly, I noticed something that was attached to the back of the refrigerator with masking tape and upon taking a closer look; it was a small, black notebook of about three by four inches. *"You have a knife on you, Russ?....I forgot mine back at the room."* He quickly reached into his pocket, opened it, and handed his Case jackknife to me. Carefully, I sliced away the several layers of tape from it, and with a handkerchief, I removed the notebook from the back of the refrigerator. Placing it on the Formica counter, Barrett appearing to be enthusiastic about his find came over to me and leaped, placing his paws on the edge of the counter and within seconds gave it a good examination by sniffing every corner of it.

With both of us staring at it for a few moments, I patted my furry sidekick on the forehead. *"That's one thing about him, Russ.... when he acts like this, something's usually up and in this case, it appears our victim was trying to hide something as it looks like an appointment book of some kind......I wonder what type of information is in it for her to take these kind of steps to protect it.......maybe we are going to learn something very interesting from this."*

Opening a few pages with my handkerchief, it was a typical calendar book for scheduling appointments as there were several passages written in it for each particular day along with some notes in the margins. As my eyes scanned it while slowly flipping the pages, I suddenly realized that my furry partner had left us. *"Where did Barrett go?"* I asked while perusing the book, page by page. *"He went into the bedroom, Shake....looks like he's not done yet....I tell you one thing, if I hadn't seen it with my own eyes, I wouldn't have believed it....that dog is truly amazing!"* Giving him a nod, I answered back, *"Yeah...he can be amazing all right, but he can be a pain in the ass too....sometimes he can get himself involved with......look at this, Russ......seems like Miss Swanson was conducting her own investigation of the Mayor's office...it says here under*

Friday, May 10th.....met with Mayor to verify Veratex affiliation with 61 campaign, illegal contributions??.....and then on Monday May 13th ...she notes, Mayor's office called....meeting at City Hall on May 15th, Wednesday confirmed with Veratex Corp. ....wasn't she killed on the fourteenth?"

My old partner's expression immediately turned sour, as he could not believe where I was going with my suspicions. *"What are you saying Shake?....you don't think the Mayor's office had something to do with this?"* Pursing my lips, I folded the notebook, wrapped it up in my handkerchief, and while placing it into my jacket pocket, I smirked back at him. *"Well, Russ...doesn't it seem a little odd that our gal who was investigating some potential problems with the big man of our city and a private organization regarding possible illegal campaign donations, suddenly winds up dead before a big meeting is to take place?....plus, why hide the notebook, if it didn't have some damaging implications?....hmmm?.....I know one thing, we'll have to go through this book with a fine tooth comb and see if its got any other damaging material on the big man or anyone else."* Just then, startling both of us, a sharp bark came from the bedroom. Grinning at him for a second, I headed for the bedroom, saying, *"Sounds like my partner might have something else for us, Russ."*

Going through the bedroom door, I discovered Barrett was at the far corner of the room staring at a ventilator duct in the floor. A small steel grate of about six inches by nine inches, it was located next to the bed by a nightstand. Barrett was pawing at the grate and as I stooped down to take a look, he promptly backed away, sat on his haunches and patiently watched my every move. *"What do you think he's found now?"* Russ asked while he moved the bed aside to make more room for us. *"I don't know....but what ever it is, it's inside this duct....can I have that knife of yours again?"* Taking Russ's knife, I pried the faceplate up from the floor and removed it, placing it off to the side. With my pen light, I examined the inside of the metal ductwork. *"Give me your handkerchief, Russ.....looks like our chief inspector has found another possible clue.*" Reaching in, I grabbed the object with the piece of cloth and showed it to my old partner who was intently looking over my shoulder. *"It's a cuff link....a nice one too,"* Russ said as he backed away, allowing me to stand. Looking at it more closely, I eyed him, saying, *"It appears to be black onyx and the body of the link appears to be solid gold....yeah...it says 14K on the back of it...see?"*

Sitting on the edge of the bed, with the link in my hand, I studied the rest of the room. Did this cuff link mean something? Did the killer mistakenly drop it? As these and other thoughts rammed through my mind, Russ seeing that I was in deep thought, blurted, *"This could have been lost by a friendly visitor of hers or by any other person for that matter that rented this apartment before her.....don't you think, Shake?"* Nodding my head slowly my mind continued to work as I looked around the room. *"Maybe, Russ....but Barrett found this by scent.....a scent that he has already associated with the various people he has met....maybe even the serial killer for that matter or should I say the possible killer of this woman."* Puzzled, Russ took a seat on the windowsill opposite me. *"So, Shake....you are back to your theory about there being two killers."* Staring back at him, I wrapped the cuff link in the handkerchief and placed it in my pocket. *"Yeah, maybe....or it could be just a coincidence that she was killed by our serial boy......but with what we have found so far, somehow I think this may be going down a different path....you know what I mean?"*

Noticing Barrett, sitting next to me, I stroked his head. *"Are you all done now?"* I asked. He gave a lick of my hand and walked towards the bedroom door, signaling he was ready to leave. Chuckling a little, I glanced over at Russ, saying, *"I guess that answers that....doesn't it."* My old partner laughed and stood up in front of the window, exclaiming, *"When the man is done....he is done!.....looks like he wants to go home for some dinner."* Barrett immediately let loose with a sharp bark acknowledging what he had just heard and made a motion towards the door. *"You see, Russ....I told you he can understand English and you know what?......I'm hungry too, it's been a long day."*

With a nod of his head, my old partner and I headed for the apartment door and as we left, he locked it behind us. Walking down the hallway, we were surprised to see a man, dressed in painter's coveralls, approaching us. He was carrying a small, metal, paint bucket along with a brush, whistling an unknown tune. Being a little nervous by not seeing Barrett, my eyes quickly began scanning down the hall, trying to figure out where he had gone. When the man was about twenty feet from us, Barrett suddenly appeared behind us from around the corner further down the hallway. Seeing the huge animal loping down the hallway towards him, the man tried to reverse his direction in an instant. Unfortunately, losing his balance, he fell over backwards, flinging the paint pail into the air and falling to the floor, the pail of paint dumped all over his chest, leaving him covered from head to toe with white paint. Still petrified, he quickly slid his butt over to the opposite wall, ramming his back up against it, and glared at the huge beast that was about to *"devour"* him. Barrett, not knowing why the man was acting in this way, promptly went over and gave him a big lick on the side of the face. Opening his mouth and not being able to at speak first, the man finally forced the words out of himself. *"Get...get him off me!"* he screamed. With both of us in hysterics, Russ stopped, bent down, and stared the man in the face. *"What's the matter fella?.....are you afraid of the big bad wolf?"* Realizing that the poor man was about to have a heart attack, I whistled for Barrett to come and he quickly joined up with us as we walked down the hallway to the stairs. Allowing Barrett to head down the stairs before us to the front door I chuckled, saying, *"Come on you big, bad thing.....you've cause enough trouble today."*

Exiting the building, I lit up a smoke and offered one to Russ. Puffing away on our butts, we watched Barrett leap through the opened rear window on the passenger's side to access the back seat. Making it look effortless, I turned to my old partner, saying, *"Wouldn't it be nice, Russ, if the both of us could do that."* Russ smiled as he gazed at Barrett in the back seat, panting with his tongue out, while he stared back at the both of us. *"Look, Shake....he's laughing at me....saying to himself, that guy with his forty inch waist wouldn't have a chance in hell of doing that."* I slapped Russ on the back as we headed to our respective sides of the car, saying, *"Yeah....Barrett really knows how to hurt a man, doesn't he?"*

Driving back to my motel room, Russ and I were more than eager to discuss the case as to what we had found back at the apartment. *"We should have these dusted for prints, don't you think, Russ?"* as I held up the two handkerchiefs. With a disgruntled look, he sighed, lowering his head slightly. *"Never mind that, Shake....this stuff should be submitted into evidence, but considering what we did with the note that we found down by the river, how are we ever going to turn this material in?"* I shook my head vehemently, replying, *"No....we are not going to turn this evidence in...I am starting to think that we might have discovered something that could put us both in a very dangerous situation....it's obvious that Swanson was onto something big here and may have been silenced for what she had learned...... and it appears to me that the murderer only made it look like she was a victim of the serial killer.....if you look at the facts then you...."*

Suddenly Russ pulled over to the side of the road and slammed on the brakes, skidding down the gravel shoulder, creating a huge cloud of dust that enveloped the car. Poor Barrett almost flew over the front seat because of the sudden stop and I had to put my arm out to hold him back. *"What the hell are you talking about?"* Russ said loudly. *"Just because we found a notebook with a notation in it about a discussion with the Mayor, doesn't mean that she was killed to keep her yap shut.....and it doesn't confirm a full scale conspiracy is going on in City Hall either.....right now, there is no way we can even go there.... not with this stuff, anyway....so get a grip, Shake.... otherwise we are both going to be on the outside looking in without a job.....I don't know about you, but I want my pension and what you do with yours is your own business......if you are going down that path at the fork in the road, I don't want any part of it.....after all, you know the old saying about not being able to fight City Hall."*

Russ was dead serious; there was no doubt about it as his eyes were glaring at me with fire in them. He seemed actually scared, something that I had never witnessed before in him. Throughout the past, we had been through some tough scrapes together and had tangled with some really bad and desperate men, but this case was obviously different in his mind. As he nervously lit up a cigarette, his hands could barely hold the match steady enough to light it, and his first drag off it almost took half the life out of the butt. For the first time in our relationship, I had the real feeling that he was about to bail on me, leaving me to fend for myself. Shocked to say the least, I attempted to counter his summation, but he held up his hand when I started to speak. *"No, Shake...don't give me any of that 'we need to do the right thing crap'.....because that won't cut it on this one....you don't know what the Mayor is capable of along with his cronies....especially that assistant of his, Marty Sloan....he's a real sleaze ball and he'll sink you quicker than the iceberg did to the Titanic.....and the worse part of it is, they have friends higher up in the State Government....real powerful people that are just waiting to take out a couple of two bit cops like us....my advice to you is to quit thinking about the Mayor's office and just do your job of catching us a serial killer.....let the true evidence speak for itself."*

I leaned back in my seat, staring out the windshield, thinking that this was what the city had finally come to as it was far worse now than when I had left. The immense political machine had everyone running scared and my old partner had become a prime example of that. *"So, Russ.... are you trying to tell me that you are going to drop out of the case and let me go on by myself?....is that how real partners are supposed to act?"* A bead of sweat rolled down the side of his face as he puffed away on his butt. Biting his lower lip and peering out the side window, unable to face me, he thought for a moment as the tension in his face bloomed while the blue veins stuck out like purple yarn along his temples. His character was sinking fast, almost overwhelming to observe, and as he pondered for a moment, I really did not know what he was going to say. With a deep excruciating sigh, he replied softly, *"You don't realize how long of an arm the Mayor has, Shake.....this place is a lot worse since you left and the things that go on here are sometimes hard to believe.....some of the money that is being passed around to all of the fellows is substantial and everybody just accepts it as doing business as usual.....we do not have a police department here anymore; it's a mob for heaven's sake.....the mayor runs the chief and everybody else in this city with an iron fist...sometimes I think this is Nazi Germany for Christ's sake and if we are not careful, we could end up in a suitcase by the river...I just want to do my few remaining years and get out, that's all, and you should split before it's too late.....leave this place, Shake.....before you can't."*

Looking at the man fall to pieces on me, I had one question spinning around in my head and had to ask it. *"What about you?.... have you taken money?"* Russ rubbed the side of his face with his hand, almost trying to wipe the stress out of it as he attempted to respond to me. With a tear starting to form out of the corner of his right eye, he looked over at me. *"When a pile of cash is offered to you and all you see in a paycheck every week is $86.46 .....what do you think I did?..... when you see hundred dollar bills stacked in front of you a foot high and all you have to do is look the other way......something that does not mean a piss hole in the snow to you personally or even the department for that matter....tell me...what would you do, Shake?....ehh?......at least now I have a little some-thing to show for working in this God forsaken town......like I said, Shake....get out while you can. "*

Wishing I had never asked that question, I looked down at my own hands, thinking what I would have done. Would I have grabbed the money and simply went on with my false and hypo-critical ways? Dishonor the badge that was pinned to my chest and say the hell with the oath I said aloud when taking the job? I was a drunk, yes, and had done many stupid things in my time, but take money? That was definitely not within my being and was something that was like the *"kiss of death"* to me. Had I ever been offered cash or other gifts? Of course, I had and lots of it, to tell the truth, as the opportunities were always there. What cop had not been offered some money sometime in his career? However, not accepting it was what kept us different from the *"bad guys"* that we were always after. Scruples and morals were supposedly molded into the badge and once a cop crossed that line, he was worse than the scum that we put in jail. Shockingly, my own partner, of so many years, had just admitted to me that he committed the ultimate sin of taking bribes and now his whole existence was a sickening sight to me. It was like a bad dream to learn that the man who had backed me up with the shooting of the young kid and who had saved my life once was now telling me he was a crook......nothing, but a low down, good for nothing crook.

As Russ put the car in gear and proceeded down the highway again, I could not even look at him. He was different in my eyes now and would never be the same to me. Silence fell between us and even Barrett, in the back seat, had gone to sleep with his head resting on his paws as a million thoughts blitzed through my mind. As we approached the motel entrance I needed to know what the game plan was going to be from here and asked, *"So, Russ...where does that leave us?.....we have been through some tough shit together, but this is another ball game....where do we go from here?"* Russ stopped the car in front of the front door to the lobby and kept looking straight ahead. Without turning his head, he simply said, *"You're on your own, Shake....like I said....my pension is worth too much to me....I'll tell the chief that we simply can not work together on this....I do not know what he will do.... maybe he will assign someone else to you and of course, that will be his decision....sorry I have to go this route, but it is the only thing that can be in the cards for me right now.........be smart for once, Shake, and leave this place....go back to where you came from before it's too late as this place will bring you nothing else, but more pain and death."*

I shook his hand and as I exited the vehicle, Barrett leaped through the side rear window to the ground next to me. He pawed the car as if he was saying goodbye to my friend as well and without looking back at me, Russ placed the car in gear. Giving me a look of empathy he said, *"Good luck, Shake....you're gonna need it,"* and hitting the gas pedal hard, he peeled out of the driveway, speeding off down the road. *"Well, partner....we are on our own now,"* I said patting Barrett on the head. Watching the car disappear down the street around a corner, I added, *"And just maybe, boy....it's for the best."*

CHAPTER ELEVEN
Pack of Lies

S tanding at the entrance, I saw Zack at the front desk through the large picture window and gave a small wave to him. Even though he definitely noticed me, he purposely kept busy and ignored my attempt to make eye contact with him, which surprised me a little. He had been a lonely man most of his life, there was little doubt about that, as he never had any wife or family that I knew of. His father died when he was very young, killed in a horrible accident while working at a construction project and this left his mother to bring him up. Naturally, through the years, he became very close to her, and she was really all he ever had that meant anything in his life. He had several relationships with many expensive, beautiful women in his time, but his mom was really the only person that he could depend upon, and talking about her, the other day probably did not set too well with him.

Pondering for a moment, I thought that must have been his reason for not acknowledging me, but I knew there were several more questions that I needed to address with Zack and like it or not, he was going to have to answer them. Opening the lobby door, the attached overhead bell rang out, which quickly got his attention. At first, he smiled, expecting another guest, but when he saw it was me his attitude instantly changed. As I approached him with Barrett, his expression became cold and lifeless, hardly the same as it was yesterday when I first saw him. With a peppiness in my voice, I asked, *"How are you doing, Zack?"* Keeping his head down at his desk, behind the glass-covered counter, and without glancing up he replied, *"Another day...what of it?"* Leaning my elbows on the glass, I peaked over the counter at his desk and glanced at the paper work that surrounded him. Most of them were bills from the Electric and Gas Company along with several other invoices from various vendors. Apparently, some of them were marked *"overdue"* in big red letters and there were several registered demand notices mixed in among them.

Realizing that these had gotten my attention, Zack quickly started gathering them up and placed them underneath one of the ledgers on the desk. *"You don't know how much paper work is involved until you have your own business, Shake...it just keeps coming at you."* Chuckling, I replied, *"Yeah, just like police work... some of the reports that we have to do are something else.....like in this case for example, there are always loose ends that we need to tie up....so....do you mind if I ask you a few more questions?"*

Zack quickly turned, facing the opposite wall behind him, and started taking down some notes and other papers from the bulletin board. While doing so, it was obvious he was nervous, which caused him to drop a few thumbtacks during the process. As he bent down and retrieved a couple of them, some of the tacks actually dropped for a second time, causing him to swear under his breath. While bending over to pick them up again he angrily replied, *"Yeah, go ahead and ask your damn questions....we all have a job to do in this shit hole that they call life."*

While scratching the side of my head, watching him fumble with the thumb tacks, and trying to be respectful of his situation, I softly asked, but still in a demanding tone, *"I won't take very long as I know you have a lot of work to do, but there are some things I need to ask you about Tina Hendricks.....you said she worked for you for several years, right?"* Zack gathered up the remaining papers and placed them in a pile on his desk while nodding his head. *"Like I said, Shake, she worked here for about seven years and was my assistant manager."* I took out a butt and Barrett quickly went to the other side of the room, as he hated cigarette smoke, knowing that it was not good for him. Grabbing a match, I asked, *"She was a little young for the job, don't you think?"* Zack quickly looked up and replied, *"She was twenty-nine years old for Christ's sake.... of course she was old enough to be on duty at night alone....besides, she had a mind of her own and was more than capable of handling herself."*

I knew that had touched off a nerve with him due to his abrupt response, which caused me to ponder for a few seconds on how to proceed with the interview. After quickly gathering my thoughts, I asked, *"Okay, Zack...if I remember correctly she was single....were there any men in her life that you knew of?"* A bewildered look came over him as I stared right back at him, waiting for an answer. Rubbing his face with his hands, he sighed a little, and sat down on a high stool behind the counter. *"What does that have to do with finding a killer?....even if she had some boyfriends, what difference would that make?"* Not saying a word, I continued to stare at him and patiently waited for another response to come out of him. From years of experience, I had learned to allow a witness to sweat a little and wonder how much I actually knew. Sometimes this caused the person being questioned for his mind to run a little and this was especially true if I remained quiet for an extended period. As the moment of silence grew in length, Zack became even more fidgety and nervous, rubbing his hands together and wiping the sweat from them on his pants.

Knowing the silence was driving him crazy and that he was having a hard time dealing with my constant stare, I decided to press him a little more. *"I need a complete look at her life, Zack....I need to understand what kind of dealings she had inside and outside of work....in fact, I need to know your exact relationship with her...was it strictly professional or was there something else to it?"* Zack reached into his shirt pocket and pulled a cigarette from the pack, but dropping it on the floor, he had to stoop down to retrieve it. Pulling a lighter from his pants, he attempted to light it, but no matter how many times he frantically flicked it, no flame was visible. Evidently, it must have been out of fluid and as he kept nervously striking the flint, I lit a match. *"Here.....this might work better for you,"* as I touched off his cigarette. Taking a puff, he glared back at me out of the corner of one eye. *"Our relationship was purely business, Shake....after all, I'm over fifty and I could have been her father....in fact, I think she looked at me as her dad because she had no one else you know....her father and mother died a few years ago...her dad passed away from cancer and her mother from a broken heart....I helped her through some tough times and she often leaned on me for support...with no boy friend or husband I was more than just a boss to her, if you know what I mean."*

Zack became teary eyed as he said those words, looking like a lost soul and figuring there was little sense of pursuing the matter further, I responded, *"Very well...we'll continue this some other time....looks like you need some time to yourself."* With a simple flip of my hand, I waived good-bye to him and hand signaled Barrett to follow me back to my room. As I walked outside, my eyes glanced across the street towards the liquor store and their lights were already on, telling people that they were open to fulfill anyone's needs. Stopping for a few moments, I stared hard at the package store and one of their signs on the glass front glared back at me. *"Smirnoff Vodka - Sale - Pints $1.39,"* and as my eyes read those words, a small amount of drool oozed from the corner of my mouth. Turning and taking a step towards the liquor store, I quickly got a hold of myself. *"No!"* I murmured. *"You can't start on that stuff now....Russ is right...you're in the shit already, maybe right up to your eyeballs....all that booze will bring you right now is a quick trip off the force or even worse like your old partner tried to tell you."* Regaining my focus, I headed towards my hotel room at a brisk pace before my will power could deteriorate and noticing a small stick, I picked it up to throw it for Barrett. Getting ready to toss it, Barrett was staring back at me as if to ask, *"What is your problem?....never mind the place across the street....let's play."*

Throwing the piece of wood, I chuckled at him saying, *"Don't worry ole boy...not tonight as we are going to bed....because tomorrow, I'm sure it's going to be a hell of a day."*

▲ ▲ ▲

The next morning we awoke early and that gave me some time to examine more closely the appointment book that we had discovered in Swanson's apartment. Having a print dusting kit with me, I was unable to collect any prints off it that were clear and readable. All of them were severely smudged and it was a similar situation with the cuff link. I really did not expect to get any prints from the notebook other than Swanson's, but getting nothing off the cuff link was disappointing.

It was clear upon reading the daily entries in the notebook by Kyle Swanson that she had begun a full-blown investigation into the Mayor's office about three months prior to her death. There were several notations at the rear of the notebook listing various individual names that were associated with his office and at the top of the list was Marty Sloan, the mayor's administrative assistant. Others included his secretary, Pamela Smith, the mayor's campaign manager, Tom Flux and the police Chief, Roland Morin. At the bottom of the list there was a series of numbers....24.....28...29... and 23, with no notation explaining their meaning. She was quite a doodler and on several of the pages where no appointments were noted, she had scribbled several strange shapes of various circles on top of each other. What meaning these might have had was anybody's guess, but next to them in several locations appeared to be phone numbers, such as 106R and 447J.

Knowing that these might be a viable clue, I picked up the phone and asked the operator to connect me to 106R, and to my surprise, the Mayor answered. If that was not enough, when I asked for 447J, another man answered. Come to find out, it was a direct line to the Chief of Police and when I did not respond to his voice right away when he answered by saying, *"Chief Morin here...*

what's up?" his patience grew short and he abruptly hung up the phone. *"What the hell is going on here?"* I thought as I slowly placed the phone back on its receiver. *"There's only one reason why the newly hired assistant planner would have a direct line to the chief of police....either she was having an affair with him or she was onto the son of bitch and was researching his involvement with the Veratex Corporation."* Chuckling to myself and thinking what the chief looked like I mumbled, *"Somehow I think it's the latter."*

The more I thought about it, even Department heads never had direct numbers like that to the Mayor or the Chief of Police, as they were usually required to go through the secretary's office like anyone else. There was little doubt in my mind now that Swanson probably had the goods on them and was just dotting the eyes and crossing the tees just before her death.

Suddenly the phone rang and startled me, breaking my concentration. Answering it, the voice on the other end said, *"Good morning, Shake....thought I would check in on you."* It was Andrea and her pleasant voice made me feel good inside. *"Hi hon....everything is fine....Barrett and I have settled in and are hot on the case, aren't we boy?"* Barrett promptly gave a short bark in response and Andrea answered back, *"Sure sounds like he is doing okay, but what about you?....you sound a little tired....are you doing alright?.... any problems that I can help you with?"* Thinking to myself that she needed to know nothing about what was really happening as it would only make her worry, I replied, *"Nah....no problems at all....we are making some very good progress on this thing and everybody here has been extremely helpful......it's actually going a lot better than I thought it would..... I should be home real soon."*

She seemed happy to hear that and as we made some more small talk for a while, I could tell by the sound of her voice that my answers were satisfying her curiosity. After all, this had been the first time I had been out of her sight since drying out from the booze, and I knew she was concerned about me. Not that she did not trust me, but as the old adage goes, *"when the cat's away, the mice will play,"* those words were probably playing in her mind.

She apologized for walking out on me and told me she had gone back to our house after we had left for Harrisburg. Being sorry for the way she acted and understanding why I had to go back, she assured me that she would be waiting for us to return. After talking for about another fifteen more minutes or so, we finally said good-bye to each other, and hanging up the phone, I looked over at Barrett lying next to the door. *"No sense telling her too much, was there?....after all, if we told her the truth, she probably would have been down here in a minute and then all hell would have broken loose...don't you agree?"* Barrett immediately leaped onto the bed next to me and placed his head on my lap, looking for attention. Stroking his fur affectionately, I added, *"I think we need to pay a little visit to the Planning Director....what do you say about that?"* Barrett quickly sat up, heading for the door, and when he reached it he looked back at me, waiting for me to follow. *"Well, that didn't take any convincing, did it?"* as I threw my sport jacket on. *"Come on...let's go then"* and out the door, we went.

Driving to City Hall, the August day was going to be a typical one in New England. The sky was a brilliant blue and the temperature was already seventy-five degrees even though it was only nine o'clock in the morning. The humidity was already building and the afternoon was sure to bring a few thunderstorms, something that Barrett was never happy about. Being fine with gunshots and other loud noises, nothing terrified him as much as thunder. In fact, he would often hide for hours before a storm, telling me that the storm was on its way and I would often find him in the bathtub, shivering and shaking with fear, completely petrified of the oncoming storm, and this was well before any human could hear it. Today was no exception, as he was already nervous and looking toward the northwestern sky, anticipating what may be coming in the afternoon.

As I pulled into the City Hall parking lot, there were several open spots and finding a parking space was not a problem. Exiting the car, I noticed there were many reserved parking spaces designated against the building, indicated by several signs. One in

particular drew my attention, which read, *"Don Birmingham –*
Planning Director." My eyes widened as I gazed upon the sign, but
that was not what was filling my mind with amazement. A light
blue, brand new 1961 Oldsmobile Starfire convertible filled the
space. With its 394 cubic inch engine and beautiful bucket seats,
it made me cringe with jealousy, as I knew the car cost at least
five thousand dollars, making me wonder how a city employee
could have afforded such a car. Could this guy be on the take, too?
Taking money at every chance, he could get? Like my old partner? Standing for a moment, admiring the car, I could not help
my mind from drifting, thinking that the person might be directly
involved with the Mayor's office. Shaking my head in disgust, I
suddenly noticed the side entrance to the building and decided to
head towards it.

The planning board office was on the second floor and rather
than taking the elevator, Barrett and I walked up the huge, wind-
ing marble staircase. The building had been built in the late 1800's
and was typical of that era with very high ceilings and marble
floors. Ornate wainscoting adorned the walls and all of this naturally gave the place a huge presence and grandiose feel. Previous
mayor's pictures adorned the walls along with huge chandeliers
on the ceilings, all of which completed the entire flavor of the
structure. Of course, we got the usual stares of the people as we
went through the building as some of the city employees walking
down the hallways purposely disappeared into adjoining rooms
to avoid us, which made me chuckle a bit. Barrett just plodded
along side of me with his toenails clicking on the marble floors,
and while noticing the people disappear as well, he never paid
that much attention to them.

Reaching the door to the planning board office, the secretary
immediately looked up from her large, oak desk. *"May I help*
you?....oh my...where did that come from?....sir, you can't bring a dog
in here." Smiling at her, I leaned on the counter while Barrett sat
beside me. *"Oh, he's got special privileges....you might say he is an*
officer of the law." The woman kept staring at Barrett, while she

glanced back at me for a second. *"Well, who are you?"* I pulled my wallet out with my identification. *"I'm Detective Madison...I don't have an appointment, but I'm here to see the Director...is he in?"* Just then, a very tall and husky man walked around the corner from another office. *"Yeah, I'm the director...Don Birmingham..... and your name again, sir?"* I noticed right away he was well dressed in a two-piece dark suit and had a bright white shirt with a business like tie. *"Detective Madison...I have been assigned to the Harrisburg police department to assist Chief Morin.....I would like to ask you a few questions regarding Kyle Swanson....and oh...by the way, this is Barrett...my partner."*

At that moment, Birmingham noticed Barrett sitting next to me and the look on his face was priceless. His eyes grew large and he even backed up a step or two. Seeing the fear erupt in him, I promptly added, *"Don't worry, sir....he's harmless unless provoked....then all bets are off."* My words only sent more fright into the man as he backed up another step, trying to put more distance between us. *"That's no dog...he looks like a wolf!"* he exclaimed as he tried to press his body up against the wall. I smiled at the secretary and then at the Director trying to put them at ease. *"Like I said, he's really friendly...that is unless you piss him off...see?"* Barrett sat upright; back on his haunches with his paws raised, and folded them out in front of him, looking more like a teddy bear. He was really hamming it up too, by looking as cute as possible with his ears perfectly erect. Taken back a little by his antics, I whispered down at him, *"That's enough for Christ's sake....you're going to ruin your reputation, acting that way."*

Seeing that the dog was not an apparent menace, Birmingham relaxed a little. *"Sure...come on in...the next room over is my office."* As we walked around the wooden counter, the secretary's eyes never left Barrett as he passed her by, and disappearing around the corner with the director, all I could hear was a huge sigh of relief behind us, which only made me chuckle a little more. *"Have a seat, detective,"* as Birmingham took his place behind his desk. *"Your friend, there...well, I guess he knows what to do as well."* Barrett had already taken a seat beside me and was staring directly back at him, watching every move that the director was making. *"You said you wanted to ask me a few questions about Kyle...how can I help you?"*

I grabbed a note pad out of my pocket along with a pencil and leaned back in my chair. *"Like I said, I am investigating the death of Kyle Swanson.....can you tell me about her work history and what her responsibilities were?.....also, what was your relationship like with the woman?"* The Director pulled opened the center drawer in his large metal desk and took a piece of chewing gum from it. While opening the tin foil he replied, *"What's this business about investigating her death?...I thought she died of natural causes."*

Watching his body movements for any clue, I calmly replied, *"Strictly routine...I know you have already talked to the department, but I have been hired to clean up a few loose ends....so tell me, when was Miss Swanson hired?"* Birmingham seeming to accept my explanation, responded, *"Kyle came to work for us about two years ago and soon became a great asset to this department as she was very diligent in her work....some of her projects involved the rezoning of several land parcels in town and she was very instrumental in getting them passed through the city council......the president of the council, Abe Stockman, and ward five councilor Willis Regan worked extensively with her on the necessary ordinance changes..... they found her to be extremely efficient and informed me of this several times during the long and arduous process......if it wasn't for her due diligence on this project, I don't think it would have passed."* Quickly, I interrupted him, *"Why?...was there a lot of opposition to the zoning changes?"*

The director chewed heavily on his gum a few times and gave the impression that he was collecting his thoughts as he looked up, towards the left for an appropriate answer. That was something that did not sit very well with me, as I did not know if he was setting me up for a lie. *"You might say that, Mr. Madison....the Veratex Corporation was seeking the ordinance change in several locations of the city to provide more housing, especially for the elderly and* low income residents." Puzzled, I promptly asked, *"That sounds like a good thing...why would there be anyone against it?"*

Birmingham guzzled a drink of water from a glass on his desk and while some of it dribbled down his chin, forcing him to wipe it with the back of his hand, he looked out the window for a second. Then he turned to me, blotting his face with a handkerchief, and placed his hands on the desk. Folding them together in front of him and wearing a smug look on his face, he replied, *"Well, most of the property was zoned commercial or business...under current laws, we have a special zone designation for apartment dwellings called APP-1....it is the only zone that allows for five story buildings and multi family dwellings...some of our residents along with several city councilors did not want to sacrifice our tax base by eliminating commercially zoned property and the public hearings got pretty heated at times....in fact, the police had to be called in on one of them to remove some of the instigators."*

Glancing down at Barrett for a second, I noticed that my partner was fast asleep; telling me he was entirely bored with the situation, but I knew this path had to be taken as the clues were starting to come together. *"But in the end, Mr. Birmingham...it did pass, didn't it?"* Taking a deep breath, chomping on his gum as if he was a cow chewing its cud, he said, *"Yeah, it did, but that was not the end of it and in fact the problems with the passage of the ordinance still marches on today....the city's tax base has taken a severe hit and revenues are way down.....this is causing alarm with everyone including the mayor.......he had to use most of the city's "free cash" that had been built up by previous administrations to supplement the current budget to keep the tax rate down......once that is depleted there will be no other choice, but to raise taxes in the city or make major cuts to the budget....that is something all of us department heads are dreading."*

As he was talking, my eyes were drawn to his suit coat, which I knew was very high quality, probably costing hundreds of dollars. His white shirtsleeves protruded the exact amount out of his sport coat indicating to me that it must be a tailored suit, but then my eyes widened. Trying not to stare, I realized he was wearing onyx cuff links, which were very similar to the one found in Swanson's apartment. *"My God,"* I thought. *"Did the cuff link we found in the heating duct belong to him?.....Am I actually looking at her killer?.....or is it just a coincidence?"*

Knowing I was right on the edge of possibly blowing the case wide open, I pressed forward with another tough question. *"So, Mr. Birmingham....what was your exact relationship with Miss Swanson?....was it truly business or did you two get a little personal with each other...or was it possibly a little of both?....hmm?"*

Immediately, he flew up from his chair and stood tall, looking over his desk at me with glaring eyes. This startled Barrett too as he came out of a sound sleep, rising to all fours, ready to do battle. *"How dare you ask a question like that, sir......I am a true professional and conduct the city's business with an utmost conviction and dedication to public service....accusing me of fraternizing with my subordinates is appalling, disgusting, and something that makes me sick to my stomach....in fact sir, you offend me."*

To be honest, his declaration of innocence did not surprise me at all. Being a cop, sometimes the magnitude of a denial expressed by a suspect usually measured a person's guilt rather than his innocence. I debated in my mind whether to present him with the evidence that Barrett had found in her apartment, but as I rolled it back and forth in my hand inside my pocket, I decided to hold off. Instead, I wanted to make him speculate for a while why I was implying a possible relationship or worse yet, his involvement in her death. My silence in response to his uproar, caused the sweat to form rapidly on his forehead, and the beads resulting from it rolled downward along the sides of his face onto his rosy red cheeks. He was primed, ready to explode, and to add a little more fuel to the fire, I asked, *"Where were you on the night of May 14, sir?"*

Asking that, promptly resulted in the redness of his face to rise like an august sun, and I could perceive his blood pressure increase before my eyes, indicating I had hit a direct nerve with him once again. Spinning his body, he swiftly moved over to the front of the window, which overlooked the parking lot below. Apparently staring at something while rubbing his chin, his expression turned to a complete blank. Caught in my trap now and desperately thinking of a way out, I knew he was hoping to find the words to unlock the cage that he now found himself in.

After a few moments, he swallowed hard and answered, *"I was home in bed with my wife....check it out....she'll tell you we went to the movies and turned in early after we got home...for Christ's sake, your department has already questioned me extensively about this."* Not letting go of the noose around his neck, I continued with, *"So...what did you see?"* He spun around like a top and glared at me, almost challenging what I had asked. Then attempting to moisten his lips by working his tongue over them, he answered, *"The Guns of Navarone....starring Gregory Peck....it was an excellent movie and if you haven't seen it, you should....it's a great war picture."* Amazingly, he kept staring at me, hoping that I would not believe him, so that he could continue his condescending attitude towards me.

Either the man had nerves of steel or he was ripe for the taking, I thought, while feeling the onyx cuff link with my fingers in my pocket. By the looks of him, he seemed to be telling the truth, but taking the cuff link out of my pocket and continuing to roll it in my hand; I decided to drop the bomb on him. *"Have you ever seen this before?"* Opening my hand and exposing it to him, the color flowed out of his face like water draining out of a bucket. Immediately, I could see the beads of sweat on his forehead turn to rivulets and watching them run down his face, he nervously wiped them away with the back of his jacket sleeve. Straightening his neck, he licked his lips, indicating that his throat was drying up as if a desert had formed at the back of his throat. Lunging his hand out to reach for the glass of water on his desk, he initially drank from it, but each swallow turned into an enormous gulp. Eventually, trying to force down as much water as he could and after draining the glass, he answered weakly, *"Ahh....no....I mean, I have never seen that before."*

With a sheepish smile, I grinned back at him and pointed to his white shirtsleeve that was exposed from beneath his expensive suit coat. *"That's funny....seems you like onyx....in fact, you are wearing similar ones right now!"* I swear the man appeared as if he was going to pass out when those words exited my mouth because he quickly grabbed the pitcher and began feverishly pouring himself another glass of water. Not paying attention and gazing off into empty space, he overfilled it and water spilled all over his desk, flowing onto the floor. The few papers on it became completely soaked, and clumsily lifting them up, he tried to find a dry place to put them. Knowing that he was on the run, I pressed further. *"Mr. Birmingham....don't you think they are similar?.....I mean, when you really take a long hard look at them, wouldn't you agree they are almost identical?"* Rubbing the sweat from his upper lip and gritting his teeth, I could see his jaw muscles flex and stick out from the pressure. By his actions, there was little doubt in my mind now, that he might be the killer, but the amount of evidence I had on him was still not enough...at least not for a conviction, anyway. Going out on a limb, I glared back at him with seriousness in my face. *"You know...it will go a lot easier for you, if come clean and are cooperative in this matter.....why don't you start at the beginning."*

With his right hand, he massaged his face several times; hoping to pull the stress from it, but it was obvious from his behavior that his attempts were futile. Wringing his hands together, he plopped back down at his desk, and hung his head, staring at the floor. He knew I had him in a box and it was only a matter of time before we would be coming for him. Sighing deeply, he replied, *"It's not what you think, Madison....I didn't have anything to do with her death....you see, I was in love with her....we were involved in an affair."* From his reaction, I perceived more bullshit was spilling from his mouth and he was now only trying to save himself. As I peered at the sniveling coward, I stood up, and placed my hands on his huge desk, peering down at him with contempt. *"Don't give me that crap, Birmingham.....you know the hounds are on you and your time is up....you killed her, didn't you?"* The director vehemently shook his head back and forth with his eyes focused on the floor. *"No...no....I didn't.....we were lovers, I tell you....we had been seeing each other for months....I loved her!.....she meant everything to me!"*

He broke out into tears and sobbed like a distressed child who had just seen his favorite toy taken away from him and as he tried to wipe his face from the wetness; his watery eyes stared up at me. *"You gotta believe me.....I wouldn't have done anything to hurt her!.....she was my life....my love.....she meant everything to me."* Seeing a grown man whimper like that was a sickening sight to me and even Barrett could not look at him, as he laid there with his head down with his eyes closed. *"Well, sir....if she meant that much to you, why didn't you inform the department of your relationship to her and help them with the investigation?"* With a closed fist he pounded his desk, answering, *"Because of my wife!....if she ever found out, the woman would have thrown me out into the street..... that would have meant that the money would have gone bye bye too!...you have to understand that she's rich!"*

My mind was running now and although I thought, the murderer was sitting right in front of me, doubts started to infiltrate my suspicions. Was he telling the truth? On the other hand, was he trying to latch on to anything that was floating on a sinking ship? Still sobbing with his head down, Barrett finally awoke and stood on all fours staring at the crying man, trying to figure out what was going on with him. My fury partner looked back and forth at Birmingham and me, with puzzlement in his eyes, almost appearing to read the director's thoughts. *"Okay, Birmingham....if she was your lover and you didn't kill her....then who did?"*

Shaking his head, he responded, *"I didn't know someone killed her....I thought she died of a heart attack....if someone murdered her I have no idea who did....she was a nice girl and wouldn't have hurt a fly...why anybody would have wanted to kill her, God only knows."*

Thinking that he may be telling the truth, I decided to go down another road with him. *"Okay....you said she was working on a special project regarding zoning changes....who initiated the ordinance change?....I mean whose brainchild was it?"* Regaining his composure for a moment, his eyes began to clear and his face became less red. Wiping his brow a few times, he looked back at me with a sympathetic expression. *"Well, the Mayor of course.....it was his idea as it was part of his rehabilitation program.....with the Veratex corporation willing to pour money into it, why wouldn't he go along with it....after all, the program was going to guarantee his reelection for many years to come."*

The pool of corruption and cover-ups that I was falling into was deeper than I could have ever possibly imagined. Did someone order the killing of the planning assistant who may have discovered a diabolical scheme, leading to the mayor's office? Alternatively, was it just a coincidence that she happened to be murdered by the serial killer along with the other women? Nevertheless, if a cover up was going on and the other girls were a separate issue, just how large was this conspiracy? Was everyone in on it? Being a detective with an imaginative mind brought these thoughts and others into my head like a freight train running out of control. With ideas constantly whirling around in my head, soon I felt as if my mind was going to split wide open from the headache that was quickly forming. Then the tempting idea of relief enveloped my thoughts and soon the bottle of Vodka blocked my vision. My heart raced with celebration on the thoughts of taking that first drink and the feelings I would have with it pummeling down my throat. *"All of this pain and misery would simply fade away, if I had that medicine,"* I thought. *"When I took this case, I didn't buy into something like this....this sewer of corruption is way beyond my control or capabilities for that matter....the state boys should have been brought in on this."*

Then, as the drunken spear tried to penetrate my armor even further, I remembered what my old partner had told me. Just how far did the Mayor's ugly hand extend? Was it actually to the

State and Federal levels? Blowing the whistle to them could bring a world of hurt down on me and to my friends for that matter. Especially not knowing whom to trust, it might be risky to divulge what was in that black book as a trip to the river could be in store for all of us. There was little doubt that it was *"decision time"* as there were two choices. It was either get out of town now or throw all caution to the winds, and go further down the road of undeniable corruption and possibly murder.

Deep in thought, I suddenly heard a distant voice say, *"Well.... don't you agree?"* Looking off to the side, Birmingham was staring at me, waiting for an answer. Problem was I had no idea what the question was even about. Embarrassed slightly and not wanting to show it, I replied, *"I guess it's the way you look at things."* I figured that was a safe answer, but the Director followed with, *"Well, the poor girl may have discovered something harmful through her work and I should have warned her about the consequences....as you must know, this town is not a very friendly place."*

At that point, in time, I did not really know if he was telling me the truth or was trying to blow smoke up my backside. The brand new car sitting in the parking lot might have come from his wife's money or from his possible shady dealings. Maybe he was tied up with the City Hall bunch and was just trying to lead me off the trail, but I had shaken the bushes and the snakes were beginning to come out everywhere. Glaring at him, I exclaimed, *"I would appreciate it if you kept this conversation we had to yourself for the time being and I'll be back in touch with you if I need anything else....in the meantime, just keep your mouth shut and go on with the city's business, okay?"*

While he nodded in agreement and after shaking hands, I turned to leave, but taking a few steps, I realized that Barrett was still standing there, closely studying him. Not wanting to waste anymore time I ordered, *"Come on...let's go, boy....we have work to do."* My partner refused to move and not knowing what his problem was, it caused me to be more firm. *"I told you it's time to go....leave it!"* Suddenly breaking from his stare, Barrett finally followed me, and as we passed the secretary's desk she happily said, *"You have a good day, now."*

As we reached the outer office door, I suddenly remembered one last question that I had neglected during my interview. *"Stay here,"* I commanded to Barrett, *"I'll be right back."* Returning around the counter and passing the secretary's desk, I heard some talking emanating from the director's office. Walking slowly up to the partially closed door and putting my ear up to it, Birmingham's distressful voice crackled. *"Well, you better do something....Madison has been snooping around here with that stinking mutt of his and that's not good for any of us.....you better get off your ass and take care of it."* Just then I opened the door and with a startled look on his face, Birmingham quickly cupped the phone, stammering, *"Ahh.....ahh.....did you forget something?"* With a slight smirk, I answered, *"No....just forgot to tell you to have a good day, that's all,"* and giving the director a slight wave along with a smug look, I left his office.

CHAPTER TWELVE

More Lies?

Getting back into the car, I was still reflecting on what I had just learned. Leaning back against the hot vinyl seat that had been directly in the sun, and caught up in my own thoughts, I suddenly felt a person's presence beside me. Turning my head and looking out the side window, I discovered that it was a uniformed police officer. Startled for a second, I looked up at him, while rolling down the window. *"Can I do something for you, officer?"* He promptly answered, *"You're Madison aren't you?"* Thinking what in the hell did I do now, I replied, *"Yeah, that's me...what's up?"* The officer flashed a small smile, appearing to be glad that he had found me, saying, *"The chief wants to see you in his office right away."*

Barrett's head quickly appeared beside mine from the back seat and peered at the officer, waiting for his next move. Seeing the concern in the officer's face I blurted, *"Don't worry....he won't do a thing....you might say, he's just looking out for my best interest, that's all.....you said the chief wants to see me.....for what?"* Backing away a few steps from the car, the officer's eyes remained glued on Barrett. *"Didn't say...but I hear another body was discovered...it might be about that."* I immediately turned the ignition key and with the engine roaring, I said loudly, *"Tell him I'm on my way."* Spinning and chirping the tires on the paved surface, I quickly exited the parking lot and sped down the street, thinking, *"Another one?....I knew it was only a matter of time."*

When I reached the station, it was in chaos. Several officers with paperwork in their hands were scrambling from one office to another and the radio in the dispatcher's office was blaring away. *"The chief is expecting you.....go right in,"* the receptionist said as I approached her. Rounding the corner and entering his office, it soon became evident that something was dreadfully wrong, as there were several plain clothed detectives and uniformed men speaking to him. I heard one of the detectives say, *"That's right, sir....I don't know if we can suppress the situation any longer....seems like the newspaper has already gotten a hold of this one."* The chief who was pacing back and forth behind his desk, shouted, *"We better get a handle on this, gentlemen, or some heads are going to roll.... Sloan, make some calls and see what you can do......your boss is not going to like this spread all over the papers."*

It was obvious that Marty Sloan, the mayor's executive assistant, did not like taking orders from the chief as the look on his face was tell tale. Talking under his breath, he slowly turned and headed for the exit, passing me by as he made his way out the door. Throwing a quick glance in my direction, he muttered something more under his breath, which I did not completely understand, but by the looks of him, it was definitely not complimentary to Chief Morin.

Then a loud voice bellowed throughout the room causing everyone to come to a complete silence. *"Madison!....it's about time you showed up.....I am so glad that you finally decided to join us..... where in the hell have you been?"* Everybody in the room turned and stared at Barrett and me, appearing as if they were going to witness an execution. *"If you would be so kind, why don't you take some time out from your busy schedule and take a seat....you can then inform us on the great progress you have been making so far.... from what I hear, you are doing so well that your partner withdrew himself from the case and is now refusing to work with you.....is that true?"* As the chief stood there with a huge smirk on his face, I knew what his game plan was going to be. Knowing there was little time to respond, I tried to head him off at the pass, but he continued before I could say another word. *"That is, if it doesn't put you out with too much trouble Madison, because it seems we have another body on our hands..........Robinson, why don't you take a minute to enlighten the man or should I say detective, if I may use that word so loosely."* Chief Morin scanning everyone in the room with his roaming eyes, smirked, and added, *"And I'm sure you won't mind if he does Madison....will you?"*

Detective Robinson, holding a sheet of paper in front of him, eyed me for a second, and his expression was tell tale before he even opened his mouth. Anxious to respond, the detective smiled, immediately stating, *"Sure chief....after all, we are all working together on this case, including the furry guy over there that badly needs a hair cut."* Snickers and laughs broke out from everybody, but the chief immediately put an end to it. *"All right, that's enough now.....Robinson get on with it."* Raising the paper to read it, Robinson tried to wipe the grin off his face and said, *"This is what we know so far...Lori Jenkins....age 22....local prostitute and known drug dealer....including a few priors for shop lifting, she was also a robbery suspect in the Village Inn holdup a couple of years ago..... well, gentlemen.....she won't be a problem anymore, as she was found dead this morning at 5:35 a.m. near the Fifth Street bridge by a woman walking her dog......strangled and partially stuffed in a large suitcase, she was entirely nude with several abrasions on her body along with severe discoloration in many areas as it appears she was severely beaten with a blunt instrument, possibly a baseball bat....her skull was badly crushed in two locations and her body was subjected to heavy blows in the torso area.....the lab boys are going over her now, looking for any evidence that may have been left by the killer.....but the worse part of the situation is, for some reason, the woman discovering the body contacted the local newspaper before calling the station.....in fact, they were on the scene before us "*

While Robinson was speaking, the chief was still pacing back and forth behind his desk like a caged lion. Puffing heavily on his cigarette, the veins in his neck were pulsating with each word that filled the room from Robinson. There was little doubt he was about to explode and as the detective finished his synopsis, Chief Morin suddenly stopped in his tracks, gazing at everyone in the room. His dark and tired eyes scanned each one of us, one at a time, almost appearing to look directly into our souls. It was obvious to me that he was trying to intimidate us into saying something foolish so he could rip us apart. That was the way the chief worked a difficult case such as this one. If a case was going badly, his first reaction always was to find a scapegoat, someone that he could pin the failure on. As the chief's eyes stopped on me, a slight grin came over his face while he examined me up and down. *"You call yourself a detective, Madison....I haven't heard a peep from you since you arrived here.....all I've gotten from you so far or should I say from that God damn mutt of yours is that my allergies are acting up.......what in the hell have you been doing all of this time?...hmm?....maybe taking a few bottles back to your room at the motel?"*

The men chuckled in the background, and hearing jeers along with derogatory comments spilling all over the place, it flooded me with disparagement towards the chief. He was acting like an asshole, plain and simple, and I was not about to take it anymore. *"Why wasn't I called sooner, chief?.....How am I suppose to contribute to this case if I can't even see the murder scene before its contaminated to shit?....letting newspaper people tramp all over the place like cattle......if that's the way this department is going to conduct its investigations then....."*

Without any warning, Morin suddenly cut me off by hollering, *"That's enough out of you, detective!....everyone out!....I'll speak to this man alone!"* He waived his right arm furiously, instructing everyone to leave, and as everybody rushed for the door, Robinson gleaming with sarcasm while walking past me whispered in my ear, *"Good luck, detective and I hope you have a real pleasant time with the chief."*

When everybody had cleared the room, Chief Morin came from behind his desk, and grabbed the door. Slamming it so hard that the hinges almost buckled, he yelled, *"Sit down, Mr. Madison!"*

As he barreled his way back to his desk, he threw his chair into the corner with so much force that it pierced a hole in the plastered wall. Startling Barrett with his act of violence my partner growled loudly, causing me to grab him by the back of the neck. *"Be quiet, boy...before you know it, both of our asses will be in a jam."* With his hand behind his neck, Chief Morin gazed towards the ceiling, and rubbed it for a moment. Then turning his head towards me, he grabbed his chair and righted it in a huff. Sitting back down in it hard, he lit up a smoke and took a heavy drag off it, almost burning the entire cigarette in one drag. Leaning back in his chair and thinking for a moment, he moved forward with his elbows on his desk and pointed at me with his cigarette, while ashes fell onto the blotter. *"If you think for one minute you are going to come into my office and chastise me in front of my men, you have another thing coming, mister as I'll throw your ass so quick in jail, that it will make your head spin......plus, I'll leave you in there for about a week, maybe even a month....that will give me some more time to think up another few charges to hold you there until you rot!"*

He was pissed all right and rather than have our *"discussion"* go further into the sewer, I figured the best thing to do was not join the fight and to let him rant. Realizing I did not throw a counter punch, he rambled on. *"I did not want your drunken ass back here in the first place, Madison....the Mayor did...why?...who in the hell knows....you were a drunken useless piece of shit when we rode your ass out of here the first time.....you killed that kid in cold blood, Madison.....you know it and I know it..... and how you can still consider yourself a member of law enforcement is beyond me....but let me tell you one thing mister, you're about to screw up big time again and when you do....bang!....I'll enjoy slamming that metal door on your ass so much that I'll probably end up dancing a little jig down Main Street."*

For some reason, the chief had always despised me, and his current rage was just some more of the same. Before I could answer him, he let go with another salvo of accusations. *"The Mayor thought you had cleaned up your act and would be a viable source of help on this, but it is obvious to me that you haven't ......* *even your old partner can't work with you because of your incompetence.....Madison, to put it mildly, you're nothing but a disgrace to the uniform!"*

The man had finally done it and it was about time that I called him out into the street. Barrett could sense I was becoming upset too as he stood on all fours beside me, closely observing the chief and wondering whether he deserved a few chomps or not. Sensing this, I rubbed the back of his ears a couple of times, hoping to calm him down a little, before I fired back with, *"This case is far more complex than you might think, chief.....there are a lot of 'outside' forces at work here and the serial killer is not the only culprit.....I think there has been a lot of money passed around this place and when all of the dirty wash is hung out, many people are going down the shit tube on this."*

The chief's eyes immediately rolled backwards as he threw himself against the back of his chair with disgust, attempting to control his temper. Knowing that he was about to blow a gasket again, I decided to drop a few more bombs to hasten the explosion. *"It's obvious by the evidence that there is more than one killer at large, chief....the crime scenes don't match up and the killer's MO is not consistent....plus, the Planning Director is probably guilty as hell for the Swanson killing and I know for a fact that there has been a lot of cash passed around City Hall.....look at the car he drives.... where does a city employee find that kind of money?"*

Chief Morin smirked back at me with defiance while I was speaking, almost laughing at my accusations as they came flowing out of my mouth. He could not wait for an opening and when I paused to get a breath, he sarcastically replied, *"You're really pathetic, Madison....I mean, you don't even have a clue who you are dealing with around here, do you?....your head is so far up your ass that you can't see one inch in front of your nose.....don't you know who the Planning Director's wife is?.....well, sir, it's obvious that you don't.....for your information, detective, and again I use that term VERY loosely, because it seems you never do your homework.....*

in fact, I think you are missing a few cards out of your deck......to add some good solid material to your notes, why don't you take this down, Mr. Madison......she is the daughter of Sam Townhill, who is one of the finest men I have ever met....he is also one of the biggest land developers on the east coast and daddy has always been really good to his little princess.....so, Mr. Detective you are worried by the car he drives and what it costs?.....maybe five thousand dollars or so?....that's pocket change to that man for it was given to them as one of their wedding presents.....so before you go traipsing around the city, spreading some shit house rumors about money being passed around here, you better get your God damn facts straight!"

The chief lit up a cigarette, grinning the entire time, thinking that he had shoved me in a hole and buried me in it. As he took a couple of puffs, wearing that smirk, I watched him gloat for a few more moments in his apparent victory. *"Should I play another card?"* I thought. Thinking, *"I guess I may have screwed that one up, but what if the chief was dirty?....could he still be involved in the City Hall conspiracy?.. ..and should I reveal some of the key evidence that I had found to him?.....possibly blowing my chances?....or should I keep it close to the vest and let this play out a little longer?"*

All of these thoughts were playing on an endless tape in my mind as I sat there looking at his smug puss. After dealing with the prolonged agony of so many thoughts, his sickening face was finally too much for me and I let loose with my massive artillery. *"Well, chief.... daddy probably would have been really ticked off if he had found out that his son-in-law was banging his Assistant Director!"* The chief's deplorable character instantly changed to even a lower level as he leaned forward on his desk, allowing the ash from his butt to drop all over his shirt. Realizing what he had done, he quickly wiped them away, and yelled at the top of his lungs. *"What do you mean by the director banging his assistant?.... what kind of shit is that?....have you actually lost your mind?....I know what it is....you're drunk, Madison....come over here, so I can get a sniff of you.....if there's even a hint of alcohol on you, mister..... your ass is mine!"*

Revenge tasted immensely sweet as I watched the chief choke on his next drag off his cigarette and he was so flustered and blazing red in the face that I expected him to drop from a stroke at any moment. Relishing the sight, I patted Barrett a few times while the chief fell back in his chair, speechless, realizing that I was dead serious and that I might actually have the goods on the Planning Director. With a contemptuous smile, I added, *"He admitted it to me, chief........Birmingham had been banging her bones for a couple of months before she was killed.....and do you know what I think now?.....maybe Swanson was going to spill the beans to his wife and he had to make sure that never happened....as he said in his own words....let me see here,"* as I pulled my notebook out. *"Yes, here it is.....quote, 'if my wife finds out...there goes the money'....far as I am concerned that puts him at the top of the list."* The chief coughed uncontrollably on the smoke that was exiting his lungs and after clearing his throat several times, reluctantly replied, *"Ahh...he admitted this to you?.....I mean about the money disappearing if his wife ever found out about Swanson?"* Smiling back, I smugly said, *"Sure did.....gives him a pretty good motive, doesn't it?"*

The chief rose from his chair quickly, looking like a jack in the box, and crushed his cigarette out in the ashtray with a hard, deliberate grinding action. Almost pushing the cigarette through the glass ashtray, he faced the window with a blank stare, looking outside in deep thought. Then expressionless and without looking back at me, he said solemnly, *"Does anybody else know about this?....I mean did Detective Wilson hear this as well?"* Knowing my spear of information had found its mark, the words flowed out of me easily. *"No....no one else....in fact, Russ had left the investigation and me prior to my meeting with the director."* Immediately, Chief Morin turned around, with eyes of a caged animal. *"Tell me...this guy just didn't admit this to you out of the clear blue as it could have meant the end of his silver spoon.....what did you say to Birmingham?....you must have discovered something, right?"*

Reaching in my pocket and retrieving the onyx cuff link, I answered, *"This, sir....found it or should I say Barrett found it in* her apartment....apparently it had fallen into a heating duct in the floor....he wears this type of cuff link all the time and when I confronted him with it, the game was up." Rubbing his chin and scratching the side of his face, Morin genuinely acted surprised. "That's very interesting, Madison.....I never would have suspected him.....there's no question that there is motive here....if the wife had ever found out she would have shut him off from the cash for sure or should I say of daddy's money....he enjoys the lifestyle he has grown accustomed to these past few years and I don't think he could have lived without it.....membership to the local country club, fancy cars, and that big house over on Windermere Drive are just some of the little tidings that her daddy's money has provided him.....yes, your point is well taken....I think we should take Mr. Birmingham into custody immediately."

I shook my head slightly, looking at the cuff link. "No, chief....I don't think he did it...besides he denied it vehemently and he has an alibi, supposedly supported by his wife....I guess they were at the movie house the night of Swanson's killing, seeing that war picture that came out about a year ago, 'The Guns of Navarone'.....besides, my little voice is telling me he's not our man, but I need to know a little more about this case.....why don't you tell me about this recent killing regarding Lori Jenkins."

With befuddlement written all over his face, Chief Morin lit up another butt, and took a huge drag from it. Exhaling the smoke into a large cloud that hovered in front of him, Barrett quickly moved over to the other side of the room to avoid the noxious fumes and laid back down. The chief noticing this, readily asked, "What the hell is the matter with him?" Chuckling, I replied, "Ever since he's been a pup, he has really despised cigarette smoke and has always tried to avoid it ....like I told you before, that dog is smarter than most people.....actually, he's been trying to get me to quit, but so far it hasn't worked." Morin took another drag, staring at Barrett and then his eyes fell back on me. "What do you mean, he's tried to get you to quit....don't tell me that the dog speaks to you.....if he does, then we have a real problem on our hands, don't we Madison?" Laughing aloud, I leaned back in my chair. *"No, he hides them on me, sir......you know, takes the pack out of my shirt pocket and puts them where I can't find them....one day, he actually chewed the whole pack up and spread it out all over the place...... that's when I lost it and really gave him some hell for I had to clean up the damn mess, but to this day he still hides them on me....you might say Barrett never quits on something once he puts his mind to it....now, tell me more about this latest murder, chief....how bad of a girl was she?"*

Morin picked up a piece of paper from his desk and handed it to me. *"This is her rap sheet....since the age of fourteen, she's been nothing but trouble....in and out of 'juvy' hall was a way of life for her until she hit eighteen.......that's when she finally did a short stretch for prostitution, but it didn't end there.......as you can see, she was a suspect in the Village Inn hold up where the owner was killed.....we could never get enough evidence on her boyfriend, Ty Phillips, but we were confident he was the shooter....your old partner, Russ Wilson worked the case and followed Phillips for months, trying to pin it on him, but he was never successful....I think it still bothers him today as the owner of the Inn was a good friend of his."*

As my eyes scanned her rap sheet, I noticed that both of her parents were deceased, the mother dying of a drug overdose, while her father was shot and killed by police trying to rob a liquor store in upstate New York. Shaking my head in sorrow, I looked up from the sheet, saying, *"Seems like the girl had a tough go of it, chief.....too bad that some of the young people go this route."* Taking another puff, Morin replied, *"Yeah, she was actually an honor student in high school until she got mixed up with the wrong crowd...then it was all down hill from there on."*

Glancing over at Barrett, he was fast asleep, not paying any attention to what was going on around him. When he was bored that was his usual way of escape and I really could not fault him for that, for when duty called, he was always ready to do his job.

Rolling the cuff link in my hand while staring at Barrett made me think without it, this case would have been still stuck in the mud. *"I'll take that, by the way,"* the chief declared pointing at the cuff link. Tossing it to him, I answered, *"Sure...I checked it for prints and there weren't any, but you're right it should be submitted into evidence."*

After carefully examining it for a few moments, Chief Morin placed it on his desk in front of him. *"Like I said, I'll take care of this, you just keep working the case Madison as it seems you are at least making some progress....the evidence points to a real sicko out there who will stop at nothing until we catch him.....in my opinion, from the severe acts of violence committed against the latest victims, he is beginning to progress.....maybe, he is even starting to like it...it's probably some nut hyped up on drugs, but I think we have little time left on this before the lid is totally blown off this thing....I hope you realize the pressure I am under to solve this thing."*

Debating in my mind if I should reveal anything more to him, especially the note that the killer left, I became hesitant to do so. The possibility of the chief being crooked and a liar was still whirling around in my head and telling him more was not the best approach. Deciding to let things play out a little more, I stood up and Barrett recognizing this, awoke immediately, and got to his feet as well. *"I guess it's back to work then,"* I said, heading for the door. Morin quickly rose out of his chair and swiftly came around from behind his desk, asking, *"Wait a minute...I need to know a couple of things before you leave.... why did Russ request a transfer away from this case?.....and who should I put with you for another partner?....I was thinking, Robinson."* Grabbing the brass doorknob, I stopped and pondered for a moment before turning my head slightly towards him. *"You might say, chief, that Russ and I don't see eye to eye any longer....I guess we are like an old married couple who can't get along anymore and it just means we need to go our separate ways....and for the partner?.....well, I have one."* Motioning with my head towards Barrett, I added, *"And like a new girlfriend, he doesn't argue with me in the slightest...he just gives me unconditional love."* Chuckling as Barrett and I went through the door, I left the chief standing there with his mouth wide open, trying to figure out what I had just said.

CHAPTER THIRTEEN
The Snakes come out

I had one more stop to make, as I wanted to speak to William Stone, the lab forensics technician, about the latest victim. Arriving at his office, which was located adjacent to the property storage building and police station, I was surprised at the size of the place. For years, it had always been far too small for a city the size of Harrisburg, and amazingly not much had been done to the structure in my absence, as all of the rooms were still crammed to the ceiling with stuff. Sadly, the entire building was still a maze of desks, tables, file cabinets and electronic instruments, which made it extremely hard for anyone to make their way through the place.

The receptionist not surprised to see us as we entered the building, told me that the station must have called ahead of time, letting her know that we were on our way over. *"Mr. Stone is expecting you, sir....you can go right in,"* she exclaimed, seeming not to be fazed in the least by Barrett as she intently watched us pass her desk. *"Mr. Madison, what a beautiful animal you have there....he's a real handsome boy."* I grinned in appreciation and replied, *"You hear that, boy....she thinks you are a good looking devil....you should thank the nice lady."* Barrett promptly jumped onto her desk, placing his front paws on it and gave her a big slurp across the face, making the woman almost fall over backwards out of her chair. Giggling and laughing like a little schoolgirl, she wiped the saliva from the side of her face. *"My!....he is quite the devil, isn't he?"* Pleased by her response, I flashed a little smirk at her. *"Oh, he knows on how to put on a show alright.....with that black fury face and that cute look of his, he can make any girl melt.... can't you, boy?"*

Barrett jumped down from the steel desk that was littered with papers and followed right behind me as we entered Stone's office. The technician seemed to be busy signing some forms as he was taking a page at a time from a pile that was to the left of him. Surprisingly, his desk was a disorganized mess, as it was covered with dozens of large manila envelopes and several manuals. Littered amongst the scattered papers were three or four ashtrays that were overflowing with ashes along with scores of burnt out butts. Along side them was an old pipe that had heavy teeth marks on the end of it and all at once the tell tale smell of stale pipe tobacco smoke hit my nostrils. There were no windows in his office and except for a few framed diplomas and certificates that hung crookedly on the wall behind him they were barren. A fake plant in one corner of the room, and two chairs along with a clothes rack in the opposite corner were the only other pieces of furniture besides his desk. With everything covered in a thick layer of dust, overall, the office was a very dismal place to work in. *"I would go nuts if I had to work in here,"* I thought extending my hand to shake his. *"I'm Detective Shaker Madison and this is....."* Quickly he held his hand up while interrupting me. *"I've heard all about Mr. Barrett....he's actually been a big hit in our city...you might say he has become a celebrity around here."*

Stone appeared to be unafraid as he swiftly moved from behind his desk to pat him. This surprised me, to tell the truth, as very few people upon seeing him for the first time reacted like that. *"You must like dogs,"* I remarked watching him vigorously rub Barrett's head. *"Oh, I love dogs....especially large ones, like Barrett here....he sure is a beauty....where did you ever get him?"* Taking my seat as Stone returned to his I replied, *"I got him from an Indian up north and we hit it off right away...in fact, you can say Barrett really found me."* Chuckling a bit, Stone grabbed his pipe and began packing it with tobacco from a pouch that he had pulled from a drawer in the desk. *"How's that?"* he curiously asked. Smiling I responded, *"He left his litter bed and bravely swaggered over to me....since that point, he has never left my side."* As Stone puffed a few times on his pipe to light it, his eyes were bright and glaring at Barrett, as if he was envious of my partner in life. *"I wish I had a dog like that.... hell, they are better than most people you meet in this God forsaken world.....especially in this type of business....right, Madison?"*

Nodding my head, I could not have agreed with him more as police life was a very dirty business. The scumbags we had to deal with on an everyday basis could bend your attitude toward the entire human race, if you were not careful about it. That was something that you had to be constantly aware of, as they were like a cancer that could spread throughout your entire body and before you even realized it, they would take you to a very dark place that was chuck full of ugliness. Unfortunately, in our line of work, many depressed cops eventually ate a bullet, quickly ending their life of misery and despair, but for me the chosen path was the bottle, which was a much slower way to die. Rather than end your existence in a flash of light, taking the bottle to your lips and sipping your seemingly useless life away was a much harder way to go. Every morning, I felt the wraith of self-destruction as I placed that one foot on the floor, getting out of bed. Each time my foot went onto the floor, I wondered how much pain was going to shoot through my head and body that day. Struggling to put food in my stomach and wondering if it was going to stay down that morning was just a part of normal day life. Sadly, more often than not, I stopped the car along the way to work, and heaved my guts out to the point of developing dry heaves. Then after emptying my stomach, reach for the glove compartment, and with a shaking, sweaty hand pour some more *"medicine"* down my throat, praying for the sickness and jitters to go away. Without fail, the calming effect I searched for came suddenly and I felt like a human being again, ready to attack the day. As I thought of the past, the images were overwhelming that were playing in my mind, and as the words, *"Isn't that right, Madison?"* streamed through the air, I came out of the trance that had temporarily deafened me.

Noticing Stone was still puffing on his pipe and staring at me, waiting for an answer to a question that I had no idea what it was about, I pushed the thoughts of the past out of my mind. However, the sadistic thoughts of booze had done it once again to me, changing a sober reality to a dirty and ugly world. *"Ahhh.... oh...what was that again?"* Stone wore a slight grin while he took another puff on his pipe. *"By the looks of you...I didn't know if you were ever going to come back.....what ever you were thinking about must have been pretty captivating."* Pursing my lips, I rubbed the side of my face, answering, *"Stone, this case has had me thinking a lot and sometimes I just get lost in it.....tell me, what have you found so far with the latest victim....what was the COD?"*

Grabbing some papers from one of the several piles on his desk, he rummaged through them, and finally selected a few sheets. *"I know it looks like a mess, Madison, but believe me I do know where everything is....sometimes it just takes me a while....in a way it's my own unique filing system, but it still drives the chief crazy....oh, here it is,"* as he began studying one of the pages. His eyes roamed the page for a second, and then he glanced up at me while reading from the report. *"Mind you all of this information is extremely rough and could change once we've had a better look at the body.....the cause of death was strangulation according to the preliminary findings of the coroner.....the blood vessels in her eyes were ruptured, the larynx was crushed, and with the parachute cord wrapped around her neck.....yeah, there was little doubt what killed her.....as with the others, her hair was removed near the scalp and stuffed in her mouth.....with the amount of hair we found down her throat, she could have died from that alone, but that was definitely done post-mortem.....there is no doubt about that as there were no hairs found in her lungs."*

Studying the paper intently for a moment, he puffed a few more times on his pipe and continued. *"There were several bruises and other severe injuries to the body...a few broken ribs, a fractured left cheek, and broken right ankle to name a few....there were many internal injuries to the spleen, liver and kidneys as well...in a nut shell, she had been badly beaten and strangled to death, but like I said previously, she was dead prior to the hair being stuffed into her throat or before most of the beating took place....all of this means a definite overkill in my opinion......let's see here....there appeared to be no evidence of sexual assault, but there were signs of venereal disease, Syphilis to be exact....she had sores within the mouth and the typical rash on the soles of her feet....the victim was probably in the secondary stage of the disease, but we won't know that until further lab tests are conducted, but like some of the others, she was a definite heroin addict as there were several needle marks on the arms and between the toes....and one more thing, this one had two large letters carved on her back with a very sharp instrument, probably a fillet knife....'AC'....damnedest thing I have ever seen."*

He handed me a couple of photographs, which were of the crime scene, and I began to peruse them. Nothing new really, it was obvious to me that she was found next to the river as I immediately recognized the area. However, one detail quickly hit me as her outer clothes were scattered haphazardly around the partially nude body, which did not agree with the MO of the previous victims. Found in a large black suitcase, the tell tale parachute cord was tied with a slip not around her neck. Being a relatively small woman of about 5'-1", 105 pounds, she easily fit into the case and this may have explained why the legs and arms of the victim were not broken. The carved letters in the victim's flesh were very apparent on her upper right back as they were about two to three inches in height. Shaking my head from side to side in disgust I asked, *"The victim's name was Lori Jenkins, wasn't it?"* Stone nodded his head while his eyes went to the top of the page. *"Yes....she lived at #3 Sycamore drive.....from the needle marks found on her body that was a good place in town for her to live."*

Stone was right, that area of town was nothing but a haven for addicts and drug dealers. For years we had tried to clean it up, but the amount of drug trafficking was immense and it always seemed that when we made an arrest, there was always another dealer to take his place and the filthy business would go on. Mumbling to myself I said, *"Why the letters, AC?....maybe the killer is trying to tell us something, like possibly his name?....somehow I find that hard to believe, but maybe his ego needs it...some of these nuts like to taunt the cops by leaving clues like this which might turn out to be useful in their own sick and demented ways......but in the end, realistically, most of these so called 'clues' are just left to throw us off the track."*

Stone took back the glossy photographs as I handed them to him and while he sorted the pictures back in order, I saw the evidence bag on his desk containing some of the victim's personal effects. *"Can I see those?"* pointing to them. He quickly handed the bag to me and the first item that immediately drew my attention was a key that looked very familiar. It was definitely for an Elgin lock as the name was inscribed on it and pulling my Spirit Arms Motel key from my pocket, it was almost a perfect match. *"Well, that's a coincidence,"* I thought to myself. *"I wonder if this key will fit any of the rooms back at the motel."*

I placed the bag containing the single key to the side and picked up a charm bracelet in another. It looked to be sterling silver and it had several, various decorative objects attached to it. A small shoe, dog, cat, and what looked like an acorn dangled from it. A silver heart with the initials *"LJ"* inscribed on it, also hung from the chain, but there was a single strand of silver wire that had nothing attached to it, almost giving the impression that one object had been torn from it. The rest of the personal effects were a woman's watch that was not working, a small handbag that contained a number of syringes, a dirty spoon, a book of matches with the name *"Blue Moon"* on the cover, and a small amount of heroin in a plastic bag. *"Was all of this stuff found at the scene?"* I asked placing the various bags back on the desk. Stone quickly answered, *"Far as I know....these drug addicts generally travel pretty light, but they do carry the essentials to keep themselves high.....we dusted all of this stuff for prints, but there was nothing.......funny thing though, her clothes had been removed, but she was still wearing her underwear, which is not consistent with the other murders, as her panties and bra are in that bag over there........Madison, whoever is doing this is real smart......the guy is very careful about not leaving us a damn thing to work with."*

My eyes drifted over to where he was pointing and on the cluttered counter along the wall were two additional evidence bags. Walking over to them, I found that they were among many other evidence bags and some loose papers. Very amazed at the disheveled mess, it seemed the pile of bags had no order or system to it. *"You say you know where everything is in this place, Stone..... well, I'm glad you do, because this is like looking at a pile of trash at the landfill."* The forensic man leaned back in his chair puffing on his pipe and smiled. *"Don't worry, Madison....there isn't a thing in this place that I can't find....the chief is always on my ass about the condition of this place, but what am I supposed to do?....you can see we need more room."*

Picking up the evidence bags with the underwear in them, I was surprised at the quality and fanciness of them. They were expensive looking and consisted of a high quality silk type material, something a strung out drug addict could never afford. *"You sure these came from her, Stone?.....I mean Lori Jenkins?....this type of expensive clothing is hardly found on a person like that."* Stone's expression immediately turned to one of surprise. *"Of course they did....in fact, the chief made sure that I bagged them separately."* Placing the evidence back on the counter I turned to him. *"Has the chief been this attentive on the rest of the girls that have been found?"* A smirk came to his face as he sat there puffing on his pipe, enjoying its aromatic smoke. *"No....this one seemed to peak his interest more.....he was real careful about making sure everything was done according to the book....you know...that all of the evidence was properly collected and categorized.....plus, he was especially concerned about the chain of custody on this one.....why, I couldn't tell you."*

Staring at Stone at his desk I blurted, *"I'm going to need to sign out this key for a few days."* Stone returned the stare and looked back at me inquisitively, immediately answering, *"You know I will have to contact the chief about this....he'll have my head if I don't."* Noticing the way Stone was staring at me, thoughts of the chief's particular interest in this victim were running through my mind. Why did Detective Robinson say the girl was found naked in the briefing? Moreover, why the chief's sudden personal interest in this part of the serial case?

Lighting up a smoke, I took a single drag, exhaled and peered at Stone through the smoke hovering in front of me. *"I'm going to call in a favor; Stone....you remember that little incident about five years ago?"* Stone's face instantly turned red at my words and he immediately puffed vigorously on his pipe. *"Yeah...I remember it....so, what do you want?"* Holding up the evidence bag with the key in it I replied, *"This...let me take this out for a few days without anybody knowing it and I will consider our little business settled."* Stone wiped the front of his face with a handkerchief, trying to keep his composure. Thinking hard for a moment, he stared back at me, replying, *"Why?....do you have a hunch?"* Now, I did not want to tip my hand, so I decided to throw a vague answer at him. *"Maybe....just really want to check out a few things, that's all."*

As Stone handed me a sheet of paper, pertaining to the release of the key for my signature, I noticed he seemed content with my answer and suddenly appeared more than willing to help me. After quickly scanning the one page document, I signed and dated it, handing it back to him. Taking it, he buried it in a folder and simply glanced up at me, grinning, looking like the cat that just ate the canary. *"Don't worry, nobody will see that....anything else?"* he slyly said pursing his lips.

Knowing I could probably press him for one more favor I asked, *"The Swanson killing....I have seen some of the crime scene photographs, but I think there might be others....would you know anything about that?"* Stone held up an index finger, replying, *"Hold on for a minute....that is something I know I can help you with."* Quickly going to a file cabinet behind him, he pulled a very large manila envelope from the second drawer and tossed it on his desk. *"Those are all of the photographs of the crime scene....you can look through them, but they have to remain here and there's no dickering on that, okay?"*

Not wanting to piss him off, I picked up the file and went over to another table. *"Yep, no problem, Stone....just want to take a look, that's all."* Cleaning a spot by pushing the piles of papers aside, I pulled the photographs from the envelope and spread them out. I knew what I was looking for and it was not long before I found the close up picture of the victim's neck. Previous pictures that I had seen were frontal shots of the head, but this photograph plainly showed three individual small bruises along the left side of her throat. *"I knew it,"* I mumbled. *"She was obviously strangled before the cord was placed around her neck....someone is playing games with us."*

Placing the pictures back in the envelope, I handed them back to Stone. *"Madison, did you find what you were looking for?"* Shaking his hand I happily replied, *"Yeah, I think so, but this case just gets more complex by the minute.....I have a feeling that what I am about to find out is not going to be in some people's interest..... we'll catch you later Stone....and thanks for your help."*

As we started to leave the office, I could sense the unbroken stare at Barrett, and when we reached the doorway Stone hollered, *"Heh...if you ever want to get rid of that dog, I would be glad to take him off your hands."* Hearing that caused me to stop dead in my tracks for a moment, thinking on an appropriate response, but all I did was look back at him, thinking what a ridiculous statement he had just made. Leaning back in his chair, puffing on his pipe, and blowing a few smoke rings, Stone's grin grew wider. *"Well, if you ever do, let me know....like I said he can come and live with me anytime."* Wearing a full smile he added, *"Have a good day, detective and good luck.....because you're going to need it."*

Not giving him the satisfaction of a response, I thought, *"Funny, someone else just told me that,"* as I continued out into the receptionist's office. Saying goodbye to her, Barrett and I headed back to the car and upon reaching it, I took out my motel key from my pants pocket and compared it to the Jenkins's key. *"Mmmmm,"* I said aloud to Barrett. *"Seems like this one is almost identical to our room key.....what do you think about that?"* Barrett sniffed both keys in my hand and then sat back on his haunches, staring at both of them. *"We need to find out if this one fits any of the locks back at the Motel, don't you think?"* Answering me quickly with a sharp bark, I replied, *"Yeah...just what I thought....get in."* Without hesitation, Barrett leaped through the opened rear side window, into the back seat, while I opened the door on the driver's side.

Getting in and pondering for a moment before starting the vehicle, I felt a presence off to side of me and to my surprise; it was Russ my old partner approaching the car. *"Heh there....how are you doing, Shake?"* Pleased to see him I replied, *"Ahhhh..... good.....where have you been hiding yourself?"* As my old partner reached towards the side window, Barrett immediately rose to his feet in the backseat. He seemed to be uneasy and a low, threatening growl actually eked out of him. *"What the hell is the matter with you?"* I commanded glaring at him in the backseat. *"You know Russ....don't you remember him?"* Barrett still not being himself and Russ considering Barrett's reaction, kept his distance from the car. *"What's up with the mutt?.....don't tell me that he hates me now."* As Barrett's upper lip slightly curled upwards, exposing his large left canine tooth, I replied, *"I don't know....he's upset about something....what, I couldn't tell you."* I offered a smoke to Russ and upon him taking it, Barrett settled down a bit, but his eyes remained fixated on my old partner. *"Have you made any progress on the case lately?"* he asked lighting up a cigarette. *"I spoke to Robinson and he tells me that you were in to see the chief....what's this about you thinking that Birmingham had something do with Swanson's murder?"*

Alarm bells started immediately ringing off in my head as I had just seen the chief not more than an hour ago, and already Detective Robinson knew about what I had told him. Additionally, in that short period of time my old partner was brought in on it as well. Now my suspicious side was screaming out to me, yelling, *"You know the chief is probably dirty....he has to be because of Swanson's research....a normal superior would have kept our conversation confidential and he never would have leaked it by broadcasting it throughout the station.....after all, there was a possible finger pointing at City Hall."*

Deciding to play along I replied, *"Well....it's just a theory.... you know how these cases can go....you have to suspect everyone."* Nodding his head, Russ took another deep drag on his butt and exhaled, short and hard. *"Yeah, you do...especially with what has been happening around here lately....be careful Shake....there is a lot of talk going through the station about you coming down on people and harassing them.....they say you are asking too many questions and poking your nose where it doesn't belong.....it's not a good situation to be in, especially in this town....people in your shoes seem to have accidents, if you know what I mean."* Crushing my butt out in the ashtray, I started the car and while looking up at him, cracked a little grin. *"Well, you tell who ever is whining that there are going to be a lot more questions asked around this place and not to get their panties in a bunch.....and for me having a possible accident?..... tell them to go to hell!"*

Slamming the vehicle in reverse, Russ made a move towards my window and it startled Barrett as he jumped to his feet again. Pointing his finger at me, he yelled, *"Don't tell me that I didn't warn you, partner.....even cops sometimes have to watch their backs!"* As I backed up the car, Russ stood there alone in the parking lot, staring at me. His look was cold and for the first time, he seemed very distant to me, and was not the same partner that I had known for so many years. Giving Russ a short, belligerent wave, I squealed out of the parking lot and headed down Main Street. My temper was flaring, thinking how my old partner had just issued a warning to me about working the case too hard and that I had stepped on a few toes. *"That's bull shit,"* I thought. *"Let them come after me, it isn't the first time and it won't be the last, either."*

Turning the wheel sharply and heading down another street, my thoughts drifted to a case, years ago, when the department busted a petty thief by the name of Sid Wilkins. Because I was the arresting officer, he swore revenge at the hearing, declaring that he was going to *"collect my chips from me."* By saying that, he had left little doubt in anyone's mind that he was going to see my ass in the damn ground before him. Well, he served his two years and after he was released, he did try to take me out one night, waiting for me outside the police station with a piece of lead pipe. Not being too smart, he had positioned himself under a streetlight, where I caught a glimpse of the asshole, and when he came at me with the weapon swirling in the air, my .357 caught him with one in the lower right side. The shock of the bullet hitting him sent the man backwards over the hood of a parked car with such force that when he smashed into the ground, he tried to smooth out the pavement with his face. In a nutshell, his quest for vengeance ended abruptly, as he was sent up for an additional ten to twenty for attempted murder.

It was already getting to be late afternoon and with the sun setting below the buildings on the horizon, it created a beautiful sunset filled with vibrant red, orange, and purple colors. In addition, the blazing rays were reflecting off a few scattered clouds that littered the skyline, only making the view that much more spectacular. Enjoying the sight for a moment, I then turned my head partially around, while still keeping my eyes on the road. *"What do you say we call it a day, boy?.....besides, I would really like to see if this key fits any door back at the Motel."* Barrett licked me on the back of the neck and began shaking his bushy tail in agreement. Pleased that he was anxious to go back to the motel as well, I turned down Spring Street to save some time. The shortcut meant taking many side streets, but being ready for the rack, that was just fine with me.

Within a few minutes, we were back at the Motel and parking the car outside the main office, when I saw Zack working at the front desk. As his eyes found me through the large picture window, he immediately disappeared through a side door into the backroom. It was obvious that he was avoiding me, but I decided that this was a good time as any to try to press him for a little more information. *"Stay here....I'll be right back,"* I ordered Barrett. Not liking my command very much, my furry partner pushed his nose up against the side window, hoping I would have second thoughts, but as I continued to the front door, loud whimpering sounds came from within the vehicle. Not wanting to look back as that would have only made Barrett crazier; I opened the entrance door quickly, which rang the little bell above it. *"Zack.... are you around?"* I said loudly with my eyes scanning the office. Hesitantly, he slowly appeared from around a corner, looking like a kid who had just been caught with his hand in the cookie jar. *"Yeah, I'm here....what's the problem now?"*

Walking up to the Formica counter, I replied, *"Just wanted to ask you a few more questions, that's all.......did you ever know a girl by the name of Lori Jenkins?"* Zack, hanging his head and staring at the floor softly replied, almost in a whisper, *"No....that name does not sound familiar at all, but you know how this business can be....I meet a lot of people....you can hardly expect me to remember all their names....can you?"* Eyeing him up and down, trying to ascertain his sincerity, I added, *"Well....would you mind if I took a look at your register?"* Biting his lower lip, the tension built up in his face almost immediately, making him grimace a little. *"No.... not at all....look all you want to....I have no problem with that."*

He slid the register on the counter over to me and upon opening it, I began thumbing the pages. *"What are you looking for anyway?"* Zack asked while nervously lighting up a cigarette and taking a swig of beer out of a bottle that he had taken from below the counter. Noticing him with the booze in his hands, I had to make a comment about it. *"Never thought you drank at work, Zack..... having a bad day?"* Defensively, he replied, *"I never get any time off in this damn place since Tina was killed.....I told you, she was essential to my business.....she was like my right arm."* I looked up at him and smiled. *"You did tell me that didn't you?.....about you being close and all....isn't that right?"* Taking another sip of beer, he almost choked on it while it went down his throat. *"Ugh..ahh... that's right, I did tell you that."*

Running my finger down the names in the register, I could not help from noticing that Zach was sweating profusely, and his hands were trembling as I continued to study the register. Closing it up, I stared back at him while his eyes glared back at me, asking, *"Did you find what you were looking for?"* Continuing to stare directly at him, while he gulped his beer, I replied, *"Oh, I found a few things....tell me.....did Lori Jenkins ever stay here?.....maybe with another person?"* The sweat was now running down the side of his face and while wiping it in desperation with his shirt sleeves, he answered, *"No...I don't think so."* Immediately, my mind went to work and I asked, *"How in the hell would you know that Zack if you didn't even know her...or even what she looked like?"* Those words pierced his weak armor as his face suddenly grew pale and lifeless, obvious signs that he was going into shock. About to pass out, he stuttered while answering me back. *"Ahh...ohh...that register tells me everything...if her name isn't in it...then she was never here....it's just that plain and simple."*

After having dealt with hundreds of people in uncomfortable situations as a cop for several years, I knew when someone was trying to buffalo me. No doubt, this was one of those times, and with my little voice screaming at me, I decided to go for the jugular. Pulling the key from my pocket, I held it up to him. *"This key looks awfully familiar, doesn't it Zack?"* He stared at the key with wide-open eyes, wetting his lips and swallowing hard. Standing there with a dumb look on his face, not understanding what I was driving at and not saying a word, I reached into my pocket and held up my room key as well. Placing them out in front of me on the counter, side by side, I exclaimed with a grin, *"This key is almost identical to mine, don't you think?....if I didn't know any better, it might even fit the lock on my door."*

His eyes broke from the key and he looked to the right, then to the left, desperately looking for an escape, but then his eyes caught mine. After a few moments of intense staring, he asked in a crackly voice, *"Ahhhh.....where did you find that?....was it left in your room?...or did you find it somewhere else?....and you know, just because it's an Elgin key, doesn't mean it's for here."* Putting both of the keys back into my pocket, I smirked at him, watching the sweat run off his face. *"Oh, it's not important....just thought you might have lost a key along the way, but you're right....it's probably not a key for here, anyway."* His mouth tried to turn into a smile, but it was impossible for him do so as he wiped the sweat from his lips. *"Well, it's been a long day,"* I said while heading for the front door of the lobby. *"I'll catch up with you later."*

As I exited through the door, my mind was on what he had just said about the key and knowing it was an Elgin without me telling him. While opening my car door, I continued to ponder his words. *"There is no way he could have seen the name on that key from that distance.....something rotten is going on here and it's time to find out what it is."*

After moving and parking the car in front of my motel room, I noticed that there were only a few other vehicles that were along side the building, signaling to me that the motel was almost void of guests. While reviewing the register, I noticed that the amount of business had been generally bad in the previous year with very few room rentals and the vacant parking lot only confirmed this.

As Barrett and I walked towards our room, the thought of the key found at the Jenkins's murder scene kept invading my mind and pulling it from my pocket, I walked pass our room down to the far side of the building, and tried it in the lock for room 100. Not fitting that lock, I moved down to the next room marked 101; I tried the key and did not fit as well. One by one, I kept trying the key in each door and had no success until I reached room 112 when it easily turned the lock. Initially surprised at the result, I looked down at Barrett, saying, *"Well, what do you know....Bingo!.... we are in!"*

Entering the room and turning on the light switch to the left of the door, nothing seemed out of the ordinary as the layout of the room was exactly like mine, with the bed on the left along with a nightstand and desk. The door to the bathroom was on the far wall and on the right side was a small table along with a luggage rack next to it, for the placement of customer's bags. The room appeared to be very clean and neat, even smelling of a fresh evergreen scent. In fact, the carpeting looked like it had just been replaced and the bedspread was vibrant in color, appearing to be new as well. Going into the bathroom, it was spotless as it glistened in the overhead light and the strong smell of disinfectant filled the air. The white tiled floor being so clean appeared to sparkle and then I suddenly realized what kind of strong smell had filled my nostrils; it was bleach and a lot of it. In fact, it was almost over powering, and as I looked down at the bathtub, Barrett was already sniffing that area. Leaping into the tub, his nose immediately went to the drain and after a few seconds of investigation, he looked up at me, and I knew he had found something. Upon closer examination, a slight thin red ring was around the outside of the silver drain. *"What did you find, boy?..... that looks like it could be remnants of blood."* Squatting down and carefully scraping around the drain with my jackknife, I removed a few flakes of the substance, and placed it in a piece of paper that I had taken from my pocket.

Standing up, I realized Barrett had disappeared, leaving me alone in the bathroom. Wondering where he could have gone to, I stepped back into the main room and to my surprise there he was, sitting on his haunches, intently staring up at the ceiling. Growing anxious, he began moving back and forth, while keeping his focus on the corner of the ceiling, telling me that it needed further investigation. Grabbing a wooden chair from the desk and stepping on to it, I recognized that it was a suspended ceiling. Reaching up and pushing some of the tiles up and away from the steel frame, unexpectedly, a clear plastic bag fell from one of the tiles to the floor. Barrett immediately began to give it a good *"sniff over"* while I jumped off the chair and as I picked up the clear plastic bag; its shocking contents were revealed to me. A syringe, spoon, and other drug paraphernalia were inside it, along with several smaller bags containing a white powder, which I immediately suspected was heroin. Upon further examination of the bag, there was also a large roll of currency with an elastic band around it. Opening the bag and retrieving the roll, I removed the elastic band, and began thumbing the one hundred and fifty dollar bills. Soon, it became apparent, that there was well over two thousand dollars in cash and my thoughts instantaneously recalled what the briefing had told me about Lori Jenkins being a drug dealer and user. *"This must have been her stash,"* I mumbled while placing the elastic band back over the bills.

Then my head turned to the bathroom, recalling the blood found around the drain along with Tina Hendricks body being discovered adjacent to the river, not more than five hundreds yards from the Motel. A young woman that had worked for Zack and supposedly was his *"right arm"* according to him. *"Two young woman....Tina Hendricks and Lori Jenkins....both murdered and obviously known by him.....it's also evident that this room was overly cleaned for some reason and the carpet was even replaced....along with the new bedspread, maybe something happened here....is this where one or maybe both of the girls were actually murdered?...... is it possible that he's the serial killer?"* My head spun with horrid thoughts of what I had just learned as the possibility of Zack being a horrific killer of young woman ripped through my mind. *"My God,"* I thought. *"He had to know she was staying in this room..... hell, Jenkins was selling drugs out of here.....there's no doubt he lied to me about Lori Jenkins and possibly Tina Hendricks...a person lies for only one reason and I'm starting to think he knows a little more about this than he's letting on."*

Standing up on the chair to replace the tiles, something else caught my eye. Hanging over the edge of one of the ceiling tiles was the end of a small black notebook. Reaching for it with my handkerchief and opening it, the book was filled with numerous names along with dollar amounts beside each one. *"These people must have been her customers,"* I said to myself as I thumbed through the book. *"There must be at least seventy names in here....* *what a great little business she had going and by the looks of this* *list, she must have been supplying drugs to half the neighborhood."* Closing the book, I wrapped it up, placed it in my shirt pocket, and returned the loose tiles. Jumping off the chair, I moved it back to its original place at the desk and patted my fury partner. *"Good boy, Barrett....you've done it again....we are about to nab us a killer."*

Confirming everything was back in its place; I carefully opened the door and peeked outside. It was extremely dark already as all of the streetlights were on and seeing no one at either end of the building, we exited, and I locked the door. My room was only a few doors down and as we strolled towards it, I was becoming excited over our recent discoveries. *"Things are finally coming together,"* I thought. *"Pretty soon we can put this guy away before he can do anymore of his heinous acts."*

Just as I thought that, we had reached our room, and while placing my key in the lock, suddenly the light by the door exploded into a thousand pieces. While broken glass showered Barrett and I, the tell tale sound of a high-powered gun shot rang out, echoing through the night air. Ramming the door hard, I busted into the room along with Barrett. Within seconds, another shot rang out, and the mirror in the bathroom on the opposite side of the room shattered, scattering broken glass all over the white tiled floor. Diving and hitting the carpeted floor, I crawled behind the wall next to the door, with Barrett right next to me. Lying there for several minutes and with no additional shots being fired, I stroked his head, saying, *"Well, boy....we must be getting close..... real close I figure....whoever did this knows it too."* As I moved the curtain away from the corner of the picture window, I looked out at the cars going up and down the street in front of the building. *"Those shots must have come from across the street, but the big question is....from where?"*

As my eyes studied the opposite side of the street, nothing seemed out of the ordinary. Traffic was still in motion as if nothing had happened and I noticed that there was even a car pulling into the liquor store parking lot. Suddenly, thoughts of Zack came into my head, and I immediately jumped to my feet. Peering around the door jam to the outside and seeing nothing, I set off on a dead run towards the office, but before I even got two steps, Zack was sprinting towards me down the concrete walkway along side the building. Seeing me, he hollered, *"What the hell is going on?....are you alright?"* Meeting him about half way, he had a look of genuine concern, as he frantically looked me over. *"I'm okay, Zack.....seems like someone wants me off this case permanently,"* as I looked across the street. *"Another few inches closer, he might have gotten me."*

As Zack came closer, I could see that his eyes were looking everywhere around him, telling me that he was just as confused as I was. *"Where did you come from?"* I asked. Surprised at my question he turned to me, blurting, *"Well, I was in the office when the shots rang out.....at first I thought it was a car backfiring, but when I looked out the window towards the street, I saw a car parked up on the hill behind the liquor store....it must have been at the end of Colby street which dead ends there....it wasn't a second later when I saw the muzzle flash from the second shot."* Not knowing if I could believe him because just minutes before in my mind I was accusing him of being the serial killer, I decided to see his further reaction to a couple of questions. *"You saw the muzzle flash, ehh?.... did you get a look at the gunman?"* Zack shook his head. *"No....he was too far away and it was already pretty dark....but, I did see the car.....it was full size.....I think it was a dark colored Chevy....like an Impala."*

He sounded convincing, but I still had my doubts. *"You were in the office, ehh?....what were you doing?"* Taken back a little from my accusatory attitude, he replied, *"Paperwork, of course.....what else do you think I was doing?"* I stared back at him with a cold glare. *"Paperwork, ehh?....why don't we go back to the office, so I can take down your answers to some other questions I have....plus, I need to call the station to get some help out here."* I did not like the reaction that came out of him when I said that, as he kept looking down and he seemed nervous while we walked back to the office. Additionally, he was quiet the entire time, which was not like him, and as we entered the main office, Zack pointed to the phone on the desk. *"You can call from there."*

Asking the operator to dial the station, I was surprised to learn that the department had already been notified and along with an ambulance had dispatched several squad cars. It seemed that the liquor storeowner had called the police to report the shooting and as I looked out across the street, I noticed a man standing outside the building. Thinking he must be the person that reported it, I hung up the phone and looked over at Zack who had his head buried in his hands. *"They're already on their way, Zack....I guess the guy across the street called them and it looks like he's standing out there waiting for them."*

Zack raised his head out of his hands and peered across the street, not saying a word. Staring at him, his eyes finally came upon mine, and by my look, he knew there was more to the incident than I was letting on. Seeming to accept defeat, he said softly, *"I suppose you have been trying to find out what door that key fits."* Smiling back with a suspecting grin, I replied, *"What do you think, Zack?.....of course, that's what I've up to and do you know what I discovered?"* Zack's face cringed when he heard those words, telling me that he was dreading what was going to come out of my mouth next. Hanging and shaking his head back and forth again, he muttered, *"I suppose that you figured out that she was staying here."* Walking up to, the counter that he was sitting behind, I leaned on it with both hands, hovering over him. *"And who might that be, Zack?....mmmh?"* Suddenly he jumped up from his chair and faced the wall, crying out, *"You know who!....why don't you just spill it for Christ's sake and stop torturing me!"*

Not responding right away, I continued to glare at him for a few moments and that is all it took. Quickly he turned at me saying loudly, *"Lori Jenkins....that's who!.....I didn't want to say anything because I didn't want to become involved."* Watching him squirm, I pulled a smoke from my pocket and lit it. After taking a deep drag,

I replied, *"You know it looks bad for you...right?"* Zack rubbed his face with one hand, thinking for a moment, and I could see that his brain was on overload as he tried to come up with an appropriate response. *"Yeah, I let her stay here....her money was good and green even though she dealt in drugs.....she paid me faithfully every week and I needed the money."*

Barrett came up beside me and I rubbed his ears a couple of times, while keeping my eyes on Zack. Not wanting to show all of my cards at once, I decided to take the *"systematic approach."* *"You know, Zack....allowing drug trafficking under your roof with your knowledge can send you away for a long time....and with your record, it could be for a VERY long time....so long, in fact, that you might come out an old man with a very long, white beard."* Biting his lower lip hard, his face grew a packed look of anguish. *"You don't understand, Shake....I needed the business as this place has been dragging me down for a very long time and I'm sure you saw the evidence of that in the register....you see, for the past couple of years, people have just stopped coming, and I don't know why."*

By the looks of him, he was becoming *"right for the picking"* and I knew with a little more pressure he was going to break. *"Zack, I found something very interesting in Jenkins's room.....specifically, in the bathroom as there appears to be some dried blood around the bathtub drain....would you know anything about that?"* He bit his lower lip even harder and the stress in his face exploded as he moved away from his desk, looking up at the large Regulator clock on the wall that was commonly found in railroad stations during the old robust days of train travel. While he continued to stare at the clock and as it was about to strike 9:00 p.m., his awareness of me became less and less.

Almost in a heavy trance, Zack's stupor was broken when several patrol cars sped into the parking lot along with their sirens screaming and within seconds, the place was bustling with cops. Detective Robinson was one of the first to enter the main office and he immediately saw me along with Barrett next to Zack. *"Are you alright?"* he blurted making his way over to me. Saying something like that seemed funny to me, since why would he ask me that question. How did he know that I was the one that was shot at? Deciding to be a little facetious, I replied, *"Yeah, I'm okay....what took you guys so long?"*

As more officers poured in, Robinson's eyes were obviously surveying the room, and I knew what question was coming next. *"The guy across the street from the liquor store said there was a shooting here, but I don't see any evidence of it....where did he take a poke at you, Madison?"* Again, this seemed funny to me as he was continuing to assume someone had tried to take me out, but I replied, *"Down near my room....room 106....the first shot took out the light beside the door and the second, the bathroom mirror."* Robinson quickly motioned for the men to go outside to secure the scene and while they were doing so, he turned back to me. *"We don't take kindly to this type of thing, Madison...did you see who it was?"* Shaking my head I answered, *"No....but the shots came from across the street...Zack saw the muzzle flashes on top of the hill behind the liquor store....the shooter must have parked at the end of the street and set up there....someone should check it out."* Robinson nodded his head in agreement, looking towards the liquor store. *"Good idea, Madison...why don't we take a ride."* That was the last thing I wanted to do, as I was so close to cracking Zack. *"I was right in the middle of something here, Robinson.... why don't you go on ahead and I'll catch up with you later."* The detective moved in closer to me and whispered, *"You better come with me....the chief gave strict instructions about making sure that you stayed with me, because he wants you totally involved in this."*

As I moved towards the front entrance door with him, I could see immediate relief come to Zack's face and thought, *"That's right Zack....think you're off the hook, do you?....well, you can be certain of one thing in this rotten world, Mr. Thompson.... I'll be back to parley with you some more."* Walking towards Robinson's car, I opened the rear door for Barrett for him to get in and the detective immediately grew a look of surprise. *"Madison, does that mutt have to go with us?....hell, I just got this car back from being cleaned at the motor pool."* Chuckling, I closed the door and opened mine. *"Don't worry, Robinson he's probably cleaner than the both of us put together.....and besides, he might be of some help up there."*

Pulling out of the parking lot, I counted at least eight law enforcement vehicles along with a few emergency trucks, including an ambulance and there were countless police officers and emergency personnel roaming the grounds. *"Looks like you guys were expecting the worse, Robinson....you probably thought Barrett and I would be sprawled out on the pavement...ehh?"* Backing the car up, the detective looked over his glasses at me and firmly replied, *"Like I said, we don't take kindly to our men being shot at....especially when they are under the chief's wing."*

When we reached the dead end of Colby Street, it became obvious why the shooter had chosen the location. It was desolate, void of any nearby homes, and it had a clear view of the entire Motel complex. Although the distance between the two locations was approximately two hundred yards and the difference in elevation was about seventy-five feet, it seemed a high-powered rifle with an adequate scope could have easily made the shot. With all of us getting out of the car, Barrett could not wait as he leaped out of the opened side window to the ground and started his search pattern. Smirking a little, Robinson chuckled as he watched the dog go to work. *"That mutt of yours doesn't waste anytime....does he, Madison?"* Pulling a flashlight from the front of the car and shining it on Barrett as he roamed the area, I replied, *"No.....when there's work to be done, he's all business....look at him, I think he's onto something already."*

Before we could reach the edge of the steep embankment, Barrett was sitting and waiting for us, indicating that he had found something. *"Well, that didn't take him long,"* I said walking towards Barrett and as we came upon him, both of us could see why he was sitting there. Next to him, lying on the ground, were two shell casings, spaced about a foot apart. Squatting down, I took a pen out of my pocket and inserted it into the end of one of the empty cartridges. Picking and holding it up to Robinson while glancing over at the motel I said, *"Looks like it came from a .308......from this distance, he should have had me cold.....especially a man of my size being illuminated by the outdoor light near the door."*

As we both gazed across the roof of the liquor store and the highway to the Motel, it became obvious to the both of us that the shooter had a clear and easy shot. *"Yeah,"* Robinson responded. *"From this distance any man worth his salt with a rifle like that should have drilled you.....maybe he didn't have a scope, ehh?.....because without one, it would have made the shot much harder."* Letting out a short sigh, I followed with, *"But why try and make a shot like this without one, Robinson?.....I knew if I had to take down a person, especially a cop from this distance, a scope would have been in the cards for sure."*

Taking my pen, I moved the casing directly under the light. *"You see anything peculiar with this casing, Robinson?"* The detective looked at it closely, replying, *"No, why?.....should I?"* Flashing a slight grin, while I twirled the casing on the pen back and forth, I added, *"The bottom of the casing has a slight bulge to it and see the rim?....there's a small crack in it....this cartridge was hand loaded and it was loaded hot.....probably a compressed load by the looks of the casing and due to the excessive pressures, the case ruptured slightly....whoever did this, wanted to make sure of the result."* Robinson glanced at the case and looked back at me. *"So....you're telling me that this was a professional hit?"* Looking across to the Motel, I replied, *"Maybe...or it's someone that knows how to reload and just plain missed the shot....because any professional that might have done this would have had me dead to rights....no question about it......I could have made this shot with ease with a 308 loaded to the hilt.... if the shooter utilized a 165 grain bullet, it would have boogied out of here at over three thousand feet a second....that would have produced with very little bullet drop at this distance.....hell, all he had to do was put the cross hairs on me....no, I think this may have been a warning to me....you know, to back off or else."*

Robinson was nodding his head as I laid out my theory and when I finished, he rubbed his chin slightly, looking over the scene and then eyed the Motel. *"Yeah, Madison....I see what you mean....maybe the handwriting is on the wall because you ruffled a few feathers, but what does this all come down to?"* Turning my head, I stared directly at him. *"Robinson, one thing I hate in this stinking world is a coward that won't face me....you know, the kind that wants to give it to you in the back, so he doesn't have to look you in the eye....well, I'll tell you one thing right now.....this bastard is starting to get under my skin and when that happens, there is one thing you can surely bet your house on..... I'm going to put this asshole in jail or in the ground before he gets me."*

Continuing our investigation, we collected both casings, placed them into evidence bags, and began looking around the scene for any more clues. Unfortunately, the ground was a hard packed gravel surface, which hampered the possibility of finding tire tracks, but off to the side, I noticed Barrett was showing some special interest at a small depression. Shining the flashlight on him, the remnants of a small dried up mud puddle became visible and in it, clear as a bell was an impression of a footprint in the thin layer of soft mud. *"That looks like it was made from a dress shoe, Madison,"* Robinson commented as I shined the light down on it. As we both studied it, I added, *"Yeah...a size nine or so.... definitely made by a relatively small man....you see the depth of the print?....I'd say the man weighed no more than one hundred sixty-five pounds or so."* Robinson nodded his head in agreement, replying, *"We need to get the lab boys up here to take a cast of this....I'll go to the car and make the call."*

As he walked away, my eyes looked down at the Motel below us. There were still several patrol cars and officers at the scene, shining their flashlights in various directions. However, one man in plain clothes quickly got my attention as he was standing away from the group at the end of the building, and he seemed to be looking for something. *"Who in the hell is that guy?"* I thought. Turning to go back to see how Robinson was making out, I met him after only taking a few steps. *"They're on their way up here,"* he said. *"It will be good to get a cast of that print."* Pointing to the man across the street, I asked, *"I wonder what that guy is doing and who is he?"* Robinson stared in the direction I was pointing in, replying, *"You mean the guy at the end of the building, Shake?.....that looks like Detective Harley....I can tell it's him by his walk....he's got a slight limp on the right side....bad hip, you know."* Continuing to stare at the man, I added, *"Well, he's been there for several minutes....what in the hell is he looking for?"* Robinson began watching the man for a few moments, as he walked back and forth near the end of the Motel. *"I don't know why he's over there, Madison, but there's no question he's looking for something.....but what?"*

Watching Harley eventually walk back to join the other men at the crime scene by my room door, I was still befuddled by his actions. Robinson still observing the man, added, *"Maybe he just dropped something, Madison....it happens you know."*

Possibly, Robinson was right, but my little voice was telling me something different, and as I turned to walk towards the car to join Barrett and him, a vehicle was approaching us from down the road. The lab boys had arrived and when they exited their car, Robinson quickly signaled to them where the foot impression was. *"I'll take you and Barrett back to the motel....the lab boys will finish up here,"* Robinson said starting the car. Piling in and as he backed up the vehicle, the headlights beamed onto the men taking the mould of the footprint, casting their long shadows against the gravel surface. Watching them pour the plaster, Robinson remarked, *"With that cast, at least we can determine the approximate size of the guy who took a shot at you and possibly the type of shoe that he was wearing......my theory makes me believe that it must be someone that you arrested in the past and hearing that you were back in town, they decided to settle some old scores....tomorrow I'll take a look at your file and pull out some of the possible suspects by looking at the smaller men with a history of gun violence.... what do you think?"*

As we continued to drive down the road, I was laughing to myself over Robinson's suggestion, thinking how far off base he was with this whole thing, and I really did not care about even giving him an answer. Talk about not being on the same page as me, he was actually a few pages behind. There was no doubt in my mind that the shooter was not from the past, but a hired gun, possibly associated with the Veratex corporation or even worse, someone who might be working for one of the crooked city officials. Observing the passing trees out the side window, I glanced over at Robinson who was trying to drive and light up a cigarette at the same time. I leaned my head back on the seat, closing my eyes, and remarked in a soft voice, *"That will be fine, Robinson.... you do that.....you know, this has been quite a day and the bed is going to feel really good tonight."* The detective, after exhaling a huge cloud of smoke, smiled, as his eyes gleamed at me. *"I'm sure it's going to, Shake.....I can't believe what happened here tonight..... we need to find and nail this bastard to the wall for what he tried to do...shooting a cop is dirty business and who ever tried it needs to pay, but I know what you mean about hitting the rack.......it will be a welcomed sight for me as well."* Not wasting anytime, Robinson pinned the accelerator to the floor and we sped off down the road, back to the motel.

CHAPTER FOURTEEN

A New Day

As the sun rose and gleamed through my picture window, its rays found my face. I had forgotten to close the drapes and although the warmth and brightness woke me earlier than usual, I felt refreshed and was ready to go. Feeling a little scrunched, I discovered that Barrett was completely sprawled out at the foot of the bed and was still fast asleep. Nudging him with my leg I said, *"Are you going to sleep the day away?.....come on, get up."* He stirred slightly and grunted, but only one eye opened to contest my suggestion and it quickly closed again. *"Get your ass up, we have a lot of work to do today."* Giving him a little push with my foot, this time both of his eyes opened and he raised his head, producing a big yawn. *"That's right, you big lazy bag of bones....it's time to get up!"* As Barrett rose, he placed his front paws out in front of him and arched his back in a huge stretch. Seeming anxious to face the day, he moved over to give me a huge lick on the side of my face, and jumped off the bed. *"Okay...okay, it's time for me as well,"* as I rose out of the bed and grabbed my pants. Barrett quickly made his way over to the door, signaling to me that it was time for his morning constitutional, and pulling my pants up I reached over and opened it. Within a flash, my partner disappeared from view and looking through the small crack between the door and the frame, I realized it was going to be another beautiful day. *"Three nice days in a row,"* I thought. *"This does not happen often in New England....I wonder how we are all gonna have to pay for it."*

Continuing to dress, I reached for my Smith and Wesson model 27, .357 Magnum revolver and placed it in my shoulder holster. It had been a long time favorite of mine and since being introduced in the mid 1930's, history had proven it a very dependable piece. With 125-grain bullets and producing over 500 ft-lbf of force, it was a far more stoppable weapon than the typical .38 carried by most law enforcement officials. Having holstered that weapon as well, which was a Smith and Wesson Model 15, I saw the ineffectiveness of that type of gun during my early years on the force, and I knew a change had to be made. Today, some of the guys were starting to carry semiautomatics, but they had proven to jam sometimes, something that revolvers never did. Call me a little old fashion, but as they say all the time, *"I would rather be living and walking around than pushing up grass with a semi on my hip."*

Putting on my sport coat, I reached for the gold watch off the dresser that Andrea had given me after completing my first year of sobriety. Often reading the inscription on the back, this morning was no exception, ***"To Shake....one year of truth and commitment...with love Andrea."*** Every time I saw it, a smile came to my face, and placing it on my wrist, I noticed myself in the mirror as I was much thinner now and my young chisel face had returned. During my drinking days, my features were bloated and the bags under my eyes were as big as a small woman's purse. Those were gone now and my face had returned to its original, normal color, not rosy red as it was during those ugly drinking and drugging years. No longer did I look more than twenty years older than my actual age and had a paunch overhanging my belt. Standing at over six feet in height and around two hundred and ten pounds, my frame looked straight and strong, something expected of a man in his mid 30's. *"My God do I look different now,"* I thought. *"If it wasn't for Andrea and my own guts, I would have never looked this good again....never mind, I might not even be alive today!"*

Lacing up my dress shoes, I heard a bark at the door telling me that Barrett was back and opening it, he promptly went over to his water dish and took a hefty drink. Grabbing my car keys off the dresser and watching him guzzle the water I said aloud, *"Come on....you've had enough....let's go and get some breakfast."* Exiting the motel room and closing the door behind us, I glanced towards the office and recalled my conversation last night with Zack before we were interrupted by the onslaught of police. Wondering if I should take another shot at him before breakfast, by asking him some more questions, I decided that it would be better to do it on a full stomach. Opening my car door to allow Barrett to jump into the front seat, I noticed that the curtain on the office window moved slightly to one side. *"Mmmm....he's worried at least,"* I thought. *"No doubt about it, I struck a chord with him....he's involved with this thing somehow, but question is how much?...I guess only time and putting a little more pressure on him will tell me that."*

After finishing breakfast at Tony's Diner, it was still early. I wanted to do some research at the assessor's office and with it only being 7:30 am there was a little bit of time to kill until City Hall opened. Driving by the Evergreen cemetery, I decided to pay a visit to my wife's grave as she had been on my mind lately. Parking the car along the access road, Barrett and I got out of the car and began walking up to my wife's stone. Sensing my well-being was on the rocks; Barrett whimpered and cried a little as we made our way to my wife's plot. Standing in front of her grave and taking his place beside me, Barrett looked up, almost appearing sympathetic to my situation. His deep yellow eyes, full of compassion kept staring at me, trying to offer support as we stood together at the grave. *"She was a good woman, ole boy.....you would have liked her,"* I said aloud as I rubbed his head and gave him a few pats. *"She was the love of my life....something a man only finds once in a lifetime."*

As we stood there, my mind went back to that time when we were together, expecting our first child, and the preparations we were making for it. The extreme happiness it gave to the both us was almost overwhelming and thinking of it, brought nothing but a smile to my face. Then as quickly as that thought came into my head, the reflection of loss crushed my serenity in an instant. *"All of that was taken away from me in a split second by someone,"* I mumbled while staring at her stone. *"Why did God abandon us and leave me with nothing but misery?....Jane was a beautiful, caring person that was full of life and should have never been taken so young.....if I could only find her killer, Barrett.....maybe I could find some peace and finally put this behind me."*

Then, my feelings suddenly turned to revenge and savagery, thinking what I would do to the man that was responsible for robbing me of everything and putting me on a path of self-destruction. *"Ole boy, I swear I'll put a bullet into that man's skull if I ever get a hold of him....that piece of shit doesn't deserve to live another day for what he did to us......the hell with the system and its whore lawyers....they'll only spare the bastard by saying he's insane and after keeping him caged up for a few years they'll let the son of a bitch out again to prey on someone else......no, when I find him, he'll be mine,"* as I patted my 357 beneath my coat.

Suddenly Barrett became alert, rigidly standing on all fours, and looked off to our left. As my eyes turned in that direction about seventy yards across the cemetery, I saw a middle-aged man getting into an old Buick. Barrett growled a little, causing me to say, *"Hold down there, boy....he's only visiting someone he knew in the past....there's nothing wrong."* My partner's eyes would not leave the man as he drove very slowly out the other exit and being too far away to make out any facial details, within a few moments, the stranger was gone.

Glancing down at my watch, I realized that it was time to leave for City Hall and while opening the door for Barrett, I looked over the roof of the car at my wife's grave. *"Don't worry hon, I'll find him......I swear to you, if it's the last thing I ever do on this earth, he will pay for what he did."* Closing my door, I started the car and sat there for a moment in my own thoughts. Barrett lying next to me on the front seat put his head on my lap, recognizing that my feelings were in turmoil and I needed a little help. *"That's one thing about you,"* I said looking down and rubbing him. *"You know how to take the pain away, don't you?"* Taking one last look at the grave, I put the car in drive and headed for the Assessor's office.

Turning into the City Hall parking lot, I noted that Director Birmingham was pulling into his reserved spot with his brand new Starfire. He definitely saw me and it was obvious by his quick walk into the building, he wanted no part of me. To avoid any more confrontation with anyone inside the building, I decided to leave Barrett in the car and not liking it at all he began to howl, but after a few consoling words I was able to quiet him down. Walking towards the building, I glanced back at him and of course, he was intently watching me through the windshield, making sure that I was okay. Once I disappeared into the building, I could not help myself from looking back through the glass in the heavy wooden doors to check on him. Seeing that my dedicated friend had promptly vanished from sight and knowing that he had lied down, I was satisfied that he had gone to sleep to await my return.

Entering the Assessor's office, there were two secretaries behind the counter at their desks shuffling paper work. They were elderly women with gray hair and looking like they were near to retirement, both of them looked up at me at the same time. Presenting my identification I said, *"Good morning, ladies.....My name is Detective Madison and I was hoping you could help me this morning on a few matters."* One of the women slowly stood up and gradually shuffled over to the counter. *"My name is Dolly, detective, and I would be glad to assist you."*

Studying the room behind her, it was filled with numerous metal filing cabinets, five drawers in height, and unlike the forensic lab technician's office, it was very neat and tidy as there were only a few loose papers stored on top of them and both of their wooden desks were very well organized. *"I would like some information on the properties owned by the Veratex Corporation..... you must be familiar with the large development company that is doing a lot of business in town, aren't you?"* There was very little reaction from either of them, but Dolly grinned at me slightly. *"Sure, Mr. Madison....that will be easy as we have a separate filing system set up for them because of their various land holdings.... which particular parcels would you be interested in?"*

Surprised at her answer, I thought, *"They actually own that much stuff in this town that they need a separate filing system?..... how much land can they own?"* After pondering for a moment I asked, *"You wouldn't have a master list of their current holdings, would you?"* Dolly looked over at the other woman and she nodded her head without looking up. *"Yes, we do,"* and she walked over to one of the steel cabinets, opening the top drawer. There, she pulled out a huge manila envelope that was about two inches thick and placed it on the counter in front of me. *"That's a detailed summary of the properties currently owned by them.....there are deeds to some of the major pieces of land in there as well....if you need deeds to the other properties, they would be filed in those cabinets.....you can use that room off to the side over there to work in and please let us know if you need anything else, okay?"*

Taking the large envelope I thanked her and moved to the adjacent room, which had a very hefty wooden table with several cushioned chairs surrounding it. The walls paneled with dark cherry wood and the floor covered with a rich red carpet, made it look more like a law firm's office than a room belonging to the city. Because there was only a picture of the mayor and a few other decorative paintings on the walls, I assumed that the room must have been generally used for meetings or conferences.

Pulling the material out of the envelope, on top of the stack was an alphabetical list, by street, of the properties owned by the corporation. Additionally, deed book and page number, acreage, valuation, and current tax bill for each property were listed for every piece of real estate. However, one thing immediately caught my eye and that was the number of pages contained in the master listing. Thumbing through them, there had to be at least twenty type written pages, listing more than sixty parcels throughout the entire town. Some of the pieces of land were hundreds of acres in size, which were in residential zones encompassing huge subdivisions that totaled several thousand homes.

By the valuations listed for each lot, they were hardly homes for low-income people as some of the recent sales involved a lot of money. Putting the figures together, I determined from the notes made by the assessors in the margins, that their calculations for assessment of adjacent land parcels for setting tax amounts were based upon these figures. There was no doubt by the calculations that people owning land next to these developments were seeing a huge increase in their property taxes due to the increases in their evaluations. As a result, with increases of their property values, the adjacent landowners could not afford the excessive taxes on their land that they were assessed. More disturbingly, according to the deed transfers, Veratex was not buying the land directly from the landowners, but was allowing the city to take the land due to non-payment of taxes through the tax title process. Once the city took possession, they would in turn sell the piece of real estate to the Veratex Company, which was much less than the inflated evaluation.

"What a sweet deal," I thought. *"At first, the company comes into town and starts buying up a few parcels of land....then they begin developing it by selling high end homes to outside individuals....when the adjacent landowners can't afford their taxes because of increased valuations of their properties, the city takes possession of it through the tax title process for nonpayment of taxes.....a few months later, the city conveys it to the Veratex Corporation for pennies on the dollar, who then develops it at a huge profit....and the biggest problem of it all.....it's all semi-legal with the city's help."*

Continuing to examine the file, it became evident that they were conducting the same scheme to acquire apartment buildings and other multifamily dwellings, utilizing the same process. By the deed transfers it was obvious too, that they were gaining ownership of these complexes at a rapid pace, rehabilitating them, and selling them at a huge profit. Additionally, they appeared to be keeping ownership of some of the *"choice"* buildings and charging much higher rents, putting some old town residents out into the street.

The most sickening part of the whole scheme, however, was that the Veratex Cooperation acting as its own bank was lending money to middle class and low-income families at an inflated mortgage rate. According to one of the foreclosure documents, if only one payment by the buyer was late by fifteen days, the company had the right to foreclose on the property. The Veratex Corporation acting through its own bank would then seize the property and sell it again, making even more money. It was obvious the corporation had cared less for the city's residents and was solely in it to make massive amounts of money. My mind rambled on with me muttering to myself. *"This is a far cry from what Russ had told me about this company and how it was beneficial to the town....oh, from the outside it appeared that the mayor's 'program' was good for the city, but in reality it was nothing but a crooked scheme to make certain people rich."*

As I continued to plow through the master list, my eyes noticed several handwritten notations in the margins next to some of the properties. Suddenly, my scanning eyes stopped at one particular parcel at #351 Spring Street, the location of the apartment building that the third victim, Kyle Swanson resided at. The Veratex Corporation did own it, but there was writing in the margin noting the name Kyle Peabody, the date, and two numbers, 1150 - 28. Pondering on it for a moment, I got up, and exited the room with the sheet in my hand. *"Excuse me....can either of you two ladies tell me about these handwritten notations in the margin, specifically next to 351 Spring Street?"* Showing them the sheets, Dolly looked up from her desk over her glasses and peered at the papers for a moment. *"Oh, detective...those are past deed transactions that we haven't been able to record yet....we use those to correctly adjust our master lists and files."*

Wanting to know more I pressed on with, *"The people that purchase these properties, do they ever come into this office to verify their ownership?"* Dolly shook her head handing me back the papers. *"No....not usually...we get the notification of the deed transfers from the Registry of Deeds....like the one for 351 Spring Street.... it was conveyed on March 26, 1962 to a Kyle Peabody and the deed is recorded in book 1150 page 28 at the Land Registry.....when we get the time, our master list and our files are updated to reflect those changes.....usually the Registry sends us a copy of the deed within a few days after the transaction and we keep that on file as well."*

My curiosity was bulging at the seams causing me to ask, *"You wouldn't have a deed copy of 351 Spring Street, yet....would you?"* The secretary got up from her desk, wandered over to another file cabinet, and took out a stack of papers. Thumbing through them she remarked, *"These are the deeds we need to file yet....let me see here....ahh....here it is....351 Spring Street."* As she handed me the deed, my eyes went directly to the top of the page. Where it read, *"The Veratex Corporation, being a company in good standing, based in Erie, Pennsylvania, hereby conveys the following property located at 351 Spring Street, located in the City of Harrisburg, Massachusetts, Worcester county to Kyle Peabody, (Swanson), for the total price of one hundred dollars ($100.00) bounded and described as follows....."*

Reading those words sent a chill up my spine as Peabody was evidently the victim's maiden name. Suddenly the realization of selling a piece of property for one hundred dollars that should have sold for fifty thousand did not make a whole lot of sense to me, unless the Veratex Corporation had tried to buy her off. Was this because she was about to expose the crooked scheme that was currently going on in the city or was she part of it? And this conveyance was payment for her assistance on the zoning changes?

Then another idea entered my mind, thinking that maybe this property was not enough to buy her silence and she had become a liability to them. Suddenly the heads of the corporation found themselves in a real pickle and with no other choice at hand; they resorted to a more permanent solution? Like having, her killed? My mind was running at hyper speed now with so many thoughts and accusations bouncing in my head that I needed to calm myself down a little. Taking a few deep breaths to bring my mind under control, I realized that the pieces of the puzzle were finally coming together and the picture was becoming clear. Knowing that her murder was similar to the others, it was also different in many respects as well. Did they try to make it look like she was just another unfortunate victim who would be thrown aside and conveniently forgotten about by everyone?

I went back to the table in the conference room and began analyzing the master list for other recent conveyances, hoping to find more clues. However, none of the other names handwritten in the margins jumped out at me as being other city employees, but one name in particular appeared many times and that was the M&S Realty Trust. They had acquired several apartment buildings along with a single large parcel of land on Hammond Street. Stepping back out into the room, I asked the elderly woman, *"Dolly, the M&S Realty Trust.....do you know anything about them?"* She politely replied, *"No, I don't......there are literally hundreds of trusts in this city, detective....you will have to research that at the tax collectors office to find out who belongs to it."*

Thinking, that the answer to this problem was probably sitting upstairs in the Planning Director's office, I thanked the women for their cooperation and asked for copies of the Swanson and other pertaining documents, which they provided me. Placing everything into my briefcase, I headed upstairs, and upon reaching the planning office, I asked for Director Birmingham. Knowing that I had ruffled his feathers the last time, the secretary was extremely cold towards me, but she still buzzed the intercom, telling him that I was there to see him.

When I entered his office, the director appeared to be very busy with some paperwork that was piled up on his desk and not looking up at me he softly said, *"What can I do for you now, detective?....seems to me we discussed everything about Kyle the last time you were here."* Taking a seat in front of his desk, I placed my briefcase on my lap and opened it. Taking out my note pad, I placed the case beside my chair on the floor. Smirking a little,

I replied, *"I want to know if you have heard of or have anything to do with the M&S Realty Trust."* He immediately looked up at me and gave me a cold stare. *"Never heard of it....don't know what you're talking about."* Smiling back at him, I responded, *"Just like you never knew anything about Kyle Swanson, your assistant?.... like having an affair with her for months and hiding it from your wife?"*

His face filled with redness as he got up from his desk and turned his back towards me. Rubbing the rear of his neck, he desperately tried to massage the stiffness out of it. *"You won't quit on that, will you Madison?.....you think I killed her, don't you?....to keep her quiet about our so called affair....well, I'll let you in on a little secret, detective.... you're dead wrong."* I watched him as he continued to knead the back of his neck and with each passing moment, the rubbing became harder. He was flustered for sure and I knew with a little more coaxing, I was going to have him for lunch. *"You had motive, sir and you knew if your rich wife ever found out about the affair, the game was over for you, and the money would have went bye bye....maybe Kyle was going to spill the beans on your relationship to your wife or maybe she was just blackmailing you for a piece of the pie?....ummh?"* That is all it took as he spun around and pointed his finger right at me, beat red in the face. *"You're a prying piece of shit, detective and you make me puke with your sickening accusations.....yes, I did have an affair with my assistant, but when I found out she was seeing other people, that's when it ended!"*

Those words really got my attention. *"Come on Birmingham, what kind of shit are you trying to spread around here now?"* He continued to glare at me with rage in his eyes and I could see his hands start to shake as he tried to wring out the stress in them by rubbing them together. Then a sadistic grin came to his face, appearing as if he had turned into Mr. Hyde. *"Big detective....thinks he has all the answers....well, Mr. Madison let me inform you of something....you don't.... in fact, you don't have jack shit....actually, your summation of our relationship is so far off base, you better go back to detective school.......you see, Kyle was a nymphomaniac.....*

*she loved her sex and one person was just not good enough for her....
she had to have many people and I was just a play toy for her as I
was nothing but a resident male for a short period of time.....you
see, she used me until something better came along and when that
happened, I was left out in the cold.....so, detective, before you go
running off at the mouth, get your facts straight!"*

He hung his head after saying that and I could hear a slight
sob coming out of him as he wiped his eyes a few times. What
a pathetic sight, I thought, as he continued to bury himself in
self-pity, trying not to lose it completely in front of me. *"Okay,
Birmingham....so she dumped you.....that still gives you a motive
for killing her."* He immediately gazed up at me with red eyes and
wetness all around them, looking like a broken man. Glaring back
at me he cleared his throat a couple of times, saying, *"I loved that
girl....not just in a physical sense, but on a professional level too....
she was everything to me as she handled the daily operations in this
office with the utmost efficiency....the records she carefully kept on
our new rehabilitation program through the mayor's office was a
model for anyone to use, but she was more than that to me....she was
my love, my life.....she was truly an amazing girl."*

Upon saying that, tears ran down his rosy red cheeks like a
schoolgirl who had been neglected to be asked to the prom. He
was about to completely break apart, but I needed to push him
a little more. *"So....when you were dumped for another man, you
killed her, right?"* Birmingham laughed and wiped his face, staring
at me as if I had two heads. *"Detective...you're not too smart are
you?.....I wasn't dumped for another man....I was thrown to the side
like a piece of garbage for another woman!"*

Birmingham's laugh grew louder with each passing second
and by the expression on my face; I guess he was getting a real
charge out of it. *"Kyle was a great girl, Madison, but she had one
flaw.....she liked to party....I mean really party....drugs, booze and
sex....she loved it all and she could never satisfy her craving for it.....
seemed the more she got, the more she wanted.....hell, she didn't care
if it was a woman or a man.....as long as she could get her rocks off,*

she didn't care who was on the other end....when I found out that she was seeing another woman and was in love with her, it made me sick....so sick, that I wanted to fire her, but before I could get the courage up to do it, she was dead.....besides, she was really good in her job and was a great asset to the city....I probably would have never fired her and just kept my mouth shut."

I lit up a smoke, studying him, trying to determine if he was giving me a ration of crap or was actually confessing the truth. His demeanor seemed to be changing as he became more relaxed and his hands stopped shaking, looking like he was finally at peace with himself. "Okay, Birmingham.....so, who was her girlfriend that she dumped you for?" A slight smirk came from the corner of his mouth as he looked up at me. "At first I did not know who it was, but I began following her as I suspected she was cheating on me.....you know, trying to find out what man she was seeing and if there might be a chance I could get her back....sounds stupid now, but I was desperate......expecting some rich guy or something, I was taken aback when I followed her over to the Spirit Arms Motel one night....that's when I was stunned to find her in bed with that drug dealing bitch and they weren't just bunking together either, if you know what I mean.....what I saw that night through that window would have made any man's hair curl."

Taking a huge drag off my butt, I exhaled the smoke slowly, looking directly at him. He had a smug look on his face, looking very content, almost telling me with his eyes to take a flying leap. Shocked by his story, I cleared my throat and asked, "Who was she?" With a glaring eye, he responded, "Jenkins, of course...the one that was found dead the other day.....she was dealing drugs out of the motel for months and playing with that bitch, Swanson..... however, what really set me off, I discovered everybody knew about it except me, including some of the cops."

Birmingham stood up from his desk, walked over to the water cooler and pulled a paper cup from the dispenser. Filling it and taking a few sips from it, he turned to face me once again, smiling to beat the band. "So, detective.....you can see it wasn't me, can't you?.....someone else killed her and that person must be the serial killer....just hard luck, I guess, her being in the wrong place at the wrong time."

Warning bells sounded in my head when he said that. How did he know about the serial killer as everyone at the station had kept it under wraps? *"What's this business about a killer being on the loose, Birmingham?.....what makes you think that?"* I asked while crushing out my cigarette in the ashtray on his desk. Again, he smiled, looking like he was glowing inside, thinking he was way ahead of me. *"One of the cops told me and of course the paper is not helping matters much.... have you seen the headline today?..... 'Possible Serial Killer Stalks Harrisburg....Police Baffled'.....you don't have to be a big time detective like yourself to figure that one out!"*

His chuckling broke out into roaring laughter as he watched me digest what he had just said. I felt like an idiot and watching him snicker and mock me just made things worse. I could only imagine what the chief was yelling back at the station at everyone, since it appeared that the *"cat was out of the bag."* Thinking for a moment, trying to think of a quick response to his ridicule and obnoxious laughter, I finally lost my temper. Swiftly grabbing him by the front of the shirt and pressing him up against the wall, I ripped into him. *"Listen you piece of shit, I know you killed her.... you couldn't take being jilted like that and your pride made you snuff her....imagine big man, another woman being more sexually satisfying than yourself!"*

Suddenly, he shook my grip of him and shoved me backwards, yelling, *"You still think you have it all figured out, don't you?.....well, mister let me fill you in on a little something....what I saw through that motel window that night made me vomit....the bitch was nothing but a two bit whore who had an itch between her legs that she let anyone scratch....yeah, at first I was appalled and wanted to kill her for what she had done to me, but then I realized something... I was totally off the hook and finally free!......I could simply walk away and be free of Swanson's spell because that's just what it was, you know....she could make a man feel things that only a hard ass drug would do....but now, seeing those two in bed I realized I could go back to my wife without her knowing a damn thing....my wife's money or should I say my money would be safe and secure!...."* He poked me in the chest, stared directly into my eyes and said loudly, *"And I could go on with my God damn life and enjoy it!"*

Again, he broke out into hysterics, almost choking on his own laughter as he sat back down behind his desk, leaving me standing there, dumbfounded. Lighting up another cigarette, he leaned back in his chair and took a few puffs, watching me wallow in my thoughts. *"Pretty bad, huh?....I mean to be caught with your pants down, detective.....just when you think you have it all figured out..... wham!....someone throws cold water on you and it's all gone....that's it!....no more case against Director Birmingham and you have to start all over!"*

Laughing and choking on the smoke, he grinned at me, appearing like the pompous ass he was. I could not stand the sight of him any longer and thinking Barrett had been in the car alone far too long I slowly headed for the door. Birmingham's laughter grew louder with every step I took and as I opened his office door he said loudly, *"You have a good day, detective.....the man that knows it all.....the man that supposedly knows everything about everybody!.....well, good luck, detective on finding another sucker to dispense your so called justice upon!"*

Slowly closing the door of his office behind me, I could still hear his loud laughter while the two secretaries stared at me as I passed their desks towards the counter. With both of them wondering what was going on, I walked gradually towards the exit door, but stopped for a second and while turning my head I said softly, *"Ladies, you both have a nice day."* Then flashing a little smile at the both of them, I slowly opened the door and disappeared down the hallway.

CHAPTER FIFTEEN
Time to Reflect

Walking back to the car my mind was a jumbled mess as the case was becoming nothing but a tangled nightmare. How could I have been so wrong and jumped to the conclusion of Birmingham being the killer? Kyle Swanson, a young respected businesswoman who seemed to have it all was actually a full-fledged drug user and a real party girl. Shockingly from what I had learned, she used men and woman like sex toys to fulfill her needs with little remorse. Was her secret life the real reason behind her death? Did the darkness of drugs, booze and sex parties finally catch up with her? By Birmingham's account, she was Lori Jenkins's lover, a known drug dealer who was walking a thin line herself. Jenkins was even dead now either by the hands of the serial killer or someone else due to a bad drug deal. On the other hand, had Jenkins been caught up in Swanson's perilous investigation of City Hall? The various scenarios were driving me crazy, but the main problem whirling in my head hit me with a vengeance. *"What was going to be my next move?"*

As I approached the car, I saw Barrett in the back seat, patiently waiting for me. Seeing that I was near, he immediately rose to his feet trying to stick his nose through the small crack in the partially opened side window. Opening the driver's side door and sitting in the seat he quickly licked the back of my neck, showing his appreciation of my return. *"That's enough, ole boy.... we are in a world of shit now.....looks like we need to take a whole* new look at this thing," I said aloud as I continued to pat him, hoping that he could provide some comfort. Barrett was always good for that and now more than ever I needed him because in the back of my head some other type of liberation was trying to bust into my mind. Trying to push the thoughts of the bottle away, I started the car and drove out of the parking lot, pondering my next move.

Heading down Main Street, passing the police station, I thought of what had happened the other night. *"Someone tried to kill me.....I must be getting close,"* I mumbled. *"After all, why try and take me out or at least give me a warning to back off?.....it must have been someone experienced with weapons as the custom loaded shells were proof of that, but the shot was not difficult and he should have had me cold..... did he miss me on purpose or did he just screw up the shot?"*

Then, my mind turned to the link of Swanson's involvement with the Veratex Corporation and the transfer of property to her. *"Was the apartment building an actual payoff to keep her mouth shut?.....or was it a fruitless attempt and since she was probably going to spill the beans, they took her out?.....but how does all of this relate to the motel murders of Tina Hendricks and Lori Jenkins, the drug dealer?.....Swanson definitely knew Jenkins as they were lovers....Birmingham stated that and he seemed believable when he did....and why would he lie about something like that?....after all, finding out that your girlfriend has dropped you like a hot potato for another woman is something that a man does not easily admit."*

As thoughts spun around in my head, I knew if Birmingham was telling the truth, he did not have anything to do with the Swanson murder or the others for that matter. However, with the evidence so far, it was becoming obvious that there had to be more than one murderer as all of the killings were similar, but different in many respects as well. Reviewing in my head what Zack had told me, I knew he had been involved with the fourth victim, Tina Hendricks, an employee of his motel. Nonetheless, he had not been very candid and my little voice was telling me that there was only one thing to do now, and that was to press Zack to the limit, as he appeared to be the key to the case.

Driving the couple of miles back to the Motel gave me some extra time to think about the small notebook that I had found in Jenkins's room. Considering the volume of drug business that she was conducting there, it had to be known by someone in the department, and if it was allowed to go on....then why? And by whom? Trying to recall some of the names in the notebook only made my head spin faster so I decided to pull over to the side of the road. With the car coming to a sliding stop on the gravel shoulder, I took the black notebook out of my pocket and began thumbing through the pages containing the numerous names, trying to recognize any of them. It was amazing on some of the amounts that were written next to the various entries as it entailed thousands of dollars and it involved not just several people, but dozens. So many, it made me start to wonder what some of the killings were actually about. *"Any one of these people had a motive for killing Jenkins,"* I thought scanning the various names. *"All this book does is complicate things even more by giving us a huge round of suspects....looking at this long list of clients, especially when drugs and money were in the mix, there are just too many people that might have wanted her to disappear."*

Studying the pages filled with names, frustration started to take hold, but finally reaching the last page of the book, a notation at the very bottom caught my eye. The initials T.H. were inscribed with an arrow through them and there was a heavy dark circle written around the letters as well. Underneath the doodling, was the word, *"betrayal"* with a sad face next to it. A light bulb came on in my head, thinking the initials T.H. might be that of Tina Hendricks. Was Zack's employee a drug user as well? This only confirmed my suspicions and not wanting to waste anymore time, I pushed the accelerator to the floor, sending gravel flying out the back of the car. Knowing that Zack might hold the key to all of this now, and since there was a glimmer of hope again of solving the case I sped back to the motel.

As the vehicle came to a screeching halt in front of the main office, Barrett knew I was onto something. He did not wait for me to open his door as he leaped through the open side window and followed me into the building. Zack was sitting behind the counter at his desk and by his look; I knew he dreaded the thought of speaking to me again. *"Okay, Zack....it's time to stop the bull shit,"* I said plowing my way up to the counter. *"Was Hendricks on drugs?....and was she being supplied by Lori Jenkins?"* Holding the notebook up I added, *"And don't try and deny it....I have her payment book right here."*

Surprisingly, Zack stood up and walked over to the counter, staring at the notebook in my hand. *"You found it, ehh?.....yeah, Tina was on drugs....she had been for a long time and I tried to get her off them, but Jenkins's hold on her was too strong......she needed the drugs all the time and Jenkins gave them to her.....that's the main reason why I let her stay and do business here....I had to keep the drugs handy for Tina, but she needed Jenkins for something else as well."*

Zack looked away from me after saying that and refused to make anymore eye contact. Staring out the window, I knew something incredible was eating him up inside as his eyes began to water. *"What do you mean she needed her for something else?"* I asked grabbing him by the shoulder and forcing him to look at me. Zack's body posturing became weak as he slumped into a submissive mode. His shoulders drooped, with his body leaning forward, and his head looked downwards at the floor as it was clear that he was having difficulty gathering the strength to answer me. *"I suppose you're going to find this out anyway, Shake, so I might as well tell you....Tina and I were lovers....I know you must think that's a little sick, but our age difference was never a problem with us.... we were happy together and really enjoyed being with each other..... at least that's the way it was until Lori Jenkins came along.....she got Tina hooked on drugs and on herself you might say.....you see, Shake, Lori could almost cast a spell over people.....making them do things they never thought possible....I should know as she forced me do things that would have caused a normal person to cringe."*

I could see a tear beginning to run down his right cheek while his emotional state went into the abyss. *"Okay...what are you trying to tell me, Zack?.....did you kill her?"* Quickly, he looked up at me with disgust and contempt on his face. *"How can you stand there and accuse me of such a thing?....especially when we have been friends for such a long time.....I loved Tina and I loved Lori too.... our wild times together were filled with unbelievable happiness and passion, but at the same time it brought us nothing but heartache..... you're probably not going to comprehend this, but the three of us together were lovers."*

As he hung his head lower, my mind was traveling at the speed of light, attempting to pull some sense out of the whole mess. *"Don't tell me you were screwing the both of them?"* I asked lighting up a cigarette. Of course, Barrett looked up at me, while I lit the match, and he promptly scampered over to the far corner to avoid the smoke. Zack watched him trot across the room and grinned slightly. *"The only smart one of the bunch....he knows what's not good for him and he avoids it....not like the rest of us who just keep doing something that makes us fall deeper into the bottomless pit of misery."* I touched him on the shoulder and Zack looked back at me with a red-faced glare. His eyes were cold, lifeless, and with nothing behind them, he continued to gaze at me with not even a hint of emotion. *"Yeah, I was screwing the both of them, if you want to call it that......you see, Shake, they were screwing each other, as well.....we did everything together and I do mean everything..... you know what I mean?"*

I had to take a deep drag on my cigarette to take in those words and as I did, a slight grin came to Zack's face. It pleased him to see me agitated about his antics and he seemed happy to elaborate further. *"The type of sex we had was something no person can describe....Lori was always full of surprises and it made Tina and I feel really good inside....so good, in fact, that I even experimented with drugs myself as it only made the sex better.....more powerful, more exhilarating.....hell, I could screw all night long on the stuff and the girls loved it......you can't even imagine what it was like, Shake....here I was almost twice their age, banging the hell out of them, just like a young kid with the stamina of a raging bull....I could make them come again and again.....their screams of passion only made me screw them harder.....I thought it would never end, but all of it did.... in one, horrific night."*

Naturally, his confession deepened my interest, as I knew something was coming over the horizon and it was not going to be good. *"Okay....go on Zack...what happened that night?"* His face turned purplish red as he replied, *"That night, after Swanson died, we were all going to have one of our little sessions together, but that's when I discovered that Tina had found out about Kyle Swanson and Lori Jenkins."* I could barely comprehend what he was telling me, but I also recalled what Birmingham had told me about seeing those two together through the window one night at the motel. Wanting to verify this fact, I quickly interrupted him. *"Don't tell me Kyle Swanson and Jenkins were lovers, too?"* Zack chuckled as he sat behind his desk, rubbing his face with a far away look in his eye, seeming to be enjoying the memories of the good times with the girls. Then suddenly his behavior changed and a look of anger came upon his face. *"Yep....and when Tina found out about it, she went ballistic, but when Lori suspected that Tina had killed Swanson in a jealous rage, that's when Lori swore revenge and that night is when she satisfied it."*

That was too much for me to process as hearing that story burnt through my mind like a red-hot piece of iron through wax. Tina Hendricks killed Swanson? Did Zack actually know this for a fact? Staring back at him I said, *"Hold on for a minute....let me try and get this straight....Lori Jenkins was having sex with Kyle Swanson while she was screwing you and Tina?.... and when Tina found out about it, she killed Swanson in a jealous rage?....are you serious?....and how can you be so certain about this?"*

He looked away for a moment and pondered, trying to get his emotions under control. Then with conviction plastered all over his face he said, *"If you could have seen what Lori did to Tina that night, there can be no doubt in my mind who killed Swanson.....that night at the Motel, Lori was her usual wild self when we started our threesome together, but later she suddenly turned into a wild animal....before I knew it, she was grabbing Tina by the hair and ripping it out....then she picked up a large heavy ash tray from the end table and began beating her with it....the savagery of the woman was beyond belief as she pounded on Tina's face and head with it..... soon, blood was everywhere and our naked bodies were covered in it.....the walls, bed linens and portions of the carpeting were all drenched in blood.....it was like a horror movie that had come alive, but I was of little help because I was pretty loaded on drugs and booze.....hell, I just laid there and tried to get my senses back, thinking that this could not be happening......before I was able to pull Lori off, the horrible deed had been done and Tina's lifeless body was sprawled out on the bed in a mass of blood. Her skull had been split wide open and with her eyes rolled backwards in her head, that's when I realized she was dead.....so I....."*

Before he could continue rambling on, I cut him off again. *"Wait a minute...just you hold on there, I need to get this straight...... you said she killed her in the motel?....was it room 112?....the room that I found the key to?"* Nervously, Zack lit up another cigarette, lighting it with the one that he had going already. His hands were shaking so badly that he dropped both of them to the floor and picking them up, he attempted to align them once again. Crushing the spent butt out into the ashtray, he puffed heavily on the newly lit cigarette while rubbing his forehead. Knowing that his ass was in a jam and I was about to slam the door on it, he forced the smoke in and out of his lungs. *"You have to understand, Shake....I had nothing to do with the murder....Lori was out of her mind with jealousy and hatred.....she went mental on Tina as the thought of Tina killing Kyle Swanson was just too much for her to take.....yes, I was there and eventually tried to stop it, but I swear to God that I never took part in it....so help me."* He continued to pull heavy on his butt, exhaling huge amounts of smoke into the room, and his eyes looked like a scared animal that had just been trapped in a cage. Glaring at him, I said loudly, *"You must have had something* to do with it, Zack....Tina's body was not found in that room, but down by the river and I know it didn't just magically appear there.... what do you have to say about that?"

Again, he looked down, hanging his head like an ashamed piece of crap, trying to gather his thoughts once again. I could sense he was desperately pulling together the right words, as he knew anything he said to me now might put him away for a very long time. "You're right, Shake....after I knew she was dead, a feeling of panic came over me....if anyone had discovered the body in my motel, I knew with my record it would have been curtains for this boy, so I needed to do something quick about disposing of the body......Lori was no help at all as she had gone into some kind of psychotic shock.....it scared me actually, as her eyes were big and full, looking like she was totally off her nut....she just sat there, emotionless and still, staring off into space not saying a word......then without warning, everything seemed to slow down.... it was like I was in a dream and my fear suddenly disappeared...then, actually being able to think, a solution came to me....why not place the body down by the river?....with all of the other bodies being discovered there, what was one more?...it just would have gotten mixed up with the other killings, right?.....so, I cleaned up the room, burned all of the linens and disposed of the mattress at the dump....temporarily, I had to store the body in the bathtub until the place was cleaned up and later I hauled it down to the river...I guess my cleanup job was not good enough because you found some evidence of blood around the bathtub drain.......and Lori?, well, she was.....” Once again I interrupted him by saying, "Why didn't you call the police?....after all, Jenkins killed Hendricks, not you....plus, how did you know about the serial killer?"

With a heavy sigh, he stared out the office window and I knew he was hoping that this was just a bad dream. "I was in love with Lori, too, Shake....or at least I thought I was....she had a talent for making a man feel things that are hard to explain....the drugs....the sex....it was all part of it and I wanted it to go on....I know what I did was wrong, but she made me nuts....crazy with desire....crazy with *a need that only a drug could provide....so I did what was needed to protect her, but in the end all of it was for nothing, for she is gone too."*

Feeling sorry for himself, he fell back into his office chair and whimpered, sobbing uncontrollably with his face clutched in his hands. What a pathetic sight, I thought staring at him. How a man could let himself be sucked into a situation like that was beyond me, but it was obvious that Zack had been broken by a woman who seemed to possess almost a demonic power over him. He had always been a very sensible man, but the immersion into a world of drugs and sex had taken all of that away from him. The number of charges against the man were many and he knew it as he cried, wiping the tears away several times with the back of his sleeves.

Walking around the counter, I placed my hand lightly on his shoulder. *"So....what about the serial killer?.....and Lori Jenkins?.... you killed her for what she did to Hendricks, didn't you?* His head quickly snapped up and with tears running down his cheeks, yelled, *"Detective Harley told me all about the serial killer rampaging this city and how all of their bodies were being found down by the river, strangled by parachute cord....he's got a big mouth, you know, especially when he has been drinking.....so I tied a piece of cord around her neck with a square knot and put her in a suitcase down by the river, but I was real careful about wearing gloves and all, especially when I staged the scene in the breakfast room when I smeared and splattered her blood around with her body by hitting it some more with a crowbar......but the main issue at hand is....I didn't kill Lori Jenkins! .....I loved her for God's sake!....like I told you, Shake I loved them both....I never would have done anything to hurt either of them....Shake, be the detective that you are supposed to be for Christ's sake and go find the psychotic son of bitch that killed Lori!"*

He returned his face to his hands and continued sobbing. No question about it, he was a total mess and I knew then I had to make the call to the station. After all, at the very minimum, he was involved in the murder of one girl and possibly another as

I watched him melt down in front of me. *"I'm sorry Zack...but I need to take you in for the murder of Tina Hendricks and Lori Jenkins.....at the very least, there's illegal disposing of a corpse and there are probably going to be a few other charges as well, but we'll let the courts decide your fate......I'm truly sorry old friend, but there is really no other choice...I have to do my job."*

As I walked over to the phone on the wall, Zack's sobbing seemed to subside and dialing for the operator, I could hear a desk drawer open. *"You just don't understand, do you, Shake?.....I loved both of those girls!...they meant everything to me.....well, I have a job to do myself....good bye!"* Just as I turned to see what he was doing, I saw the revolver being hauled out of the desk drawer. Quickly drawing my own weapon from its holster in an attempt to shoot him before he got me, a weird type of smirk came to Zack's face as he placed the muzzle tightly under his chin. With his grin growing wider, he pulled the trigger. Bang! The top of his head exploded from the muzzle blast and pieces of skull, blood, and hair splattered on the wall behind him, creating a red sun of scattered debris. Startled by the shot, Barrett jumped to his feet, trying to ascertain the situation, while I stood there in awe with my eyes glaring at the disfigured head of my long time friend. The top of his skull was completely gone and as he slouched in his chair, the strange grin that was painted on his face remained as his eyes stared downwards at the floor. Rivulets of blood ran down the side of his face and as it slowly dripped onto the linoleum floor, a small puddle formed next to the smoking .38 Smith and Wesson snub-nosed pistol.

After a few moments had passed, Barrett walked cautiously towards him, and placed one paw on his knee, almost trying to speak to him, but after recognizing it was hopeless, he turned his head at me. I reached out with my hand and patted Barrett on the forehead a couple of times, looking at my furry partner with sadness in my eyes. Trying not to let my voice crack and attempting to hold my emotions in check I said aloud, *"He's gone, boy....there's absolutely nothing we can do for him."*

CHAPTER SIXTEEN
All Hell Breaks Loose

After calling the station, I waited for the ambulance to arrive along with members of the department. Since it took them several minutes to get there, I sat down in the office and tried to understand what had just happened. My old friend that I had known for so many years had just taken his life and *"for what?"* I thought. No doubt, that drugs, booze, and sex had taken its toll on my long time friend and it had finally caught up with him, but should I have seen it coming? Looking at him sitting there, staring at the floor with his arms drooped by his side, I could not help remembering him trying to help me through the death of my wife. He had been a good friend during that horrible period as he was there for me when I needed it most. If it were not for Zack during those tough times, I probably would have ended up just like him as I stared at his lifeless body in the chair.

It almost killed me when I arrested him several years ago for the bookie operation that he was conducting at his place, but as always, being a cop; I had a job to do. Now, he was gone....at his own hand....because he had slipped into a world of wickedness.....a world of drugs and sex that in his mind had really left him only one way out, but why as I thought, rubbing Barrett's head as he sat beside me. How could have Zack allowed himself to get in so deep? To be involved with two women half his age, one being a drug pusher and the other who experimented with the wild and fast life. How could he have done this to himself?

Then, like turning channels on a TV set, my thoughts went back to my own existence less than three years ago when I was lying in the gutter, waking from a drunken stupor and how I had nearly died from it. Luckily, I was saved by a woman who cared for me and set my sickened body on the path of recovery. Yes, Andrea had helped to save my life and there was little debate regarding it, but as I looked over at Zack, sitting there lifeless, with a few houseflies already crawling over his bloodied face and starting their natural process, the irony of the whole situation hit me like a ton of bricks. The stark recognition that his road was an entirely different one, where women had been his actual demise not his savior, robbing him of everything. The thought of it shook my inner soul as they had taken his dignity, integrity and eventually the ultimate thing we all have.... and that is life.

As the many officers eventually invaded the scene, it was extremely chaotic at first with emergency personnel trying to attend to Zack, but within minutes, everyone realized it was hopeless. Detective Robinson naturally questioned me on what had happened and to my surprise Marty Sloan, the mayor's assistant was at the scene as well. *"What's he doing here?"* I asked Robinson pointing at Sloan. The detective turned his head and glanced in the direction I was pointing in. *"Him?....I really don't know...all I was told is that Sloan has a free reign in this case and is not to be interfered with.....at least that's what came down from the chief..... why, I couldn't tell you."*

As we both stared at Sloan, his eyes caught ours and realizing this, he walked over to us with a look of concern and disgust all rolled into one. *"Can you tell me what's going on here, Madison?..... can't you even arrest someone without causing a mess?.....I suggest you get this cleaned up and file your final report ASAP as it looks like we finally have our serial killer."* With a glare in my eye I replied, *"It's pretty God damn obvious what happened here, isn't it?....I'm sure even a man with a small intellect such as yours can comprehend it......besides, Zack was a really good friend of mine and for him to go out like this is a God damn shame....a tragedy actually....I* think...." Suddenly Sloan came nearer to me and pushed his finger into my chest. Loudly, he exclaimed, *"Listen up, Madison....your so called friend was a serial killer....a real sick son of bitch who preyed on woman and treated their bodies like garbage.....and to top it off, the chief is getting real tired of your incompetence and lack of judgment on this case.....he wants you out of his city, so you better wrap this thing up, file your damn reports and go back to Hicksville where you belong......and you can take that stinking mutt with you!"*

With a burst of temper gone bad, I shoved him backwards into the wall and hitting it hard, Sloan shook his head in a daze while rubbing the back of his head. Barrett knew I was beside myself and promptly took his position next to me, just waiting for the man to counter attack. Sloan regaining his senses looked down at Barrett and then to me. *"That's why this city got rid of you, Madison.....I suppose you are still hung over from the night before and can't wait to go back to your hotel room to numb that pickled brain of yours....that the reason why no one will even work with you anymore......and to be truthful and blunt, that's why you have that smelly animal as your sidekick."*

Just then, Barrett took a few steps toward Sloan, seeming to understand every word the man had said about us. The mayor's assistant reached into his jacket and within seconds, I saw the butt end of a revolver, begin to appear. *"If that mutt takes another step at me, Madison, I'll blow him away!"* he said loudly, attempting to pull his gun. In a flash, I lunged at the man, grabbing him by the front of his suit coat, and forced the piece of crap up against the wall. With a deep growl Barrett was right behind me while I hollered, *"You better leave that stinking piece of hardware in your jacket, Sloan....that's if you know what's good for you....otherwise, I'll stick it up your ass and pull the trigger, giving you the enema of your life!....then I'll hand you over to Barrett so he can have his way with you!"*

My temper was out of control as I whipped Sloan over a small wooden chair into the far corner. Crashing into a wooden table with a vase on it, the noise exploded throughout the room like a cannon shot. Suddenly, everyone stopped talking and all of their eyes were trained on us as they watched me reach down and pick the sleaze ball up off the floor. Grabbing him by the collar with both hands, I hauled him up against the wall, ramming his head into a picture frame, busting the glass. His feet were dangling in mid air and his look of fear told me that he was seeing his life flash before his eyes. His two-inch snub nose fell out of his jacket pocket, hitting the floor with a thud and Barrett seeing it, quickly trotted over and picked it up with his teeth. Swiftly carrying it away, he gently placed the gun on the floor about ten feet away and then immediately sat back on his haunches. Staring at Sloan with his deep yellow, menacing eyes, his lip curled upwards exposing his huge canine teeth and along with it came a loud hair rising growl. Chuckling I said, *"Looks like my partner doesn't like your talk as well, Sloan.....maybe I should let him go a few rounds with you....what do you think?.....are you ready to take him on for the title?"*

Detective Robinson, like a shot moved over quickly, grabbing me by the back of the shoulder, yelling, *"That's enough, Madison!.... he's the mayor's right hand man for heaven's sake....do you want to end up in the cooler?.....let him go!"* Disgusted from the sight in front of my eyes, I released my hands in a huff, and Sloan dropped to the floor in a heap. Looking up at me, the despicable man wiped his mouth from the saliva that had leaked out of him due to the untold fear he had inside. Brushing himself off, the mayor's assistant gazed at me with hatred painted all over his face. *"Madison, you're nothing but a relic....a drunken piece of shit that can't hold it together...and that mutt of yours should be put in a cage or put down for that matter as he's no better than you...obviously, the booze still has its claws in you and it won't let go......I'm gonna see to it that you never work again!"*

Barrett instantly lunged at Sloan, sending more fear up the man's spine while he threw himself backwards to avoid the attack. Quickly standing up, the mayor's assistant watched every move the dog was making as he stepped backwards up against the wall, standing perfectly still, and pressing his body hard against it. Barrett slowly moved in sniffing his groin and I could see the sweat pop from Sloan's forehead as he prayed for the menacing animal to disappear. The mayor's assistant stuttering with torment in his face, looked down at the huge black head while it nosed and smelled his groin. *"Ahh....Ahh....what's he doing, Madison?"* Enjoying, the man's suffering I replied, *"Just checking you out to see if you have a pair....that's all."* Chuckling and with a grin, I added, *"But then again....he might be hungry."* A few laughs and snickers started to sprinkle throughout the room as Barrett put his nose closer to Sloan's crotch and before I knew it, everyone in the room was laughing and ridiculing Stone, sending the whole room into an uproar.

As Sloan looked around the room, glaring at all of the laughing faces, he yelled, *"The hell with all of you!....it's not funny in the least!....that beast is nothing, but a ...."* Suddenly, out of the clear blue, an officer yelled out, *"Madison's right....he's a hungry son of a bitch!....and he wants a piece of you, Sloan!"* With that, the whole room became hysterical with laughter and seeing that no one was on his side, Sloan whipped his head at me. *"Madison, I'm going back to the mayor's office....plan to be there within the hour or start packing your bags!.....and you keep that God damn dog away from me!"*

As Sloan moved carefully sideways on his tiptoes, with his back against the wall, Barrett kept careful watch and followed him towards the front office door. Sloan's eyes were all over the place as he kept turning his head around making sure Barrett was not going to take a chomp out of him. The sight brought nothing but more comments and laughter from everyone and with each expression of fear on Sloan's face, only made everybody laugh even harder. Within a few seconds, Sloan was out the door and running down the sidewalk to his car leaving Barrett sitting there, yawing at the whole ordeal.

When I was through at the scene with the detectives, Robinson reminded me about what Sloan had said about going back to the mayor's office. To tell the truth, I was fed up with the case, and just wanted to head back to Middleton. I would have left in a minute, but there was still one thing holding me to the despicable City of Harrisburg and that was the thought of, *"Who killed my wife?"* Another problem that plagued me was letting them think my long time friend was the serial killer as that was entirely wrong. I knew Zack was not the murderer as he was just a poor unfortunate man who was caught up in a world of drugs and sex who decided that life and him did not get along anymore.

However, there was little doubt that Lori Jenkins killed Tina Hendricks and Zack had disposed of the Hendricks's body, trying to make it look like the work of the serial killer. His admission of tying the square knot and beating along with his version of events was proof of that.

As I thought more about the evidence, my little voice was still telling me that Tina Hendricks's death was the result of an unfortunate vengeful mistake by Lori Jenkins, as Hendricks probably did not kill Kyle Swanson. I was sure that there was much more to the case, as Swanson's murder was possibly linked somehow to the Veratex Corporation. Swanson was onto something big, it may have made some very powerful people of that organization extremely nervous and it probably cost the poor young woman her life.

Driving to the mayor's office, my mind was still running, trying to put together the other aspects of the complex puzzle. The picture was beginning to appear, but many pieces were still missing, as the remaining killings were similar, but there were inconsistencies as well. No doubt, that there was serial killer on the loose, but how many murders he was responsible was a big question and it was still plaguing me.

Unfortunately, Lori Jenkins and Zack believed in all sincerity that Tina Hendricks had killed Swanson in a jealous rage, thus setting the stage for that horrible night at the hotel. Unfortunately, Zack killed himself thinking that he was at a dead end, and due to his previous record was going to jail for the rest of his life.

That may have been the case, but knowing that he was not the murderer, I would have stood up for him at his trial. Of course, once he entered the legal system, anything might have happened, as there would be little chance of him coming out of it clean.

Pulling into the lot and parking the car, Barrett and I went through the main entrance to City Hall that faced Main Street. Climbing the immense granite steps that led into the building, a car caught my eye that was parked further down along the street. Two men were sitting in it and their eyes seemed focused on us as we reached the top of the stairs. While I pulled on the large glass door framed in oak, both their heads suddenly looked down to hide their faces when they realized I was looking back at them. I could tell they were well dressed by their dark suit coats and ties and they appeared to be middle aged. Neither of the men looked up at me again, but I did notice the make and model of their car. Because of its heavy chrome grille in front, it was easy for me to recognize, since the front of the car had always reminded me of a ferocious animal. It was a black 1953 Buick Roadmaster.

Entering the building, the mayor's office was the first office on the left, and as I rounded the corner, the echo of everyone walking through the building filled the air. City Hall, with its tremendously high ceilings created an echo chamber as everyone's heels clicked on the shiny marble floor, and the loud clattering noise made it sometimes hard to speak over. *"The mayor is expecting you,"* the secretary said while cupping the phone receiver as I entered the office. *"You can go right in."* As the mayor came into view, in the room behind her, I saw an open seat to the left of him and while grabbing a chair to sit down, a loud voice suddenly exploded from behind me. *"That's the man!....I want his job now!"* Quickly turning my head and looking at the wall behind me, Sloan was sitting along side it with another man who was dressed in a three-piece suit. His shiny black leather shoes glistened in the sunlight that blazed through the huge windows and as he moved, brilliant flashes of light emanated from the rest of his body. Even

Barrett was taken back by the appearance of the strange man as he moved to the other side of the room.

Once the well-dressed man reached the wall to the right of us, he pulled up a chair and sat down. Not wasting anytime, the strange man pointed directly at me, yelling, *"That's the one I have been telling you about, mayor!....he's been causing nothing, but trouble ever since he arrived here....the nerve of the man, spreading vicious rumors about me and my company...telling everyone in this great city of ours that we are robbing this place blind and getting rich......all he's accomplished so far in this case is spewing untold lies about our vital work we have done in this city....Mayor, I want that man fired right now and thrown out of town!"*

Cautiously taking my seat, I glanced over at the mayor whose head was still down, appearing to be studying some paperwork on his desk that was in front of him. With no immediate reaction coming from Mayor Logan, my attention was drawn back to the man in the five hundred dollar suit. He was middle aged and had thick black hair, which was cut very short, almost appearing to be a butch style type of hair cut. In reality, along with his heavy black eye brows, hooked nose, and puffy face, I thought I was looking at Al Capone. Then I noticed that the sporadic glistening was coming from a heavy gold chain around his neck that was adorned with a very large medallion, embedded with several diamonds. As his hands waived in the air while he was speaking, many of his fingers adorned with wide golden rings, sparkled in the sunlight, causing flashes of light throughout the room. *"He looks like a pimp for Christ's sake,"* I thought to myself taking my seat. *"I wonder how many girls are in his stable."*

Then the well-dressed man rose to his feet quickly and moved in closer to the mayor. Facing the chief executive by placing both hands on his desk and leaning on them, he gave the appearance that he was going to pounce on him. Staring the mayor down for a few moments, he demanded, *"Well, mayor?....are you going to fire this man and take care of business or should I?"* The mayor did not utter a word, but kept looking down at his paperwork, almost seeming to ignore the belligerent man. After a brief period had passed, the mayor finally looked up and softly said, *"Cool down, Charlie and take a seat.....don't worry, we'll get this straightened out."*

The well-dressed man, surprised at the mayor's response, backed up a few steps, and glared at me with red-faced anger. *"You're nothing but trouble, Madison....I built this town and we don't need people like you around here."* With purple veins bursting on each side of his neck, he moved over towards his chair and plopped down in it. Still focused on me he said loudly, *"You think you can come into this town and stir the shit up....ruining everything we have accomplished in this great city ....well, let me tell you one thing, mister......your ass is about to go down the road quicker than you can blink an eye!"*

The mayor suddenly looked up at the well-dressed man and Sloan, who were sitting side by side. Then his eyes moved over to me, saying, *"Seems like we have a problem here, Madison..... what have you been spreading around town about Mr. Shield's company?"* Immediately, I realized who the man was in the fancy suit and wondered what was going on. What sort of rumors was I supposed to have been spreading? It was obvious to me by the way Shields was looking at me, that he was fit to be tied, and whatever it was, it must have hit a touchy spot with the man as he was livid. Then without warning, Shields exploded again. *"And that dirty mutt you have there....how dare you bring that thing in here.....this is the people's house and that is the kind of respect that you show towards it?....of all places, bringing that flea bitten piece of shit into the mayor's office....you should be ashamed of yourself.....the best thing for all of us is for you to pack up your shit and get the hell out of here!"*

Marty Sloan, the mayor's assistant, suddenly flew out of his chair and blasted lightning bolts with both eyes at me. *"Yeah, Charlie's right, mayor....get rid of this son of a bitch as he's nothing but a drunk who can't even find his way to bed!.....send him down the road!"*

The mayor's eyes scanned everyone as he leaned back in his chair. Turning his head at me, he said, *"Well, Madison it looks like you have finally hung yourself, but at least you solved the case for us, and we are grateful for that."* Hearing those words sent a cold chill up my spine as I thought, *"Solved the case?......they can't be serious, can they?"* The mayor's response was beyond my comprehension and before I could answer him, Shields went on another tirade. *"Mayor!....I want that man out of here, now!....he is damaging our city and before he totally destroys it, we need to send him on his way!....I realize that he has found our serial killer, but that does not mean he's not dangerous to our community and still a menace... and far as I am concerned, that furry ball of shit can go with him!"*

At my wits end, I could not take the bullshit anymore. *"I don't know what everyone is talking about, Mayor.....I have never said anything detrimental against the Veratex corporation or any of its employees for that matter....besides, this case isn't over by any means....there is...."* Shields swiftly approached the mayor at his desk and looked down upon him with fire in his eyes. *"Don't listen to that drunken hick, mayor....he's just trying to save his skin and make himself still seem relevant....well, he's not!....it's obvious we have the serial killer....hell, he killed himself rather than go to prison or get burned in the chair...even a child can see that....so just throw him out of town so we can get back to the business of rebuilding this city as we don't need his kind in here anymore!"*

As Charlie Shields was speaking, Sloan was nodding his head in agreement and smiling at me. His smug look made me burn with anger inside as I wanted to pop him. *"Just one punch,"* I thought to myself as he continued to wear that smirk on his face. *"That's all it would take to wipe it off....that guy's a weasel and he should be the one that is sent down the road."* The mayor looked up at Shields with firmness in his face. *"I told you to take a seat, Charlie....now go and sit down."* The sharply dressed man, immediately straightened himself, and stood tall in front of the mayor's desk. His eyes were wide, glaring at the mayor, and his lower jaw clenched as he tried to hold his temper. Then with contempt and disrespect, he

pointed his stiff index finger directly at Mayor Logan. *"Listen....*
has it slipped your mind who put you in that chair?.......anybody can
be replaced and that includes you!" Then he raised his hands in
front of him, wiggling all ten of his fingers with decorative golden
rings on them. They glistened and produced bursts of bright light
in all of our eyes, almost blinding everyone. Then with a smug
grin he added, *"You're forgetting, mayor.....the man with the gold*
makes the rules!"

That was even too much for the mayor to take, never mind
me. The arrogant son of a bitch in front of the mayor had touched
off a nerve in both of us and before I could call the man an asshole, the mayor's face turned red, biting his lower lip in frustration. I thought he was going to blow his stack, but surprisingly,
his behavior was not a man of rage, but a somber one as he calmly
answered, *"Now, Charlie.....he was just doing his job.....after all, all*
of us wanted the serial killer captured.... I'm sure the detective is
more than willing to apologize and set things straight between you...
aren't you Madison?" I was willing to *"set things straight between*
us" all right, as I stared at the man in the monkey suit, glittering in
gold, like some two-bit pimp. However, before I could speak the
mayor sent a glaring look my way, telling me that I had better take
his advice or else. Receiving his mental suggestion loud and clear,
I knew that in order to finish this case, I had to be on it, and there
was only one way to do that. *"That's right, mayor....I didn't mean*
to offend anyone in my investigation....if I caused any hardship to
Mr. Shields or his company, I sincerely apologize for it."

Saying those words, almost made me vomit, but I realized it
was the only way. This case was far from being solved as they had
the wrong man, but most of all I wanted to stick around to investigate my wife's death. Yes, the serial killer had to be stopped, but
the man who ran down my wife needed my personal attention too
and I was praying for that day to come as I had something special
planned for him. The mayor looked over to Shields, anticipating a response, but the man remained silent. Grinding his teeth
in frustration, the company executive got up from his chair, and

began walking towards the door. Grabbing the knob and turning it, Shields looked back at the mayor. *"You know my feelings on this, Logan....get rid of him or else."* Then he opened the heavy oak paneled door and quickly exited into the secretary's office. Slamming it shut, the loud noise made us all jump a bit, and even Barrett's head perked up, awakened from a sound sleep.

The rest of us just sat there looking at each other, trying to figure out who was going to speak next. With the silence becoming very uncomfortable and awkward, Stone finally decided to break the ice by blurting, *"Well, Mayor.....I guess we all know where Charlie stands on this, don't we?.....why don't you do us all a favor, Madison....just pick up your shit and go back where you came from, okay?"* As he said that, he was still wearing that grin of his, which only sparked in me a growing hatred for the man. Just as I was about to say something, the mayor cut me off. *"Detective, you say this case is not over with......are you certain about that?.....seems to me, everybody is telling me that we already have our man and the city can rest easy again, but I take it that you don't agree?"*

To tell the truth, at this point in time I did not trust anybody, especially the mayor. Someone had put Shields on my trail, even though I had said absolutely nothing detrimental about him or his company. Either Shields was directly involved with the attempt on my life and Swanson's murder, or he was being played by someone to get at me. That is, someone who wanted me out of the picture bad enough and suffer through the heat of killing a cop. No doubt, I was getting close and the snakes in the grass were starting to slither out, as there was little doubt now that they wanted me gone.

The mayor, staring at me, waited for my response, but knowing whatever I was about to say might rock the boat even more I said softly, *"Zack was not the serial killer, mayor....he had gotten himself tied up in a mess, but he was no killer....knowing the man as long as I did, I can almost guarantee that and the evidence so far just doesn't support it."* The mayor took out his pipe and began stuffing it with tobacco from a pouch on his desk and while listening intently, replied, *"Okay....so what's your evidence that makes you think your buddy Zack hasn't been killing woman all over this city....according to the crime report submitted to me by the chief, he was responsible for killing the Hendricks woman and disposing of the body down by the river....and if that is not enough, your friend Zack was having sexual relations with the Jenkins woman who was later found dead by the river as well.....whose to say he didn't kill all of them including a city employee who we valued very much.....he pulled the wool over your eyes, Madison, but when he was discovered and things were going bad for him, the man simply decided to take the easy way out."*

Not wanting to play all of my cards, I contemplated for a minute on what the mayor had just said. Sighing a little, I replied, *"Well...I don't have all the pieces of the puzzle yet, but there is an obvious difference in the way the girls died....some are identical, but several of them aren't....take the Hendricks woman for an example....she was obviously beaten to death, but Sullivan was stabbed multiple times...this is not the same MO of the serial killer as most of the others were strangled to death.....we already know by Zack's confession that Jenkins beat Hendricks with a heavy ash tray during a jealous rage thinking that Hendricks had killed Swanson, but that's where there's a rub....you see mayor, I don't think it happened that way at all...Jenkins killed Hendricks alright as there is little doubt about that, since men that are about to blow their heads off don't take to lying when they are about to meet their maker.....plus the evidence I recovered supports his account of the killing.....additionally, Swanson was strangled in her apartment and she was a relatively large woman, being 5'-8 inches tall and weighing close to 160 pounds....Tina Hendricks was much smaller, 5'-2 inches in height and was only 110 pounds....there is little chance that she could have overpowered Swanson and strangled her....besides, woman don't normally commit murder in that way....it's up close and too personal for them, if you know what I mean....additionally, Tina Hendricks had access to a handgun....she worked many years for Zack and must have known where he kept it, so why not use* it?....no, I think someone else killed Swanson and it wasn't the serial killer, either."

The mayor looked off into the distance, thinking about the facts I had thrown at him. Not saying a word for several moments, we all sat there patiently waiting for the chief executive to come back to earth and enlighten us with his thoughts. After a minute or so, he woke from his slight stupor, and raised an eyebrow while peering back at me. "So, detective.....you really think we still have a problem?.....I mean there is still a nut running around loose out there that's ready to kill again?" I nodded my head vigorously, replying, "Yeah...and it won't be long before there is another body found down by the river."

Logan rubbed the side of his head, trying to get a handle on the desperate situation that the city was still in, but I could tell by the look on his face that he was having a hard time coming to grips with it. "Okay, Madison....how much more time are you going to need on this?....you have to understand with Charlie Shields on my back along with the city councilors, before you know it, my job is going to be on the line.....I wouldn't be surprised to see impeachment proceedings begin to start in the next few days." Puffing heavily on his pipe, he leaned back in his leather-covered chair and pointed at Sloan. "And you....I thought I told you to take care of this mess.... so far, you haven't produced diddly squat."

Sloan gazed across the room at me with a dark glare in his eyes, giving the impression that this was entirely my fault for the mayor's disappointment in him. Knowing that another barrage was probably coming from Sloan, I quickly stood up and addressed the mayor's question. "I need another few days, mayor....then you'll have your killer or should I say killers because with the evidence that has been collected so far, everything points to that."

Motioning to Barrett to come with me, my partner promptly stood and walked over as I headed for the door. Sloan with a face full of awe blurted, "That's a pretty bold statement that you just made Madison....what makes you think you can solve this case in a few more days?.....you must have more than you are telling us." Stopping for a second at the door, I turned my head and gave Sloan a small grin. Chuckling, I reached down and rubbed Barrett's head, replying, *"Well, I have the best partner in the world, that's how.......or didn't you know that?"* Motioning with my head for Barrett to follow me and while walking out the office door I added, *"Don't you worry, mayor.....we'll have your killer behind bars or in the ground before the middle of next week.....right partner?"* Immediately, Barrett licked his chops, nodded his head, and let out a soft bark to acknowledge me. The two men observing the spectacle and not believing what they had just witnessed, gawked at Barrett following right behind me as we both left the office. The mayor looking over at Sloan flashed a grin, as he eyed us going out and said, *"Well, I'll be....the dog really does understand English, doesn't he?"*

CHAPTER SEVENTEEN
Backing up the Talk

Leaving the mayor's office, I knew my bold statement of capturing the serial killer in a couple of days was going to be a tough one to fulfill, but to be honest I was getting a little tired of their crap and just wanted to shut them up. In reality, I was almost back to square one, and where the Veratex connection was going to lead me was anybody's guess. Being desperate for answers, it was obvious by the latest killing and the newspapers grabbing a hold of it, that the politicians would be running scared and by the mayor agreeing to give me more time, it only let the political scumbags line themselves up with someone that they could use for a whipping post. Unfortunately, that escape goat was me and if the situation suddenly turned for the worse, I knew Shaker Madison was going to be first person in line to take the fall.

Later that afternoon when I arrived back at my hotel room, my bed was still in disarray, telling me that housekeeping had yet to service the room. With Zack being dead, I wondered who was going to take over the place as he was not married and did not have any children that I knew of. To determine if the place was even going to be in business anymore, I decided to take a walk up to the main office to see if I could get some answers. As I walked towards the main office, it was clear that all of the department's personnel had left the scene and when I entered through the main door, I noticed a strange man behind the counter that I had never seen before. Dressed in a grey pinstriped suit, he was a relatively small man, that was partially bald, and in his late fifties. Wearing steel-wired rim glasses, and appearing to be extremely frail with shaking arthritic hands, he was attempting to lift the huge ledger books above his head onto the shelf behind him. Hearing the overhead doorbell and sensing me behind him, he promptly turned around and placed the books back on the counter in front of him, saying, *"Can I help you, sir?"*

As Barrett and I approached the desk, I could tell his eyes were on my partner as he was trying not to appear alarmed on what was in front of him. *"Yeah, you can....who's in charge of this place now?"* The man pushed the ledger books on the counter to the side, and folding his arms, he leaned on it. *"Mr. Shields is, sir....my name is Ben....Ben Wilding....I work for Mr. Shields."* A little surprised at his response, I countered with, *"My name is Detective Madison and I'm staying here.....you say Mr. Shields owns this motel?....do you mean the Veratex Corporation?"* He nodded his head while taking out a cigarette. *"Yes....he has owned this motel for about a year now....Mr. Thompson was an employee and since he is no longer with us, I am the new manager."*

My mind started to run with several suspicious thoughts as I gazed upon the man. *"So...you say he owns the motel....did he purchase the place from Zack?"* Taking a few puffs on his butt, the man grabbed a few papers off the counter and stacked them on the shelf behind him. With his back towards me, he answered, *"Don't know anything about that....all I know is Mr. Shields acquired the establishment more than a year ago....you'll have to check with our main office if you need more information."*

As my eyes examined the room, the appearance of the office was amazing as there was no evidence of the horror that had recently taken place. All of the throw rugs had been replaced and the linoleum floor was spotless, along with the room having been entirely cleaned up, it surprised me how quickly the crime scene had been officially released, even though it was a suicide case. *"I'm a little amazed on how the place looks, sir....you can't even tell what happened here."* The man chuckled as he moved some books

240

off to the side. *"Well, you know how Mr. Shields can be.....I heard the construction crew is going to be in here next week to rehabilitate the place....its going to get a whole new face lift from what I am hearing, sir....that's how Mr. Shields operates his business and when there's work to be done, my boss never wastes any time."*

Watching the man go on with his duties, it shocked me a little on how familiar he seemed to be on where everything was located. Arranging the various ledger books on the shelves and filing the papers in the various steel cabinets apparently did not present a problem to the man. Curious, I asked, *"You appear to know your way around here pretty well, Mr. Wilding.... You seem to know where everything goes."* Turning around, he faced me with a slight smile. *"That's because I have worked in here, from time to time, going over the books ....you see, I am one of Mr. Shields's accountants."* That was interesting I thought as I noticed a huge ledger book on the right side of the desk. *"Well, then you must know how the Veratex corporation came to be the owner of this place,"* I asked, staring at the black ledger. Realizing on where I was looking, the man moved slightly towards the book and casually picked it up. Watching him place it in a drawer, I added, *"You might as well tell me....or do I need to bring you in for questioning?....I am sure Mr. Shields would not like it at all, if one of his employees was identified in the local paper as being a possible suspect in a murder case....it would probably put Mr. Shields and his company through a lot of heartache and it might not go very well for the employee, either..... what do you think?"*

Nervousness overtook the man almost immediately as he slowly closed the drawer, looking down at it. Rubbing his sweaty face with his hand and biting his lower lip, he let out a big sigh. *"No...that won't be necessary as I really don't want to cause him any inconvenience.....I believe Mr. Shields acquired the property about one year ago this past March and actually, the city took possession of the motel before that for nonpayment of taxes....Mr. Shields then purchased the property from the city and allowed Mr. Thompson to work here as the manager....However, Mr. Thompson was in the process of buying it back from the corporation when he died."* After dangling that carrot in front of me, I could not wait to ask, *"And how was he buying it back from them?....who was the bank?"* Wilding quickly looked down again and went back to work, saying softly, *"Well, the Veratex Corporation was the bank as they were going to hold the paper on it .....I guess you could say that Mr. Shields felt sorry for the man."*

That was a new one as the man I met in the mayor's office was hardly a man of passion and understanding. There was little doubt in my mind that he was a vicious businessman who would stop at nothing to make money, and was hardly a person who would give charity out by giving a poor soul who lost his place a job. *"So... the motel was auctioned off by the city?"* I asked while taking out a cigarette. That question hit the man hard as he stopped what he was doing and thought for a moment. After a few seconds had passed, he looked over at me, saying, *"Well....not exactly....you see the mayor is passionate about his urban renewal project and Mr. Shields is a big part of it, so he is given liberties."* That struck home with me as I took a drag off my butt and exhaled the smoke, sending Barrett to the opposite corner of the room and knowing the answer I asked the question anyway. *"What do you mean by 'liberties'?"* Stuttering over his words at first Wilding replied, *"Ahh... ahh...the property was transferred to him by the city at a fair and equitable price."*

Staring at Wilding while taking another drag on my cigarette, I peered through the exhaled smoke at the little weasel. *"And what amount, would that have been?"* Seeing the anxiety building rapidly in his face as it took on a red glow, Wilding's voice became very low and weak. He seemed to mumble something, which made no sense at all, causing me to ask, *"What was that?....I couldn't hear you."* Knocking the ashes off my butt into the receptacle, which was sitting on the edge of the counter, I stared at him waiting for an answer. Not being able to look me in the eye, Wilding shook his head slightly, with his eyes rocking back and forth. Still trying desperately to get some words out, he apprehensively replied, *"Ahhh...ahhh....I think it was one thousand dollars......yes, one thousand....a fair and equitable offer."*

Now, I have heard of good deals before, but this was one for the record books. I knew the motel was worth at least one hundred thousand dollars and acquiring the property for a thousand bucks was a little more than just a bargain...it was stealing, plain and simple. Not wanting to tip my hand, I appeared nonchalant and tried not to show any emotion, but what he had just said to me was ridiculous. The sweat rolled down the side of Wilding's face and his troubled feelings were becoming evident due to his body posturing while he waited for my reaction. Not giving my true opinion I promoted a lie by replying, *"That's the good thing about the tax title process....people can pick up properties at a reduced cost, which allows them to rehabilitate the buildings......it really gives the city a needed face lift....don't you agree?"* With a halfhearted smile the timid, little man replied, *"Oh, yes......yes...ahh...oh, I agree......it's a really good program."*

The sight of him made me sick actually and because he worked for a crook, all I could dream of was arresting him and throwing his ass in a cell. White-collar crime in many ways was worse than the criminal element on the street. Those men preyed on the weak that through some unfortunate incident had fallen on hard times and in this case, with help from their own government, they were stealing properties for pennies on the dollar. Tired of dealing with him I blurted, *"So....when is someone going to clean up my room?....the bed's a mess."* Glad that I had changed the subject he happily answered, *"I'll get someone right over there, sir....her name is Mildred and she will take good care of you."*

Waiving to Barrett to get his attention, I proceeded to the door to leave and before I could open it Wilding blurted, *"That's quite a dog you have there....I'm sure glad that he's friendly."* Opening the large, glass entrance door I grinned slightly. *"Oh, he's friendly alright....but he hates crooks....especially the ones that cheat and steal by taking property from others for their personal gain....that's when he gets really mean and nasty."* Barrett stared at Wilding behind the counter with his gleaming yellow eyes highlighted by his jet-black fur. A small amount of drool leaked from his open mouth and dripped to the floor, causing his teeth to glisten in the overhead lights. Then, Barrett's long pink tongue swiped the side of his muzzle while he focused in on the man and a low deep growl emanated from him, making the man's eyes bulge with fear. I think Wilding may have been on the verge of a heart attack as he cautiously watched us from his desk leave the front office through the double glass doors. While we walked by the large picture window, Wilding's eyes remained totally locked on my furry partner, giving the perception that he was unaware of anything else around him. Looking down at Barrett as he followed beside me I said aloud, *"Well, chalk up another one ole pal and I hope you're proud of yourself......there's no doubt the guy back there probably pissed his pants."*

As Barrett loped behind me walking back to the room, my mind was conjuring up all kinds of scenarios regarding the Swanson killing and the reasons for it. It was very clear now that the Veratex Corporation headed by Charlie Shields was stealing land away from the local inhabitants, including some business-men, and making millions. Realistically, the previous owners of the *"stolen"* properties had three choices, either pay higher rents in the newly renovated buildings; buy their properties back by taking a mortgage through the Veratex Corporation or leave town. On the other hand, what was worrying me was the Veratex Corporation supposedly contributed heavily to the mayor's cam-paign fund. Was the mayor truly aware of this property scheme or worse yet, did he approve the possible silencing of Swanson to protect his source of funding? However, if that was true, what had Swanson discovered during her work on the rehabilitation pro-gram that made her such a threat to the organization? It appeared that they had attempted to buy her off by transferring the apart-ment building where she lived to her, but if she had agreed to it, then why kill her? They must have known that someone like me, investigating the crime, would have uncovered this fact and determined the direct tie to the Veratex Corporation, putting the whole scheme in jeopardy. There were still dozens of questions that needed answering and as they whirled in my head, without realizing it, I soon found myself back at my motel door.

Putting the key into the lock, Barrett immediately put his nose to the threshold and pawed at it. Looking down, a folded piece of paper caught my eye as I opened the door. It was of normal letter size that had been folded into quarters and as I reached down to pick it up, Barrett seemed to be quite interested in it as his *"sniffer"* was busy at work. Opening it, the message that it contained was made from various sized misaligned letters that had been cut out from the local newspaper. It read:

<blockquote>
Whom do you think you are kidding?
Your performance on this case has been dismal at best
Look at the real evidence to begin the test
And not before it's too late
For you may find another by the river
With no time left and still at the gate
</blockquote>

Immediately I looked at the surrounding area, trying to see if anyone was watching me and Barrett sensing what I was up to began doing the same. Each of us carefully scanned the parking lot and the stores across the street, but there was no one in sight and as a few lone cars passed us on the adjacent street, it became obvious that the person who had left the note was now long gone. Slowly closing the door behind us, I placed my car keys on the dresser and took off my suit jacket, hanging it on the chair beside the desk. Tossing the note onto the end table, I sat on the edge of the bed, massaging the back of my neck. Barrett sensing my frustration, placed his head on my lap, and tried to cheer me up by rubbing his nose against me. Stroking his head, Barrett closed his eyes enjoying my kneading of his ears, and it was not long afterwards a few low grunts emerged, signaling his approval.

My mind continued to run again as I stared at the killer's note on the end table. Looking away from it, my eyes drifted out the large picture window towards the package store across the street. Seeing the large lit up neon sign with the words *"Spirits"* caused me to drool at the corner of my mouth, thinking how easily I could take my inner frustration away. Quickly wiping the streak of saliva off my chin with the back of my hand, I turned my focus to the note. Obviously, it was from the killer, there was little doubt about that, but one sentence had really caught my attention. *"Look at the real evidence,"* I said aloud while my eyes stared at it on the end table. *"What is the real evidence?"* I mumbled, picking it up again and reading it once more. *"What do you think, ole boy?.....where do we go from here?"*

As I said that, Barrett went over to my suit jacket that was draped over the chair and sat by it. His head turned at me and then back to the jacket several times, telling me to pick it up. *"What the hell does he want me to do now?"* I thought. *"There's nothing in my jacket, but my wallet and....."* Suddenly realizing what he was trying to tell me, I grabbed my coat from the chair and took out Jenkins's notebook that I had found in the ceiling. Immediately, Barrett let out an exuberant bark and panted heavily, telling me I was on the right track. *"So this is what you wanted me to look at, ehh?"* Barrett was on all fours now, dancing up and down showing his approval, and as I opened the small black notebook, he quickly came over to me and nudged it with his nose. *"There must be something more about this book that I'm not seeing,"* I thought to myself, thumbing the pages as I had done a hundred times before. *"But what could it be?"*

Sitting back down on the edge of the bed, my eyes studied the pages containing the names of Jenkins's clients. Along each name were numbers, signifying the dollar amounts that were owed for the drugs she had sold them. Flipping through it, the pages were filled with dozens of names and some of the amounts next to them were staggering. She was far from a small time drug dealer; her amount of business was way beyond that. Jenkins had a huge operation going that was raking in thousands of dollars in drug money, which was making her a very wealthy girl. Scanning the pages, I acknowledged to myself that I had been over all of these names a hundred times before and none of them seemed to have any real bearing on the case. Unfortunately, most of them had turned out to be nothing but ill-fated addicts that had been simply lost to a horrific world of drug addiction.

Feeling uneasy, I could sense eyes were staring at me, and as I looked up, sure enough Barrett was looking directly at me with his tongue out, panting to beat the band. Sighing a little I said aloud, *"I don't know what has you all worked up about this book......I've looked at this over and over again....there's nothing more in here."* Tossing it on the bed in frustration, I rubbed my face with both hands and while doing so, Barrett pawed the book several times, coaxing me to look at it again. *"For Christ's sake, Barrett....what is with you and this book?"* Extremely annoyed, I grabbed the notebook and opened it, showing it to him while thumbing the pages. *"There is nothing more in here, I tell you.....you know I have looked at this a thousand times....there's just nothing more in here that can help us."* Tossing the book back on the bed, I bent my head backwards and closed my eyes, hoping to get some peace.

Surprisingly, Barrett moved over and nudged the book with his nose again. Sitting back on his haunches, his deep yellow eyes glared at me, encouraging me to pick it up once more. *"Okay... okay,"* I said in a huff, reaching for the book and opening it. *"Have it your way....you know, sometimes you can be a real pain in the ass!"*

I knew there was nothing more in the book, but to get my furry friend off my back, I began thumbing the pages again, appearing as if I was studying it. In reality, I was thinking more about Andrea and what she must be up to as I really missed her. She loved Barrett too, almost as much as me, and we were a family now. That was something that I had longed for since the death of my wife and turning the pages one by one, I glanced back at Barrett who continued to stare at me. *"I don't know what you expect me to find in here...but this book really has nothing more in...."* Just as I said that, something dropped to the floor, and as I looked downwards, lying there was a very small piece of paper. *"Where in the hell did that come from?"* I said aloud while picking it up. To my surprise, written on the paper were several numbers and letters:

L12 R41 L25

Examining the notebook cover more closely, at the bottom of the binding was a very small opening. *"It must have fallen out of there,"* I thought to myself. Studying the piece of paper in my hand, I said to Barrett while patting him, *"Looks like I owe you an apology, ole boy......seems that nose of yours has been working overtime."* Reciting the numbers to myself several times, it became clear that the series of numbers were a combination to a safe. Placing the paper in my wallet I mumbled, *"But there are no safes in our motel rooms....at least I don't think so....after all, there isn't one in mine, but on the other hand, could there be one in her old room?"* Grabbing my suit coat off the chair, I headed for the door. *"Come on....we need to take another look at room 112."*

Opening the door, I waited for Barrett to follow me, and as we headed down the long concrete sidewalk in front of the other units I thought, *"There's only one reason anybody has a safe and that's to keep something valuable away from other people, but where could it be?"* Suddenly, my sixth sense told me that something was very wrong and quickly my eyes patrolled the area around me. Almost instantly, I noticed the parked car facing towards us in the paved lot that was across the street next to the liquor store. There were two men inside and as soon as I turned towards them, their car started. Within seconds, they exited the lot and headed down the street. With the setting sun directly in my eyes, I moved quickly to change my vantage point, attempting to avoid the glare coming off the windshield, but it was still impossible to make out any of their faces before they were gone. *"Seems like our fans are still with us, Barrett....they'll be back and next time we will be ready for them, right?"* Barrett's eyes were trained on the vehicle as it sped off down the street and as it disappeared around the bend, he looked back at me. Realizing it was futile, with no chance of us intercepting it, he trotted back to me and we continued on to Lori Jenkins's room.

Trying the doorknob, I found the door still locked, and utilizing the key that I had gotten from the evidence room, we entered the premises. *"You know what we are looking for....get busy,"* I told Barrett as I looked behind one of the pictures on the wall. Continuing to look for almost an hour and finding nothing, I sat on the edge of the bed and mumbled, *"We have gone over every square inch of this damn place....there's no safe in here.....in fact, this room is exactly like ours."*

Realizing it had been a big waste of time, Barrett and I exited the room, and as I closed the door behind us and locked it a familiar voice behind me said, *"Heh...what are you up to?"* Quickly turning my head, it was Detective Robinson walking down the sidewalk. Flashing a grin at him, I quickly moved away from the door and responded, *"Just tying up some loose ends, Robinson..... thought there might be something that we had missed."* When he reached me, a partial suspecting smile came to his face. *"The results just came back from the lab on that footprint cast we took the other night....it was a size nine alright and it was definitely made from a dress shoe....probably a Dack's or something like it with a pointed toe....pretty common I'm afraid, but we might have had a stroke of luck.....if you remember, it was a left shoe print..... come to find out, it had a small chunk of the heel missing near the instep of the shoe.....if we can find the person who wears that shoe, then we'll have the guy who tried to take you out."*

Nodding my head, I quickly placed the key back in my pocket without him seeing it. Not trusting anyone, especially someone so close to the chief I replied, *"Well, at least that's something to go on, Robinson.....this case hasn't given us much so far.....just a bunch of dead ends."* The detective offered me a smoke and as we both lit up, we felt the hopelessness of the situation fall over us as our eyes looked in various directions, trying to make sense of the situation. *"Yeah, Madison....I just left the chief and he's on a rampage today.....I guess the city councilors are really on his back and there's rumors going around that they are going to have a special meeting to call for his resignation.....in fact, we just took in Jenkins's boyfriend and there's pressure coming down from up above to charge him for the murders."*

As I took another drag and expelled some smoke, I replied, *"You must mean Ty Phillips.....they actually have him in custody, downtown?"* Robinson nodded and I added, *"Then, I would really like to speak to him."* The detective let out a big smile, almost seeming exuberant on my request. *"Why?.... do you really think he might have something to do with all of this?"* Dropping my spent cigarette on the ground and grinding it out with my shoe I replied, *"Maybe......but somehow, I don't think so....there's more going on here than meets the eye I believe, but it's worth a shot."* Taking a long drag off his cigarette Robinson exclaimed, *"Well, let's go then....after all, it can't do any harm.....I'll take my car and meet you there."*

Walking along side him back to our vehicles, my mind was busy deciding how much I should tell him. My little voice kept telling me to be careful, as I knew someone in the department was trailing me. Evidently, the person was feeding the chief information on my whereabouts and what I was doing in the case. Could it be Detective Robinson? Maybe, but that was something I was just going to have to deal with especially if Robinson was assigned by the chief to be with me. In order to try to put my mind at ease, I decided to test him. *"I would really like to know your opinion on this, Robinson....do you think Phillips is the serial killer we're after?"* Hearing that, the detective abruptly stopped, causing me to halt in my tracks as well. With a surprised look, he stared back at me. *"At this point in time, Madison, I don't know what to think.....as far as I know, this Phillips guy is nothing but a good for nothing pimp and a drug dealer....he's a piece of shit for sure, but a serial killer?.....*

no, he's not crazy enough and he doesn't have the balls to do something like that....plus, he's as dumb as they come......the guy we're after is real clever and smart.....the killer knows what he's doing and always leaves a clean trail behind him.....if I didn't know better, I'd say he has had some training in law enforcement or security because that's just how good this guy is....so, to think a lowlife like Phillips had something to do with it, is in my opinion a real stretch of the imagination."

With that type of response, it made me feel a little better, as I knew he was telling me the truth, but I needed to push the envelope a little more. "Okay....so I take it you had nothing to do with taking Phillips in......have they charged him?" Pursing his lips, Robinson crushed out his butt on the sidewalk and ground it heavily with his shoe. "Not me....it was the chief's idea.....he's convinced that Phillips is our man.....his theory is that Ty Phillips was partnered up with Lori Jenkins in their drug dealings and was her pimp.....when Phillips discovered her extra curricular activities, being in a jealous rage, he killed her....the chief also thinks she may have even found out about him being a serial killer and that might have been the actual reason Phillips silenced her....the chief concludes that Phillips must be...."

This was making little sense to me as I listened to him spout off about the chief's brilliant reasoning so I was forced to cut him off. "Wait a minute, Robinson....Zack Thompson told me that he saw Lori Jenkins kill Tina Hendricks right in front of him....if Ty Phillips actually killed Jenkins like the chief thinks, then Zack would have known about it.... knowing Zack Thompson like I did and how he felt for the Jenkins woman, I know for a fact that he would have killed Phillips to get revenge rather than take his own life by blowing his head off..... after all, they all knew each other and were lovers for Christ's sake.....Zack would have done anything to settle the score and killing Ty Phillips would have made him a very happy man."

Robinson stood their thinking on what I had just said and by the look in his face; I knew he was getting ready to fire another round at me. *"I know the chief's version of the case is tough to swallow, Madison....its even hard for me to chew on, but when we took Phillips into custody, the murder weapon was found in his apartment.....I know it sounds crazy, but it looks like Phillips might be our man."* Not believing what I was hearing, I immediately responded with, *"What do you mean the murder weapon was found?.....what was it?......and who discovered it?"*

The detective rubbed the side of his face for a second, trying to relieve the tension in it as he reached for another cigarette. With pressure written all over his face, he went on to explain that Russ Wilson, himself and Detective Harley had gone to Phillips apartment, under the chief's instructions to question him. To avoid a possible escape by the suspect, Wilson went around the back to cover the rear entrance while Harley and he approached the front door. They heard the TV playing in the background so they naturally assumed that someone must have been home, hoping it was Ty Phillips. After knocking on the door several times and announcing that they were from the police department, not a single word was offered in response. Not hearing any response, they tried to further explain that they only wanted to talk to him, but all they heard coming from inside the apartment was the TV.

After several minutes of waiting, they finally tried to open the door, but it was locked. Knowing that he was probably in there, they rapped the door with their nightsticks and waited again for a response. Suddenly, the sound of a loud crash came through the door, followed by dishes and glass breaking, which startled both of them. Realizing a fight was in progress, they rammed their shoulders to the door, busting it off the hinges, and entered the apartment. To their amazement, Detective Wilson had Phillips lying face down on the floor with his knee on the back of his neck. Flashing a huge grin, Wilson blurted, *"What took you guys so long?.....he thought he was going to split from our little party here.... caught him going out the back door."*

As Robinson went on, he told me Phillips struggled as he tried to break the hold that Russ Wilson had placed on him. However, my old partner, had things well under control as he bore down heavily with his knee on the suspect's neck, pinning him to the floor even harder. *"Get off me, pig!"* Phillips hollered while he violently tried to move his body back and forth along the floor. Smiling ear to ear, Wilson slapped the back of Phillip's neck with his Billy club. *"Hold on there, boy.....pretty soon you're gonna get my friend here, the hard way!"* While Wilson slapped the cuffs on him, Harley and Robinson searched the apartment for any evidence. It was not long before Harley produced a blackjack that he had found in a drawer in the bedroom along with some parachute cord. *"Take a gander at what I found,"* Harley announced, holding up the blood-covered blackjack for everyone to see. *"Looks like we found ourselves a serial killer, boys."*

Robinson took a deep drag off his cigarette and exhaled the smoke quickly. Looking directly at me, his eyes were full and wide. *"That really sent Phillips into a rage Madison....he claimed that we had planted the stuff and all the way back to the station he was cursing and spitting on us....that's when Wilson lost it and gave it to him with his club... believe me, after your old partner got done with him, the poor bastard shut up."*

Suspicions were flying in my head now, as it seemed Phillips was possibly being set up as a patsy for the killings. Robinson must have seen I was deep in thought, because he touched me on the shoulder to wake me. *"Heh, man....you don't think we planted that stuff, do you?"* I heard his words, but I could not speak because my mind was blank. I knew we had some crooked cops on the department and things were a lot worse now than when I had left a few years ago. Fixing a few tickets for friends and overlooking some traffic violations, we did all the time, but planting evidence to frame someone even if they were drug scum for a charge of murder was an entirely new ballgame. Shocked beyond words I managed to say, *"I want to talk to Phillips...I need to ask him some questions."* Motioning for Robinson to follow me, I added, *"Come on....let's go....we need to get this straightened out."*

CHAPTER EIGHTEEN
The Fog Lifts

When we arrived back at the station, Robinson and I headed directly to the holding cells at the rear of the building. Entering through the steel door, I noticed that Detective Harley was speaking to Chief Morin at the end of the long corridor and as we approached them, I noticed a smile develop across the chief's face. *"You're a little late on this one, Madison....we already have our boy....he's in there."* Looking to the right of me, there in the holding cell was Phillips, a scrawny man of about thirty years old. With long, black, stringy hair and a ratty beard, he looked like something that had been dragged out of a cardboard box from a back alley. Dirty and disheveled, his dark eyes peered through the steel bars and the glassiness of them told me that he was higher than a kite. Hardly the appearance of a serial killer that was terrorizing the city, I was having a hard time swallowing that Phillips could have committed the murders.

It was a good thing that I had left Barrett in the car, because the sight of Phillips would have really bothered him. He never liked bearded people and seeing the long dirty hair as well, my furry friend would have definitely made a move on him. *"Yep... he's the right one alright....we even found the murder weapon in his apartment,"* the chief said with a glow in his face. Instantly upon hearing that, Phillips lunged at the bars, squeezing them in both hands with a wild look in his eyes. *"You planted that shit in my place, you assholes!.....I don't know where that came from!.....and I didn't kill anyone!"* Around the corner, my old partner suddenly appeared and he swiftly approached the bars, waiving his nightstick at Phillips. *"Anymore shit out of you and you'll get another taste of this!"* Seeing the heavy black stick Phillips instantly backed away from the bars to the opposite corner. It was evident by the look on his face and the tears running down his cheeks that he already had a taste of my old partner's *"instructional"* club.

Moving closer to Wilson I whispered, *"Go easy, partner...the man has had enough....look at him, he's like a whipped dog."* The extreme amount of fire in my old partner's eyes was something that I had not seen before. Although, in the past, we had been in a few skirmishes together and had to *"lay the law down,"* this time his attitude and actions seemed to be a little out of line. While Wilson continued to stare at Phillips, Chief Morin observing the whole mess suddenly blurted, *"What the hell are you doing here, Madison?....like I said, you're dead last in this race.....we already have our man."* Noticing that the chief seemed to be really enjoying the spectacle that was unfolding in front of him as he watched me stare at the prisoner in the cell, I knew there was only going to be one chance at questioning Phillips so I decided to carefully choose my words. *"I need to ask him a few questions in order to complete my report, chief......after all; you want an iron clad case, don't you?"* The chief's grin turned into a broad smile as he nodded his head in agreement. *"That's very good, Madison....you're finally on board with us on this thing....that's very good.....go ahead and ask your questions."*

As everyone turned their eyes on me, waiting for me to open my mouth, I knew asking the type of questions that I wanted to with witnesses around was not going to fly very well. From previous experience, the chief on occasion had looked the other way while we interrogated our prisoners, so I decided to play with his aggressive side a little. *"I want answers to some very difficult questions, chief and it might require a little coaxing of the prisoner..... you get my drift?"* I gave him a wink while saying that, hoping he would go along with me and within seconds, he took the bait.

"Okay, gentlemen....lets give Madison some space here so he can clean this case up!" the chief declared, while heading for the door and motioning for everyone to follow him.

Surprised, Wilson gazed at me with bewilderment and before he could say something, Detective Harley handed me his nightstick. *"Here...take this in case you need it for that animal in there....seems he only understands one thing and this might get you what you want from him."* Not wanting to rock the boat I grabbed it willingly and said, *"Thanks....this might come in real handy."*

Tapping my palm with it, in a rhythmic motion, my eyes peered at Phillips in the cell. The prisoner's full attention was focused on the stick as it struck with every blow to my hand and with his eyes wide and glaring, he knew what was in store for him. To add to his horror, my eyes focused in on him with coldness, while I continued to tap the nightstick in my palm, looking like I was going to be his worse nightmare. In a full-scale panic, Phillips grabbed the bars again and yanked on them in desperation, screaming, *"Don't leave me with this nut!....he's going to kill me!....I beg to God, please don't leave me alone with him!"*

Phillips pleading went unanswered as the other detectives along with the chief exited the hallway and as they left they joked among themselves, which only added more anxiety to the prisoner's demeanor. As I turned at him, he backed away from the bars and rammed his back up against the opposite wall. *"What are you going to do?"* he asked with a timid and pathetic voice. Tapping the nightstick in my hand I replied, *"Nothing....if you answer my questions, but if you don't....then....well let's just say we are going to resort to other methods....so what's it going to be?....answer a few questions or this?"* Again, I took the club and walloped my hand with it, flashing an evil grin towards the man. As Phillip's eyes stared at the black nightstick, I saw the fear blooming in them as he intently watched the up and down motion of it, striking my palm. Stuttering at first he managed with a weak voice to utter out, *"Ahhh....ahh....okay....go ahead....ask your questions."*

Pleased that he was going to cooperate I firmly asked, *"So... how long did you know Lori Jenkins?"* Rubbing the side of his face, he thought for a moment. *"About two years, I think....she was my partner."* Quickly I rebutted, *"Yeah, dealing drugs and destroying people's lives, right?"* He sat on the bench at the opposite wall and folded his hands in front of him, trying to squeeze the sweat out of them. *"I don't know what you're talking about....I have never dealt drugs in my life....so why don't you take a flying..."* Realizing that this was not going to go anywhere I abruptly cut him off. *"You just wait a minute...I'll be right back."*

It was not long before I returned with my *"coaxing medicine"* and as I opened the door to the cellblock, Phillip's eyes immediately saw what it was. There for him to see, walking beside me was 130 pounds of the meanest piece of flesh on the planet. I swear Phillip's eyes grew three times their normal size as he stared in total terror at the thing walking beside me. *"What the hell is that?"* he yelled. *"Where did you get that black devil?"* Barrett took a seat beside me in front of the cell and instantly began playing his part to the hilt as his huge canine teeth became totally exposed when his upper lip slowly rose. His deep yellow eyes shined in the partially lit hallway and the jet- black fur on his back stood up, showing that he was definitely ready to do what ever was necessary if I commanded him to do so. *"This you might say is my chief interrogator, Phillips.....he has a unique way of bringing out the most out of a scum bag like you.....pretty soon you'll be telling me everything that I want to hear....the only question now is......are you going to answer to me or to him?"*

Barrett almost on cue, growled deeply, and stared at the prisoner while licking his chops. Phillips darkened eyes, due to years of drug use, were completely fixated on the huge beast and I knew his mind was trying to comprehend the terror that was about to be unleashed upon him. As I put the key into the cell door Phillips cried out, *"You're not going to let that thing in here, are you?.....he's a killer....look at him!.....he can't wait to get at me!"* Barrett moved closer to the cell door, seeming anxious for me to open it and

Phillips seeing this quickly stood on the bench on the opposite wall, pressing his back against it. *"No!"* he screamed. *"I'll tell you anything you want....just don't let that thing in here!"* Chuckling a bit I removed the key saying, *"Too bad, ole boy....looks like you are not going to be able to question him....I guess this one is mine."* Hearing that, Barrett laid down at my feet and placed his head on his paws. His eyes became less alert and solemn, appearing to be disappointed that he was not going to be able to have some fun.

"Alright then....tell me about Lori Jenkins....and let me remind you, scumbag....any lies or bullshit and my partner takes over....you got that?" Nodding his head, he got off the bench and sat down on it, still keeping his eyes on Barrett. *"Okay....ahh.....as I said Lori and I were partners....drug partners that is....I supplied the dope by getting it out of New York and she was one of my main dealers."* As I lit up my cigarette, Barrett looked up at me and moved to the far corner of the hallway, signaling his distaste of the tobacco smoke. *"What the hell is the matter with him?....is he afraid of fire?"* With a small chuckle, I smirked at Phillips. *"That dog isn't afraid of anything....he just hates cigarette smoke....you should have seen the last crook we took down together that had a cigarette in his hand......poor bastard hasn't gained the use of that arm yet.....to tell you the truth, after Barrett got done with it.....the sight of that arm even made my stomach turn a bit .....by the way, I forgot to ask....would you like one?"* Phillips face immediately turned to a look of disgust. *"Oh, that's real funny lawman....I bet you get your jollies off that, don't you?"* Taking a puff, I answered, *"Well, never mind that....tell me more about your relationship with Lori Jenkins, Tina Hendricks, Zack Thompson and of course, Kyle Swanson."*

In my time, I had seen many different reactions come from prisoners when I questioned them and this one was no different. The surprise reaction from Phillips was choice as he stood up and walked to an adjacent wall, rubbing his forehead, not believing what names he had just heard. While he collected his thoughts and before he could spill any lies to me I blurted, *"And remember....no bullshit....I think I know what's going on here and if you try to pull the wool over my eyes, I'll open this cell door and leave....* *you can then tell my partner all about it....you got that?"* The sweat beaded up on his forehead and his greasy hair became shinier while the perspiration came out of him. The prisoner turned his head at me and with a petrified look, replied, *"I know some stuff, but I don't know what you think I know....you gonna have to give me a little slack."* Taking a few steps toward the bars, I glared back at him. *"Listen scumbag, I don't like your kind and never will....as far as I am concerned you are something that I scrape off the bottom of my shoe when I step in it......you don't know it yet, but I'm your best friend right now as they're getting ready to pin a murder rap on you and that means life if not the death penalty in this state.....and the funniest part is, I don't think you did it....so get your shit together and tell me what I want to know as I'm your only chance of beating this....otherwise you are going to spend the rest of your days in the slammer."*

Phillips sighed a little, nodding his head, and I could see him clench his teeth by the protrusions of the small muscles in his jaw. Submissive and beaten, in a soft voice he responded, *"Yeah.... go ahead..... ask me want you want to know.....I'll answer anything you ask."* Exhaling a drag off my butt, I peered through the smoke with a cold stern look, confirming the bullshit was over and he was ready to come clean. *"Okay.....then, tell me about your relation-ship with the girls and Zack Thompson."* Phillips sat back down on the bench and clasped his hands in front of him, looking directly at me. His skinny frame and dark inserted eyes spelled nothing but years of drug abuse as he beckoned me for a smoke. Reaching for it and as I lit it through the bars he answered, *"We were all friends.....especially Lori Jenkins and I.....I met Lori through a drug deal several years ago, and she eventually became my bitch....you see, sometimes the girls could not afford their habit and they had to pay for the drugs with something else, if you know what I mean..... anyway, Lori and I were busted one night for breaking into a liquor store because we were desperate for cash.....since it was our first rap, we both got probation and that did not sit too well with some of the cops and from then on, they constantly harassed us and roughed us up a little, especially me......however, one of the cops, took a liking to Lori and tried to make it with her....imagine, one of your boys in blue trying to put the boots to a heroin addict who was half his age, but she refused him and told the bastard to get lost....needless to say, the cop didn't like that at all and he beat her up pretty badly....that's when she became friends with the Hendricks chick as Lori needed a woman's shoulder to cry on and that's how we met Zack ....it wasn't long after that, we were both staying at the motel where Hendricks worked."*

As he paused to take a heavy drag from his butt, his hands were shaking, indicating he was longing for a fix. All the signs were there as sweat beaded on his forehead and the man's fingers trembled with anxiety, while he attempted to hold the cigarette steady in his mouth. Looking at him reminded me of myself only a few years ago when the *"whiskey devils"* were knocking at my door, trying to make me stay on the path of self-destruction. Trying to squeeze the nervousness from his palms by wringing them together, Phillips glared at me with bloodshot eyes and knowing I was becoming impatient for more he continued. *"Within a short period of time, Lori and I had a great business going together....you know, with the drugs and all....the cash was pouring in and before long we had bags of it..... so much, in fact, that we didn't know what to do with it all.....the funniest thing about it, the cops knew what we were up to as well, but we took care of them as we spread the cash around a little and in turn they left us alone...that is, all except for one cop who still had the hots for Lori."* Abruptly I cut in. *"You mean you were greasing the cops? Who were they and which cop was after Lori Jenkins?"*

Suddenly, his attitude changed to a look of worry as fright overwhelmed his eyes. *"I can't tell you that!...they'll kill me for Christ's sake.....just like the city woman."* Hearing those words sent shock waves to my brain as I watched the man lose it completely in front of me. He began sobbing uncontrollably and buried his head into his hands, trying to hide himself from the world. *"Well,*

I can tell you one thing right now, Mr. Phillips....while you're in here, your ass is hanging out the window......if you think someone in the department is out to kill you, they'll sure do it while you are in here....so you better spill it and come clean if I'm going to be able to help you out of this mess."

Wiping his eyes with the back of his sleeve, he looked up at me, bleeding through the whites of his eyes with desperation. *"If I tell you...you'll protect me, right?"* Upon seeing me nod my head he added, *"The big cop who took me in tonight....he's the one that had the hots for Lori and roughed her up....he's a jealous bastard and wants me dead!"* Rapidly my mind went to work, thinking that both Robinson and my old partner Russ Wilson were fairly big men, standing six feet tall. *"Which one was he talking about?"* I thought. Phillips lunged at the bars, holding on for dear life, pleading, *"The man is a maniac, I tell you....what he did to Lori was something only an animal would do.....I know we all had sex and did drugs together along with the city woman, but there was never any violence, but when that cop came around it was a different story.... he liked it rough and loved doing it that way....you have to protect me!"* With that, he collapsed to the floor, still clinging onto the bars looking like a pile of jelly. I knelt down and instantly Barrett came over as well to investigate what was going on with the man. Both of us stared at the pathetic Phillips who had just become a crushed human being. Reaching into the cell, I grabbed him by the front of his shirt and pulled him into the steel bars, saying loudly, *"Phillips, you say a cop killed the city woman?....which one was it?....tell me, who it was!"*

Crying like a kid who had lost its stuff toy, he stared up at me. *"The big cop...you know the one they call Harley."* Quickly releasing him and throwing him back a little, I looked to the side and downward, not comprehending what the man had just told me. My head felt like a buzz saw and with a terrible headache coming on fast, my mind whizzed with thoughts of, *"Detective Harley?....a crook and a murderer?....he killed Swanson?.....can it be true!"*

Quickly looking up and staring back at him I asked, *"Are you positively sure it was Detective Harley?"*

Phillips attitude seemed to change as I think he realized that I was anguishing over one of our own being possibly a killer. His head slowly rose and a slight evil grin came to his face. *"Yeah.... the big man....the one that likes to use that stick of his and I'll tell you another thing, Mr. Policeman..... he likes his sex rough, I mean real rough....I know it for a fact because we used to play sex games together all the time and one of his favorites was to strangle the girls while we screwed them."*

I fell backwards a little, not wanting to believe the scumbag behind the bars, and losing my balance I was forced to lean up against the opposite wall. Glaring up at the ceiling, I hoped that the dizziness would pass as the room was beginning to spin out of control. Forcing myself to get a grip, I detected that Phillips was smiling back at me and giggling slightly, enjoying the spectacle that was unfolding in front of him. *"Makes you kinda sick, doesn't it lawman?.....knowing that one of your so called 'brothers' is a real sicko......makes it a little hard for you to swallow, doesn't it?"* As he said those pretentious words, his eyes glowed with pleasure, and he snickered while he approached the steel bars. Still holding a sickening smug look he softly said while almost whispering, *"And do you know what lawman?....the girls loved it too....they came over and over again when he tied something around their necks, choking them to almost death......especially the city woman......she even liked it up the ass!"*

That was it, I lunged at the bars grabbing him by the shirt and yanked him towards me, smashing his face into the cell door. *"You filthy piece of shit!...you're lying!....there's no way an officer would act like that....time to turn my partner loose on you!"* I pushed him away and signaled for Barrett to join me by my side. Putting the key into the cell door, Phillips grabbed the door with all his might, pulling on it, preventing me from opening the door. *"No!...I'm not lying!....we had several romps together with the girls and Zack was there too!.....you gotta believe me!"* he hollered, holding onto the cell door for dear life.

Suddenly realizing my temper was getting the best of me; I motioned with my head for Barrett to back off and took the key out of the lock. Gathering my senses, I counted to ten under my breath and calmed myself down. *"Okay...okay, Phillips....but if you are lying I swear I will kill you myself!.....so, what's this about the city woman?.....you say she was in on these drug and sex parties, too?"* Relieved that I was not going to sick my dog on him, Phillips let out a huge sigh. *"Ahh....ahh...she was, but drugs were not her main thing and the booze wasn't either, but the sex?.....she loved it and she was good at it too.....it was amazing what she could do to a man and that friend of hers even liked to watch."* My eyes must have almost popped out of my head asking, *"What friend?...who liked to watch?"* Shaking his head back and forth, he replied, *"I don't know who he was....never got his name, but he worked for the city, that much I do know....I think he worked with her at City Hall."*

"For heaven's sake," I thought to myself. *"Was it Birmingham the Director of Planning who was screwing Kyle Swanson on the side anyway?........was he part of all of this?....and had he conveniently left this part of it out while he dumped his load of garbage on me?"* When they say curiosity killed the cat I was right on my way, since it seemed with each question I asked, my elevated feelings towards my profession were slowly being wiped away by the low-life, but I needed to know more. *"The city woman's name was Kyle Swanson, Phillips....she worked in the Planning Department....her boss's name was Birmingham....sound familiar?"* The man sat back down on the bench and rubbed his face with both hands. *"No, it doesn't....but Kyle's name makes some sense as we used to call her 'Super Kay'.....you know because she was soooo good at what she did."*

Lighting up another cigarette, I threw the match into the ashtray in the corridor, and looking over at him, I asked, *"So the man that used to watch....describe him."* Again, Phillips rubbed the back of his neck, answering, *"He was a very small man and* was well dressed.....I think he had black hair and he didn't have a beard or a mustache....he was probably in his mid forties, but I never knew his name or who he was...one thing that always struck me odd about the dude was that he had a nervous twitch....it used to bother me and make me a little nervous as he used to do it all the time...he liked to tap the side of his leg while he watched.....it seemed the more intense the sex became and the greater he enjoyed himself, the harder he slammed his leg.....I tell ya, it really spooked me out sometimes."

With sweat running off his forehead and trembling hands, Phillips looked like he had just been put through the wringer. To be frank, I think it was the combination of recalling the sex parties and his withdrawal from drugs that were causing him to approach the breaking point, but he was spilling his guts now and I was not going to let him off the hook now by stopping the interrogation. "Okay, Phillips....you said the city woman joined in all of the time and was a big part of your little sex ring.....then, you must have gotten to know her quite well." Nodding his head vigorously he answered, "Yes....like I said, I never knew her real name, but she used to tell Zack and me a lot of shit that was going on in the city... you know, private stuff......in fact, she gave me something to put in my safe, in case anything happened to her." This raised one of my eyebrows as I stared back at him. "What kind of stuff?" I anxiously replied while watching him fidget with his knees bouncing up and down as if they were spastic. Swallowing hard and trying to get a breath, Phillips peered up at me. "It was books and shit along with some papers....I never looked at them really....I just put them in my safe....she told me that if anything ever happened to her that I was to contact the State Police and give the stuff to them, but when Lori was found dead, down by the river, I took off...... I figured Harley must have had something to do with it and I was next.....he's a real nut case you know, and he's capable of anything....that's why you have to protect me.....I know he can't wait to get his hands on me because he probably thinks I going to sing.....hell, I won't last a week in here with that nut job around."

Weeping like a small child, Phillips was losing it and I knew a total breakdown was well on the way for him. What he had just told me was hard to comprehend, but the thoughts of obtaining what was in his safe made me crave for additional information. *"Okay...you say the stuff is in your safe....where is that?"* With his face all red and puffy, he raised his head with his eyes glaring at me. *"That's the trouble...the floor safe is back at my spare apartment in a closet under a box of old shoes over on fifty-two Laurel street, apartment 3C, but the real problem is I can't remember the combination to it....I tried a hundred times, but no matter how I spun the dial, it wouldn't open......I guess because of all the drugs, my mind is just a bowl of mush.....I can't even help the city woman who was so good to me....she really made me feel like a real man and the sex I experienced with her was beyond....."* Not wanting to hear anymore about his sexual escapades, I shut the man down with, *"Okay...okay...I know all about your feelings for her....just one more thing Phillips....what makes you think that Harley killed the Jenkins woman?"*

Swaying his head back and forth, he became almost delirious, trying to speak. His words were garbled, hard to understand, and as he mumbled something back to me, I knew time was running out. Without a recent *"fix,"* DT's were surely on their way and it meant that he would soon become a useless piece of meat. With little time left to get anymore-useful information out of him, I opened the cell door. Suddenly he looked up and threw himself into the far corner. With fear spilling from his eyes he hollered, *"I told you what you wanted to know!"* Rushing over and grabbing him by the front of his shirt, I rammed him up against the concrete wall. With his feet dangling off the floor, I pushed my face into his saying loudly, *"Get it together you drug ridden piece of crap!....tell me, what makes you think Harley killed Swanson and Jenkins?"*

Looking up at the ceiling, begging for words to come to his lips, Phillips cried out, *"When Lori Jenkins finally rejected him and told the guy he was old enough to be her father, Harley took up with Tina Hendricks and he eventually became obsessed over her too as he was hooked on the sex that she had given him during their romps together....it was like a drug to him and when Lori killed Tina that was too much for the man to take.... she had taken the one thing away from him that he treasured!"* Wanting to hear more from the useless human being in my grasp, I shook him, yelling, *"And the city woman?....why her?"*

Again, Phillips stared at the ceiling; wishing the nightmare was over and that I would leave his dream. Still not hearing anything coming out of him, I banged his head against the wall in frustration and Barrett instantly rose to his feet to be my side. His upper lip curled, which signaled to Phillips that he was about to be made into lunch. Seeing the mean look in the dog's eyes and crying out with fear Phillips loudly said, *"She knew about all of the corruption and the money that was being passed around City Hall......she told Zack and me that she was going to blow the whistle on everybody..... hell, the woman had been gathering shit about everyone for months and had a pile of stuff on them.... they even tried to buy her off by giving her a place to live, but she was better than that....she was a sex maniac, yes, but she wasn't crooked and corrupt....you know how the Mayor runs this town with his Gestapo sons of bitches and Harley is one of the worse!......she had to be silenced and what better way of doing it than to use that psycho bastard of his!"*

I threw Phillips to the side and he fell hard on the floor next to Barrett. Gathering himself together and sitting on the floor he blurted, *"And when Lori was killed, I knew I was next.....I tried to get that damn safe open to get at the stuff as I figured it would buy me some insurance, but when I couldn't remember how to open it, I split."*

As Phillips looked upwards with sympathetic eyes, hoping that I had bought his story, my furry partner stood over him, letting the man know that he was more than ready if he had to act. Seeing Barrett's threatening look caused Phillips to slide himself on the floor against the wall, trying to put distance between them. Barrett turned his head and glanced at me for a second and then his eyes returned to the prisoner, hoping that I would release him to do his work, but I said, *"Leave him alone, boy......he's had enough for today.....we need to get the hell out of here and get back on the hunt."*

Closing the cell door behind me Phillips jumped to his feet and lunged at the bars. *"You gotta protect me!....they're going to snuff me for sure!"* Walking away from him down the long hallway I turned my head slightly, saying, *"Behave yourself and you'll be fine....they wouldn't dare do anything to you until they find out what you might have told me....so, just sit tight."*

As I opened the door to enter the back offices, everyone was there waiting for me, and it did not take long for the chief to ask, *"Well?....did he confess, Madison?"* The others peered at me with anxiety written all over their faces in anticipation of my success. Not wanting to tip my hand on what I had learned, I chuckled replying, *"In a way he did....after he sobers up and with a little more coaxing later, we'll get a complete confession out of him...I'm sure of it, but he has had enough for now."*

When I finished saying that, you could see the relief come to their faces as the grins and smiles came forth. Detective Harley, however, kept a stern look and while I handed his nightstick back to him he asked, *"Did you have to persuade him a little?....I hope you did.....that thing back there is nothing but a cancer on society....he deserves anything that you gave him."* That brought a chuckle out of him as he placed the stick beneath his jacket on his belt. I wanted to arrest Harley right there, but without any of the evidence from Phillip's safe, I was still unsure about what Phillips had told me. After all, it could have been just a junkie talking to save his own skin, trying to pin the murder rap on someone else, and what better person than a rogue cop? *"Yeah, he's a scumbag alright, Harley....the lowest of the low,"* I replied heading for the exit door. Exhibiting a great deal of concern the chief immediately moved in my direction and grabbed me from behind. *"Where do you think you're going?....a report needs to be filed on your findings so far."* I shook loose his grip and stared directly into his eyes. *"I don't have anything to file yet.....I need to check a few loose ends first and then you'll get your damn report."*

Not giving him the chance to grab me again, Barrett and I headed out the door along with the chief hollering, *"I want that God damn report, Madison.....and I want it tonight on my desk or else you'll be cleaning toilets in cell blocks for the rest of your stinking career!.....you hear me!"* While Barrett walked beside me as we exited the building, I could still hear the chief yelling at the top of his lungs, but we just kept going. There was little time to waste, considering what was at stake, and with Phillips still in jail, if what he had told me was the truth, it would only be a matter of time before he had an unfortunate *"accident."* After all, one more killing would have meant nothing to the Veratex Corporation at this point so they could protect their real estate scheme of making millions of dollars. In my own mind, I had little skepticism left that the serial killer was probably a figment of everyone's imagination, as I still believed that most of the murders had been committed to serve as a cover up for the Swanson murder. All except for Tina Hendricks, that is, Lori Jenkins had undoubtedly killed her, since both Zack and Ty Phillips confirmed that and all of the evidence discovered so far backed up their version of events.

Zack's theory about Tina Hendricks killing Swanson for revenge over a love triangle was probably wrong; however, as it did not make a whole lot of sense as the evidence did not support it. I was convinced Swanson had been murdered to silence her, but I needed the ledgers and other materials to prove it. With the hounds on my trail, it was becoming increasingly apparent that I had to reach the safe in Philip's apartment before anyone else. Opening the door to my car for Barrett, the only thing on my mind now was to retrieve the documents before they could be destroyed by the Veratex organization or even by someone in our own police department. Starting the car and revving the engine, I peeled out of the parking lot and blasted down Main Street. Headed for Phillip's apartment, I hoped that I was not going to be too late, because if Swanson's records were already gone, there would be little chance, if any, of bringing anyone to justice.

CHAPTER NINETEEN
The Race is On!

It only took me about twenty minutes to reach Ty Phillip's spare apartment on Laurel Street, which was on the southern part of town. That was common with major drug dealers as they usually had several places to live in order to avoid the police or unsatisfied customers. However, I always hated the Laurel Street area, as it was the poorest section of the city, filled with nothing but drug addicts and the *"undesirables"* of our society. Prostitution was commonplace here as there were girls constantly working the streets, looking for prospective clients. We constantly arrested them and threw the *"ladies"* in jail, but their pimps bailed them out as quickly as they were put in. Without fail the next night, they would be back on the street and the vicious cycle would start all over again. Even after several offenses, the courts went easy on them and gave most of the girls' probation. In fact, the more repeated offenders, if they got any jail time at all would receive less than thirty days and then they were back to work again. Because of this, the departmental personnel mainly stayed out of this section of the city, unless political pressure came down on the chief. When it did, we were forced into a token appearance and made a few arrests to please the politicians, but normally once a few girls were taken into custody our *"big take down operation"* would fold up shop and then we would worry about more pressing matters. In a nut shell, that is the way the system worked and unfortunately, there was little in the wind to change it.

Pulling up to his address, Phillips lived in a four-story apartment building that should have been torn down a long time ago. The rat-infested structure was crumbling from years of neglect and the bottom of its brick facade was almost fully covered in graffiti from neighboring gangs. Several of the windows were boarded up with plywood and most of the remaining uncovered glass was broken. The single flight of stairs leading up to the front entrance was made out of concrete and even those had been badly chipped in places along with markings of various colors of paint.

As my eyes continued to survey the premises, the deplorable shape of the building reminded me of the structures that were bombed over in Europe during the war, making it very hard to understand how any person could have lived under those conditions. Standing in front of the building the dead silence which enveloped the area added to the eeriness of the place and even Barrett carefully tip toed up the concrete stairs while his head turned from side to side, looking for possible trouble. Opening the front door to go inside, the ceiling of the main lobby looked like it was going to fall in at any moment, since several sections of the old horsehair plaster were hanging everywhere. Several punched holes and graffiti littered the walls along with broken windows. Climbing the stairs, trash consisting of old food wrappers and garbage were scattered in the stairwell, and upon reaching the third floor, I noticed the stairs to the right of me that led to the fourth floor. I was glad Phillips lived on the third floor as the stairs leading upwards were in horrendous condition, looking like they could collapse just from their own weight. Walking past a few closed doors his apartment number eventually came into view and even that was crooked with the number three missing a mounting screw, allowing it to fall at an angle.

Pulling my gun from its holster and turning the doorknob the door went ajar, surprising me a little that it was unlocked. Glancing down at Barrett, I instructed him to stay so he could watch my back while I entered the apartment. Instantly, upon opening the door a horrid odor filled my nostrils as the tell tale smell of body odor and urine filled the air. Peering inside, the apartment was in total disarray with soiled clothes thrown everywhere and the kitchen table was covered in dirty dishes with decaying food on them. As my eyes scanned the living room area and kitchen, which consisted of one large room, the wallpaper was hanging off the walls and there were several holes in the sheetrock, telling me of the numerous *"battles"* that had occurred here in the past. *"If these walls could talk,"* I mumbled to myself, working my way over to one of the bedroom doors. *"I bet the stories they could tell would make your hair stand up."*

Carefully taking a couple of more steps over some piled trash on the floor I suddenly heard the sound that could make any cop cringe with utmost fear and that was the pulling back of a hammer on a handgun. *"Hold it right there, mister....don't make a move or I'll blow your fucking head off,"* a weak, but convincing female voice said behind me. *"What the hell do you want here Mister?"* Not responding at first she further demanded, *"Get your hands up or I'll give it to you in the back!"*

Before I could answer her and while raising my hands, a familiar sound filled the room. *"Grrrrrr"* echoed through the place, causing a deadening silence to fall over it. I could hear the woman's heartbeat pound throughout the room as she whispered, *"What the hell is that?"* Glancing backwards over my shoulder I could see Barrett at the front door, crouched, and ready to kill. *"Lady, if you don't put that gun down right now, you are about to meet hell itself....I'm a cop and I am here to help you....so be a good little girl and put that gun of yours on the floor because even if you pull that trigger and get me, it will be the last thing you ever do on this earth....that, I can promise you."*

I could see out of the corner of my eye that her head had turned towards Barrett's direction and she found what I was talking about. All one hundred and thirty pounds of my partner was ready as the hair on the back of his black back was standing straight up and his yellow eyes gleamed with fiery hell in them. It even made me nervous seeing Barrett like that, as he was no longer a controllable beast, but a pure demon from hell that would tear a person's throat out as a wolf often does to a deer or an elk. *"You better decide pretty quickly my dear or else you are going to meet your maker in a few seconds.....put the gun down, now!"*

Slowly turning my head, I saw her stoop and place the gun on the floor. As she stood back up she fearfully said, *"You said you are here to help us?....where's Ty?.....what's happened to him?.....is he hurt?"* Gradually turning around, my eyes fell upon a young girl in her late teens whose blonde hair was stringy and greasy due to all of the oils in it. The petite girl's face was dirty and her clothes were severely tattered. Along with several holes in her blue jeans and wearing no shoes, she looked more like a refugee than a normal citizen. Scanning her up and down, I determined that if she weighed ninety pounds soaking wet, she was lucky and the needle marks in her arms told me that she lived on something else besides food. Her once stunning eyes were encompassed by dark circles and her Lilly white skin was puck marked with scabs, telling me this once beautiful young girl had now become a full-fledged drug whore. *"I'm a cop......your boyfriend is being held downtown for questioning and if he doesn't get my help, I'm afraid they are going to pin a murder rap on him for killing Lori Jenkins..... and the way things are going for him, they might just add some other murders as well."*

I saw her lifeless eyes start to go backwards in her head as she passed out in front of me. Quickly, I grabbed her from falling to the floor and while putting my gun back in its holster I placed her down into a kitchen chair. Squatting down and holding the young girl from falling forwards by placing my hands against her shoulders I said, *"Hold on there, miss......you're going to be alright....just take it easy for a moment."* In the meantime, Barrett had walked over, trying to figure out what was wrong by sniffing her up and down. It was only a few seconds later that I saw life return to her eyes and gaining consciousness, she gazed up at me, screaming, *"Oh my God!.....get that fucking thing away from me!"* Barrett immediately backed up a little, surprised at the girl's reaction.

"Don't worry miss...he won't hurt you now...he's your buddy," I said as I motioned with my head for Barrett to back up a little more. Seeming to have calmed down a little the young girl grabbed my arm, pleading, *"Ty didn't kill anyone....he's never done anything like that in his life!.....Ty's a kind and gentle person that wouldn't hurt a fly....oh, we've done drugs together and stole for sure, but we never hurt anybody....you say you're here to help him?"*

Patting her on the head like a small child I answered, *"Yeah, I don't believe he killed anyone either, but unless I can get some information out of you, your boyfriend will be heading for the chair or the can for the rest of his life....so what's it going to be?"* Suddenly tears began flowing down her cheeks as she grabbed one of my hands, pulling it towards her, wanting to be held and protected. *"I'll help you anyway I can, sir....just ask me what you want to know....I'll do anything for Ty."* Slowly and gingerly, she brought my hand to her lips and kissed it, rubbing her cheek against my fingers. *"Do you like me?....we can party first, if you want to....I'll make you feel real good."*

Trying to stomach the stench that was coming from her and the deplorable condition she was in, the sickening sight was even making me queasy. During the war, it was a common sight for homeless civilians to look and smell the way this girl did and her offer of *"pleasing me"* was something I wanted no part of. Watching her blood shot eyes bleed from their sockets down her rosy, scabbed cheeks while she made a gingerly move with her hand towards my crotch, caused me to back up a step. *"No.....that's quite alright, Miss.....maybe some other time.....the main thing now is for you to tell me where the safe is."*

Distress came over her as she stood up, looking like I had invaded her mind. *"How do you know about that?....did Ty tell you?"* Pulling a cigarette from my shirt pocket, I lit up and took a drag from it, while peering back at her through the exhaled smoke. *"Yeah, he told me all about it....where is it?"* As she hesitated for a moment and then attempted to move away from me, I placed my hand on her shoulder. *"You're in trouble too, Miss....*

if you aren't cooperative, by the looks of those tracks on your arms, drying out in a prison cell won't be a pleasant experience.....have you ever seen anybody 'Jones' out before?.....it's not a pretty sight, I tell ya......it starts off with the cold sweats and the jitters....then you get the uncontrollable shakes.....soon, the clothes on your back will become drenched with sweat and a deep coldness will set in, making you curl into a fetal position to bear the pain....you will begin to beg for God to take you and end your miserable suffering, but no help will come as your frantic pleas and screams will go unheard.....then the little bugs will come to visit you....at first there will be a couple, then a few more.....soon, thousands of them will be crawling all over you.....frantically, you will try to pick and brush them off, but no matter how hard you try, they'll keep coming and coming.....you'll scratch and scream, pleading for sanity to return, and when you think you have lost your mind, that's when the little animals will appear to help you along your way.....they'll crawl out of the walls and emerge from the floor, chattering.....squealing....taking bites out of you......oh, you'll try and fight them off too at first, but it will be useless as nothing will stop them..... and just when you think you have reached the epiphany of suffering and despair and can take no more, the demons from hell will magically appear, taking you to a......" Almost out of her mind with trepidation and not being able to withstand it anymore she grabbed me with both arms, screaming, *"Enough!....enough already!....the safe is in the closet....there, in that room!"*

As the girl pointed to a door beside the bathroom, I picked up her .38 revolver and headed that way. Barrett began following me, but holding out my hand I instructed, *"You keep the lady company....I'll be right back."* My partner took a seat beside her and with drool leaking out his mouth, he licked his chops while looking up at her. Repulsed by his actions the young girl took a seat at the table, keeping her distance away from him.

Upon opening the door to the spare bedroom, it became evident that it was only used as a place to collect junk, as the room was something right out of a hoarder's house. Several piles of debris consisting of old typewriters, books, magazines, and other loose papers littered the floor. Little furniture was in the room except for a pullout couch that contained dirty, yellowed sheets and a sofa chair, which had several burn holes in it. On the opposite wall was the closet door and opening it, the small room was stuffed to the ceiling with cardboard boxes filled with more books and dirty clothes. This was a common occurrence, since drug addicts and dealers often did not wash their clothes as they had piles of drug money at their disposal. To put it simply, they usually bought new clothes when they needed them and threw the dirty ones away.

Moving the numerous cardboard boxes aside, a filthy carpeted floor was revealed. Surprisingly at first, there was no evidence of a safe, but upon closer examination, I detected a slight bulge in the carpet. Taking my pocketknife I determined that the carpet easily lifted and rolling it back, a dial to a safe was exposed. Reaching into my pocket and retrieving the combination I thought to myself, *"This whole case depends on what is in here.....if its what I think it is......a lot of people are going down."* After turning the dial left and right according to the numbers, I grabbed the handle and tried to turn it left, then right, but it did not budge. Trying the combination again, the safe still did not open. Attempting the combination for a third time I mumbled, *"This must be the right safe....what else could this combination be for?"*

After several more futile attempts, I sat with my back against the wall in total frustration. Staring at the small piece of paper, the combination L12 R41 L25 seemed clear enough and the thoughts of busting into the safe started to enter my mind. *"Calling a safe company is just what I need right about now,"* I murmured, staring at it. *"To bring more attention to this is not good....at least right now it isn't."* Not giving up I spun the dial and tried the combination again, unfortunately with the same result. *"I can't believe this!... what the hell is going on here?"* I said aloud, gazing at the combination on the small piece of paper. Suddenly, I sensed someone standing over me and glancing up the young girl along with

Barrett were peering down at me. *"What's the matter, sir?....I bet you can't open it, can you?"*

Standing up to confront her, the grin on the young addicts face pissed me off. *"Yeah, that's right....I can't open the God damn thing and I guess you know the reason why, don't you?....well, I'm going to let you in on a little secret, Missy....if you don't open that son of a bitch right now I'm going to haul your little ass down to lockup and then you'll lose that shit eaten grin of yours."* Pointing my finger into the center of her chest I smiled, adding, *" and when you eventually wind up in the pen with big Mama Cass, a young, sweet thing like you walking down the cell block won't last two minutes.....she'll get a hold of your little ass some dark and lonely night and show you how nightmares are born!"*

Not seeming to be fazed in the least with my threat, the young addict sat down in the old sofa chair and folded her hands together in front of her. Chuckling, she looked at me waiting for a reaction, but not seeing one she said, *"You cops are all alike....you think you're so smart.....you look down at all of us like we are the scum of the earth....well, mister we aren't scum....we are just every day folk who are trying to make it in this damn, stinking world.... look at you, sitting there among all our garbage, feeling sorry for yourself that you can't open a little safe.....and do you know why?..... it's because you aren't so smart after all....you're really...."*

Having enough of the whore's bullshit, I grabbed the bitch and lifted her out of the sofa chair, pulling her smelly body in close to mine. *"Listen, you drugged up little piece of crap....your boyfriend that you supposedly care so much about is being set up to take the rap and that could mean old 'sparkie' for him......do you know what that means?....death by the electric chair or worse yet, living his remaining years in a stinking hole that they call a jail cell.......but by the looks of him he will clean up real nice for Big Bubba who will certainly make him his favorite bitch......yeah, you're right about me having to wade in your filth....that's because it's my job and do I like doing that?...hell no....sure, I'd like to be in a nice, clean office somewhere writing reports and stuffing manila envelopes rather than dealing with this crap....so little girl, you better smarten up pretty God damn quick or I'll have your drugged up ass downtown within the hour!"*

Probably seeing the fire in my eyes the girl quickly answered, *"I don't know how to open the safe as the combination was never given to me....Ty kept that a secret as he set aside all of his stash and money in it......he felt the fewer the people that knew about it, the better, but Lori was his business partner....she knew how to open it."* Staring at the paper in my hand she grinned and said, *"But I might know what's wrong with those numbers written on that piece of paper.....what's it worth to you, big man?"*

Losing my patience, I grabbed the back of her head and filled my hand full of greasy, blonde hair. Yanking her head backwards and forcing her to look at me I hollered, *"Okay, bitch, this is it!... ..I'm going to give you one last chance.....tell me what you do know or else!"* Wincing from me pulling her hair she desperately replied, *"Lori got everything backwards all the time as she was forever making dumb mistakes with money and things....you know, giving wrong change back by mixing up numbers.....we used to kid her all the time about it, especially when she gave a false social security number to apply for a driver's license......she got in real trouble for that...... but it wasn't that it was a false number, she just got the numbers backwards.....maybe you should look at that combination in a way like she would have."*

Pondering a moment on what she had just said, I studied the numbers on the sheet and wondered if she had a point. Deciding to reverse the first number from twelve to twenty-one I tried that set of numbers, but the safe still did not open. Then I noticed that the numbers on the dial went only as high as fifty. Reversing the third number from twenty-five to fifty-two was impossible, but reversing the second from forty-one to fourteen was feasible to coincide with the range of the dial. Finally, coming up with a combination of L21 R14 L25, I tried spinning the tumbler again. Coming to the final number of twenty-five and letting out a huge sigh of anticipation, I turned the handle to the left and the safe opened easily.

Glancing up at the girl, she was smiling down at me. *"You see, lawman....us druggies aren't so dumb after all."* Giving her a sincere look of appreciation, my eyes then returned to the contents of the safe. It was loaded with cash and bags of what I suspected were heroin, but the main thing that caught my eye was a large Manila envelope with the name *"Veratex"* marked on the outside. Reaching in and pulling it from the safe, I must have been smiling because the girl quickly said, *"Looks like you found what you were looking for....what's going to happen to all of that cash and other stuff?"*

I stood up with the envelope in my hand and peered down at the cash in the safe along with the drugs. Staring at her with a serious look I answered, *"Never mind the money or the drugs.... your life right about now means about as much as a piss hole in the snow.....there are people out there that will kill for the information that's in this envelope and I bet someone is on their way over here to look for it now.....these people will stop at nothing to get at this stuff and putting you to sleep with a bullet to the brain is something that they would enjoy doing, if you get my drift."* Reaching down I pulled a wad of cash out of the safe and handed it to her. *"Here, take this.....you'll need this to get out of town and lay low for a while."* Retrieving a piece of paper from my pocket, I jotted down a few lines, and handed the note to her. *"This is my girlfriend's address.... her name is Andrea and she'll take good care of you....I am going to take you down to the bus station today and have you go there....if you want to live, you'll do exactly what I say, otherwise your naked body is going to be found in a suitcase down by the river."*

I do not think she believed me as she took the cash from my hand because a smirk developed across her face. *"What about the white powder?....can I take some of that, too?"* Her glassy, bloodshot eyes shined in the light as she stared at the huge treasure trove of drugs in the safe and looking mesmerized by it, it was obvious to me that the only thing on her brain now was to get a buzz from the shit. Not wanting the girl to blow a gasket from withdrawal, I handed one of the smaller bags to her. *"Alright....take this too....at least it will keep you from trying to find the shit somewhere else....I need your ass on that bus to my girlfriend's house."*

Anxious, I opened the large, manila envelope. It was loaded with what I had hoped for as it was filled with copies of deeds and other papers outlining the Veratex land holdings along with dozens of bank account numbers. Additionally, there was a long list of names adjacent to the various property holdings along with deed transactions of numerous parcels of land. Most damaging was an itemized list, outlining how thousands of dollars had been paid to various city officials for building permits and approvals. There was even a cross reference of the various individuals with their ownership to fake corporations and land trusts. *"It must have taken Swanson months to gather this amount of information,"* I mumbled to myself. *"Look at these names....everybody is listed here,"* as my eyes scanned the lists. *"The health director, the city treasurer, the tax collector and the city accountant...they were all in on it...even the chief is listed here....wow!...did he ever hit it big with this operation."*

My eyes returned to the girl and as I extended the documents for her to see I said, *"Do you know what these are?.....they're a bunch of nails in people's coffins regarding their careers and lives...... some of them are very powerful people with a long reach and with this stuff it means a lot of people are going down the shit chute...... lives like yours won't mean a hill of beans once this stuff hits the streets.....that's why it's imperative that we get you out of town as soon as possible....go pack a bag, I'm taking you to the bus station right now!"*

Reading the seriousness in my face, she retrieved a medium sized suitcase out of the hall closet and began throwing some clothes into it. Closing the safe, I replaced the carpeting and piled the boxes back on top of it. *"What are you going to do?"* she asked while stuffing some toiletries in the upper portion of her suitcase. *"Won't they be coming after you as well?"* While reorganizing the materials back into the manila envelope I replied, *"Don't worry about me, it's you that we need to get out of here because I don't know who can be trusted at this point....the biggest problem we have right now is that I might have been followed here....I want you to go out the back way and meet me two blocks over on Day Street..... there's a gas station on the corner....hide in the ladies room until we get there.....Barrett and I will go out the front and make sure that we are not being tailed before we come and pick you up."* Noticing that she was half listening to me because of her drugged up state, I grabbed her by both shoulders and shook her a little, trying to knock a little sense into her. *"And whatever you do, don't leave until we get there....you got that?"* Nodding her head, I let her go and giggling slightly, she headed for the door. Before she opened it, I reached out and grabbed her shoulder from behind. Spinning her around, I tried to make her realize the seriousness of the situation we were all in by glaring directly into her eyes, with a cold heartened stare. *"Remember, don't let anybody see you on the way and stay at the gas station until we get there, okay?...... and wipe that stupid grin off your face as there is nothing funny about this my dear.....your life depends upon it."* With a simple nod, her grin dissipated and I watched her cautiously walk down the dark hallway to the back of the building. Stuffing the manila envelope beneath my shirt, I looked down at Barrett. *"Come on...we'll go out the front and make it look like we got nothing from here."*

As we exited the building, there were several cars parked along the street. It was evident by their condition that some of them had not been moved in weeks or even months. One car was entirely up on blocks with the tires removed while two others across the street had their windows smashed out of them. *"What a Zoo,"* I thought walking down the deteriorated concrete steps and as I reached the bottom, a flash of light hit my eyes. Trying to ascertain the direction it was coming from, it became apparent that it was a reflection of some kind and continuing to walk to my car I suddenly realized that the light was coming from a pair of binoculars in a car further up the street. The vehicle was parked about sixty yards from me on the opposite side of the paved way and I could make out the definite outline of two men in the front seat. *"Don't look now ole boy, but it looks like we have company,"* I said to Barrett letting him into the back of the car. Walking around to the driver's side and opening the door, I noticed that the man in the passenger's seat of the other vehicle was still looking through his binoculars at me. Climbing into my seat, I closed the door in a casual manner as to not tip them off that their cover had been blown. Starting the car, I pulled out into the line of traffic and noticed in my rear view that the car behind us did the same by making a U-turn. *"You better lie down and hold on,"* I said aloud to Barrett sitting in the back seat. *"Any minute here, things could get pretty rough."*

Heading my warning, Barrett snuggled close to one of the doors to brace himself and looking for a possible escape route, I decided to take a hard left down Holly Street. Flooring the gas pedal, instantly I saw the car in my rear view lunge forward as they accelerated towards us. With the engine roaring, I banged another hard left onto Proctor Ave., speeding at over seventy miles per hour down the narrow street and while taking the sharp corner the car slid sideways, smashing into several garbage cans along the sidewalk. Hurling them into the lawn area of an adjacent house, I quickly glanced in my rear view mirror and saw trash strewn everywhere, leaving dozens of loose papers floating in the air.

To my surprise the other car was still not far behind as they crashed through the toppled cans and rubbish. Pushing the accelerator to the floor, trying to get more speed, I took a hard right down Pearson's Alley Way, which was nothing more than a wide footpath between two rows of run down houses. As small limbs from trees and bushes hit the windshield I was almost driving blind, but still holding the *"pedal to the metal,"* I busted through a white, picketed fence onto Fifth Street. Not letting off the gas, I swerved the car to the left and slid almost twenty feet, broad siding a parked car. Poor Barrett went flying through the air in the back seat into the passenger's door on the opposite side while I hammered the throttle again, speeding off down the street.

Taking still another right onto Chalmers Street, I grabbed a quick glance in my rear view mirror while going down the street and saw no one behind us. *"That must have done it, Barrett....looks like we lost them,"* I said aloud taking a hard left back onto Berry Avenue. Barrett was sitting up again, looking out both side windows at the passing scenery. He appeared to be actually enjoying the wild ride and I swear he was smiling, while he looked over his shoulder out the rear window. Seeming to confirm my suspicions, he added a few exuberant barks of approval while his head turned around and looked at me.

Taking no chances, I took the long way around to get back onto Day Street where the young girl was supposedly waiting for me at the gas station and pulling into the pumps the attendant immediately came out to greet us. *"Fill her up?"* he asked while looking the car over. Not believing what he was seeing, he began closely examining the heavily damaged passenger's side of the vehicle, which had a major portion of the rear quarter panel dangling in the air and the rear bumper was missing. Taking his cap off and scratching his head, I could see that his attention was then drawn to the hood, which had several branches and debris on it. Continuing to survey the car, he noticed that there were very large dents and scrape marks along both sides, the hood was buckled and the passenger's side window was among the missing. Noticing that the windshield was severely cracked as well, with a confused look and still gazing at the vehicle he asked, *"What the hell happened to your car?......were you involved in an accident or something Mister?"*

Before I could answer him, the young girl appeared and yanked the passenger's side door open. Throwing her suitcase in the back and hopping in the front seat she hollered, *"My ass...it's full of broken glass!"* and immediately raised her butt, wiping the broken pieces off the seat onto the floor. Still cursing while she removed pieces of glass from her backside, the attendant looked on saying, *"Where in the hell have you been with this car, Mister?.... it looks like you went through the woods with it!"* Slamming the car into gear and hitting the accelerator I yelled back, *"Took the short cut....saved a lot of time too!"* Speeding out of the gas station and glancing in my rear view mirror I saw the attendant still standing there, scratching the back of his head, trying to figure out what he had just seen.

"What the hell happened to your car?....it looks like you were in one of those demolition derby's," the young girl asked while she picked up the last few pieces of glass from her seat before sitting back down. Suddenly, while she rested her head back against the seat, a large wet tongue gave her a greeting on the back of the neck. Lunging forward she said loudly, *"For Christ's sake.... do you have to bring that thing everywhere you go?"* Smiling back at her, I replied, *"Yep....where I go, he goes, Miss......never mind.... that 'thing' back there as you call it, has saved my ass a few times during our safaris together."* Furiously wiping the back of her neck from the gooey saliva she answered, *"Well, he's gross; licking me like that.....he should learn some manners."* Laughing out loud, I reached back and grabbed Barrett by the head, giving him a few rubs. *"He's just saying that he likes you and is glad that you made it back to us...that's all."*

Still wiping her neck she added, *"You didn't tell me what happened to your car and from the scenery that is going by, this is not the way to the bus station... I thought you were taking me there."* As I took a turn down a back street, keeping to the side roads, I glanced over at the young girl who was still fidgeting. *"We are going to the bus station, but not in this town.....that would be the first place that they would look for you.....I'm taking your ass over to another city and put you on a bus to my girlfriend's place from there.....and far as the condition of the car?.....that will be the condition of your head if they ever get a hold of you......you have to realize little lady, one more killing won't mean a hill of beans to them, especially a drugged out bitch like yourself."*

I knew she was pissed because for the next hour there was not another word uttered between us and as we made our way over to the bus station in Greenfield, she kept her head down with her eyes closed. Even Barrett tried to nuzzle his nose at her neck a few times to get some attention, but she shrugged my partner off, not wanting to acknowledge him. When we finally reached the bus depot, I pulled down a side street and stopped. Putting the car in park, I turned slightly and smiled at her in the passenger's seat. *"Okay...we're here....remember what I told you....take the bus directly to Portland....my girlfriend Andrea will be there waiting for you and will pick you up there...when you get off the bus, just stand there and do nothing.....when a woman approaches you, she will say, 'Barrett is a good boy' and that will tell you, she is Andrea......don't worry, my girlfriend is a great gal and will take good care of you..... remember, this is not a game little lady and if you ever want to see that boyfriend of yours again, you'll do what you're told....otherwise it will be a one way ticket to the river for you....you got that?"*

Not looking up she continued to hang her head, looking like she was going to cry. Without muttering a word for several moments, I finally reached over and grabbed her by the shoulder. *"Are you listening to me?"* She shook loose my grip of her and flung open the door, getting out of the car. Reaching over the back seat and grabbing her suitcase, she slammed the broken door shut. With bits of broken glass flying everywhere, she turned to me and yelled, *"Yeah...I got it, but you better let nothing happen to Ty.... otherwise I won't testify to shit!"* Flipping her middle finger at me with a vengeance, I watched her quickly turn and walk to the bus station. Stomping her feet with every step, she threw open the door and entered the building, dragging the suitcase behind her. As she disappeared, I put the car into drive and glanced at Barrett in the rearview mirror. *"Now you know why I never got married again, partner......when the female species gets a hair across their ass, you better watch out.....do they ever get pissed!"* Barrett's eyes were on her as well and after saying that, his head turned to me. Panting, he gave two short woofs and put his right paw on the back of my shoulder. Putting the car into gear, I chuckled, saying, *"I thought you would agree with me,"* and stepping hard on the accelerator we headed back to Harrisburg.

CHAPTER TWENTY
Where to Go From Here?

I t took us less than an hour to get back to the city and while driving there; my mind was turning with options on what do go next. Gazing down at the large manila envelope on the seat, I knew what was sitting beside me was the hammer that was going to crush many of people's lives and put them away for a very long time. *"There is no telling what they will do to get this....I need to protect this evidence, but how?"* I thought while taking a right turn onto Main Street. *"This is the foundation of the case...without it, we have no case, but to whom can I give it to?....who can I trust?.....it seems almost every city employee has become a crook in this town and our department is no exception....with even the chief on the list, how far has it spread throughout the force?..... what if something happens to me?....none of this material will ever see the light of day and those bastards will be let off the hook....there's got to be a way of securing this stuff."*

As the post office came into view, it suddenly dawned on me what needed to be done. My chief back in Middleton, Maine was the answer and mailing the package to Ben Morse was the obvious solution. *"Yeah, I know he can be trusted as there is no doubt in my mind that he is as honest as the day is long......plus, there's no way he has been associated with any of this."* Nodding my head in agreement with my own assertion I chuckled aloud and thought, *"My loyal friend, Ben Morse doesn't know it yet, but he is about to* become a big part of this whole mess....hell, once he sees what I have gotten him into, he'll probably throw my ass out of town."

Pulling into the post office parking lot and stopping the car, I reached into the glove compartment while noticing a patron walking by. By the befuddled look on his face, it was obvious he was examining the damage to my vehicle and trying to figure out what had happened to it. Smiling back at him through the broken windshield as he passed me by I said, *"You should see the other car.....it's got some real problems."* Even with my smile, it did not break the ice as the man quickly turned and scurried to the front door. Chuckling and taking out a pen I began writing a short note to Ben about the material I was sending him along with a brief summary of what I had discovered so far in Harrisburg.

"Ben....the material contained in this envelope is a summary of the corruption that is going on here.....it is running rampant throughout this city as it seems everybody is on the take and the worse part of it is, I think a Detective by the name of Harley is actually a suspected serial killer or should I say a contract killer.....I believe he has been covering up his crimes of eliminating threats to an organization known as the Veratex Corporation by murdering other people at random.....I suspect that Detective Harley probably killed a woman by the name of Kyle Swanson, the author of the materials in this package, who worked for the city planning office..... she had been gathering evidence related to the corrupt real estate transactions that were being conducted by the Veratex Company headed by Charlie Shields, but before she was able to expose them, she was murdered.....but to cover up the killing, Harley murdered others to make it appear that a serial killer was on the loose in the city......they know I am hot on their trail as they have already tried to kill me and I expect them to try again....I don't have to tell you how valuable this stuff is....keep it in a safe place and tell no one about it, including the state boys as I believe the corruption goes at least that high or even higher.....I will contact you when I have more.......Shake."

Placing the note in the manila envelope, I sealed it, and brought it into the post office. After paying for the postage and as the envelope left my hand, I watched the package drop into a huge mail basket behind the clerk. I uttered a sigh of relief, since the package was now under the protection of the federal mail system and not in my hands where it could be stolen or destroyed. Leaving the building my eyes constantly scanned the street and parking lot, seeking the car that had chased me only a few hours before. To my relief, everything seemed normal enough as several patrons were hustling back and forth to the building and with no sign of the vehicle; I quickly got back into my car and headed down the street.

I was still undecided on what to do next, so to give myself some time I drove around the block a few times, analyzing in my mind the different alternatives that were before me. *"I need someone here that I can trust too,"* I thought. *"Someone that is in the department preferably, but who could that be?.....the only person that I can even think of would be my old partner Russ Wilson, but he walked away from the case, leaving me to fend for myself......as he put it, he just wanted to finish up his stretch, retire, and receive a pension..... after all, he had made that pretty clear to me, but I desperately need someone now, so I guess there is little choice....Russ will have to be the one."*

Content with my decision and since it was Saturday I headed for his house hoping that he might be home. Russ lived on Hill Street, which was on the Northeast side, a nice part of town. Being a cop, he liked to get away from it all and this area was the place to do it in, as this area was usually quiet. However, this part of town was both blessed and cursed at the same time since it had extremely low crime, but the property taxes were sky high as well. Because of this, Russ lived a relatively simple and conservative life, as it was the only way he could afford to live in this area on a detective's salary.

As I pulled up to his house, I noticed that his car was parked in the driveway and not in the garage. Opening my door, I exited the vehicle, but before I could close it, the side screen door of the house opened and Russ emerged. *"Heh there, partner,"* he called out. *"What brings you around?"* Noticing that Barrett was staring at him from the back seat, I saw that his ears were at full alert and when a slight snarl came out of him, I promptly instructed the unruly pup to behave himself. Telling him to lie down I answered back, *"Nice day isn't it?.....we don't get many days like this in New England, do we Russ?"*

As Russ approached me, he chuckled saying, *"Well, I'm sure you're not here about going on a picnic....what's on your mind?"* Knowing he was not a person for small talk, I got right to the point. *"I really need your help, Russ....this case is about to be blown wide open and a lot of people are going to be headed for the slammer, but the biggest problem I have is, who those people are."* My old partner's eyes grew wide as I started to explain what I had found out and how bad the corruption was, leading possibly to the chief himself. Lighting up a pressure butt, Russ glared at me through the exhaled smoke while he leaned his back against the car. *"I tried to tell you Shake, but you didn't listen......now you know how bad this city really is.....it's a sewer for Christ's sake and just about everyone who works for it, is a big God damn rat....and the sad thing about it is, you have probably only scratched the surface."*

Watching him enjoy his long drags off his butt, made my cravings come alive and I lit one up myself. Exhaling a large cloud of smoke into the fall air and leaning on the car next to him, I lowered my head thinking about the mess we were in. *"Oh, it's bad, Russ....I think it might even go all the way up to the chief.....it seems everybody has been wetting their beak on this as the real estate scheme that the Veratex corporation has been running in this town for the past several years has been throwing money at almost every public official in City Hall.....but the real problem that's looking at us in the face now is the actual reason for the killings."*

My old partner's eyes grew even larger when I said that as he took a deep inhale of his cigarette. Exhaling slowly, he gazed at me through the cloud of smoke with astonishment in his face.

*"What do you mean by the real reason behind the killings, Shake?....
we are dealing with a serial killer....aren't we?"* I did not know what
kind of relationship Russ had with Detective Harley, whether
it was a good or bad one. The different roads our conversation
could possibly take ran quickly through my mind as I pondered
for a moment. How was I going to drop the bomb of telling him
that one of our own was probably a contract killer? Almost biting
my tongue, I looked at him out of the corner of one eye, replying,
*"What I am about to tell you, Russ, may shock you a little, but I
believe we are not hunting a serial killer....I think we are mixed up
in a bucketful of corruption by city officials who are working with
a corporation that will stop at nothing in order to keep their money
making machine in operation....Kyle Swanson, a very intelligent and
dedicated employee, who worked for the Planning Department, was
about to bring everybody down by her research and development of
key evidence, exposing the massive corruption in this city.....upon
discovering this, the powers to be decided to have her killed, but in
order to do that, they needed to create a diversion....something that
would throw us all off the track and that would take our eyes off the
ball, so to speak.... and what better way to screw with a cop's mind
than to mix in a few other killings, making it appear it was the work
of a serial killer?"*

Wilson listened intently as I went on to describe the evidence
that I had found and the testimony by the various witnesses,
including the young addict that I had discovered at Ty Phillip's
apartment. He appeared to agree wholeheartedly with my assessment and nodded his head vigorously at various stages throughout my layout of the case and seemed to be genuinely interested
about my discovery, but when I informed him of the fact that
Harley might be the so-called serial killer; his eyes bulged out of
his head. Folding his arms across his chest he peered back at me,
saying, *"Wow...you just said a mouthful, but it's about time someone
found out the truth of what's really been going on in this town....but
Harley?.....I'm a little surprised at him, though......I never thought
he had it in him....oh, taking money and roughing up a few suspects*

was always within the man's reach, but killing people?...that part of your theory is a little hard to believe and realistically, to hang a cop for all of this?....now, that's something else."

Taking another drag on his cigarette, I could tell Wilson's mind was at work as his eyes stared off in the distance and after a brief pause he continued with, *"So, where do we go from here, Shake?....I'm sure that they must have had something to do with trying to take you out the other night.....and with what you're telling me, with everyone as dirty as they are, there's not many people in this damn place that we can trust anymore."*

My old partner had hit the nail on the head as this only caused additional problems, but one aspect of the case kept spinning in my head and I decided to throw it out at him. *"Russ.....were you involved in getting me back here?.....I mean did you have any discussions with anybody on it?"* Looking perplexed he replied, *"Why, Shake?....what does that have to do with all of this?"* I took a few steps away from him and placed my hands on my hips, looking down the street at the kids playing. Allowing my mind to drift back, I thought to myself when I was their age and how simple life was at that time. *"Back then, we had no idea what this world was really like, did we?"* I mumbled to myself. Lost in thought I suddenly heard, *"I didn't quite get that, Shake?....what did you say?"* Coming back to reality, I turned my head towards him. *"Mayor Logan....he was the one that wanted me on this case, Russ....isn't that right?"* Crushing his cigarette out on the ground with his shoe, Russ looked up at me. *"Yeah...so what?"* Working my head from side to side and trying to get the kinks out of my neck I answered, *"That's what bothers me about this whole mess.....if the mayor was involved with the crooked dealings around here, why look to bring someone from the outside to poke their nose around?....especially me?....I'm someone that this city rode out on a rail to get rid of.... that part of it doesn't make any sense."* Russ grew a smile from ear to ear. *"Who the hell cares, Shake?....it's possible the man has some real guilt down deep inside him and its eating at his gut.....you know, like a cancer that is slowly sucking the life out of him....maybe the* mayor just can't take it anymore and wants to be caught....who in the hell knows what goes through a mind like that."

I was hearing the words, but my mind was blank from them while I listened to my old partner try and psychoanalyze the mayor's mind. *"Keep it simple, stupid,"* kept going through my mind as my head spun with crazy ideas and conspiracy theories. Listening to Russ go on about the mayor I realized that this case, although complicated was beginning to unravel and it was becoming more clear to me. *"Russ...I'm going to see the mayor again and dissect him a little more....he needs to answer a few of my questions before I can decide on how I am going to proceed on this thing....so, are you aware of anyone else at the station we can trust?"* With a grin, he answered, *"Let me think on that and I'll get back to you.....I'm sure there's a few of us left.....in the meantime, I'll head over to personnel and see if I can get my hands on Harley's file....that may help us out on this, what do you think?"* Nodding my head, I reached for the handle on my car and while opening the door, answered, *"Sounds good.....check on Ty Phillips for me too while you're at the station...like I told you, they are trying to pin all of this on the poor kid and I'm afraid he might just have an accident, especially with Harley hanging around.....we'll get in touch with each other later and compare notes....say eight o'clock tonight at my place, over to the motel?"*

Russ gave a simple nod and waived at me as I started the car and backed out of his driveway. Driving down the street, I saw him in my rear view mirror still standing there, shaking his head in front of his house, watching me go down the road. *"I just really screwed with his mind,"* I thought to myself as I took a right turn onto Main Street. *"Like me, the poor man will never be the same."*

CHAPTER TWENTY-ONE
The Mayor's Office

It was not long before I found myself turning into the parking lot at City Hall. Naturally, it was a busy business day as it was nearing the end of the quarter for people to pay their property taxes and not being able to find a parking space in the lot, I decided to park along the street across from the building. Upon exiting the car, out of the corner of my eye while opening Barrett's door to let him out, I noticed a parked car across the street about seventy yards from us. Immediately, I recognized that it was the same black Buick, which had previously chased me and I had given the slip to. Looking closer, two men were sitting in the front seat and it was obvious by their body posturing that both of them had their eyes trained on us. *"They're back, ole boy....seems like they're not going to give up....why don't we pay them a little visit for a change."*

Barrett, eager to go with me, followed close behind as we strolled down the sidewalk towards the parked car. Because of the sun shining on the windshield, I could not make out their faces, but I did see the beginnings of some movement inside the car as I got nearer to them. Not knowing what to expect, I drew my .357 from its shoulder holster and held it out of sight behind my body as I cautiously continued towards them. Looking for available cover if things went bad I spotted a mail collection box about ten yards further down the walk and a large oak tree not far from it.

All of a sudden, I saw a gun barrel exit the driver's side window and realizing everything was about to go down the shitter, a loud crack suddenly exploded from the car. Buzzed by whizzing noises I dove behind the mailbox and fired back two shots back at the vehicle. To my surprise, the man on the passenger side climbed partially out of the side window and positioning himself overlooking the roof of the car, he let loose with a machine gun, pulverizing the mailbox in seconds with dozens of rounds. The few passerby's' ran for cover as well, as the entire scene went chaotic with gunfire, and suddenly, I imagined myself back in Korea during the war when something like this was a common occurrence. As the bullets ricocheted off the sidewalk and tree lawn, exploding dirt into the air, out the corner of my eye, I saw Barrett head for cover behind the tree. A loud screeching noise cut through the air as the car swerved from side to side and seeing the car speed off, the smell of burning rubber and smoke filled the surrounding area. Throwing all caution to the winds, I stood and fired my remaining four shots at the car, blowing out the rear window, but the vehicle kept speeding away, eventually disappearing around a corner.

An officer, who was directing traffic beyond City Hall in the town square, immediately came running towards me when the chaos started. Drawing his weapon, he had emptied his revolver at the car as well, but I doubt any of the shots found their mark as he was too far away. *"Are you alright?"* the officer yelled. Burning with rage and brushing myself off I answered, *"Yeah, I'm okay.... enough with this crap!....something has to be done about this!"* Walking swiftly past him while reloading my gun, Barrett came up along side me as we crossed the street and headed directly to City Hall. Passing the officer, he attempted to grab me by the shoulder to stop me, but I quickly pulled away from him. *"Where do you think you're going?"* he asked. Yelling back at him I answered, *"I'm going to put a stop to this shit right now!"*

I picked up my pace again, shoving my gun back in its shoulder holster and hit the front steps to the building almost on a dead run. Barreling up the granite steps, I blasted through the huge glass doors into City Hall and took an immediate left towards the mayor's office. Marty Sloan, the mayor's executive assistant was standing in the secretary's office as I rushed in and being surprised to see me he blurted, *"Can I help you?"* Not paying any attention to him, I pushed him aside into a planter, but as I attempted to continue into the mayor's personal office, he reached out and grabbed me by the shoulder. Shaking his grip, I shoved him harder this time with both hands into the wall behind him. Hitting it with great force, he cracked the plastered wall and immediately collapsed to the floor. Barrett, who was behind me growled loudly at Sloan with fierceness in his face, letting the man know that if he dared to touch me again, he was surely going to have a butt full of canine teeth.

"You can't go in there....he has..." Sloan hollered, lying on the floor, but it did not faze me in the least as I kicked the closed door off one of its hinges and busted into the mayor's office. Mayor Logan, sitting behind his desk was completely startled and jumped up, moving backwards away from his chair. With apprehension in his face, he gazed at the two of us bolting towards him, fearing the worse. Unexpectedly, out of the corner of my eye I realized that there were two other people sitting on the opposite wall from the mayor and to the left of me. They were dressed in expensive suits and had opened briefcases, filled with papers, sitting on their laps. Red faced and full of anger I turned towards them, yelling, *"Pick up your damn shit and get the hell out of here!....I need to talk to the man!"* To speed them on their way, Barrett let out a loud, deep, threatening growl, exposing his canine fangs, letting the men know in no uncertain terms they were not wanted. In a total rush the men slammed their briefcases shut and like a shot, scrambled out of the room. In fact, they almost trampled Sloan on their way out who was lying next to the doorway and upon noticing the little weasel there; I slammed shut what was left of the door in his face.

Turning my attention back to the mayor I shouted, *"Let's cut the shit right now you son of a bitch!....I know what the hell has been going on in this city and you must too!....everybody is on the take in this place and you are probably the man calling the shots..... this is nothing but bullshit, calling me back here to take this case, hoping that you can order your henchmen to take me out.....well, mister that isn't going to happen because you're the one that's going down!"* I reached across the desk, yanking the mayor over it and threw him to the floor while setting myself on top of him. The mayor was so scared that I think he wetted himself in the process and while looking up at me, all he saw was my raging eyes and Barrett's huge white teeth in his face.

Almost on a dry drunk I screamed, *"With what I have on everyone in this place, everybody's going down including you.....you piece of shit!"* Just then, the damaged door to the mayor's office flew open with Sloan, yelling, *"Mayor!...I told him he couldn't come in....."* Losing all sense of self-control, I drew my weapon, cocked the hammer back and pointed it directly at him. *"If you don't get your ass out of here right now....I'm gonna fill that stupid looking face of yours with lead!"* Like a timid chipmunk, he quickly shut the crooked, hanging door and vanished. With him gone, I swung the gun barrel around and pushed it into the mayor's face, making him wince with untold fear. *"Alright, mayor...you and I are going to have a nice private chat on your crooked dealings and murders that you have orchestrated here!"*

In complete shock, the mayor stuttered, trying to expel a response. *"Ahh...ahhh...I don't know anything thing about any murders......oh....I know there's been something crooked going on around here, but that's why I got you back here in the first place.....there's no one that I can trust anymore and I needed a person like you to help me find out the truth!....please, Madison!....you gotta believe me!"* Hearing him beg like that, caused my mind to recall the Swanson documents with practically everyone's name listed in them from City Hall. Then a shocking revelation came to me, since there was one name that I did not remember seeing....and that was Mayor Logan.

The possibility of the mayor speaking the truth suddenly entered my thoughts, causing me to gradually lower my weapon. Easing the hammer down on my 357 and wiping my face from the sweat with the back of my hand, I got off him. Sitting to the side of Logan on the floor, the mayor sat up with panic still in his eyes. Grabbing my arm, he shook it several times in a begging manner while saying, *"That's why I had to get you back here, Madison.....I have known for a very long time that something hasn't been quite right around here.....with the constant whispers, the unusual actions of public officials, and the constant rumors of money being tossed around, I knew I had to do something.....don't you see?....I needed someone from the outside....someone that wasn't involved and a person who I could trust that would investigate the whole mess....... and considering what just happened outside City Hall in broad daylight, it definitely appears that you have aroused the people that we need to worry about.....and there's no doubt now that some of them in this God forsaken place are becoming so desperate that they want to silence you.....permanently!"*

I wanted to believe the mayor, but he was the one that had led the charge to drive me out of this town in the first place. He let me sink like a rock to the bottom when my shooting incident became a political problem for him, as there was no support from his office at all. Glaring at his desperate eyes, my anger was weakening and suddenly I realized that my severe accusations were beginning to go up in flames. Could it be true that he was straight and honest? That he had no part in this at all? Not knowing which way to turn, the damaged door to his office suddenly busted open and several officers with guns drawn, pointing in my direction entered. *"Don't make a move, Madison or you're a dead man!"* someone hollered from the pack of men. Recognizing the voice immediately, I attempted to respond to the chief, but Mayor Logan cut me off, saying, *"Hold on boys.... there's nothing to worry about here....the detective and I just had a little misunderstanding, that's all....put your guns away and leave us."* The officers began slowly lowering their weapons when the chief stepped forward, blurting, *"But mayor, he assaulted you.... we even have an eye witness with Sloan here....he's willing to testify that this madman busted in here and pointed a gun at you and him....let me take this nut and put him away where he belongs."*

The mayor stood up and rearranged his suit while I moved off to the side. Barrett seeing that this could go possibly very wrong at any second, quietly took a seat beside me and stared at all of the officers while they still held their weapons on me. The mayor casually walked around his desk to his chair, reaching for a cigarette from the pack that was next to the telephone. *"Chief Morin....I told your men to leave us alone and that includes you!"* Looking disappointed, the chief while peering at me signaled with his hand for his men to lower and holster their weapons. *"Madison....I don't know what's going on here and right now I really don't care, but in the future if you even simply jay walk or spit on the sidewalk, I'll throw your ass in jail....you got that?"* Mayor Logan observing the belligerence in the chief quickly came to my aid. *"Do you want to keep your job, Morin?.....I was the one that appointed you and I can fire you, too.....so, if you don't get all of your asses out of here right now, you'll be going down the road before you know it!.....and just maybe, your ass will be the one that goes to jail!"* With total disgust on his face, the chief waived his arm at the other men, telling them to back off and leave. Following the other officers out of the room Chief Morin stopped for a second, throwing a glance my way and while pointing directly at me with conviction in his voice said, *"Remember what I said, Madison....I'll be watching you."*

When they had left, Marty Sloan entered the office and the mayor immediately glared at the man, sending lightening bolts with his eyes, screaming, *"I told everyone to get out and that means you too, Mr. Sloan!.....leave us and don't let the door hit your ass on the way out!"* Staring at the mayor for a second, not believing what he had just heard, the mayor's assistant timidly moved towards the large oak door. Not wanting to leave, but realizing the mayor was dead serious he hesitantly closed the damaged door behind him.

"There....now we can get down to business, Madison....so where were we?" Realizing the mayor was shooting straight with me I lit up a butt and like always, Barrett moved to the opposite corner of the room to avoid the smoke. The mayor chuckled as his eyes observed my partner plop down in a huff, licking his chops a few times and placing his head down to rest. *"Maybe he's the only smart one in the room..... ehh, Madison?"* Smiling back at him, I replied, *"He's never liked tobacco smoke, sir....even when he was a pup he shied away from it.....if the smoke got too bad, he often escaped to the outside by clawing out a screen in a window....that's one thing about Barrett, he always goes where he wants to."*

The mayor leaned back in his high back, leather chair and folded his arms across his chest, glaring at me with full conviction in his eyes. *"This better be good, Madison because I just threw the chief of police out of my office in front of several witnesses and he has a lot of friends on the council.....I'm going to hear about this one for sure."* Exhaling a huge amount of smoke my eyes peered back at the man, telling him that what I was about to reveal to him was going to be shocking. *"I have direct evidence mayor that half of City Hall has been on the take....they have been receiving bribes through cash payments and the transfer of properties via the Veratex Corporation....the materials that I have in my possession point to the Planning Office, the Tax Collector, Police Department, the City Accountant and the Health Director to name just a few. They all have been conducting secret and illegal activities through the issuance of illegal permits, preferential tax assessments, misleading assessments of property values, and have used the police department as their enforcement agency......the most shocking part of this, however, is the murder of Kyle Swanson who worked in the Planning Office.....her death was not the work of a serial killer....evidently, Swanson discovered the wide spread corruption when she conducted the zoning reclassification changes for the city council......*

her research and findings are impeccable as the evidence that she gathered can not be refuted by anyone, especially the Veratex corporation who was at the center of her investigation.......I believe the poor woman was going to blow the lid off this scam and that's why they killed her, but the most horrific part of all of this, others were murdered to make it look like it was the work of a serial killer.....and when...."

The mayor's eyes were wide open now and before I could continue he blurted, *"Wait a minute, Madison.....are you saying my whole administration is full of crooks, liars, and murderers?.....even the God damn police?.....I can't believe it.....the Veratex Corporation along with Charlie Shields has been really good for this city.....countless homes and apartment buildings have been constructed and rehabilitated, making this city one of the most progressive places in the state, if not New England.....never mind, he has created hundreds of jobs in this city and put people back to work, giving them a decent living....how can you accuse the man and his company of such corruption?"*

I knew by the mayor's face that he was genuinely astonished and blindsided by my accusations. My words had definitely hit his core and watching him grab the pipe off the desk, I could see the nervousness in his hands as he attempted to light it. There was no turning back now as I realized that I needed to tell him all of it. *"Mayor, I also believe there's a detective by the name of Harley from our police department that has been killing people throughout this city in order to cover up the murder of Swanson which was the primary objective as all of the other murders were committed to throw us off track....all except for the fourth victim, Tina Hendricks that is.....she was killed in a jealous rage by Lori Jenkins who later became the fifth victim of the so called serial killer....she murdered Hendricks because she was cheating on her with Kyle Swanson of the Planning Department.....you see, mayor, now hear me out before you go ballistic....most of them were bisexual and all of them engaged in wild sex parties with other city officials, including some* of the cops.....even Zack Thompson of the Spirit Arms Motel killed himself over one of the girls....he was involved with...."

Suddenly the mayor jumped out of his chair, throwing his arms up in the air. *"What kind of ludicrous crap is this, Madison?......you expect me to believe this shit?....have you totally lost your mind and gone completely off your rocker?.....do you need psychiatric help or something?.....you know we can get you some professional help, if you need it......for your information, Kyle Swanson was a sweet and innocent girl....she was like mom's apple pie for heaven's sake......hell, she was someone that you would take home to mom for Christmas....she wouldn't have been involved in such queer and sickening acts such as this.....I've never heard of such crazy charges in my life!....and to think I trusted you!"*

Rubbing my chin at first, I tried to keep a straight face, as I knew how preposterous all of this was sounding to him. Knowing I was about to lose him I opened up the bomb bay doors and dropped some more. *"All of the evidence points to it, mayor.....Kyle kept a detailed log of her investigation into the Veratex corporation.....there are deeds transferring land and buildings to city officials along with evidence of city personnel issuing illegal building permits and passing defective and deficient health and zoning permits for the development of the raw land by the Veratex Corporation.......additionally, there are detailed written records of individual's bank accounts showing large amounts of money being issued to them from the Veratex corporation through dummy trusts and false names......Swanson did a great service to this city, sir, but she had a big weakness and that was sex.....several witnesses have testified to that fact and some are still alive....one of them I put into hiding until we can get this thing under control and the other is in our jail right now.....his name is Ty Phillips and if we don't get him some protection pretty soon, he'll probably be conveniently found dead in his cell, due to some unfortunate 'accident'........there is no doubt about it, sir....Kyle Swanson was good at everything she did and that included sex games and wild parties.....in fact, someone from City Hall used to watch her while the others engaged in their* sexual fantasies......I have not found out that person's identity yet, but I will.....all I need is just a little more time....she put on a good act and had all of you fooled, but like I said, Swanson is ultimately the one responsible for blowing this thing wide open."

I think the mayor was completely shell shocked when I finished saying those words. The look of bewilderment and amazement was telling on his face as he slowly lowered his pipe onto his desk. Plopping back against his chair, he rubbed his face vigorously with both hands and peered at me through his fingers. "Jesus Christ....what the hell has this place come to?.....a fucking mess that's what." Red faced and with blue veins sticking out of his forehead, the mayor shook his head several times, trying to wish the nightmare away. Looking up at me with pain throughout his face he asked softly, "What the hell are we going to do, Madison?..... where do we go from here?" Crushing my cigarette out in the ashtray on his desk I stared directly back at him. "To be honest with you....I don't think we can trust anybody in this place as they have already attempted to kill me twice......it has to make think that when they try and take out an officer of the law right in front of City Hall in broad daylight, you have to realize then, that they will stop at nothing....hell, because I'm in here talking to you, you're probably going to have to check your car for wires before you go home, if you know what I mean."

Those words put a dreadful fright into the man as he jumped up from his desk and went to the window, rubbing his left arm. After staring out at Main Street for a few seconds, he quickly turned towards me. "You have to protect me!....that's your job isn't it?.....after all, I'm the one that got you here in the first place....to serve and protect, right?.....well, Madison here's a man that needs some help, so start serving and protecting me right now!"

To tell the truth, I felt sorry for the poor man as I could see him coming apart at the seams. He was losing it for sure and right about now that was something I could not afford. "Mayor, do you have any real friends in the State Police that you can trust?.....I'm not sure, but with a large organization like Veratex, they might have even *infiltrated that department as well.....better yet, how about the feds?"* The mayor wiped the sweat from his forehead with his hand while biting his lower lip and you could see the smoke coming from his ears as he pressured his brain to think. *"Yeah, I know a few people in the bureau that I can trust....one of them I went to school with....he's an old friend by the name of Steve Ross and I know he's a straight shooter."* Smiling back at him, I replied, *"Good....that's very good.....you get in touch with him at the FBI and let the man know what's been going on here as I'm sure he's going to be quite interested.....ask him to bring out a few agents and we'll meet here tomorrow morning, say about 10:00 am....at that time, we'll go over everything that I have discovered and maybe get some protection for Ty Phillips as well.......that will give me some more time to tie up a few more loose ends....how does that sound?"*

The mayor nodded his head and while I turned to walk out he suddenly blurted, *"Wait a minute, Madison....I have some more information that may help you.....Marty!....come in here for a moment."* The damaged office door slowly opened and in walked the mayor's assistant dressed in a three-piece suit looking like a million dollars. *"Yes, sir....what can I do for you?"* The mayor pointed at the several file cabinets to the left of him. *"Pull the files on Kyle Swanson, Detective Harley and Don Birmingham."* With puzzlement on his face, he answered, *"Can I ask why, sir?"* A look of anger immediately enveloped the mayor while he commanded, *"Just do what you're God damn told for once....get those files out now and give them to the detective."*

Standing next to him, I watched Sloan retrieve his keys from his pocket to unlock the metal cabinet behind the mayor and while doing so I was amazed at the amount of keys that were on his ring. Then in a flash, my eyes caught what I could not believe at first. Hanging off his key ring was a small silver heart and my detective mind went into hyper speed, remembering the charm bracelet that was found next to Lori Jenkins's body. *"My God!"* I thought while he opened the cabinet and started retrieving the files. *"Could it be?"*

Pulling the several manila envelopes from the drawers and holding them in his arms, Sloan struggled to re-lock the cabinet while trying to turn the key. *"Here let me help you,"* as I grabbed the keys from him and turned the lock. Pulling them out of the cabinet, I quickly glanced down at the ring and examined the silver heart before handing them back to him. With all my might, I tried to keep my eyes from popping right out of my head, as the initials KS jumped out at me, telling me another important clue. Trying to keep my cool, I calmly handed the key ring back to him, all the while knowing that the man standing in front of me was probably the well-dressed man that watched during the sex parties. Was he involved with the killings as well? I could not shut off my mind as it went wildly out of control with additional theories and possibilities. *"Was I wrong about Harley?"* I thought. *"Or were they both involved?.....there was little doubt that something had been torn from the charm bracelet at the Jenkins's murder scene, the dangling piece of wire told me that.....after all, Swanson and Jenkins were lovers, that fact had been verified by many people, so why wouldn't Jenkins be carrying a heart with Kyle Swanson's initials on it?... and there was probably no other way Sloan could have gotten that heart with Swanson's initials without being at the scene of the murder....and the well dressed man that watched?....a chill drove up my spine because I was looking right at him."*

Taking the files from Sloan, I nonchalantly handed back his keys, trying not to raise his suspicions. *"Thanks,"* he said and while Sloan placed them back into his pocket, his eyes caught mine. Sloan's stare was cold and I could sense from his look that he possibly suspected something. A seasoned cop could feel these types of things and often I thought that we had the same intuition as dogs, but we just did not use it or at least we were not aware of it, but this time it was loud and clear. He was onto to me.

CHAPTER TWENTY-TWO
The Case Blows Up in My Face

When I left the mayor's office, I knew a major league curve ball had just been thrown my way. I was certain that Harley was probably Veratex's hatchet man, but evidently, Sloan was involved as well, but to what extent? We were meeting with the Feds tomorrow morning and there was little time left to firm up the case against the both of them. With cash payments from the Veratex Corporation to Harley along with land transactions to him, there was little doubt as to his guilt. In addition, his violent tendencies and Phillip's testimony about him choking the girls with parachute cord to get his kicks while they were having sex was a sure way to seal his fate. Because of those facts, there was little doubt in my mind now that he was the *"serial killer,"* but Sloan was a different matter. He was probably crooked, but was he also an accessory to murder as well, or worse?

Stopping for a bite to eat at Tony's Diner and recalling that I was supposed to meet my old partner Russ, at my place tonight around eight o'clock, my mind was in high gear. Remembering that he was going to get Harley's file from the police station and having already retrieved a copy from the mayor's office I decided to give him a ring, hoping to save him the trouble. Asking Tony to use his phone I had the operator dial the number, but surprisingly after several rings there was no answer. *"That's funny,"* I thought. *"He had the afternoon off today and should have been home by now...his shift ended over an hour ago."* Gently patting Barrett's head and massaging his ears my furry partner rubbed his head back and forth on my leg, enjoying the affection. *"What do you say we head home and get a few Z's ourselves?.....Russ will be over later and we'll get some work done then."* Nuzzling his head against my body in the affirmative, we got up from the table and headed for the car.

When I stepped outside, several teenaged kids had surrounded my vehicle and were laughing and making snide comments about it. One of the larger kids sarcastically asked, *"Where did you try and do with this?.....did you try stump jumping with it?"* Backing away from my car as I approached it, all of their eyes immediately fell on Barrett as he leaped through the rear window into the back seat. *"That's quite a dog you have there....can we pat him?"* Opening my dented door, it creaked and groaned from the damage to it. Smiling at the boys, I replied, *"Sure, go ahead....if you want to lose an arm or two."*

While getting into my car and not intimidated by my answer, two of the boys approached the vehicle and with their hands out, attempted to pat Barrett through the open rear window. Barrett sitting there calmly, looking straight ahead and playing his cards close to the vest allowed the boys to reach inside the car. Just when they were close enough he lunged at them like a snake, snapping his powerful jaws and sent the two boys hurling backwards to the ground. Horrified by Barrett's response and seeing him with his head out the window, snarling, and showing his lily-white teeth, they frantically slid themselves along the pavement on their butts further away from the vehicle. *"That dog is a killer!"* one of them hollered as I started the engine. Sticking my head out the window, I yelled back, *"No...he's not a killer...he just doesn't like little assholes like you!"* Hitting the gas pedal and screeching out of the parking lot I saw the boys in my rear view mirror vigorously flip me the bird as I bolted down the street. Snickering, I said aloud, *"A few more happy customers, ehh?....they just won't learn not to screw with you.....will they?"* Barrett turned his head and looked back at the mischievous boys through the rear window who were still yelling at us. Turning back around and facing forward again while panting and flashing a huge smile at me it was obvious that he was more than content with what he had just done.

Driving back to the motel, I kept going through the case in my mind and what possible involvement Sloan had in it. Partly in a daze and not realizing where I was, suddenly before I knew it, my turn was coming up. Pulling into the parking space in front of my room and while exiting the car, a piece of paper caught my eye on the threshold. Partly stuck beneath the door, I bent down and retrieved it. Opening the note, it shocked me a little, as it was a similar type of message that I had received before from the serial killer. It was carefully scripted from letters cut from various newspapers and magazines and it read:

You think you have it all figured out, don't you
my friend?
Without following the evidence like you have
been told
You could be out in the cold
Well, I hate to tell you this, but you're in the dark
without a clue
As you have it all wrong
But don't be too long
Because we will be waiting for you

Was Harley or Sloan taunting me now? In addition, had one of them put an order in already to make sure that I did not see the sunrise tomorrow? With little doubt that the snakes were coming for me, the thoughts of them taking me out only raised my blood pressure some more. Unlocking and opening the door I walked into my room along with my furry partner who immediately jumped on the bed. Sprawled out and taking most of it for himself I was only able to sit down on the edge of it. Looking behind me I said aloud, *"If you think you're gonna hog all of it....you got another thing coming....move over, you flea bag."* Giving him a little shove, he grunted and groaned a little, showing his dissatisfaction as he rolled to the side.

Staring at the note in my hand, my mind was whirling on what it had said. *"Without following the evidence.....you have it all wrong."* Those words kept burning in my head as I stared at them, hoping their meaning would jog something loose. *"Follow the evidence....,"* I kept repeating to myself, trying to make some sense out of it. Just then, snoring filled the air and I realized it was Barrett who had fallen fast asleep. *"What a detective you turned out to be,"* I said aloud. *"Sleeping like this case is over."*

Pondering the note again, my eyes drifted over to the piles of evidence on the desk and the coffee table. Consisting of countless photographs and reports on all of the murders, my eyes quickly scanned them, while the words, *"follow the evidence"* kept running through my thoughts. Picking up some of the papers, I began perusing them. *"I have been through this stuff so many times, I should have it all memorized by now,"* I mumbled flipping through the pages. *"There's nothing new here....after all, how many times can you look at the same shit and expect to find something new?"*

Tossing the papers back on the coffee table, I rubbed my blood shot eyes and when I opened them, through the picture window the liquor store sign came into view. It was fully bright now and its lights lit up the night as darkness had completely fallen. With its sign being bright and inviting, I thought of all the potential patrons that might be drawn to it, telling them that relief was only a bottle away. Suddenly the thoughts of opening a quart bottle and pouring its quenching liquid down my throat made me dry and parched. So parched, in fact that I swallowed hard, trying desperately to get some saliva down it. Shaking my head and forcing the stinking thoughts from it, I held my face in my hands rubbing it vigorously, hoping and praying the horrid cravings would finally leave my mind.

As I peered down at the coffee table, the photograph of Lori Jenkins's partially nude body came into view. The poor girl had been beaten to a pulp, leaving no doubt that the killer had his way with her. As I studied the picture further, I imagined him tossing the girl like a piece of garbage down the embankment towards the river and laughing about it. *"The son of bitch must have really enjoyed this one,"* I said mumbling to myself as I continued to look at the photograph. The side of her heavily disfigured face immediately jumped out at me along with the heavy contusions about her torso and legs, as they were horrendous. Then as my eyes moved up along her spine to the parachute cord tied tightly around her neck the carved letters AC on her upper back came into view. *"The son of bitch had to carve her up, didn't he,"* I mumbled to myself. *"Could he have beaten this one up any worse?"* I thought, looking at the mangled body of the once beautiful girl.

I had studied the photograph a hundred times before, but there was nothing more to see and as I tossed it back onto the table, the clock on the nightstand caught my eye. It was 8:40 p.m. already and my old partner, Russ Wilson had not arrived yet. *"Where in the hell could he be?"* I said to myself. *"He was supposed to be here by now."* Seeing the flashing neon sign across the street, it pummeled my eyes with the word *"liquors"* and all it did was remind me how thirsty I was. Yearning for the initial taste and the calming feeling that went along with it, I began to rationalize with myself. *"Maybe when I'm finished with this case,"* I thought. *"That's when I'll deserve a little treat....not too much, just a little bit."*

The *"ism"* in alcoholism was bearing down on me hard now as I fought the tense feelings building inside of me. *"Just one,"* I thought staring at the lights across the street. *"All I need is just one now....one won't be so bad, will it?"* Trying to rid my mind of those horrid thoughts I glanced at the radio clock again and was surprised to find that the hands were approaching nine p.m. *"What the hell happened to him?.....for God's sake, we don't have much more time left on this thing,"* I murmured while desperately trying to keep my sanity from going into the garbage pail. *"Russ is always on time....he's never late to anything."*

My anxiety was reaching the boiling point as I flew off the bed and started pacing back and forth across the room. Wringing my hands together, they were beginning to shake and as I stared at them, I wondered if they were ever going to stop. My will-power was rapidly leaving me and I knew it would only be a matter of time before I ventured across the street to retrieve the badly needed *"medicine."* Then the thoughts of Andrea and Ben came into my mind and how they helped me almost two years ago through the darkest time of my life. *"They pulled you from the gutter, you idiot and made you well.....you were nearly dead when Ben found you......how can you let him down and yourself for that matter?....you're sober now and life is finally getting back to being good for a change ......don't screw it up now by going across the street.....you know what that will bring you."* All of those feelings kept whirling in my mind like a twister and I continued to try to convince myself. *"She's a good woman, a woman that you can be proud of and depend upon....without her, where would you be?....lying in some ditch, puking your guts out?...or worse yet, in an insane asylum or dead from an alcohol binge?"* Quickly reaching for a cigarette I thought, *"Some day Russ will get to know Andrea better and I think he'll really like her....she'll probably end up reminding him of Jane a little."*

Pausing my pep talk to myself, I struck a match and lit my butt. Suddenly a cold chill came over me, recalling the meeting with my old partner in the coffee shop when I first arrived back in town. How did he know Andrea's full name when he asked me how she was? No one in Harrisburg knew I was even dating her, as I had never mentioned her to anyone. We had always kept our relationship private and few people in Middleton even knew we were living together. So how did Russ know her last name? And how did he know she was a nurse? Sweat started to bead on my forehead as the pieces of the puzzle rearranged themselves, creating an entirely new picture.

Then as my analytical mind worked, some more, additional sickening thoughts started to reveal themselves, causing even more confusion. Why did Russ abandon the case on me? Previously, Russ and I had lived through some terrible scrapes together and he never quit, no matter how bad the situation was. Now, because of his pension I was supposed to believe that he would simply give up on the most important case we had ever worked on together? All of this was just too strange to internalize and as my mind wandered with additional suspicious thoughts, my eyes drifted downwards and the photograph of Lori Jenkins's back shined in the overhead light. There in despicable horror were the carved letters AC in her flesh. *"Oh my God....'follow the evidence'...."* I said slowly aloud. *"That's almost what Russ told me the day when he quit on me....'let the true evidence speak for itself'... ..I'm sure that's what he said when he left me that day....and God forbid....Andrea Carlson.....is that what those letters stand for?.... could it be?"*

Then my hand reached for the note that was left by the psychotic killer and I read it again. *"We'll be waiting for you,"* and as I read those words aloud, my heart sunk to my knees. I cried out, *"Dear God, it can't be....can it?"* Reaching for the phone in fear, I quickly said the number to the operator and listened to the dialing sound as I anxiously waited for Andrea to pick up the phone. I kept telling myself repeatedly, *"Please pick up, Andrea...you got to pick up and end this horrid nightmare."* The phone seemed to ring forever and after several moments had passed; my feelings sank even deeper as the operator came back on the line. *"There is no answer, sir.....please try again later."*

Hearing those words and in a full-scale panic I grabbed my suit coat off the chair while reaching into the desk drawer for some spare ammunition. Placing some in my pocket, I banged the side of the bed, startling Barrett from a sound sleep. *"Get your ass up!....there's no time to waste, partner!.....Andrea could be in real trouble!"* Hearing the urgency in my voice, Barrett immediately leaped off the bed and headed for the door. Throwing it open, I ran to the car while Barrett jumped in the back seat and within seconds, we were on our way down Main Street at over eighty-five miles per hour. *"That dirty son of a bitch!....dear God, I hope I'm wrong!"* I yelled, pounding the steering wheel with both fists.

With each passing mile, everything was becoming clearer to me now. It was if a dark cloak had finally been lifted, revealing all of the hidden horror. Even the shooting in the alley years ago involving the young kid popped into my head, as there was nobody else around except for my old partner when the shooting went down. An old rummy had testified to that, but why? Why would have Russ set me up like that? Then, like a spear piercing my heart, the thought of my dying wife hit me, almost causing me to go off the road. That horrible afternoon many years ago, Russ was first to come on the scene as well, supposedly helping me through my grief. Did he run her down? The faster I went, more horrid visions popped into my head as my brain was seeing images of everything at light speed, trying to make sense out of it. *"How could I have missed all of this shit?....why was I so blind!"* I yelled while taking a sharp corner. Then hitting me like a shock wave after saying those words, I remembered one of the lines from the killer's messages. *"There are none so blind as those who will not see,"* I mumbled to myself while the tires squealed and dirt from the gutter sprayed out the back. Lucky to keep the car on the road as I floored the gas pedal even harder I said aloud, *"The man was my friend....my partner.....a man that I trusted....a man that I would have given my life for......how could he have possibly done such a thing?"*

I was on the main road now and speed limits were a distant memory as I jammed the accelerator to the floor. The old 1953 Buick was at its limits as the speedometer reached one hundred miles per hour and Barrett, knowing something was very wrong, paced back and forth in the backseat. At times, he stared out the side windows, growling, and seemed to be envisioning things himself as the car barreled down the highway.

The normal four to five hour drive had only taken me a little over three hours as I raced down the street to my house in

Middleton. Locking up the brakes and coming to a screeching halt, I slammed the car into park and shut off the engine. Andrea's car was in the driveway and having received no answer by telephone that only added to my fears as I headed for the house with Barrett right behind me. Approaching the front door my eyes grew larger, seeing that it was unlocked and ajar. Immediately, pulling my gun from its holster, I carefully and slowly pushed the door open, looking in all directions. Suddenly Barrett began to growl and he crouched, ready to attack. Just as my head turned to the left, I heard a sudden rush of air and felt a tiny pinch on the side of my neck. Touching the affected area, I felt what seemed to be a small dart of some kind and all of a sudden, the room began to spin out of control. Trying to stay on my feet, I staggered forward, looking for something to grab onto and in the background, I vaguely heard two gunshots. Feeling my legs going out beneath me, I tried desperately to hold onto the banister at the foot of the stairs, but my body collapsed to the floor. After lying there for a few seconds, a distinct voice softly whispered in my ear. *"Welcome home....we have been waiting for you,"* and then there was blackness.

I was unaware on how much time had passed when I opened one eye. Not really knowing where I was since my vision was blurry, I slowly started to recognize that I was still at home because lying on the floor I saw the living room couch next to me and the old grandfather clock in the corner, which was given to us by Jane's parents when we were married. My head was still spinning and it felt like I had cotton balls stuck in my throat as I gagged and tried to clear it. Lying still on the floor, I saw the black dress shoes of someone sitting on the couch, but focusing in on the person was impossible. *"Nice to see you coming around, Shake.....we were starting to get a little concerned about you, but we are glad that you could finally join our little party that we have set up for you,"*

a dark voice said from across the room. Still gagging and trying to focus I heard the voice add, *"Don't worry, Shake....the effects of the drug will pass in a few minutes and then we can get down to business."* Even though I knew whom to expect, the sound of his voice still enraged me. Still feeling like I had a mouthful of cotton balls I replied, *"Russ....what the hell is wrong with you?....where's Andrea?....and what did you do to Barrett?....if you hurt them you son of a bitch, I swear I will......"* Suddenly laughter filled the room and the voice said loudly, *"You'll do what?....kill me?......let me fill you in ole buddy......you are in no position to do anything!"*

Not wanting to take anymore of my old partner's crap I attempted to stand up, but I quickly realized that it was hopeless as my feet were bound with lamp cords and my hands were tied behind my back. Struggling to loosen my bonds, the voice began to laugh again. *"You're pathetic, Shake....look at you, trying to break loose.....a little girl could do better....you're no cop and you're no man either!.......you're nothing but a useless drunk that pretends to be sober!"*

My vision was beginning to clear and objects were coming into focus as I looked up at the person sitting on the couch. It was my old partner all right, Russ Wilson, grinning from ear to ear, watching me struggle like a fish out of water. As my eyes glared at him, I suddenly saw Andrea tied up on the sofa chair to the left of Wilson and tears were streaming down her face, causing her mascara to run. A gag had been shoved in her mouth, which was held in place by pieces of parachute cord encircling her head, the same cord we had seen so many times around the murdered girl's necks. *"You bastard!....what the hell is wrong with you?.....why are you doing this?"* I hollered trying to break my bonds again.

Not seeing Barrett anywhere my thoughts quickly turned to the gun shots I heard before passing out and with my anger growing exponentially I yelled, *"and Barrett?....what did you do to him?"* Wilson chuckled as he got up from the couch, tapping the side of his leg with a .38 Smith and Wesson. *"Barrett?...well, you might say he went to that big doggie place in the sky....I think he's out there* somewhere right now with two .38's in him wondering what the hell happened......to tell the truth, when you started to pass out he took off on you, but I'm sure I hit him....he yelped like a little bitch when the first one got him."

My hatred for the man was bursting at the seams as I tried to wiggle my hands free. "If I could only get my hands on you, I'd cut your heart out you son of a bitch....gunning down a defenseless dog, I suppose that makes you feel like a really big man." Still laughing he circled me a few times and glanced over at Andrea, pointing his gun at her. "Oh, it does.....taking out a big animal like that with just a couple of shots from a .38 gives me a great feeling......but enough of that ....all of us are sure glad that you could join our little party, Shake....look at them over there, don't they look anxious to join in on the fun?"

His eyes glared with exhilaration when he said that and I could tell by his appearance that he was totally mad. Leaving me, he walked over to Andrea and placed his hands on her shoulders while he stared back at me with contemptuous eyes. Rubbing them and putting his head beside hers, he gently kissed her on the side of the cheek, causing Andrea to grimace from the ghastly contact. Trying desperately to move away from him, Wilson uttered, "What's the matter little girl?.....don't I turn you on like your big boyfriend over there?" Rearing back with laughter, he stood straight up and patted her head as if she was a dog. "Don't worry hon....once I'm through with you, your desire for the guy over there will be but a distant memory......I can hear you saying later, if I've had the best, why try the rest?....but first, I am going to warm up a bit with that little thing over there."

The roar of his laughter made me nauseous and while he moved over towards me, I sat up and leaned my back against the sofa. That is when I saw the young drug addict that I had sent on to stay with Andrea as she was lying on the floor next to the sofa chair. The poor girl had been hog tied as well and her clothes had been partially stripped off, leaving her bare breasts for him to enjoy.

Fearful on what he was going to do next I asked, *"So....what's going to happen to us?.....what sick kind of crap do you have planned in that demented mind of yours?"* Rapidly moving towards me he got right in my face. *"So you think I'm crazy do you?....well, Mr. Detective I'm not crazy, in fact I am probably the sanest man you have ever laid your eyes on.....besides, don't you want to know all the facts about your 'big case' before we start having our fun together?"* Not answering him, Wilson grew anxious while he continued to tap the .38 on his leg. *"Well, don't you?"* he said loudly. Still not bowing to his wishes he shook his head several times and raised the pistol into the air, looking up at the ceiling. *"What a detective you are.....I would think a man of your standing and stature would be dying, ahhh...no pun intended...."* as he snickered to himself, almost breaking out in total laughter. Regaining his composure he continued with, *"to figure out this whole mess.....well, even you don't want to hear it, Shake; I think it's important that you do, so I'm going to tell it anyway."*

Struggling to break my bonds, I wiggled my hands behind me back and forth, but the ropes were knotted far too tightly. Unfortunately, my deranged partner had done a good job of tying me up and as my eyes caught his, it appeared he was enjoying my efforts. *"You won't give up on it, will you, Shake?.....why don't you just sit back old buddy and relax while I tell you all about your case that you couldn't solve, okay?"* I glared back at him with hatred in my eyes, but Wilson just smiled. *"I tried to warn you, Shake about coming back here and working on the investigation, but you wouldn't listen, would you?....I really didn't want it to end up this way, after knowing you all of these years, but as you well know, being a cop isn't easy....they pay us all jack shit and expect us to work miracles, and its always been that way......you see, it will never change because the politicians in this city are like the ones everywhere else, but that's where I fooled them, ole buddy because I got myself some smarts.....a way to get paid for my true worth in this worthless society that we all live in.....when I joined up with the Veratex corporation, I was making a little over one hundred bucks a week with the city....now I make ten times that and even get a few bonuses along the way for doing some 'special overtime' work...if you know what I mean."*

Sitting down next to me on the sofa, he nudged the side of my shoulder with his gun while he said that, making me detest the man even more. *"Everything was going fine, Shake until that bitch, Swanson, came to town....why that numb skull Birmingham ever hired her, I don't know.....being a real nosy bitch, soon she was sniffing around everywhere and gathering up a lot of shit....too much shit, to tell the truth, and the bosses had to make a decision....so do you know what they did?.....they hired ole Russ here to take care of things."*

My delusional partner reared his head back and laughed hysterically, looking like a lunatic who had just been let out of an insane asylum. *"That's right, they hired good ole Russ, to make things right......so do you know what I did?.....I know you must have figured some of this out because you were about to nail Harley for it....poor old Harley....his pecker got him into trouble as he just couldn't leave those bitches alone, including that nosy Swanson.... they had him so riled up that he couldn't even think straight as those girls drove him crazy with their sex games and drugs....you should have seen what they did to him, Shake....they took a big, strong man and turned him into a pile of mush with that vaginal wrench of theirs......you know what they say all the time, Shake..... that thing between their legs has no teeth, but it has eaten a lot of men."*

Wilson reared back and laughed while eying the two women, hoping to install some more fear into them. Collecting himself he smiled at me and said, *"But those bitches could not have set him up to take the fall any better, Shake.....you see, all of those girls liked it rough....you know with whips and chains, shit like that...it was really something to see I tell you....they even loved it when the rope went around their necks and he choked them half to death.....hell, they used to cum so hard that their screams could be heard downtown."*

Chuckling, he stood up and walked over to Andrea, taking a piece of her long black hair in his hand. As he twirled it in his fingers, it made her cringe with revulsion as she moved her head, trying to dislodge her hair from his grasp. With a sickening look of ugly anticipation he added, *"Maybe I can teach your woman here about some of those things, ehh?"*

Again, I strained to break my bonds wanting so badly to tear his head off, but recognizing the fact that I was accomplishing nothing but cutting my wrists to ribbons, I finally accepted that it might be hopeless. Hanging my head in defeat, I could hear the sick bastard laughing at me, making my vengeance explode inside of me. *"I can't believe you, Russ.....what the hell got into you, anyway?.....why are you doing this?"* Scratching the side of his temple with the barrel of the pistol, Wilson smiled back at me. *"What got into me?.....the money of course, my stupid, devoted partner..... the sweet, beautiful smell of money......to think, all I had to do was kill a couple of lowlife prostitutes that didn't mean anything to anybody....and why not, to make thousands?....however, all great plans have their little snags and that's when Sloan almost screwed it up..... that stupid bastard panicked when I started the killings to set the stage for the final acts....I guess he didn't have the stomach for it and that's when he went to Swanson's apartment to reason with her, you know to try and get the woman to back off.....I'm sure you're aware that Sloan was desperate to keep the money flowing into the mayor's campaign fund as he was responsible for getting the man re-elected and the Veratex Corporation was going to guarantee that in the future through their considerable contributions...."*

"Unfortunately, for everybody, things got a little out of hand and Sloan ended up killing the girl, but by not knowing the entire MO that I was trying to establish in creating the serial killer, he botched the murder by strangling her with his hands.....personally, I thought the strangling with the parachute cord and the touch with the suitcases was brilliant....I even thought by cutting off their hair and stuffing it into their mouths, it gave the impression that a real psychotic killer was on the loose, leaving everyone with fear of who was going to be next.....and of course I had to leave them naked, that eliminated any so called evidence from being left behind and that

only added to the horror of the crimes, but I am sure you must have gathered that......anyway, with all my hard work I knew a serial killer was going to be born, but the damn fool panicked and Sloan never did most of those things....the asshole never even dumped the body down by the river."

The detective in me caused my interest to peak even though what he was saying disgusted me. As my analytical mind went to work I thought to myself, *"That's the reason why the Swanson crime scene was different from the others....Sloan did the killing and it explains the bruises on her neck along with the cord being placed there afterwards with the wrong knot.....evidently he wasn't privy to all of the previous crime scene information when he staged the scene.....plus, that explains why Zack tied a square knot around Hendricks's neck when he dumped her down by the river....Sloan not knowing what knot was used in the previous two murders must have just assumed his version of the improperly tied square knot was the right one....Detective Harley being drunk during one of their wild sex escapades together, must have told Zack about the previous girls being strangled with parachute cord and just by chance, Zack being a Boy Scout in his youth, utilized a square knot and tied it properly."*

Wilson must have seen or realized my mind was running because he grinned at me. *"Starting to figure it out, are we?..... well, here's another little tidbit for you to swallow and dissect with your great detective intellect.....when things really started to get messy with Jenkins killing Hendricks in a jealous rage, believing that Hendricks had killed Swanson, you're probably thinking that I needed to silence Jenkins....well, partner you're wrong on that too.....Sloan killed her, but not for the reasons you're thinking....oh, Jenkins sexually screwed around with Swanson and probably knew what information she had been given gathering on everybody associated with the Veratex operation, but it was Sloan's fascination with Lori Jenkins that caused him to do the job for me.....Jenkins rejected Sloan when he eventually tried to have sex with her for she knew he was a sick bastard because he liked to watch.....I never got to Jenkins before Sloan beat her to death and when he called me in a panic for help, I had to go over there and clean up the mess.... there was little time to dispose of her body and keep with the same MO......in fact, Sloan had pulverized Jenkins's face so badly, that I had to bang her up some more with a crowbar to make it look like the killer needed more than just strangulation to fulfill his needs..... plus, I had so little time I was forced to throw everything including her clothes down by the river.....and I'm sure you know by now that I disposed of the fifth victim, the Sullivan woman, to help the serial killer thing along before that, to make it look like the killer was still on the loose.....even with the Sullivan woman I had to cut her up a bit, following the beating death of the Hendricks woman to make it look like the killer was progressing.....the funniest part of this whole mess, Shake is that Sloan was impotent.....that's why he liked to watch, but he couldn't handle seeing Lori Jenkins with other men....it drove him crazy with jealousy and rage and when she refused his sexual advances and demands ....well, you now know how it all turned out."*

Sitting there in total amazement, I could not believe that there had been three killers involved, but it also explained why Barrett was confused by the multiple scents on the various pieces of evidence. There were too many people involved with the later killings and that is why Barrett could not single out the killer. However, one thing still puzzled me. *"Okay, Wilson....you've told me about the murders, but who tried to take me out the other night?....was it the guys in the black Buick?"* Wilson walked around the couch, chuckling to himself and when he got in front of me he replied, *"Don't tell me that you're that dumb, Shake....think about it....if I or the guys in the Buick with a high powered rifle took a shot at you from that distance, what do you think would have happened?.... yeah, you wouldn't be here right now....think about the evidence for a minute....use that detective reasoning you supposedly have....what did you find there?.....an imprint of a dress shoe, that's what....and who wears that type of dress shoe?...a Dacks wasn't it?...hmm?"* He made my mind ramble with thoughts even though the sight of him made me sick. Without saying anything for a moment Wilson snickered, exclaiming, *"Sloan of course!....the idiot stole a rifle out of the chief's house and tried to take you down that night with it.... poor bastard couldn't hit the broadside of a barn....that's why you're still here with us to enjoy this beautiful night!"*

Wilson took his seat on the sofa beside me and poked me with the .38 revolver. *"Well, that's about it, partner.....you know all of it now....well, almost all of it....all except for your wife and the shooting in the alley."* Immediately, my head sprung up like a jack in the box with suspicion in my eyes. *"Russ, don't tell me you actually had something to do with that....did you?"* Wilson stood up and walked over to the window, throwing the curtain aside to look out. *"No...but I know who did,"* he answered while releasing the curtain back to its original position. Smiling as he walked towards me, he pulled a cigarette from his pocket and lit it. Taking a few puffs he smirked at me, saying, *"Are you thinking that I actually had something to do with the killing of your wife?....how could you ever think that, partner?....after all the things we have been through together....I never would have harmed Jane....she was a real sweetheart."*

I was so glad to hear him say that and my spirits actually lifted a little, knowing my old partner thought that way about my wife. Wilson grinned at me knowing I was taking all of it in and I must have had a puzzled look still on my face because he asked, *"You really have no idea, do you?.....that surprises me a little....you being a detective and all."* As I stared back at the sick and demented man, my head was spinning. So much so, it was hard for me to gather my thoughts. *"Ahh...no, I don't,"* I answered while trying to move my legs from going to sleep. Chuckling, Russ took another drag on his butt and looked over at Andrea. *"She reminds me of your wife, Shake....she even looks like her....too bad she won't be around much longer, but if I don't do it, somebody else will."*

Not wanting to hear anymore of his crap I said loudly, *"Okay, Mr. Answer Man....who was it then?....who killed my wife?"* Crushing his cigarette out in the ashtray on the end table by Andrea and growing a grin from ear to ear he answered, *"Who could have set* up a thing like that?....I mean run your wife down and make it look like a hit and run.....plus set you up in the alley to take the fall for a bad shooting?....but the real question you should be asking your-self is why?" I had no idea what the maniac was talking about as my memory searched for the answers, but after several moments, no thoughts came to mind. Seeing that I was speechless Wilson added, "Who was jealous of you and wanted you out of town in the worse possible way.....come on man, think!" Those words suddenly hit home with me and before I could answer, my face must have told Wilson I was on the right trail. The maniac while staring directly at me answered, "That's right....the chief!.....he hated you and saw nothing but a competitor, maybe even taking his job away from him someday....you know there was even some talk among the city councilors of replacing him with you....did you know that?" Shaking my head I replied, "No....I wasn't aware of that....but my wife?....why her?.....I can understand trying to set me up with the bad shooting of the kid, but her?"

Wilson peered at me and looked bewildered because of my naivety. "He despised you, Shake, just as I did...you thought you were better than the rest of us and we didn't measure up to your standards.....the chief thought by killing your wife, it would mean the end of you as your life would have been turned upside down and with your days numbered, you would have just faded away...... Morin told me that when he ran your wife down, he really enjoyed it....watching her bounce off his hood was one of the best things he had ever experienced until he backed over her a few more times to make sure the deed was done....that's when he really got his rocks off." Hearing that, I spit at him. "You're just as bad as that sick son of a bitch, talking about my wife like that....both of you are the low-est form of scum!"

Wiping the mucus from his cheek Wilson chuckled. "You know, the chief was right about you....about you crashing and burn-ing....the drinking took care of that part, but when you didn't leave the force after your wife's death, it ate at him and he resorted to the killing in the alley....of course, since he's my boss, I helped him out with that one.....*you never saw me coming up from behind, did you?.....that's when I struck you on the back of your head, putting you to sleep for a while..... and the killing of the kid with your own gun?....well, that was easy, the poor kid had no idea what was happening when I plugged him with it.....he was nothing but a low life, anyway....if I hadn't done it, somebody else would have, somewhere down the line......then, all I had to do was go back in the store and take care of the owner, but the old bastard died of a heart attack when I pointed the gun at him."*

Laughing aloud, Wilson took another drag off his cigarette and let the smoke loose from his lungs slowly as he pondered for a moment. *"Shake, life is full of its little disappoints from time to time and you have to realize that...... the chief?.....well, he's deep into the Veratex deal and you were becoming too much of a liability back then....we were scared that you might figure it all out and that prompted the planning of the shooting incident......after all, we couldn't have you running around and screwing up our big happy family....could we?"*

Chuckling at the look on my face, which must have been a remarkable sight he stood over me, pointing the gun down towards my head. *"Well, partner I guess this is where we have to part company, but first you are going to watch me have some fun with the girls.....I was going to start with the young one over there, but your girlfriend.....look at that face, Shake....don't you think she can't wait to have the party start?"* Saying that, he slowly walked towards her and drew a knife from his pocket, looking like a predator that had just caught his prey. The familiar click of a switchblade blitzed through the air as the opened blade glistened in the light emanating from the lamp on the end table. Taking Andrea by her long black hair he gleamed with excitement as he pulled her head backwards, exposing her neck. Cutting a hunk of her hair off and holding it in his hand, he smelled it while removing the gag from her mouth. *"Smells pretty good, Shake....but I guess you get to smell that all the time....okay little lady, if you utter a sound, this goes in and I will slit your throat from ear to ear."*

Even though my wrists were raw from my previous attempts to slip free, I struggled again, trying to break the ropes. *"You piece of shit!....what are you going to do to her?"* With a huge smirk on his face he placed, the blade against her shirt and with one full swipe cut all of the buttons off, sending them flying in different directions throughout the room. Andrea's bra became exposed, showing her ample breasts and enough cleavage to satisfy any man with Wilson gloating, *"I told you....her and me were going to have some fun."* Bending down he kissed her softly on the cheek while stroking the side of her mouth and eying me the entire time. Tears poured out of Andrea's eyes, mixing with her mascara, which formed black streaks down her cheeks, amplifying the horror on her face.

As his hands rubbed her breasts from behind, they drifted downwards towards her waist and with one unzipping her pants the other disappeared beneath them. With Wilson still smiling at me he made Andrea wince and I knew exactly what he was doing as his hand moved back and forth in her pants. *"You like this, don't you little girl.....daddy knows how to make you feel real good, doesn't he?"* Andrea raised her butt off the chair attempting to squirm herself free from the sickening lunatic's intrusion, but he suddenly grabbed her shoulder. *"Oh, no!... my dear!"* he said placing the knife hard against her throat, causing a small amount of blood to appear. *"If you move too much, you won't be able to fully enjoy our precious time together!"* With that came a look of surprise and shock on her face as he shoved his hand into her groin, making her cry out with pain. *"You rotten son of a bitch!"* I hollered. *"Let her go....I'm the one you want!"*

Suddenly Wilson removed his hand, exclaiming, *"No wonder you found this gal so attractive, Shake....I can't wait to feel her with ole Herman here."* Grabbing his crotch, he snickered as he sliced the front of her bra with the six-inch long blade, exposing her beautiful, lily-white breasts. Pushing her to the floor by the chair, he severed the rope that bound her legs and waived the knife at her. *"Remember, if you resist, "I'll do an autopsy on your innards right in front of him....you got that?"* Andrea nodded her head in hopelessness as Wilson pulled her pants off, throwing them to the side. Seeing her pink-laced underwear Wilson's eyes grew twice their size as he reached down and ran his hand slowly up her thighs. With his hands, reaching for her underwear Wilson looked back at me grinning from ear to ear. *"Pretty nice, ehh?.....I wonder what's beneath them....I bet its paradise....is it Shake?..... after all, you should know."*

Grabbing her underwear to tear them off, suddenly everyone heard a clanging noise coming from outside. Wilson's head immediately turned in the direction of the sound, trying to determine what it was. *"Hmmmm.....seems like we have company.....I'll be right back.....don't you run away now."* Quickly jumping to his feet Wilson pulled his weapon out of his holster and went to the front door. Slowly opening it and after peering out through the crack he disappeared outside. *"Help me untie my hands, Andrea,"* I whispered. Unfortunately, no response came from her as she was sobbing uncontrollably and completely oblivious to her surroundings. Knowing that time was of the essence, frantically, I said in a loud whisper, *"Andrea!....get it under control!....you got to help me!"* Finally coming to her senses, she slid over on her side to me with her hands bound behind her back. Propping herself up and putting her back to mine, she started to loosen the knots. After a few anxious moments, she cried, *"I can't......they're too tight!"*

Trying desperately to remove my hands from the bindings I answered, *"Keep trying...it's our only chance!....if he comes back we are all dead!"* Furiously trying to untie the knots I felt Andrea shaking from the stress and knew it was only a matter of time before she lost it again. While I desperately tried to help her I noticed that the young girl was staring straight ahead, not showing any emotion at all. Thinking to myself that she must be in a complete state of shock and was unaware of the situation I mumbled, *"Look at her.....the poor girl is totally out of it.....maybe she's the lucky one."*

The feeling of hopelessness started to overwhelm me as the realization of our dire situation was becoming a stark reality when suddenly; a familiar odor filled my nostrils. Out of the corner of one eye along the floor, I saw four furry feet coming at me from the kitchen. It was Barrett! Limping towards us, I could see that he was injured in the left front shoulder as blood was running down his leg onto the floor. *"Good boy....you know what to do,"* I said softly as he reached us. Lying on his belly, he nestled his head between us and started chewing at the ropes with his sharp canine teeth. Both my hands shook violently from the chewing action as the dog that once saved my life was at the job again. Within seconds along with Andrea's help, my hands were free and I quickly loosened the lamp cords that bound my feet.

Suddenly through the large picture window, I saw Wilson returning. *"Get out of here before he sees you boy,"* I said and like a shot, Barrett disappeared into the kitchen. *"Andrea, get back to where you were....he's coming back!"* Quickly she slid herself over by the chair while I looped the lamp cords around my legs and repositioned my hands behind me, giving the appearance that nothing had changed. At the last second, I noticed a smear of Barrett's blood on the floor and quickly slid myself over, trying to hide it. In the process of doing that, the front door flew open and Wilson entered. *"It must have been a cat or something,"* he announced as he came through the door. Smirking as he approached us he holstered his .38, saying, *"Now....where were we?....hmm?"*

Staring down at Andrea's pink underwear Wilson's eyes once again grew large with excitement, anticipating his sick intentions as he walked slowly towards her almost drooling at the mouth. Taking the knife from his pocket the blade flipped open as he released the locking mechanism. *"This is going to be a real treat, Shake.....thanks for bringing such a sweet thing like this into my life....you're a real buddy!"* As he moved towards his prey with the eyes of the hunter I waited for my opportunity to pounce, but Wilson's eyes were suddenly drawn to the floor and to my despair, I knew what he was looking at. Touching the spot of blood, Wilson's piercing eyes scanned the room. *"Looks like we had a visitor....I guess my aim must have been a little off.....where is* he, Shake?" Smirking back at him I replied, *"Who do you mean?"* Pulling his gun again, he said loudly, *"You know who....the mutt.... where is that flea bitten bag of shit so I can put another one in him."*

With a grin on my face I answered, *"You never should have said that, Russ....he's never liked that kind of ......"* Suddenly out of the corner of my eye, a flash of black fur appeared flying through the air and before Wilson knew it a set of canine teeth were at his throat, ripping and tearing his larynx out along with pieces of vein and ligaments. Smashing him to the floor, Barrett pinned him, continuing to chomp viciously at his throat area and with blood spurting into the air, it was only seconds before they were both covered in blood. Quickly jumping to my feet I hollered, *"Enough!"* Barrett hearing my voice immediately backed off and sat next to Andrea, panting heavily while still keeping his yellow eyes on his victim. Wilson lying on his back looked up with horror, bug eyed, and grasped his throat, trying to hold back the blood that was flowing from it. Gurgling and attempting to speak he peered up at me with coldness in his eyes. Spitting blood and with it running down his chin he mouthed, *"F..u..c..k you!"*

Stretching his arm out to grab his weapon off the floor he raised his gun with a shaking, bloodied hand and aimed it directly at Andrea, squeezing the trigger. Leaping through the air at him, I seized his arm and forced it to the side while the gun fired. The bullet whizzed by my face, missing me by less than an inch and buried itself in a lamp on the end table by the sofa chair, knocking it to the floor. Falling on top of him, I could feel the gun between us and realizing that he was trying for Andrea again, we wrestled with it. Grabbing the barrel, I reversed the direction of the gun in his hand and all of a sudden, the gun fired and Wilson's eyes glared back at me with astonishment and awe, telling me that the bullet had found its mark. His eyes glared up at mine and I saw his last desperate attempts at life through them, but with them rolling backwards in his head, stillness came over his face as it turned a grayish white. The man who I had trusted with my life for so many years was now on his way to meet the maker of us all.

Looking across the room Barrett was still sitting beside Andrea as she stared back at me with bloodshot eyes and a blackened face. *"Is he.....dead?"* she asked. *"Oh, he's dead alright....I hope the son of a bitch burns in hell!"* I said as I got up and walked over to her. Barrett looked up at me, panting heavily and covered in blood, with a look of contentment on his face. *"Yeah, I know....you saved my ass again, partner......thanks,"* as I patted him on the head. *"But we're not finished yet as we have one more stop to make.....Andrea, are you going to be alright here for a while?....can you take care of the girl?......Barrett and I have some more work to do."* Nodding her head, she replied, *"Yeah, don't worry about us...we'll be okay."*

Untying her and helping Andrea over to the couch, I covered her with an afghan that had been draped over the sofa chair. Carefully I picked up the partially nude girl in my arms and set her on the couch next to Andrea. She was still staring off into space, oblivious to anything around her and while Andrea put her arm around the young girl, I cut and removed her bonds. Unfolding the afghan further and gingerly covering the young girl I gently touched her on the side of the face, trying to reassure her that it was finally over.

Taking a piece of paper off the end table, I grabbed a pencil off the desk and wrote down Mayor Logan's number. Handing it to my girlfriend I said, *"This is the Mayor's telephone number in Harrisburg, Andrea....call Ben and give it to him....let him know what happened here.....he'll know what to do."*

Kissing Andrea on the forehead I said softly, *"Don't worry... ..I'll be right back,"* and as I moved away, she grabbed my arm. *"Don't go...it's over now, isn't it?....you have all the proof that you need.....don't you?"* Staring at the body on the floor and then back to her with a far away look in my eyes I declared, *"No...not every-thing....but I will."* Kissing her again, this time passionately, I held her tightly and as we separated, I gave her a little wink. *"Like I said....don't worry about me hon.....after all, I have the best partner in the world.....he's always got my back."*

As Barrett and I walked to the front door, I turned and looked back at Andrea sitting on the couch next to the young girl. Trying not to cry anymore Andrea attempted a smile, followed by a wink back at me. With her eyes looking at me first and then glancing over at Barrett, Andrea said softly, *"I'll be waiting for you, Shake.... and you!....you take good care of him, you hear?"* Barrett hearing Andrea's words licked his chops and whimpered at her, telling Andrea he was on the job. Patting him and smiling at Andrea I motioned to Barrett with my hand to follow me and we quickly left the house.

Walking to the car I noticed that Barrett was limping more severely now as he tried to keep up with me. His head was hanging lower, showing the effects of the blood loss from his wound. *"Are you going to be all right?"* I said aloud looking at him as he followed close behind me. *"You're not going to quit on me before we see the end of this, are you?"* Squatting down to examine him, I stroked his black shiny fur back and discovered that the wound was on his upper left shoulder. Looking at it more closely I was thankful that the bullet had only grazed him and had not penetrated the muscles or any other vital tissue. While I continued to stroke him, Barrett licked his muzzle and rubbed up against me while closing his eyes and grunting a little. Still concerned over him I said, *"Well, are you going to be alright?....are you still able to see this thing through?"* Barrett's face immediately perked up and he raised his head, looking at me with determination in his eyes. Standing strong and perfectly erect, he stared back at me, erupting with a loud, vivacious bark and with a wagging bushy tail; he danced on all fours while glancing back and forth at the car and me. *"Okay, boy.....okay....I know what you want.....lets go and get us our man."*

CHAPTER TWENTY-THREE
Revenge is Bitter Sweet

A s Barrett and I got into the car, I thought back to the day of my wife's death and the years of suffering, it had caused me. That horrible day years ago, a piece of me died as well and with little left in my soul, but anger, I began on a path of hating myself, my friends, and everyone else in the world. As time went on, my hatred had turned into a hideous revenge and what I had from there on was a head full of retribution that I wanted to expunge on my wife's killer. During those years, the thought of finding my wife's murderer was the only thing that actually got me out of bed in the morning as I constantly dreamed of putting my hands around his throat and squeezing the life out of him, like water from a sponge. It had become my sole purpose in life and as the memories continued to haunt me, it only drove me more insane with hatred and revenge.

The day I had wished for, even prayed for had finally come as the man responsible for her death was nearly within my reach. Why Chief Morin crushed Jane and my unborn child beneath his car, taking the only precious things I ever had in life was beyond my comprehension. How the man could have been so thoughtless and cruel, had not sat well with me for all those years and my whole attitude towards God and society changed for the worse. No longer was I the happy go lucky type of person, enjoying life and being thankful for it. I had become a cruel, thoughtless, and empty man who had no kind feelings to give anymore as my quest for the killer had plagued me like a sinister disease with the cure seeming to be a wishful thought. Now that was all going to change as the man responsible was only minutes away.

Glancing at Barrett in the rear seat, I could not help to think what I would have done on this case without him and how he reacted to my old partner, Russ Wilson the day he met him. *"Heh boy.....I owe you big time....looks like your first impression of my old partner was a good one and why I never paid attention to you is beyond me.....you should have bit his ass the first day you met him."* Listening to me intently, his ears were totally erect and seemed to be taking in each and every word. When I smiled at him after saying that, he quickly jumped into the front seat and vigorously licked me several times on the side of the face. Wiping my cheek with a shirtsleeve I added, *"Yeah....yeah... I know..... you were right.....next time I will listen to you."*

Taking a right down Main Street, Holly Street was coming up fast and that was where I would find the resolution to my vengeance. I knew the chief lived alone as his wife and family had longed abandoned him, because he cheated on her. The chief was a womanizer as all of us knew about it on the force, but we had kept quiet about it. All of us were afraid to say anything due to the possibility of the chief assigning us traffic detail or some other meaningless task for the rest of our lives. That was always in the back of our minds as the chief was an extremely vengeful man that did not hesitate to ruin anyone's career over the slightest sign of not being loyal to him or the department. His victims littered the landscape during his reign as chief and they only reminded us of the consequences if we ever stepped out of line.

The thoughts of Jim Murphy entered my head as I made a right turn, a cop that had joined the Harrisburg force about two months after I did. He was a young and eager kid, who like the rest of us, wanted to make a difference in serving the public citizenry. Being a good cop and always having the public's interest at heart, Murphy immediately became a favorite of everyone in the department. For some reason the chief never liked the man and was always on his case about everything. Either his uniform was never in order or his reports were inadequate, in fact, Chief Morin addressed even the simplest of things and the kid was always chastised for it. Soon, it became obvious that the head of our department was out to get Murphy and none of us ever understood why. I thought it was pure jealousy, but others in the department attributed it to Murphy's father who was once a council member several years ago. The rumor had it that Jim's father had opposed Morin's appointment of becoming chief and worked behind the scenes to torpedo it, going so far as to have several citizens gather names on a petition to prevent it.

Whatever the reasoning, Chief Morin eventually got his wish when the kid was on duty during a break-in one night at a local liquor store. Not following departmental protocol by calling for backup immediately, he took it upon himself to try to apprehend the bad guys alone. Unfortunately, one of the thieves armed with a crowbar, attacked him from behind and put him into intensive care for several weeks. When Jim Murphy was finally discharged from the hospital, being lucky to have survived the ordeal, the chief actually brought him up on disciplinary charges and ruined the kid's career. A few short weeks after that, Murphy was thrown off the force because of it and was picked up several months later for breaking into a drug store. The poor kid had resorted to crime in order to feed his family and all it was due to the despicable actions of the chief. None of us on the department ever forgave the asshole for what he did to that kid and to this day, poor Jim Murphy suffers in prison for armed robbery.

Driving to his house now, I could feel my heart pounding inside my chest, knowing that the man who had killed my wife was going to be in my hands. Having been up all night I was running on full adrenaline and thoughts of giving up now seemed like a joke to me as I mumbled, *"Finally...soon my wife's death will be avenged.... once I put the cuffs on him and toss his sorry ass in jail, my mind will finally rest easy as the cons in that place will surely have their way with him."* Chuckling and almost laughing aloud while turning down his street, I continued to say, *"His life will be nothing but a living hell for the rest of his days.....because in that place he will surely have a target on his back........how sweet is that?"*

Pulling into the driveway, I knew he was home as his city police vehicle was parked in front of the garage. His house was a plain two story with a detached garage, something any average person would own. Although structurally good, the buildings needed some work as the paint was peeling off the walls in several places and there were numerous shingles missing from the house roof. Being two stories the building footprint was small, but it still covered the very tiny lot of land that was associated with it and by the appearance of the place it was obvious that the chief had always lived modestly, not flaunting the cash that he had received through the Veratex Corporation.

As my eyes scanned his home, my thoughts about him were many as I closed the driver's side door. *"With the thousands of dollars he was taking in from the real estate scheme he could have lived in a house twice this size, but being smart, he kept his apparent lifestyle on the low side making it seem that he was struggling on his city's salary.....you have to give the man credit.....he was smart, wasn't he?.....hiding all of those years like a snake under a rock....living like he should on a police chief's salary and giving everybody the impression that he had not broken the trust that was bestowed upon him......meanwhile, completely fooling everyone by hauling in bags of corruption money into that home of his....I wonder how much of the dirty money he stuffed in that mattress of his, dreaming of the future lifestyle that he would enjoy once he was done working for the city...living the high life in the Caribbean or some other exotic place.....well, mister, you are going on a little trip, but it's not to a place that you had in mind."*

Walking up to, the front step I kept chuckling about my last thought, and looking down I noticed that Barrett was limping less now as he followed me. Glad that he was doing better and knowing that my partner was going to be all right I stood and rapped the knocker a few times, waiting for someone to answer. After a few moments had passed and when no one answering I looked in a side window. The house appearing to be still and quiet, definitely gave the impression that no one was home and this surprised me a little as his car was parked in the yard. While hammering the doorknocker a few more times I called out, *"Chief!... are you here?....it's Shaker Madison!...I'd like to talk to you!"*

Finally, after a few minutes had passed, I heard a voice from inside say, *"Hold your horses...I'm coming."* Just then the door opened and upon seeing me, the chief exclaimed, *"What are you doing here?....do you know it's seven o'clock in the morning?....never mind, I gave you* explicit *instructions Madison to work this case until you were finished....I need your final report and here you are screwing around again...what the hell is the matter with you?...... can't you ever follow orders?.....after all, the citizens of Harrisburg are paying you good money to do your damn job."*

I could tell he was honestly surprised to see me as he stepped back away from the door while glancing at both sides of him and to tell the truth, it appeared that he was looking for a way to escape, if he needed one in a hurry. Trying to hold my temper, since the sight of the man sickened me, I calmly answered, *"Thought we would pay you a little visit, chief.....Barrett and I have a few matters to discuss with you.....seems, Wilson had a few interesting things to say about what's been happening in this town and I would like to get your input."*

Obviously looking disturbed about my invasion the chief took a few additional steps to the side and reached for something to his left. Suspecting heavily what it must be, I rammed the door into him, sending Morin across the entryway into the stair banister. Smashing into it, he fell to the floor by the bottom step, showing signs of confusion and bewilderment. Lying on the floor for a brief second, he regained his composure and immediately stood up. Reaching again for his weapon on the small table by the door, with a swift kick I connected at his breastbone, rearing him backwards into the curio cabinet. With broken glass flying everywhere and him falling to the floor, my initial thoughts were to pull my gun and end his useless existence right then and there. However, holding my temper I walked over and picked Morin up by the front of his shirt. *"You lousy piece of shit....Wilson told me everything about you and my wife.....how you ran her down in cold blood and enjoyed every minute of it, saying 'it was one of the best times of your life,' you sick bastard......plus, how you set me up with the killing in the alley, you son of a bitch.....I should blow your God damn head off!"* Hollering that, I threw him across the room through the air into the TV set. The picture tube violently exploded, thrusting glass dust particles into the air and forming a cloud above him. Desperately wiping his bloodied face the chief crawled on his hands and knees away from me into the living room. In uncontrollable rage, I grabbed a very large decorative vase off a shelf and smashed it over his back, knocking him flat to the floor.

Reaching down for him again the chief screamed, *"I don't know what you're talking about, Madison!....I had nothing to do with your wife's death....you know very well she was killed by a drunk driver and what's this shit about the kid in the alley?.....that was your own damn fault and no one else....you panicked and killed the boy....end of story....after all, we all make mistakes, you know that!....so let's put all of this behind us, shall we?.....besides, I can make you rich....richer than your wildest dreams.....in fact, so rich, you'll never have to work again!"* Hearing those sickening words come out of his despicable mouth only enraged me more as I let loose with a powerful kick, hitting him in the side and breaking a couple of ribs. Crying out in excruciating pain he shrieked, *"I can make this right for you, Madison.....I know we can work this out!"*

His words meant nothing to me as I knew he was lying through his teeth and the chief seeing no reaction from me quickly countered with, *"Just hold on for a minute...I'm sure we can settle this.... as far as what Wilson told you, all of it is a lie.....he is just trying to protect himself by pinning all of this on me...he is actually one of the ring leaders of this whole operation.....I tried to make him see the light, but it was no use as he was in too deep, too far gone......I was* going to arrest the man once I found out about it, but him and his cohorts threatened me.....that's why when you came back to town, I had hoped that you would discover the truth and help me put a stop to all of this."

As his disgusting words flowed out of him, I grabbed him by the left hand and twisted it, hyper-extending the arm at the elbow, causing him to bellow in pain. Losing what little control there was left in me I screamed, *"Is this how my wife felt when you ran her down!....like I said, Wilson told me everything.....you were the mastermind of this and not him....plus, I have the documentation to prove it!"* Grabbing him by the front of his shirt, I got right in his face. *"And that piece of garbage that you call my partner?.... he tried to rape and murder my girlfriend.....plus, an eye witness that I currently have under protection, but they're both safe now.....and your boy, Wilson?.....well, he's got a piece of lead in his gut from me and has already taken the trip to hell!"*

Fed up with the sight of him I threw him backwards and kicked him again, squarely in the groin. Holding his genitals with his hands in excruciating pain, I knocked the chief to the floor with another sidekick and pulled my gun from its holster. Caulking the hammer back and getting on top of him, I jammed the barrel of my .357 into his mouth. Glaring at him with redness and fire in my eyes, I let him know that hell was surely on the way. Terrified while reaching out with his good arm, Morin gagged on the barrel, pleading, *"Mmmh...mmmh....no.... no.....you don't understand.....Sloan was the one.....the man was out of control and had become a liability....we didn't know what to do with him.....Christ, the pompous ass was killing women left and right, thinking it was the best thing for the mayor and the Veratex Corporation, but we all knew something had to be done about him.....Madison, those men from that company are vicious murderers with no feelings at all for anyone ....they'll kill their own mothers for heaven's sake, if it means keeping their operation from closing up shop, but they gave me another chance to fix the problem.......so I took care of it."*

That grabbed my attention for a moment and made me ask, *"What do you mean by that?....you took care of it?"* Getting off him Chief Morin tried to stand by bracing himself on an overturned chair. Off balance and wavering he vehemently replied, *"What did I do?.....about Sloan?........well, he's at the bottom of a concrete footing underneath one of our high rise buildings....he won't be any-more trouble to us, that I can promise you as his killing days are over with."* Taken back a little I did not let the chief's confession change my attitude towards him. *"What about my wife?....what do you have to say about that?"* Wiping the accumulated sweat and blood from his brow he fired back, *"During those years, they would have done anything to see you out of this town, Madison and do you know why?.....because you were too close.....way too close to find-ing out the truth about their operation....the Veratex group knew they couldn't waste a cop, but a woman?....she was just in the wrong place at the wrong time!.....you gotta believe me!"*

With the butt end of my revolver and with a tremendous right cross I pulverized his big mouth to eliminate the crap that was spilling from it. Falling backwards and hitting the floor, he crashed into the dining room table. Spitting blood and teeth all over a throw rug, he looked up at me with desperation on his face, hop-ing that there was still a chance of reasoning with me. Mumbling and leaking blood out of his mouth he blurted, *"It's a good thing you took up with the bottle, Madison....otherwise we would have found you down by the river as well."* Spitting some more blood out of his mouth onto the floor the excess ran down his chin onto his white tee shirt. *"Don't you understand, Madison?....they are going to kill us, now....they realize that you want to expose them and that is something that will not happen, just as sure as the sun is going to rise tomorrow....you have become nothing but a liability that needs to be eliminated.....you see, Madison, people like you aren't around here for very long....they soon disappear, just like Sloan did......you might think you have a chance now, but those people will never give up....no matter where you go, they will hunt you down and squash you like a bug."*

Hearing his contentious words only made me soar with rage as I spun and kicked him again to the other side of the body. Sending him sailing backwards into the broken curio cabinet again, he fell into the shattered glass on the floor and lying there on his back, writhing in pain, he coughed up some more blood all over himself.

Observing his deplorable condition I suddenly felt good inside and watching him suffer I had no idea that the real fun was about to begin. Within a few short moments, he started to beg relentlessly and upon hearing that, I almost leaped out of my skin with pleasure. *"Please, Madison......please, don't hit me again as I can't take it anymore.....I'm just an old and tired man who wants to live out the rest of his days in peace, so I'll be straight with you, okay?..... you're right about your wife.....I did run her down, but it was an accident as I was only supposed to scare her...that's what they told me to do....you have to understand that I had no other choice because they own me, just like they do now with you....they know you have the goods on them, but it won't do you any good....you see, they have friends in high places and pretty soon you'll end up in a drainage ditch beside a cornfield somewhere, if you don't play their game."*

Saying those words Morin tried to keep a straight face, but I knew by his look that he was enjoying the sight of a supposed dead man. Seeing that stupid grin only incensed me more as I squatted down pushing my face almost into his, yelling, *"And the set up.... were you part of that, too?"* Answering me, he flashed that stupid smirk again. *"Of course I was....actually, it was Wilson's idea if you want to know the truth....a real buddy of yours, don't you think?.... letting you take the rap for something that you didn't do, but all of that doesn't matter now....because you see, Madison, you're a dead man as we speak and you don't even know it, yet... that will be the case unless you hand over those damaging documents that you have in your possession.....and maybe after you do that, I can talk some sense into them.....you know, calm the boys over to the Veratex Corporation down a little and convince them that we are on their side now and are willing to go along with the 'program'.....you like money, we all do....I think there's a big amount of cash just waiting for you if you can get some smarts for once......I know you must think having those documents are an insurance policy for you, but in reality they are your death warrant."*

After saying that, Morin's head reared back with laughter, causing him to cough and spray blood all over the floor again and with blood dribbling out of his mouth he stared back at me for a reaction, but there was none. My eyes glared back at Morin with a coldness that would have frozen anything in its tracks and seeing that in my face, Morin's grin turned to a full look of weariness. Not breaking out in laughter again he pressed his lips together and swallowed hard, saying, *"So....I suppose you want to kill me now, ehh?.....for all of the bad things I've done that you have cooked up in that righteous mind of yours?......well, go ahead, kill me.... and you'll burn for it, too....but the funniest thing about this whole mess is, before you can get two steps with that so called evidence of yours, you'll be shoved in a deep, dark hole somewhere with a bullet in the brain."*

I grabbed his gun off the table by the door and placed it in my belt, thinking what a poor excuse he was for a human being and holstering my weapon I started for the front door along with Barrett. *"Where in the hell do you think you're going?"* the chief yelled as I grabbed the knob and slowly opened the door. *"You don't think you can simply walk out of here and get away with this?....I'll see you in jail for what you've done!...as soon as you leave, Madison, I will be on the phone to the station, telling them that you assaulted me because I had discovered that you killed your old partner to keep his trap shut....an informant that I had depended upon in letting me know how bad you were bungling this case......besides, the information you gathered from that Swanson bitch has probably been destroyed by now and your ass is mine!"*

Morin's snickering turned into hideous hysterics as he watched my head lower, pondering his words. His eyes were full of evilness, thinking that he had me cold and there was nothing else I could do, but see it his way. Slowly I turned and faced him while easing the front entrance door closed. Then the chief's eyes suddenly grew a look of contentment, recognizing that I had finally come to my senses and were willing to play his little game. With a slight grin I responded, *"That information is already with the Feds and they are more than likely rounding up your crew right now.....everyone associated with the Veratex Corporation is probably in custody and are headed off to jail where they belong...... so Chief Morin, in reality, your little empire is finished......as they say, it's all down the shitter."*

Laughing as I opened the door the chief shouted, *"What about me?.....aren't you going to call for an ambulance?... look at me, I'm in pretty tough shape!....you can at least do that!"* Showing no mercy towards the man I replied, *"Alright, Morin...get your ass up, it's time to go to jail."* Realizing I was dead serious he struggled to his feet and spit some blood beside him, looking at me with hatred in his face. *"You're nothing but scum, Madison....a man who doesn't see his opportunities even if they hit him in the face....you make me sick!"* Ushering with my hand for Morin to follow me out the door the chief spit in my direction, narrowly missing me. *"Madison, you're a bad cop to boot and that woman of yours was nothing but a two bit slimy whore!....that's right, I killed the bitch and she deserved it....she begged and pleaded for her life and for the little bastard that was inside her, but do you know what I did?....I slammed the car in reverse and laid a little more rubber on her!"*

Laughing hideously, he walked back a few steps, relishing in his horrid torment of me. The pressure building within my skull almost blew the top of my head off as I walked away from the door a few steps closer to him, trying with all my might not to pull my gun and send six shots into the sickening piece of flesh that was standing before me. Biting my lower lip so hard in grief and anger, blood oozed from it while I softly replied, *"You won't need an ambulance where you're going."*

Perplexed, the chief stared back at me with confused eyes, trying to figure out what I meant by that. Then, as I looked to the side of me, I noticed Barrett was sitting by the door, anxiously waiting for me to leave. With his long, pink tongue hanging out and panting heavily he constantly stared at Morin, hoping that the man would make a wrong move. In a methodical and calm manner, I took a few steps towards Barrett and rubbed his forehead and the back of his neck. Patting him a few times and telling him that he was a good boy I then glanced back at the chief with a big smirk on my face. Taking his revolver from my belt, I opened the cylinder and checked to see if it was loaded. Confirming that it had six fresh shells in it, I snapped it shut and slowly placed it back on the table by the door. Smirking at Morin my eyes looked over at Barrett and I chuckled, saying, *"Let's see how fast you can be with that big sack of potatoes hanging over your belt."* Still not knowing what I was getting at, the chief 's eyes were wide and glaring at the both of us while I added, *"Barrett....this is the man who ordered Wilson to hurt you.....he's a very **bad** man.....I'm going to leave now, so you can play with him......just remember while you do, he's your **friend.**"*

Barrett's deep, yellow eyes surrounded by jet-black fur immediately glowed with the exuberance and craving of the Alpha wolf. As he rigidly stood on all fours, the fur on his back bristled upwards with his muscles rippling beneath his coat, readying himself to attack. Saliva dripped from Barrett's huge canine teeth to the floor and as his head lowered, his eyes became fixated on the panic-stricken man. Then a long, deep growl filled the room, sending even a shiver up my spine as Chief Morin screamed, *"No!....not that, Madison....don't leave me with that!.....I'm sorry!.... really I am!.....I didn't mean to hurt your wife!....they made me do it.......you have to listen to me!.....I'll say and do whatever you want!....I'll tell them all about the corruption, the crooked land deals....even the murders....I'll tell them everything!.....you gotta believe me!"*

Slowly I walked outside and closed the door behind me. Suddenly, screams reeked through the air along with deep growling sounds and the tearing of clothing. As the screams grew louder and louder with every passing second, the house rumbled with deafening crashing sounds and my smile enlarged along with it.

Then as I walked further down the driveway to my car and leaned up against it, I chuckled to myself while lighting up a cigarette. Taking a few puffs and looking back at the house I heard another loud penetrating scream emanate from it along with the breaking of furniture and the shattering of glass. With the house, actually rocking back and forth from the ruckus inside it the gleam in my eyes grew brighter and knocking the ashes off my butt I began to laugh aloud a little, something I had not done in years. For once in a very long time I felt alive again inside and the horrible feelings of hopelessness and despair were no longer hanging over me and listening to the increased uproar throughout the house only caused me to laugh even harder as I knew justice was finally being served.

The building shook from the chaos for a few more moments, but then fell suddenly silent and the only sound filling the air were a few birds sitting in nearby elm trees, chirping their morning ritual. Gradually, the sun began to peek out from behind a puffy white cloud, illuminating the yard with life and I felt the warmth of its rays fall upon my face. Then, an unbelievable feeling of utmost joy and relief came over me as if I had just climbed out of the profound depths of depression. No longer did I find myself in the darkness of the abyss, wandering about it like a blind man, trying to find his way. For everything seemed to be clearer now and I was finally at peace, ready to go on with life. Staring back at the dwelling with a huge smile I took another long drag off my cigarette and as I exhaled the smoke into the crisp fall air I said aloud, looking upwards up at the vibrant blue sky. *"God, it's a great day to be alive."* Then, grinding out the cigarette on the paved driveway with my shoe I paused for a moment and glanced back at the house, realizing that my life meant something again.

With the house remaining silent, I walked back to the front door and slowly opened it. Just as I cracked the door, a black snoot projected through the opening and Barrett came barreling out with a spring in his walk. Glad to see him I squatted down to his level as he trotted over to me. Rubbing his fir and smiling at him, I said aloud, *"Well....have you had enough fun for one day?"*

Turning my head back at the doorway and looking through the opening, I saw Morin lying on his back on the floor next to the foot of the stairs. Standing up and walking into the entryway the house was in shambles as there were broken knickknacks scattered everywhere throughout the room and a large mirror that once hung in the hallway was nothing but a pile of shattered glass on the floor. All of the furniture was turned upside down and the highly decorative lamps that once adorned the end tables were nothing more than a pile of junk. As my eyes continued to scan the room, streaks and splotches of blood plastered the walls and the displaced throw rugs, strewn against the baseboards were stained in blood.

Chief Morin moaned several times while I approached him and glaring up at me with bewilderment, his eyes were wide and filled with pain as he looked wildly in all directions. His clothes were almost completely torn from his body and his arms were hammered by dozens of teeth marks, which had blood oozing from their punctures. The man's pant legs, shredded to ribbons, had blood dripping from them and his shoes had been torn from his feet along with one sock. With his right foot exposed, it showed the devastation of Barrett's jaws as his foot was chewed heavily, leaving it severely discolored with an array of black and purple colors. His left foot, partially covered by the white sock, was heavily soaked in blood from the gash on his heel, which extended to the big toe along his instep. *"Well....he didn't kill you Morin, but he should have,"* I said, gazing down at the man. Noticing that his throat had not been touched I knelt down and peered into the chief's eyes. *"You'll live, Morin....you should be thankful that Barrett kept his oath of being a good cop who brings his prisoners in alive to face justice....to tell you the truth, I don't think I could have done it."*

While I assessed his mutilated body the chief gazed up at me, wincing from the pain and while barely able to remain conscious he uttered weakly almost in a whisper, *"I'll see you in hell, Madison for what you did to me....someday I'll get your ass."* Standing up I chuckled and looked down on Morin with a smirk, saying, *"Where you're going....I think you're going to have to worry about your own ass."*

Stepping through the door to the outside, Barrett upon seeing me immediately leaped up and loaded me with kisses by anxiously licking the side of my face. His eyes were happy and full of life, telling me that he was glad to be with me. With my grin turning to a full smile, I tried to stop him from licking and nosing me, but he wanted nothing of it. Laughing to myself, I said, *"Okay, okay.....hold on there, settle down, boy.....I believe it's over now."*

Hearing those words, Barrett immediately let out two vibrant barks and bolted for the car. Upon reaching it, he turned and looked back at me, standing there with all one hundred thirty pounds of him in a perfect rigid stance. With his head held high, tail curled upwards and ears at full alert he appeared prouder than ever of his arrest. Appreciating the impressive picture that was before me I said aloud to myself, *"Yes, the city can rest easy tonight, ole boy and it's all because of you......okay, partner.....let's go home...."*

About the Author

Steve Whitman is the author of the true survival story *Winning Life's Lottery*, the thrilling *Killer in the Mist* series, and the new detective novel *Shaker Madison- The Suitcase Murders*. He has also written numerous articles on survival and lethal force for various websites.

Whitman has more than forty years of hunting and fishing experience. He left his civil engineering and land-surveying firm to open a sporting camp in the beautiful woods of northern Maine near the Canadian border. Whitman is a Registered Master Maine guide and has extensive knowledge in emergency first aid, outdoor survival, and weapons training.

Made in the USA
Middletown, DE
02 July 2017